D1329956

GRADY
BARR

Other books by Jack Donahue

Someone To Hate

The Confessor

Erase My Name

Divorce American Style

Pray To The Hustlers' God

The Lady Loved Too Well

Wildcatter

Other books by Michel T. Halbouty

Spindletop (with James A. Clark)

The Last Boom (with James A. Clark)

GRADY BARR

A Novel by

Jack Donahue
and
Michel T. Halbouty

ARBOR HOUSE   New York

This book is a work of the imagination. With the exception of the obvious historic personages, the characters are fictitious, and any resemblance between them and persons living or dead is coincidental.

For Genie and Billye—our ladies

Oh that I were as in months past, as in the days when God preserved me . . . when I washed my steps with butter, and the rock poured me out rivers of oil . . .

—Job

BOOK
ONE

MARACAIBO

Chapter One

The man the Galveston *News* had described as a "whoremaster" and had labeled "the King of Tarts" leaned against the deck railing of the small tanker several yards away from Tom Fairbanks. Fairbanks had read about the man and had seen his front-page photograph three weeks before while waiting in Galveston for passage on the *Caribe* to Venezuela. The man had been identified as one Grady Barr, for two years the operator of the city's largest and most lucrative brothel, the Shark's Head. The brothel had been raided by big-hatted Texas Rangers and, according to the newspaper report, a score of male patrons and as many daughters of joy had been allowed to scurry into the night and freedom. Only Grady Barr had been arrested and fined. The Shark's Head had been padlocked.

Fairbanks had assumed that Galveston's many whorehouses and gambling casinos flourished with impunity. The *News*, apparently sharing his assumption, had implied that the raid on The Shark's Head was a snide political move by the Texas governor to mute criticism among his reform-minded supporters. Fairbanks suspected that Barr's brothel had been the target simply because it was the most notorious establishment in the state's most notorious city.

Several days after the raid—and the newspaper story—Fairbanks had seen Barr come aboard the *Caribe*. He had recalled that Barr was only twenty-five years old—a tender age, he mused wryly, for a man who apparently had gone so far in such a demanding profession. Yet he himself was only twenty-six, and the

11

attorney for British Meridian Oil Company of Venezuela—no mean position either in 1923.

The *Caribe* had been scheduled to dock at the busy Dutch island of Curacao, but instead it had anchored off Oranjestad, chief city of the neighboring island of Aruba. Aruba was a dreary wasteland; before the Venezuelan oil boom, its only industry had been the exporting of bitter aloes. Now Oranjestad was an oil terminal. Small tankers steamed to the island from Lake Maracaibo and discharged their cargoes into a large, stationary tanker which in turn pumped the petroleum into heavy tankers bound for the States and Europe. On their return trip to Lake Maracaibo the small tankers were usually loaded with oilfield workers.

Together with Fairbanks and Barr, perhaps a dozen "boomers" had disembarked from the *Caribe* and, while waiting for a lake tanker to discharge its cargo, had sought sustenance in the nearby Amsted Bar. There was no food to be had, a towering bartender had informed them, and only one drink—gin and tonic. The bartender had shaken his head wearily against the boomers' complaints and had proceeded to mix drinks. "Better drink up," he had rumbled. "It's a pretty rough ride to Maracaibo. And you'll get none of your American bootleg poison there, either. It's rum you'll get, and you'll learn to like it or else!"

Barr had stayed to himself aboard the *Caribe*. In the bar he had drunk alone at a corner table. Fairbanks had stood at the bar with the roistering boomers, from time to time studying the silent man in the corner. Barr simply hadn't suited Fairbanks' idea of a pimp. Certainly he bore no resemblance to the slouching, cajoling creatures Fairbanks had seen in the vice towns along the Texas–Mexico border. And he didn't look like the dead-eyed, pale-faced, sleek-haired youths who had run strings of whores in and out of hotels when Fairbanks was attending the University of Texas and later Princeton. Pimps, like store clerks and bank presidents, came in all shapes and sizes, Fairbanks supposed; still he had looked for an identifying mark. But Barr bore none, nor had he revealed his calling in word or action.

Under Fairbanks' covert scrutiny Barr had not appeared to be a man accustomed to silence and solitude, either. His was an extrovert's face, composed now but promising to become mobile with smiling warmth. It was a blond face, lean, fair-skinned, sharp-featured. Hair almost red fit the skull closely in curling waves and hat-tousled ringlets. The eyes were bright blue. But the most distinctive features were a pair of startlingly dark brown eyebrows and a wide, though somehow feminine mouth. The pointed chin and snug ears lent to the whole a flicker of sardonicism.

Barr's body was lean, also. He was slightly above medium height, but the way he carried himself made him appear taller and suggested a wiry strength. In the bar he had been dressed in brown—brown shoes, brown suit, white shirt and brown tie. His brown felt hat rested on the table by his drink.

As Fairbanks studied Barr's hands, with the broad palms and fingers which were long and thick and tufted with red hair—hands, Fairbanks decided, which were outsize by any measure—he was interrupted by a heavy-drinking salesman who wanted to share his passion for rotary drilling rigs.

"They're knocking hell out of the old cable tool rigs," the salesman had declared firmly. "Texas. Louisiana. Oklahoma. All the oil states." He had pounded the bar. "They'll do the same here, too, by God, and that's the truth!"

Barr had risen from his table and was making his way to the door as the salesman whirled to accost him. "Am I right or Amarillo? Ain't the rotary rig the one for this country?"

Barr had answered courteously. "From what I've heard I figure it's better suited. Cable tools are better for hard-rock, and I ain't heard about any down here."

Barr had turned to the door. A boomer who had heard the exchange said loudly, "Ain't that somethin'—asking a god-damned pimp about a drillin' rig!"

Barr had turned slowly around, seeking the shouter among the boomers. His face was pale, and the big hands were curved, not quite fists.

So swiftly that Fairbanks had been taken unaware, the huge bartender had made his way from behind the bar carrying a two-foot length of lead pipe. The salesman scampered away. "No blood on the deck, mates," the bartender had said softly. He had looked from the boomers to Barr and then back to the boomers.

Barr had turned abruptly and departed into the gathering darkness. The bartender had let the pipe drop to his side. "One of you is a very lucky man I was here with my thumper," he had said in the direction of the boomers. "A very lucky man."

Fairbanks had silently agreed. He had seen considerable violence in his time, had seen *vaqueros* fight to the death with awesome savagery on his family's great South Texas ranch. But never had he seen such anger as he had glimpsed in Grady Barr's narrowed blue eyes. Perhaps such passion, he had thought, might manifest itself in other directions, other ways. . . .

Now, in the early morning darkness, only Fairbanks and Barr among the small tanker's passengers remained standing on deck. They were near the bow. The others, succumbing to the Amsted Bar's gin and the tanker's wicked motion, had bedded down on the stern or had found space in the crew's quarters.

Fairbanks was no longer occupied with thoughts of Grady Barr. He was enjoying the night breeze and the shifting stars cut loose from their mooring by the tanker's antics. And he was looking forward to seeing the Maracaibo Basin after a four-year absence. A new job with a new employer awaited him, and he anticipated it with just enough uneasiness to make the prospect thrilling.

He was startled out of his reverie by a great flash of light in the distance and to the starboard. It was so dazzling and of such duration that it appeared as if the earth had caught on fire. As he settled back to watch he heard Barr stir restlessly. It was lightning, but streak followed streak so closely that they appeared to be fluid bands of flame. It was, for all those watching, a gigantic, magnificent display of unlimited power.

A squatty Chinese seaman soft-shoed between Fairbanks and Barr. "No rainee," he said to both of them. "Flashem all time, but no rainee." His black pigtail gleamed under the deck lamps. "Yes, gentlemen," the Chinese went on, his manner of speech suddenly different. "That is the Catatumbo Lights, a navigational aid in the old days. It is simply lightning playing across the face of the Perija mountains to the west of the lake."

"Thank you for educating our passengers, Charlie," a voice behind them said dryly. The tanker captain, a tall, hunched man, had come out on the bow with a storm lantern in his hand. "God save us from a well-read heathen," he muttered as he clomped on past the men. The Chinese hastened away. The captain leaned over the bow, peered into the darkness ahead and signaled with the lantern to someone in the wheelhouse.

"Let's watch him," Fairbanks said to Barr.

They moved closer to the captain. Directly ahead of the tanker they could see in the growing morning light what appeared to be two rows of fencing about two tankers wide. The captain was maneuvering the tanker into this watery avenue. Once inside,

14

the fencing became palm fronds and thick sticks which had been driven into the sandy bottom.

"This is the channel over a sand bar," Fairbanks said to Barr. "We'll be in the lake pretty soon."

Barr shook his head in bewilderment. "Why don't they dredge it out? Big tankers could come right on in if they'd clean that sand out."

Though Fairbanks was interested in Barr's reaction, he didn't want to continue the subject. "I guess the government doesn't want it," he said carelessly.

Finished with his job, the captain turned around to them. "Government!" he said harshly, bitterly. He lifted the lantern to blow it out. His lighted face beneath the seaman's cap was grooved and furrowed, and his lips were as grim and cold as a mailbox slot. Lowering the lantern, he spoke directly to Fairbanks. "You mean the dictator, may the devil roast him in hell's hottest corner." His voice was edged with sarcasm. "The evil bastard is afraid that some other evil bastard will bring gunboats into the lake and cut off this part of the country from the rest. Or even some decent bastard, for that matter." He pointed dramatically off the vessel's port. "Some of his handiwork is over there on solid ground. San Carlos prison. It's so stuffed with suffering souls that sometimes I think I can hear a single heart beating."

Suddenly he sobered and forced a smile. "Forgive me," he said. "I'm an old revolutionary, and it's hard for me to put aside my soap box."

"Are you one of those bolsheviks?" Barr asked.

"Of course," the captain said shortly.

"Wouldn't this dictator ream your ass if he knew how you talked?"

"You'd tell him?"

"I don't squeal on people, mister. Now, is there anything you can do about this dictator?"

The captain smiled. "Not right now, of course."

"Then I'd cut out all that fancy talking until I *could* do something," Barr said evenly, and turned and went back to his place at the railing.

The captain raised questioning brows at Fairbanks. But Fairbanks was saved from thinking of something to say for at that moment the sun burst over the Perija mountains and it was brightest day. He heard Barr whisper, "Jesus!"

The city of Maracaibo lay to the starboard. In the distance, across the smooth, shimmering water, it seemed to be a man's dream of a tropic haven suddenly found after weary years of searching. Palm trees lined the shore in front of it, and behind them the adobe huts and buildings and the mansions of the wealthy rose up white and clean. The red roofs were brilliant as the sun hit them. There was a magic aura about it all, Fairbanks thought, a charm that hinted that the fragile beauty was hiding even more wonders; eager, lovely women beyond compare, cool drinks, productive idleness, time without end . . .

The captain broke the spell. "It's an illusion," he said gutterally. "It's a filthy, stinking, fly-breeding hole, and the lake edge is slimy with waste and garbage. It has no standard water supply. No sewage system. The streets are dirt, and they melt in the rainy season and crack in the dry." He paused. "It was all of that before the boom started last year. Now it's a madhouse."

There was a moment of silence after the captain's harsh pronouncement. Then Barr, still looking at the distant fabled city, said mildly, "If you ain't careful, they'll elect you president of the Chamber of Commerce."

As if someone had cut a string binding his emotions, Fairbanks began laughing with a roar that shook his broad, heavy frame, and he could not stop. Barr looked at him with shrewd eyes, sensing that perhaps the laughter was heartier than his sly remark merited. Fairbanks laughed on as if he were experiencing a release of tension he had not realized had possessed him.

Barr grinned at the sight. Then he was laughing, too. The two men faced each other at the ship's railing, laughing into each other's faces, their eyes acknowledging a warmth beyond reason, admitting a kinship of spirit.

The captain watched them, apparently drained of his virulence by their unconcern. He seemed to weaken there on the deck, as if he had lost his capacity for indignation and hatred in the face of this youthful laughter. Once he tried to speak, but he couldn't find the words to defend himself against such an onslaught.

The Chinese seaman had shuffled up. His dark eyes gleamed with triumph as he beheld his shattered captain, but he touched his forehead deferentially as he said, "Sir, the shore boats are coming for the passengers."

The captain had been right. Maracaibo was a madhouse. As Fairbanks and Barr made their way from the docks to Plaza Sucre

16

by horse-drawn carriage it seemed as if every one of the city's forty thousand regular inhabitants and a horde of boomers had mobilized to impede their progress. The narrow streets of the inner city were jammed with people, each one apparently trying to out-shout the one next to him. From the doorways of shops and cantinas came the noise of player pianos and tinny phonographs, all grinding out the same tune, "Valencia." There were few automobiles, but their squawking rubber horns created a constant, throbbing din. And adding to the assault, open trolley cars with clanging bells pushed through the crowds, and barefooted boys hawked water from five gallon kegs strapped on the backs of tiny burros. There was a sort of insanity in it all, a mad carnival flavor.

Cursing both the crowd and his horse with professional impartiality, the driver made it across Plaza Baralt and finally into Plaza Sucre. He reined his horse to a halt and turned in his seat inquiringly.

Barr had already seen his destination. He pointed to a white, two-story building where painted above a high archway in black letters were the words COSMOS CLUB. The driver reined the horse in that direction. The crowd was smaller and it was quieter here.

"Where you heading?" Barr asked Fairbanks.

"Across from you. The International Hotel. They're supposed to be holding a room for me." Fairbanks smiled. "I hope they are."

"If they ain't, I can find you a place to bunk here for a day or two," Barr said.

"Thank you." Fairbanks restrained a smile at the offer. There had been no Cosmos Club in Maracaibo on his previous visit, but he had heard from others in Houston that it was a high-rolling gambling joint and fancy bawdy house. It was hardly the place, he thought, for a dignified attorney on a new assignment to bed down.

Barr stepped down from the carriage and Fairbanks, on impulse, joined him. The driver began sorting out Barr's luggage. Fairbanks thrust his hand out to Barr. "I'm Tom Fairbanks." Barr shook his hand. "I'm a lawyer, for British Meridian Oil Company, and I hope to see you again."

Barr studied Fairbanks unabashedly, but the man did not flinch. Fairbanks was an inch or two taller than Barr, wide-shouldered and thickly built, wearing a dark gray suit and gray felt hat. His broad face had been burned by the south Texas sun for so

17

many years that it was as brown as any Venezuelan's. Dark brown eyes were set wide apart under heavy brows as black as the shaggy mop of hair. The nose, however, was as sharp as Barr's. The mouth was full and well-shaped, the chin wide and strong.

Finally, Barr spoke. "You know who I am, don't you? And what I do."

Fairbanks nodded, "I do."

"I'm going to buy part of this place here. Half of it."

"All right," Fairbanks said.

One of the huge double doors of the Cosmos Club opened and a man stepped outside, leaving the door ajar. He was a white-haired man in his sixties wearing a snowy-white shirt and a black bowtie. He said pleasantly, "The gambling rooms are not open until three o'clock, gentlemen, the upstairs rooms at four. You have quite a bit of time to wait."

The door behind him was flung open. An auburn-haired woman in loose, pale-blue pajamas stood on the threshold for a moment, then went quickly to Grady Barr. He took her in his arms. She nuzzled his neck, murmuring softly, "Grady, Grady, Grady . . ." She lifted her head to look into Barr's face, and Fairbanks thought he had never seen such love shining in a woman's eyes.

Barr smiled at her. It was not a smile of love, Fairbanks thought as he watched, but certainly one of great pleasure. Barr's big hands held the woman tightly, and she closed her eyes and shivered as if anticipating the satisfaction of his hunger.

The driver tugged at Barr's elbow, demanding payment. Still smiling, Barr paid the man in silver United States coins, completing the transaction in the Spanish of the working class of Mexico and South Texas. Fairbanks had been surprised at Barr's fluency earlier when the men had cleared customs at the dock, and he now wondered when and where Barr had learned the language.

The woman turned to the white-haired man. "Marion, have someone take Mr. Barr's bags to my room."

The man nodded, his face impassive, and went inside the club.

Barr slapped Fairbanks lightly on the arm. "We know how to find each other, Tom." He took the woman's arm and escorted her into the club.

Fairbanks had no problems with his hotel reservation, the manager having assured him that although boomers were sleep-

18

ing four and five to a room in every available hostelry, the attorney for British Meridian would share his room with no one.

"I knew your father," the manager said. "He was a great man."

"Thank you," Fairbanks said.

"I met him when he was here back in nineteen-nineteen. You were with him, but I never met you." The manager shook his head sadly. "I heard about him dying. Something with his heart, wasn't it?"

"Yes. He died in his sleep."

"Shame he died before the boom, wasn't it?" The manager leaned across the hotel desk. "He predicted the boom, you know," he said confidentially. "That's why I built this hotel. Converted it out of a warehouse. Yes sir, I've heard it said that Americans never would have been allowed in this country if it hadn't been for Walter Fairbanks."

The statement was a gross exaggeration, but Fairbanks nodded anyway.

"Say!" The manager stuck his hand across the desk. "I'm Harry Little." Fairbanks shook his hand. "Now," Little said, "I've held you up long enough." He got the key from the slots behind him and handed it to Fairbanks. "You just remember," he said solemnly, "that Harry Little is always ready to help you." He grinned. "Not much happens in the Maracaibo Basin that I don't hear about."

Two hours later Fairbanks found the office of British Meridian. It was a huge single room on the ground floor of an aging structure near the docks, with walls which were covered with maps from ceiling to floor. Three brown desks with three brown chairs and a wooden crate crammed with papers constituted the furnishings. Only one of the chairs was occupied. Its occupant, a small, elderly man with a green eyeshade, rose to greet Fairbanks.

Loud voices outside distracted them both. The clerk sighed and resumed his seat. Two men came into the office. Both were clad in khaki shirts and trousers, laced boots and wide-brimmed straw hats, the oilfield uniform. It was obvious to Fairbanks that they had been arguing furiously and that only the sight of him standing there had stopped them.

One whipped off his hat. "Are you Fairbanks?" he demanded curtly. He was a short, compact man in his thirties, deeply tanned. Anger gleamed in his small blue eyes.

"Yes, I'm Tom Fairbanks."

19

"Well, you'd better get some work clothes if you're going to hang around here. You can save that suit for lawyering."

The other man laughed and shook his head in resignation. "You'd better save your advice until you find out who outranks who," he told his companion. He turned to Fairbanks. "Phil Carter, Mr. Fairbanks. Geologist, engineer and jack of all trades for British Meridian." He winked at Fairbanks. "This splendid fellow is Joe Reid, the company manager. As you can see, he's one of the sweetest chaps in all creation." The man's fat face split in a wide grin and he stuck out a moist pudgy hand for Fairbanks to shake. He winked again. "All it takes is a bit of adversity to put Joe in a bother."

"There's enough adversity to go around," Reid said. His anger had apparently subsided. He shook Fairbanks' hand, a faint sheepish smile on his lips.

"I heard about the three dry holes before I left Houston," Fairbanks said, his voice filled with interest and concern.

"Four now," Reid said. "And two broke-down drilling rigs."

Fairbanks looked rueful.

"That's not all," Reid continued grimly. "A Shell subsidiary has drilled *six* dry holes on acreage adjoining our other concession."

Fairbanks looked inquiringly at Carter.

"It condemns our stuff, I'm afraid," the geologist said. "In fairness to Joe and to myself, if you will, we would never have taken those concessions. They're too far south, to my mind. They were gotten, you see, before we got here."

Fairbanks was incredulous. "Do you mean that's all we've got?"

"Oh, no," Carter said. "We've got lots of acreage out in eastern Venezuela." He paused. "And, of course, we've got a small concession in the Kilometer Strip."

Now Fairbanks was getting annoyed. "What the hell is the Kilometer Strip?"

"Why, it's a zone that encircles the lake and extends from the shore one kilometer out into the water," Carter said coolly. "Our strip is about six miles long."

Reid broke in. "The dirty bastards make you take some stuff in the Strip before you can get something you want," he said bitterly. "They know you can never use it. It's just a way of increasing their payoff."

"I assume you can't drill out there," Fairbanks said.

"Of course not! Nobody's ever drilled over water. It's impossible! And the dirty bastards know it."

Fairbanks looked at Carter for confirmation.

The geologist shrugged. "You see, Mr. Fairbanks, that's what the arguing is all about. I think we *can* drill in the lake." He looked at Reid. "There's a great field beneath the lake, Joe. There simply has to be. My every geological calculation says so."

Reid grasped his forehead and closed his eyes. "Goddamn it, Phil, I've told you a hundred times that we'd have to drill right on the kilometer line. That's more than a thousand yards from shore and the water's asshole deep on a tall giraffe. Can't you understand a goddamn thing? It's the law."

Carter seemed unperturbed. "Perhaps Fairbanks can get the law changed. Lawyers do that, you know. Then we could drill practically on the shore line."

"Oh, Christ!" Reid said.

"What if I can't manage that?" Fairbanks asked Carter. "Where does that leave us?"

Carter shrugged. "We'll just have to manage some way to drill out on the line, won't we. Before the money runs out."

"And stockholder confidence," Fairbanks said.

"Yes. In any event, it's our job, isn't it?"

Reid said quickly, "It'll take a better drilling rig than we've got."

"You mean, if we decide to try it," Fairbanks said.

Reid nodded, and Fairbanks turned a measuring gaze on Carter. "Can you convince me that you know what the hell you're talking about?"

"Only if you know a slight smattering of geology."

Fairbanks grinned. "My smattering is the slightest."

Carter returned the grin and took Fairbanks by the arm. He led the way to a big map tacked on the wall behind a desk. "Let me show you the key to the treasure chest, old boy."

"Oh, shit." Joe Reid said disgustedly.

Rested, freshly bathed and shaven, Grady Barr stood naked in the middle of Louise Bremond's bedroom. It was a small room, almost overflowing with vines and flowering plants and dominated by a wide bed with carved posters of polished black wood. Three whirling fans hung from the ceiling, one directly over the wide bed. The bed's covers had been pulled back exposing a white sheet and three pillows.

Barr was slim, but his arms were so heavily muscled that the big hands did not seem incongruous. His chest was covered with a thick growth of golden hair, and his long, thick penis hung from a golden thatch. Waiting for the woman, he stood with the pride of a young man who knew his body was beautiful because women had told him so.

A door near the head of the bed opened and Louise Bremond appeared. She was naked. She took several steps into the bedroom, then began turning slowly, preening, showing herself to Grady Barr. Barr watched her without moving.

She was a year or two past thirty, tall, narrow-shouldered, slim-waisted. Though her buttocks were too full and heavy for beauty and her hips too wide, both promised a sensual harvest. Her breasts were small and well-shaped, slightly droopy. The nipples, however, were astonishingly large for such small breasts, dark red with only the shadows of aureolas. Two stretch marks of childbirth stood out dully on her abdomen. Her legs were long, slim and shapely.

Her pretty face was open, guileless, the face of a woman who had been the high school beauty queen in some rural community in her youth. As she preened for herself and Barr, there was nothing in its texture or expression to indicate that she had been a whore for six years, a madam for four, and that she had full-serviced fourteen celebrating soldiers in a six-hour period at war's end in 1918. Her wavy auburn hair, parted in the middle, hung several inches below her shoulders.

She stopped turning to face Barr, her eyes on his stony erection. He moved toward her several strides but halted when she held out an imploring hand. "Let me, Grady," she said.

She went to him. She began kissing his mouth, his cheeks, his eyes, his neck, caressing his shoulders, his back, the golden chest while Barr stood without moving, his eyes closed. She moved soft, trembling hands about his buttocks while she kissed his nipples and rested her cheek against his chest.

She dropped to her knees before him. While she cuddled and caressed his testicles, she kissed his penis from base to rosy tip and back again. Then, with a soft cry, she took the tip into her mouth as if it were a rare, exotic fruit and she were ravenous with hunger. Barr began trembling and the big hands clenched into tight fists.

She rose to her feet. Touching him continuously, she forced him to lie down on the bed on his back. She knelt beside him and once again put her mouth over the head of his penis, taking more and more of him in her mouth until he could feel the hot juices of her throat. Once Barr involuntarily reached out to grasp a breast and she angrily brushed his hand aside as if he'd broken an agreement.

Suddenly she pulled away from him. "Oh, God!" she said hoarsely. She positioned herself above him, spread herself with her fingers and mounted him, uttering soft, meaningless cries and going into orgasm when his penis had hardly penetrated. Orgasm followed orgasm as she moved slowly inch by inch down the rigid member. In one last movement she enclosed him, and she cried out, "Now, Grady! Now!"

Barr needed no urging, driven as he was almost to the edge of madness. Now he grasped her buttocks to open her wide. He pulled her down firmly but not roughly and set his hips into a rocking motion that kept his penis in constant movement against her clitoris.

"I'm coming, Grady, I'm coming!" she shouted, and beat on his chest with her fists. "Again, Grady! I'm coming again!"

A half dozen more times she cried out before Barr was caught up in the throes of his own orgasm. Harsh, choking sounds came from his throat as he lunged against her. She uttered one last cry and fell on his chest. Barr's arms encircled her as she sobbed against his cheek. His shaking hands stroked her back and shoulders.

"Oh, Grady . . ."

"Don't try to talk now," Barr said gently.

They lay there, with Barr stroking her hair, caressing her body, until her spasms ceased. She moved her body so they lay side by side. He held her close and kissed her mouth. She snuggled contentedly against him.

"One more and I'd have fainted," she said.

Barr chuckled.

"I know what women like about you, Grady. Do you?"

"I think so."

"No, not that! Something besides that jackass dick."

Barr raised up on an elbow and looked at her with mock indignation.

"Do you want me to go on?" she asked.

Barr kissed her.

"It's because you act like women amount to something," she

said seriously. "I don't care who they are or what they are, you act like they're worth something. Did you know that?"

"I never thought men had all the brains, Lou. Guts neither."

"But I think you *like* women, and I don't mean just in bed."

"Of course I do."

"And you're a loving man, Grady. Most guys are cleaning up in the bathroom and thinking about business three minutes after they shoot their load. You know that. With their wives or whoever they're with."

"I like it all," Barr said. "Before, during and after. I reckon it's my nature."

"Yes," she agreed, "It is your nature. Now," she said crisply, "you've probably got the longest dick in town, what about its circumference?"

"What?"

"Circumference. Do you know what that means?"

Barr was alert. "Circumference," he said slowly, drawing out each syllable. "Has it got anything to do with a circle? It sounds like it."

"Yes," Louise said with satisfaction. "It's the distance around a circle. Now, do you know what diameter means?"

"I do." His voice was sober. "I learned that in the oilfields. When they talk about a joint of four-inch pipe, they mean it's four inches across. That joint of pipe has got an outside diameter and an inside diameter. They call it OD and ID."

"All right. Now, I remember this from high school. If you know the diameter of something you can figure out the circumference without having to measure it."

"How can they do that?" Barr asked quickly.

"I don't know, Grady. I've forgotten that, if I ever even learned it."

Barr was propped up on his elbow. "By God, Lou, I've got to find out how they do that."

She pulled him down to her. "And you're going to have to quit saying *ain't*. You're as bad about that as ever."

"It's hard not to say it when everybody else does."

"I don't," she said, her voice seeming to Barr almost prim. "And you're still saying *orter* for ought to."

"Yes, ma'am." He would have said more, but her hands were on his penis, and he was becoming hard again. He began kissing her breasts, now and then scraping the nipples with his teeth, pushing a nipple with the end of his tongue until it was buried

24

in the soft tissue of the breast. His fingers were caressing her clitoris.

"It's so *hard*," she said, squeezing his penis. Then, urgently, "Let me have it." As he moved to mount her, she cried, "Hurry, Grady! Hurry. . . ."

Two years after her graduation from a small Central Texas high school, Louise Bremond ran away from home to marry a handsome flour salesman from Fort Worth. She bore him a son, but the child died within a year of its birth. Louise deserted the salesman at that point and began selling that which she had been giving away for free to men who caught her fancy.

Fort Worth was an open city then. Gambling and prostitution flourished under police protection. Louise was gathered up by a pimp named Chester Bent with whom she quickly fell in love. Bent had a stable of seven girls working the city's hotels. She worked for him for four years, turning over her earnings to him and receiving in return food, clothing, shelter and pocket money. One night while he was drunk he beat her.

The next day she left for Houston by train. She found an apartment near the downtown area and began plying her trade, taking her tricks to small hotels at first, then later to her own bed. Three times she was slapped around by pimps whose protection she refused, but her country girl independence would not allow her to again subject herself to a pimp's discipline. When a fourth pimp threatened her she took a decisive step.

She managed to pick up a vice-squad captain as he dined alone in an expensive restaurant. He knew she was a whore, but he was captivated by her daring and by her good looks. And he was surprised and gratified by her passionate response to his love-making. Within a month he set her up in a large frame house on Rusk Avenue with himself as protector and silent partner. She selected a dozen girls to work for her; the vice-squad captain silenced the squeals of pimps outraged by their losses of property. Business thrived.

The captain was her only lover. He was an adequate sexual partner, but at times she longed to couple with a man like Chester Bent, the only man who had ever really satiated her. Then Louise began hearing her girls talk about a new pimp in town, one they described as virile, friendly but firm in his dealings with his stable. The vice-squad captain told her a story about the new pimp. One of his girls had gone to a hotel to turn a trick. The trick stood in his doorway and fondled the girl's breasts while he pretended to haggle over the price. When he achieved orgasm, he slammed the door in the girl's face. The new pimp had gone to the hotel, had gained entry to the trick's room by saying he was the night manager and had slugged the trick on the jaw.

"He made the guy pay him the girl's regular fee," the captain said, "then took an extra dollar for himself for taxi fare. I kind of appreciate his touch. He didn't make a hog of himself."

Intrigued, Louise Bremond made a date to talk business with Grady Barr in a room at the Rice Hotel. They stayed in the room for two days and two nights, having food and drink delivered to them. Thereafter, she saw Barr whenever she could manage it without interfering with business or alerting the captain. She was in love again.

In 1921 Barr moved to Galveston as managing partner of the Shark's Head. In the spring of 1922 a reform movement shut down Houston's gambling and prostitution establishments. Months passed while Louise Bremond waited for word to reopen. She spent much of the time in Galveston with Grady Barr.

She had heard about Maracaibo and Venezuela from a stockbroker. "They've found some oil in piddling amounts in the Maracaibo Basin," the stockbroker had said, "but I've got a feeling somebody is going to strike it big some day. It might be a good idea for you to get in on the ground floor, Louise. It may be a couple of years before Houston opens up again."

She talked it over with Barr, and he urged her to go to Maracaibo.

"From what I've heard, I think that guy's right, Lou. You've got enough money to open up a good place. Give me eight months or a year and I'll be right there with you. I'm tired of this place, but it's too much of a gold mine to hurry away from."

Reluctantly, she left him. In October 1922 she opened the Cosmos Club on Maracaibo's Plaza Sucre, anticipating the boom by two months. In late March 1923 she received a telegram from Barr announcing his expected arrival date in Maracaibo. Believing that he had advanced his departure from Galveston to be with her sooner, she was overjoyed. When he told her of the Texas Ranger raid on the Shark's Head over drinks in the Cosmos Club, she forced herself to keep from smiling. . . .

Now she lay on his arm, resting in the menthol coolness that came with satiation. Barr slept silently. She thought, as she had thought many times before, that Barr would be successful in any field. He was attractive to both sexes, was smart and resourceful, a good businessman. She had seen him fix things; tools seemed to be made for his hands. Once he had told her, laughing, that machinery, like women, purred at his touch. And she had been pleased and flattered when he had asked her to correct his grammar.

He had told her that he had left school in the fifth grade. She knew that he read a newspaper with difficulty, that his infrequent letters to her had been scrawled with a childish hand. She thought to herself suddenly, I can make him learn to read and write better now. I'll be with him all the time. He's so curious about so many things . . .

There was a knock on the door at the far end of the bedroom. She slid out of bed and went to the door. "Who is it?" she asked without opening the door.

"It's Marion. Hernan Robles just left downstairs. He says for you to join him in an hour at the Blue Book restaurant on Plaza Baralt. He says Captain Ramirez will be there, too." There was a pause. "He says for you to bring Mr. Barr with you."

"Thank you, Marion."

She returned to the bed. Barr was sitting up. "Who the hell is Hernan Robles?" he asked. "And Captain Ramirez?"

She shrugged. "Robles seems to be some kind of bull of the woods. I've never met him, just heard about him. Ramirez is a cop. He comes in pretty often and sits around accepting free drinks. He's never done anything more than speak to me."

"But you're worried, ain't you?"

"No, not exactly worried. But I haven't been here long enough to know *all* the rules."

"Do you think you've broke one?"

She shrugged again. "Not one that I can't mend."

Barr smiled. "Always plead not guilty on account of ignorance, Lou. A good-looking woman can always get away with that." He leaned forward and slapped her gently on the buttocks. "Let's get cleaned up and go see this bull of the woods. Maybe he'll buy our supper!"

Chapter Two

Christopher Columbus discovered Venezuela in 1498 on his third voyage to the west. It was his first glimpse of the American mainland, and the great navigator was convinced that he had found the Earthly Paradise. His report on his discovery stirred the imagination of Europe, and in the wake of his caravels came the adventurers and the conquerers.

The following year a Spanish seaman, Alonso de Ojeda, explored much of the country's coastline. As he edged his small craft along the coast a sudden wind bellied the sails and the vessel glided over a sand bar and into one of the world's largest lakes. Indian villages built on stilts over the lake waters reminded the seafarer of Venice; he named the region Venezuela—"Little Venice."

The Spaniard found the Indians making use of oil and asphalt from seeps in the lowlands around the lake. The oil was balm for aching joints and a healing agent for open sores and wounds. The asphalt was excellent as a caulking for fishing boats. The Spaniards promptly caulked their caravel and oiled their weapons.

In 1529 a tall, bearded German, Ambrosius Alfinger, arrived in Venezuela to establish a settlement on the west bank of the lake. Alfinger was the agent for a German banking house, the Welsers of Augsburg. Charles V had granted the territory to the bankers, to whom he was deeply in debt. He also had sent along a contingent of Spanish soldiers to protect Alfinger and his small band of settlers.

The protection was needed. Only several small sheds were under construction when a band of Indians, led by their great chief Mara, attacked without warning. The Spaniards rallied in combat while Alfinger and his band huddled at the lake shore.

"Mara! Mara! Mara!" the Indians shouted as their chief charged among the soldiers wielding a heavy black club. But a Spaniard caught Mara on his sword point and drove the weapon through the Indian's body. "Mara cayo!" the Spaniard shouted. *Mara has fallen.*

His comrades took up the cry. Shocked by Mara's death, the Indians retreated. The Spaniards pursued them until they were outdistanced and even then "Mara cayo!" burst from their dusty throats. Safe on the lake's edge, Alfinger said to a settler, "Mara cayo. It's a good name, a proper name, for our settlement here."

Thus Mara cayo—Maracaibo as it became known—was born in violence, and it was to know more violence in the years to come. But somehow it managed to cling to life, and give its name to the lake.

Spanish mining laws had placed ownership of underground minerals in the hands of the government. An ordinance in 1783 also made deposits of oil and asphalt the property of the Crown. After liberation—when the country rose up under the leadership of Simon Bolivar and broke the power of Spain—Venezuela retained this principle of government ownership. And a policy was established that the country's president had exclusive right to grant mining and oil concessions.

In 1907 President Cipriano Castro granted leases to four private citizens which totaled ten million acres. The citizens promptly sold the leases to foreign oil companies. Most of the acreage wound up in the hands of Royal Dutch-Shell, a British-Dutch combine.

The next year Castro was deposed by Juan Vicente Gomez, a despot's despot. He immediately granted a tremendous lease of more than sixty-five million acres which after some maneuvering also came into Shell's possession. The lease covered fourteen states across the country.

On July 31, 1914, Shell completed the first commercial oil well in Venezuela at Mene Grande, a community about twelve miles east of Lake Maracaibo. Other wells quickly followed and Shell built a pipeline to the lakeside town of San Lorenzo. A refinery was constructed at San Lorenzo, and in 1917 the first shipment of oil from Venezuela was made.

Southwest of the lake Shell brought in two more fields, and

another field, El Mene, was discovered by a British company about thirty-five miles east of the top of the lake.

The fields were not prolific producers. Because of World War I equipment was hard to acquire, supplies sometimes impossible to obtain. Drilling was suspended in some fields, slowed in others. War's end, however, found the European companies ready to exploit in earnest other more promising sections of their leases.

War's end also found large U.S. companies eager to gain a toe-hold in Venezuela. But Gomez made no move to welcome them. He had a great admiration for all things British, and it appeared he was content to let British companies find his country's oil, if oil was to be found.

It was at this point that SeaCoast International—SCI—the largest U.S. oil company and Shell's greatest competitor, engaged Walter Fairbanks, Tom Fairbanks' father, to pry open Gomez's door.

Walter Fairbanks had successfully combined two business careers. He was the manager of his family's vast Sombrero ranch in southwest Texas and he was a corporation lawyer of considerable reputation. His negotiating talents were ever in demand, occasionally by the U.S. government. He was courtly, persuasive, shrewd as a roadrunner. And he spoke beautiful Spanish.

With young Tom in attendance, Fairbanks set up households in Maracaibo and Caracas and proceeded to entertain lavishly those members of the government who were alleged to have great influence with Gomez. He was wittier than the British, more charming than the Dutch, and he was quick to murmur advice on domestic legislative matters. He was soon the most popular and most sought after foreigner in both cities.

He met Gomez at a party given by the Minister of Development. He had learned that after power Gomez loved cattle, which he raised on a ranch near Maracay. Fairbanks turned the conversation from oil to breeding, and soon was comparing methods with the dictator. Gomez invited him to the Maracay ranch.

On that visit Fairbanks began his campaign to convince Gomez that the British government, through Shell and other companies, was in a position to exert more influence on Venezuelan policies than a prudent president should tolerate. American capital, he suggested, would effectively counterbalance any British initiatives.

As the days passed and the visit lengthened, Fairbanks also suggested that the country's petroleum laws be overhauled to protect the country and the people. Gomez was impressed by Fairbanks' solicitude, and he had a suggestion of his own: Fairbanks should draw up a new law which Gomez could present to the Congress for passage. Fairbanks permitted himself to be persuaded in that direction. Gomez predicted that American oil companies would be welcomed to Venezuela under the new law—if the Congress enacted it.

After token debate, the Congress adopted Fairbanks' proposals. The new law provided for national reserves, and there were provisions covering government inspections, proper drilling methods and fair treatment of Venezuelan employees.

But Fairbanks had not forgotten his employer. Supplies needed for oil operations as construed by the companies could be imported duty free. The various taxes to be paid by the companies were minimal. Royalty payments were so low that oilmen estimated that Shell, for example, would pay the government only eight cents per barrel for the country's oil. Walter and Tom Fairbanks returned home, the son to complete his law studies at Princeton, the father to die of an unexpected heart attack. Through the door the elder Fairbanks had opened U.S. oil company representatives swarmed by the dozens to pick among Shell's leavings. They bought and sold leases. They drilled in outlandish places. Shell also drilled on new locations. Still nothing occurred to fulfill the country's geological promise.

Then, in December 1922, Shell's hopes and dreams were realized on the outskirts of the village of La Rosa. La Rosa was a primitive suburb of the town of Cabimas which sprawled on the eastern lake shore just where the neck of the lake began broadening out into the lake proper. Across the lake to the northwest the city of Maracaibo stood like a sentinel.

Shell had decided to drill deeper in an old abandoned well about three-quarters of a mile from the lake shore. At six AM on December 14, the well began to flow. Because it had come in unexpectedly, no gate valve had been installed to control the flow and the oil ran smoothly out of the ten-inch casing. As the valve was being readied the flow from the well increased.

At seven AM there came a mighty rumbling from the bowels of the earth. Suddenly, with a roar that froze the blood, oil leaped from the well in a spout that towered two hundred feet above the derrick and fanned out in the air like a titan's umbrella.

Almost one hundred thousand barrels of oil per day were shooting out of the jungle well. Oil covered the trees, coated the vines, and in ever-growing streams flowed through the under-brush like black serpents. The streets looked as if they were paved and the ditches beside them ran bank-full.

Shell sent out calls for help from its other installations. Villagers, those bolder than the rest, were recruited. Sumps were dug and the oil pumped into them, but workers and pumps could not keep pace with the roaring giant.

As the days and nights passed without a sign that the flow was diminishing, a rumor spread through La Rosa and Cabimas. The local padre, it was said, had declared that Shell's drill bit had plumbed the depths of hell itself. For a people who bolstered their Catholic faith with memories of pagan gods, the rumor was terrifying.

Nine days passed before the well sanded in at the bottom and choked off the flow. News of it had been flashed around the world. The New York *Times* described it as "the most productive on earth." And in Houston, where Tom Fairbanks by now was practicing law, the newspapers ran stories on page one for six days.

The stories made Fairbanks restless. He was established in an old, successful firm, but he was bored with his routine work. Several times he thought of applying to SeaCoast International for a job in Venezuela. Each time he dismissed the idea; he didn't want to be hired on the strength of his father's labors for the company. As it turned out, his father's reputation got him on the British Meridian payroll.

At a cocktail party he was introduced to Charles Lapham, a Texas oilman who had invested in British Meridian and held a seat on the board of directors. Lapham was on his way to London for a board meeting. He was empowered to engage a Spanish-speaking lawyer, he said, and was certain the board would be pleased to have the son of Walter Fairbanks as the company's legal representative in Venezuela. He thought a three-month's salary advance was reasonable, he said, and wrote Fairbanks a check.

"I hope you demonstrate some of your father's ability in repre-senting us," Lapham said pleasantly.

Fairbanks waved the check. "I certainly don't command his fees," he said dryly.

Lapham laughed. "Good man! You'll do fine."

Two months later Fairbanks stood in British Meridian's Maracaibo office while an overweight, balding geologist explained what he called "a most notable geological process."

"This is the Maracaibo Basin," Phil Carter said, using his forefinger as a pointer. "As you see, it's formed by the Perija Ridge on the west and by the Andes on the east and south. To give you an idea of its size, the lake here in the center covers only about a fifth of it, about five thousand square miles. The lake is a hundred and fifteen miles long and seventy miles wide. It is very shallow for a lake so large. It . . . ."

"Get on with it, for Christ's sake!" Joe Reid, the company manager, had walked over to stand by Carter and Fairbanks in front of the big map on the wall. "He don't need a geography lesson."

"I travel at my own pace, old boy," Carter said, unruffled. "I know this area as no other man knows it, and Fairbanks is entitled to hear my say." He continued with his lecture. "You know, of course, that oil is organic matter," he said to Fairbanks. "For millions of years streams and heavy rainfall washed sands and muds saturated with organic matter into the basin from the mountains. So why didn't the lake run over with mud and dry up? Why didn't the heavy rains wear away the mountains?" He smiled at Fairbanks. "The lake didn't dry up because the bottom sank at the same speed at which the mud was deposited." He paused. "And with perfectly marvelous balance, old boy, the mountains grew in correct proportion. Are you with me so far?"

"I think so," Fairbanks said slowly. "If what you say is true the lake has never been very deep."

"Correct. It's been shallow from its beginning. We'll prove that when we get to drilling. I don't know how deep anyone will have to drill to reach the granite bottom, but all of the sedimentary material will have been made up of rocks formed by the hardening of muds and sands that were deposited at shallow depths. Why do I think that? Because I believe that those deep rocks, the hardened mud, if you will, will contain fossils of snails and other aquatic creatures which lived in shallow waters. Are you still with me?"

"Oh, God," Joe Reid sighed. "Is anybody with you?"

"I'll admit that much of what I've said about the lake is conjecture," Carter went on, "but I've definitely established what I said about the mountains growing."

"How?" Fairbanks asked.

"I've studied the rocks in the mountains. Now listen. I found fossils of marine creatures which lived when those rocks were at the bottom of the sea."

Fairbanks stared at the man's earnest face. "Is this process still going on," he asked slowly, "the lake bottom sinking on the one hand, the mountains growing on the other?"

"It is. Imperceptibly, of course." Carter's pale brown eyes were dancing.

"Then do I understand that the entire basin may be an oilfield?"

"Precisely!"

"And the oil-bearing formations would be thicker and richer in the lake because it's almost in the center of the basin. Is that correct?"

"Oh, absolutely!" Carter was fidgeting with joy at being understood. "Absolutely, Fairbanks."

Fairbanks turned to Reid. "Is anyone in agreement with him on this?"

"Nobody in the oil business," Reid said sourly. "At least I've never heard of it if they were."

Fairbanks abruptly changed the subject. "What's the reasoning behind this law that says we have to drill on the kilometer line?"

Reid grunted. "Typical Venezuelan reasoning. They don't want anybody drilling in the lake so they make it impossible. Gomez is supposed to want to protect the fishing for the natives." He shook his head. "The law even says you have to give up your lease if you foul the lake."

Fairbanks sat on the corner of the desk. He rubbed a hand across his face. "What about our leases in the eastern part of the country?"

Reid shrugged. "Phil says they look good. Plenty of oil signs. But they're way to hell out in the jungle. The company would be broke before we got halfway started." His face twisted with frustration and anger. "You've got to be a God damn giant to get oil in this country!"

Carter's voice was almost tender. "There's still enough money in the kitty to drill the lake. One well, at least. And then we'll be rolling in clover."

34

Reid ignored Carter, and turned to Fairbanks. "Do you think there's a chance in hell that you might get the law changed so we can drill closer to shore?" he asked.

"I don't know. I've been thinking about it."

"How much longer are you going to take to think about it?"

"It would take a trip to Caracas, maybe to Maracay," Fairbanks said evenly. "I suspect it would cost a great deal of money just to make the effort."

"You could trade on your father's name," Reid said with intentional crudeness. "Well, wasn't that why you were hired in the first place?"

Fairbanks didn't answer, and his face was impassive as he looked directly at Reid. Color spread from Reid's neck to his cheeks and shame crept into his small blue eyes. Finally he looked at the floor, mumbling, "I'm sorry, Fairbanks."

"All right," Fairbanks said. "I think you were just trying to make me nudge you toward the lake."

Reid looked up in gratitude. But then he said, his voice despondent, "I guess it's all we've got."

Before Reid finished speaking Carter was all over him, patting his shoulders, pumping his hand, saying, "Oh, Joe! Oh, Joe!"

Reid pushed Carter away. "Quit it, you damned fool. We've got to have a drilling rig and a hell of a lot more." He turned furiously on Fairbanks. "You got any other bright ideas, Mr. Lawyer?"

Fairbanks grinned. "Let me sit down and I might come up with one or two."

Reid snorted. "You sure as hell better!"

The Blue Book was crowded with boomers and with Venezuelan businessmen who somehow had managed to cope with inflation and could afford the outrageous prices for food and drink. The bolivar had stood at five to a dollar at the boom's beginning, but the influx of American oil workers earning five hundred dollars a month had sent the bolivar bobbing. Merchants began refusing Venezuelan paper money, demanding American gold and silver for their wares. Only beer had escaped the economic madness; it still sold for seven cents a bottle, and boomers bought it by the gunnysack.

A waiter led Louise Bremond and Grady Barr past the throng at the bar and between crowded tables to the rear of the room. Two men waited for them at a table that was completely bare.

Anchored to the wall above the men was a stuffed jaguar in a stalking stance, ready for slaughter. One of the men rose and indicated where the waiter should seat Louise. The man stood erect; he was six feet of slim, masculine elegance in a lightweight suit of funeral black, pale blue shirt, black tie. His close-cropped hair was graying, contrasting sharply with his smooth mahogany complexion. His dark eyes were pleased with himself, his visitors and the world at large.

The other man rose. He was tall, on the verge of being fat. He had a large round head with thinning, wildly curly dark hair and large, shadowed eyes. He was dressed carelessly in uncreased white trousers and a stained white shirt. He looked half asleep, anxious to resume his seat.

"Miss Bremond. Mr. Barr. Will you please be seated," the elegant man said. "And you, too, Captain Ramirez," he said to his companion.

When the three were seated, he sat down. He leaned forward and said warmly, "First, Mr. Barr, let me congratulate you on that handsome suit. It looks like gray silk."

"It is," Barr said. "I got it from a Cuban tailor in Galveston. I can get his address if you want it."

"Perhaps. But we're here to talk business, if you don't mind, and business talks should be straight to the point, in my opinion. Agreed?"

Barr nodded.

"Very well. Miss Bremond made a routine trip to police headquarters when she opened the Cosmos Club and paid the customary operating fee for such an establishment. Since that time Captain Ramirez has inspected the club from time to time, on my instructions." He jerked his head at Louise. "I must say that it is being operated quite properly—and quite profitably. To the point, Mr. Barr, that I had decided to become a partner."

Barr lifted a hand in interruption. "You didn't say so, but I reckon you're Hernan Robles."

"Yes, I am Hernan Robles. I thought you knew."

"Well, if you're not going to buy us a drink, I'll order a round. A drink orter help this kind of business talk. And it might keep the captain awake."

Robles flushed. "Brandy is on the way, Mr. Barr."

As if on signal, the waiter appeared. On his tray were four glasses, linen napkins and a bottle of brandy. He broke the seal on the bottle to assure Robles that the contents were genuine. He departed, and Robles poured drinks. Robles lifted his glass. "To understanding," he said.

Barr sipped from his glass, nodding appreciatively. "This sure beats hell out of rum." He turned to Louise. "Don't it, Lou?" He didn't wait for an answer, but said to Robles, "You had just decided to be a partner in the club, you said. Is that right?"

"Yes," Robles said coldly, his charm gone. "And then today I learned that you propose to buy a half interest." He glanced at Louise. "And that you are on such terms with Miss Bremond that she had your baggage taken to her living quarters."

Barr grinned. "The cab driver."

"Yes, the driver. I have ways of learning things about visitors to Maracaibo. Visitors who interest me."

Barr jerked a thumb at Ramirez. "I figure he's a cop. What the hell are you?"

"I'm a very powerful man with very powerful friends, Mr. Barr, and soon to be a partner in the Cosmos Club. My plans do not include you."

Louise spoke for the first time. "I won't sell you an interest," she said to Robles.

Barr laughed. "He ain't talking about *buying* an interest, Lou. Not Mr. Robles." He had kept his gaze on Robles. "Powerful people like Mr. Robles here, they *take* what they want."

"I've paid my fees," she said stubbornly.

Robles ignored her. "I'll deal with Miss Bremond, and deal fairly," he said to Barr. "But I warn you, if you attempt to interfere in any way, Captain Ramirez will be happy to lose you in his commodious jail. In fact," he added as if just arriving at a decision, "I want you out of Maracaibo, out of Venezuela, just as fast as you can arrange transportation. Captain Ramirez will see that you don't dally. Any questions?"

Barr nodded. "Where did you learn to talk English so good? You sound like some kind of schoolteacher."

"You can't run him out of town," Louise said. "I don't care who you are."

Barr covered her hand with his. "Simmer down, Lou."

Robles said, "To answer your question, Mr. Barr, I am an honor graduate from the Virginia Military Institute. And I have one more admonition for you. You may spend the night at the Cosmos Club, but I want you to find other quarters tomorrow. After that, stay away from the club until your boat leaves. Understood?"

Barr stood up lazily and lifted Louise to her feet. "Oh, I heard every word you said, Mr. Robles." He began moving away from the table, guiding Louise before him.

"Mr. Barr!"

Barr stopped and half-turned to face Robles.

"If you heard my words, heed them," Robles said.

Barr grinned and waved a friendly hand. Then he escorted Louise out of the restaurant and onto the plaza. She pulled him against a store front. "I'm going with you, Grady. We can go to Dallas. I've heard it's a good town again."

Barr smiled at her. "I ain't going anywhere, Lou. Hell, I just got here."

She studied his smiling face. "What are you going to do?"

He took her arm to move on. "I'll think of something," he said, and the smile was gone.

Chapter Three

Hot and weary, Tom Fairbanks made his way across Plaza Sucre toward his hotel. For four days he had searched in vain for the drunken rotary rig salesman who had so extolled the virtues of his equipment in the Amsted Bar on Aruba. Joe Reid had not been able to buy or lease a serviceable drilling rig of any kind in the Maracaibo Basin, and plants in the States were loaded with back orders. Then Fairbanks had remembered the drunken salesman, but it seemed that he had vanished like a wisp of smoke once he had reached Maracaibo. The police had been no help.

As Fairbanks neared the hotel he saw Grady Barr push through the crowd near the entrance and go inside. He had thought of Barr occasionally in the days past; now he wondered if Barr was in the hotel to see him and renew their acquaintance. He reached the lobby just as Barr turned the corner of the stairs and disappeared. Harry Little, the hotelkeeper, saw Fairbanks looking at the stairwell.

"Know that fellow, Mr. Fairbanks?" Little asked. "Grady Barr?"

"I've met him." Fairbanks held out his hand for his key. He was in no mood for Little's garrulousness.

But Little held onto the key. "He's living on borrowed time," he confided. "Hernan Robles told him to get out of town, and as far as I can see he hasn't made a move in that direction."

Fairbanks was trapped. "Who the hell is Hernan Robles?"

Little whistled softly. "Big man. Some kind of kin to Guillermo Cerro Soto, and you know who *he* is. Just the president of the state of Zulia, that's all."

"Why would this Robles want him out of town?"

"I don't know that."

"How do you know any of it?"

"It's all over town, Mr. Fairbanks. The Pig told me. He's a cop. Said Captain Ramirez was with Robles when he told Barr to skedaddle. Like I said, he's been staying here three days and he don't act like he's worried." Little shook his head. "He's a fool, I'll tell you that. Ramirez will starve him to death in that jail of his . . . that is, if he don't just out and out have him killed."

Fairbanks stared at Little in disbelief, but Little nodded knowingly. "It wouldn't be the first time. They're in everything together, and Ramirez will do anything Robles tells him." He looked at the staircase significantly. "That man's in bad trouble."

Fairbanks let out a deep breath. "What room's he in?"

"Room ten," Little said. He handed Fairbanks his key. "Going to try to talk some sense into him?" he asked eagerly. "One man to another?"

"Later," Fairbanks said. He went to the stairs.

"There's four other men in the room with him, but they won't be in till evening. He's by himself now."

Fairbanks paused on the stairs. "Thanks, Mr. Little," he said.

He went on up and found Room Ten on the second floor. He knocked at the door. "It's Tom Fairbanks," he called out.

Barr opened the door almost immediately. He was dressed in the gray suit which Hernan Robles had admired in the Blue Book restaurant. "Hello, Tom" he said, smiling. "You caught me on the way out." He closed the door and locked it. "What's on your mind?"

Fairbanks said quickly, "I'm of a mind to buy drinks and supper this evening if you're interested. You name the time and place."

Barr hesitated, then nodded. "How about eight o'clock at the Bull Wheel. It's a good place."

Fairbanks was disappointed; he had wanted to meet earlier. But he said, "That's fine, Grady. I'll see you then."

As Barr turned to leave he touched Fairbanks' sleeve. "I'll be there," he said, as if he were acknowledging Fairbanks' concern.

Fairbanks watched him until Barr went down the stairs, then he went on to his own room to clean up and rest.

When Barr reached the lobby Harry Little was talking with a stocky young Venezuelan in a white linen suit. Little called out, "Man here to see you, Mr. Barr!"

Barr did not move, but let the stocky youth approach him. He

40

handed Barr an envelope. Barr didn't open it. "What's it say?" he asked.

"He's waiting for you," the youth said.

Barr put the envelope in his pocket. "Let's go."

The youth led the way out on the plaza and to a parked Studebaker. He drove them through the crowd, honking his rubber horn vigorously. They had traveled less than a quarter of a mile when Barr rested a big hand on the steering wheel. The driver stopped the car. "This is not the way to the mansion," Barr said. The driver nodded. "He is at another place. Don't be afraid." He drove on. Near the outskirts of town, on a shady lane, he stopped in front of an imposing two-story house of stucco and tile. "His daughter's house," the driver said. "Come on."

A woman of uncommon beauty opened the door before they even reached it. She wore a green skirt and a pale beige blouse with a low neckline that showed the swell of her breasts. Large golden rings hung from her earlobes on inch-long threads of gold. The dangling rings accentuated the lean triangularity of her face and the bold thrust of her thin, sharp nose. Her lips were full cut and warm with brilliant red lipstick. Mischief swam in the black pools of her eyes under arched, inquisitive brows. She was Indian dark, and her long black hair was pulled back and gathered at the nape of her neck by a green bandana.

She stepped back to allow Barr and the youth to enter a long hallway. "He's in the study, Eduardo," she said to the youth, but she caught Barr's eyes with a boldly curious glance before the men passed by her.

Eduardo stopped at the first door to his left. It was open. "He is here, Excellency," Eduardo said.

The man, seated behind a long, broad desk, raised his gaze from some papers he was studying. He looked like a bull. He was naked to the waist and his heavy shoulders and thick chest were covered with black hair. He was completely bald and his big, round head seemed to rest directly on his shoulders. A thick black mustache bristled under a beaked nose and above thick lips. He took an envelope from a desk drawer, and Barr could see that his hand was as large as his own.

"Wait in the car, Eduardo," he said huskily. "Have a seat, Mr. Barr."

Barr sat down in a heavy leather chair in front of the desk. The room was small and uncluttered. Shelves full of books were on all the walls save the one behind the big man. On this wall was a painting of a man in gray military trappings astride a gray horse. Two shining shotguns were crossed beneath it. Barr kept his gaze on the painting a moment longer than he had intended.

"Your Robert E. Lee, a military genius," the big man said. He took a slip of blue paper from the desk drawer and waved it. "You have aroused my curiosity, young man, sending me a check for five thousand dollars and asking for an appointment. I know of your confrontation with Hernan Robles. Are you a fool, or has Guillermo Cerro Soto been smeared on the streets as a bribe-taker? I must know."

"I haven't heard anything bad said about you, sir, and I don't think I'm a fool," Barr said. "I know you've got plenty to do, running a government, but I had to get your attention. I had to find out how strong this Robles is. I've been running around with my ear to the ground and from what I hear he ain't necessarily your favorite kinfolk."

"I don't interfere in his business dealings. From what I understand, he offered you free passage out of the country."

"Yes, sir, he did. But I don't want to leave. It goes against my grain to get run off from somewhere." Barr paused. "I ain't going to be run off."

"Then you will die. Captain Ramirez will surely have you killed."

"I don't think I'm the kind that dies easy, sir," Barr said earnestly. "There'd be a lot of scratching and yelling. Enough to attract some attention."

Cerro Soto grunted. "Who would notice the death of a pimp?"

Barr stood up. "Thank you for seeing me, sir."

Cerro Soto waved the check. "What if I had simply cashed this when I received it?"

"There'd been hell to pay," Barr said, shaking his head.

"Why is that?"

Barr grinned. "Because it ain't no good."

Cerro Soto stared at him a moment. Then he fell back in his chair, short, barking laughter shaking his big body. Still laughing he waved a hand for Barr to be seated. Barr sat down, smiling at the man's amusement.

The woman who had met Barr at the door whisked into the room. She was laughing also, and ignored Barr. She said to Cerro Soto in Spanish, "Isn't he delightful in his crudity? The waitresses and shop clerks call him the golden man, and he is, isn't he?"

Cerro Soto stopped laughing. "He also speaks Spanish," he said sourly, glaring at the woman. "Will you never cease eavesdropping?" He dismissed her with a wave of his hand. "Be gone."

She whirled out of the room without a glance at Barr. Cerro Soto leaned forward on the desk. He tore the check in two. "Now," he said quietly, "what will you do if I assure your safety? You can't hold an interest in the Cosmos Club. That would be too much."

"I'll think of something, sir."

"What about the oilfields?" Cerro Soto asked thoughtfully. "You're a resourceful young man, and you look healthy." He smiled faintly. "Have you had time to learn about anything but women?"

"I started roughnecking in Mexico when I was sixteen and I turned out a driller when I was nineteen," Barr said with a hint of pride in his voice.

Cerro Soto spread his hands. "Well," he said with finality. He stood up. "You will not be disturbed unless you disturb others."

Barr stood up. "Thank you, Excellency."

Cerro Soto nodded and turned toward a book shelf. "Eduardo will take you where you wish to go."

The woman was waiting at the doorway, her hand on the knob. "Do you do the cooking and washing, too?" Barr asked. "Or do you just tend this door?" In the dim light cast by a single wall lamp he smiled and covered her hand with his. She pulled free.

"Aren't you afraid to be forward with me?" she said in English.

Barr opened the door. "I reckon I orter be," he said gravely. He cupped her chin in his hand and brushed her lips with his. "Good night," he said. She stood in the doorway and watched him walk to the Studebaker in the growing darkness.

When Barr got in the car, Eduardo said, "She's an adopted daughter. He took charge of her when she was only ten. She has been married."

Barr said nothing. Eduardo put the car in motion. "He gave you safe conduct?"

"Uh huh."

"I think she sleeps with Hernan Robles at times."

Barr sank back against the seat and closed his eyes. "Take me to the Bull Wheel, Eduardo."

Eduardo nodded. "As you say."

As Fairbanks walked into the Bull Wheel at ten minutes before eight o'clock, the first person he saw was the rotary rig salesman.

43

The man was eating alone, his brown derby pushed back on his head, his napkin tucked in his vest. As Fairbanks approached the table, the salesman looked up at him without recognition. He was eating soup from a large bowl. He wiped his mouth with his napkin when Fairbanks sat down opposite him, but he held firmly to his spoon. He was a red-faced Irishman, and the broken purple veins on and around his nose testified to years of heavy drinking. "And to what do I owe this pleasure?" he asked Fairbanks.

Fairbanks introduced himself, then reminded the salesman of the layover at the Amsted Bar on Aruba. "I've been hunting high and low for you," Fairbanks said.

The salesman rolled his eyes drolly. "You should have been looking across the lake. I didn't leave the tanker here, and I've been spending my time in the unlikeliest place on earth." He winked at Fairbanks. "Since he was there, however, nobody back in Houston can say Pete Hanlon didn't try to make a dollar for the company. No, sir!" He put down his spoon, and his moist brown eyes were sad. "Dozens of rigs running, but all of them cable tools. Nobody even wanted to talk about rotary rigs. No time, they said."

"I've got time," Fairbanks said.

Hanlon pointed past Fairbanks. "My, what a fine-looking suit that fellow's wearing. Looks like silk."

Annoyed, Fairbanks twisted his neck, saw Grady Barr approaching the table and felt a sudden surge of relief. He stood up quickly and arranged a chair for Barr. He wanted badly to talk with Barr but he couldn't afford to lose Hanlon now that he'd found him. Barr took the seat without hesitation. "The rotary rig man," he said to Hanlon. "Are you selling lots of 'em?"

Hanlon obviously didn't recognize Barr or recall meeting him, but he answered promptly. "Like my backwoods cousins say, nary a one. I was just telling our friend here my sad story."

"I'm interested in one, Mr. Hanlon," Fairbanks said. "I'm with British Meridian and we're looking to get one. Could you . . ."

Hanlon held up a hand for quiet. "Don't shit an old shitter, Mr. Fairbanks. British Meridian couldn't make a down payment on a free lunch." He was no longer the apparently careless salesman but a man who knew his business. "All you've found down here is dry holes. You haven't got a prospect in the whole Maracaibo Basin." He picked up his spoon. "My soup's getting cold."

44

Fairbanks persisted. "I'm not joking with you, Mr. Hanlon. We've got a lease in the Kilometer Strip and we need a rig to drill it. Our equipment is worn out."

Hanlon smiled faintly. "Jesus *walked* the water, he didn't drill a well in it." Amused by his own wit, he added, "He turned water into *wine*, not petroleum."

"Nevertheless, we want a rig and we've got the money to buy or lease one," Fairbanks said. "I can show you our bank statement in the morning."

Barr broke in. "Is he the only rig salesman in the country?" he asked Fairbanks.

Hanlon answered, "I'm the only *rotary* salesman. And they're selling so fast in the States it would be three months before I could get one delivered here." He wiggled his spoon. "That is, if I was thinking of selling one to British Meridian."

"Why do you have to have a rotary rig?" Barr asked Fairbanks. "It would take longer, but you could do it with cable tools."

"Hah!" said Hanlon. "Nobody but a fool would drill over water. Nobody ever has and nobody ever will."

"Gulf has," Barr said. "I've heard my daddy talk about it. They drilled in Caddo Lake long before the war. That's in Louisiana. Somewhere around nineteen-ten, I think."

Hanlon shrugged. "Then they must have forgotten it. They've got Strip acreage, and they haven't wet a tool joint."

Barr said slowly, "Mr. Hanlon, you ain't the salesman I figured you for when I first saw you. You ain't got no imagination at all." He reached out suddenly and grabbed a passing waiter. "Bring Mr. Hanlon here a fresh bowl of soup, and drinks for all of us."

Hanlon started to protest, but Barr said, "You got it coming. You sat here and let it get cold while we jawed at you. Now let me tell you what I was thinking about. You want to hear it?"

Hanlon grinned. "Well, I've never been accused before of not having an imagination. I guess I'll listen."

Barr nodded. "All right. You ain't sold a rotary rig since you've been here. Way you talk, everybody's loaded down with cable tools and they like it that way, right?"

"It looks that way now, but give me a little time. I'll crack through. Believe me."

"I don't know how much time you've got, but why wait? If it was me, I'd *give* Fairbanks a rig if he'd use it on the lake. It'd be a million dollars worth of free advertising. People are going to come from everywhere when he starts drilling out there. They'll be talking about it around the world. Damn right, I'd give him a rotary, and if it worked out I'd have 'em standing in line begging for 'em."

Hanlon's watery eyes narrowed and his lips were pursed in thought.

"Drilling the lake ain't the problem," Barr continued. "It's getting set up to drill. *I* can drill it, by God." He leaned back in his chair, casual now. "Course Fairbanks can't wait no three months for a rig. Somebody's liable to jump in out there ahead of him—and with cable tools. Gulf's loaded with cable tools, in case somebody remembers them drilling in Caddo Lake."

Fairbanks had listened to this remarkable presentation first in trepidation, then with wonder and finally with excitement. *He's got him hooked,* he thought; *by God, he's got him hooked!*

The waiter brought three large glasses of rum and Hanlon's fresh soup. The salesman ignored the steaming bowl. He put a hand on the glass of rum but didn't lift it from the table. His lips moved as if he were talking to himself.

"You'd be a hero back in Houston," Barr said. "You'd . . ."

Hanlon had lifted his glass, and he was smiling. "Boys, if Peter Anthony Hanlon can't have a complete rig at the Maracaibo docks in three weeks he's not the best salesman Lone Star Rigging ever had—and he is!"

Fairbanks and Barr lifted their glasses. "I'll be telegraphing tonight," Hanlon said. They all drank. Hanlon wiped his lips daintily with his napkin. "I'm taking your word about the bank statement," he said to Fairbanks, "and I'll want to see it first thing in the morning."

"I'll have it," Fairbanks said.

They all drank, Hanlon draining his glass. He pushed back his chair. "I'll pass the soup by, if you don't mind. I want to get to the telegraph office." Fairbanks and Barr stood up and shook hands solemnly with the salesman. "In the morning, then," Hanlon said, and he was gone.

Fairbanks and Barr sat down. They looked at each other, obviously pleased with themselves. "You silver-tongued bastard," Fairbanks said finally, shaking his head. "You practically had him slobbering, thinking about all that money he's going to make."

"I was thinking about myself, too," Barr said. "I want to help you show the world how to drill a well in that lake."

"Can you?" Fairbanks asked evenly.

46

"My problems are over, if that's what you mean. I figured you heard about them."

"No, I mean can you help us drill the well?"

"I think so. They said my daddy was the best driller in Mexico, and they said he learned me—taught me—everything he knew." Barr opened his hands and looked at them. "When I'm working on machinery or something it seems like my hands have got eyes and ears." He looked up at Fairbanks. "When I was drilling, I could feel every strain on the derrick, every strain on the machinery *before* it got there." He shook his head. "I don't know how, but I could *feel* every formation the bit went through." He paused. "Can you understand what I'm saying?"

Fairbanks nodded. "I think so." Then thoughtlessly. "What I *don't* understand is why you . . ." Fairbanks bit his tongue. He flushed, embarrassed and disgusted with his prying.

But Barr said, "Maybe some day I'll tell you. Are you hungry?"

Fairbanks smiled. "More thirsty than hungry. You?"

Barr picked up his glass. "I'm as dry as a cotton-mouthed snake."

Eduardo was waiting outside the Bull Wheel when Barr and Fairbanks emerged at midnight. The Studebaker, its engine running, sat on the plaza, parting the surging crowd like a boulder splitting stampeding cattle. Both Barr and Fairbanks were more than a little drunk. Barr grinned. "Keeping tabs on me, Eddie? Spying on me for His Excellency?"

Eduardo shook his head. "He told me you were going in the oil business. Then tonight I heard you were going to drill in the lake. I thought . . ."

"Who told you about the lake, Eddie? The waiter inside?"

Eduardo smiled. "A cook. He got it from the waiter."

For the first time Barr really looked at Eduardo. The Venezuelan was about nineteen or twenty, Barr judged. His smooth face was bland. His black hair was sleek and oily. His black eyes, however, were bright with awareness, intelligence.

"You want to help me drill the lake?" Barr asked. "Is that what's on your mind?"

Eduardo's face came alive with shining interest. "Yes! I don't know what I can do, but I'll work hard. That's a promise."

A sudden movement in the Studebaker caught Barr's attention. He bent over and looked past Eduardo. "Is that the princess in there, Eddie?"

"She drove me here."

Barr lurched past him to the car and opened the door. Cerro Soto's adopted daughter was at the steering wheel. Barr got in the car beside her. She was still wearing the green skirt and beige blouse, but the golden earrings were gone and her hair hung loosely about her face.

"Are you drunk?" she asked.

"I've been drinking pretty good, but I ain't so drunk that I don't know that you're the prettiest woman in Maracaibo. Or maybe anywhere else." Barr was smiling.

"Is this the way a pimp pays court to a woman? Half drunk and on a public plaza? Speaking like a schoolboy?"

Barr's smile faded.

"I am Hernan Robles' mistress. Do you think to strike back at him by making love to me?"

"If I decide to do something to Robles, it won't be that way," Barr said. "I don't need any kind of reason to try to make love to you. You're enough by yourself."

Her laugh mocked him. "How flattering!" She moved until she was tight against her door. "Now get out of this car," she said coldly.

"I'll see you again," Barr said.

She stared straight ahead through the windshield, ignoring him as he got out of the car and onto the sidewalk.

"What was that all about?" Fairbanks asked Barr.

Barr laughed sheepishly. "I just got stood in the corner." He turned to Eduardo. The Venezuelan's eyes seemed troubled, and Barr took him by the shoulders. "Do you work for him or for her, Eddie?"

"For him."

"Did he set you to spy on me?"

"No."

"You just decided on your own that you want to help me drill the lake."

"More than anything," Eduardo said earnestly.

Barr shook him gently. "All right. You keep in touch and we'll see what we shall see." He gave him a gentle shove. "Now, go take the princess home."

The Studebaker's horn honked and honked again. Eduardo turned toward it.

"As you say," he said to Barr.

48

Chapter Four

In the days before the arrival of the rotary rig from Houston, Grady Barr emerged as the "driver" for the lake adventure. Joe Reid surrendered his authority grudgingly; for every expeditious move Barr made, Reid took him through a snarling catechism.

The water was twenty feet deep at the spot Phil Carter selected as the drill site and the lake bottom was soft and shifting. Barr saw at once that the drilling equipment could not be placed on cribbing, as had been discussed. He had some giant trees felled and fashioned into pilings.

"I'll drive them to a safe bearing and build the platforms on them," he explained to Reid.

"What are you going to drive them with, for Christ's sake, a fucking sledge hammer?"

"The little company that built Shell's loading docks is going to drive them with a piledriver. They're going to float it out on the lake on a barge."

"Jesus Christ! That'll cost a goddamned fortune! Don't you know that?"

"They're doing it for nothing."

"Jesus!"

"They figure if we make a well, they'll have more business than they can handle."

When the pilings were being driven, Reid wanted to know why so many were being used. "You're going to cover the lake with the damned things!"

"We've got to have seven platforms. One for each piece of heavy equipment."

Later, when the platforms were being built, Reid demanded, "What in the goddamned hell are you doing with all those natives? Those monkeys can't do a goddamned thing!"

"They can do this kind of work, if I show them what to do. And they'll do it for five bolivars a day."

"Where in hell did you get them?"

"Eduardo Vigas picked them out, and he's helping me work them. He's getting twenty bolivars a day."

"Great God from Godville!"

Later, Reid hit upon the subject again. "Why in the hell are we giving Eduardo Vigas a hundred bolivars bonus?"

"Him and his buddies rounded up those joints of thirty-inch pipe for us. They got them for nothing."

"They're just streaks of rust, for Christ's sweet sake! What do you want them for?"

"I'm getting them welded together. I'm going to drive them to safe bearing and drill inside them."

"What?"

"It'll stick up out of the water under the derrick. I'll just drop the bit and drill pipe into it and get to drilling. It's the only way to do it."

"Who's this Vigas anyway?"

"I met him in town. A friend. I'm going to use him as a roughneck when we get to drilling."

"Oh shit."

Fairbanks, though, was not completely surprised by Barr's assertiveness. He had suspected his strength from the first, and he had seen Barr work his will on Pete Hanlon, the rig salesman. With no more evidence than Barr's word, Fairbanks had believed that Barr was a top-notch driller. And he was convinced that Barr's actions for British Meridian were not a cold-blooded usurpation of power and a bid for Reid's job, as Reid had apparently assumed. Barr simply saw what had to be done and he got busy on it, acting as if it were expected of him. For all of his bluster, Reid was a solid man, Fairbanks had concluded, but he hadn't the imagination to be a leader. He was a vacillator. And Barr was a man who couldn't tolerate vacillation.

Fairbanks *was* surprised at Barr's handling of the Venezuelans he had hired to help build the platforms. He never laughed or joked with them, never had a word of commendation. He was not disdainful of them, nor was he harsh. But they existed for him only as robots who took his orders and obeyed them.

"He speaks their language, but he treats them like they're subhuman, some other species," Phil Carter observed critically. "I imagine it's most demeaning."

Fairbanks had been thinking the same thing, but he said, "They're grateful for what he's teaching them. Most of them never had a hammer or saw in their hands before."

"Oh, I admit he takes pains with them." Carter said quickly. "It's just . . ."

The conversation had died on that note.

Carter found no other reason to fault Barr. When he surveyed the Kilometer Strip concession, he selected the drill site in a direct line with the village of La Rosa and the Shell gusher. "We'll be on the down dip from the gusher," he said to Barr. Barr nodded and said, "When we hit, we'll drain their oil right from underneath them." Carter had been pleased with Barr's understanding, and further pleased at his optimism. He later told Fairbanks, "He's a born engineer. Shame he's had no education." He chuckled. "Guess what he asked me. How to determine the circumference of a joint of pipe if the diameter was known. I explained to him about *pi.*" Carter chuckled again. "I suspect he's still wrestling with that one."

Fairbanks had rented a thatched-roof house on the edge of La Rosa about two hundred feet from the lake shore. It was to serve as lodging for the American drilling crew when drilling began. In the meantime, Barr and Carter slept there. The Venezuelans slept where they could, in a hovel in Cabimas-La Rosa or out in the open.

Shell rigs were running around the clock, bringing in well after well. Shell crewmen slept in tents and hastily constructed bunkhouses. Their beds were never cool. When one man awakened to go to work, another dropped on the bed. The Venezuelans who swarmed to the area in the wake of the gusher built huts of flattened tin cans. The shores of the lake, for the most part, were no more than mangrove swamps, but the tin huts—rancheros, they were called—sprang up from the fetid soil.

As in Maracaibo, cantinas and gambling joints jumped up in Cabimas. On a Saturday night, following a payday, Cabimas' main street was crowded from building line to building line with Venezuelans, all striving to spend their money. Pushing through them were Shell's American workers, eager for a go at the bars and gaming tables.

Barr returned to Maracaibo by water taxi when the drilling equipment arrived at the docks. Vigas was with him. Fairbanks had never seen Barr so excited. With loving hands he went over the equipment piece by piece, explaining the various parts and their usage to Vigas while Pete Hanlon stood beaming as if he had invented each of them. "First time I ever had a brand new rig," Barr said to Fairbanks. "It's sure some sight."

At the British Meridian office Joe Reid told Barr that he had hired two drillers and that the drillers would hire their own crews. "I want you to drill when you want to or feel you have to, Grady," Reid said. "You're the boss. I want you to run the operation."

Fairbanks had the feeling that Barr had been expecting to hire the drillers, but Barr said, "That's fine with me, Joe."

The two drillers were introduced as Bill Watkins and Homer Day. Day was in his fifties. He was heavy-set, clad in blue overalls and blue workshirt. A chew of tobacco deformed his left cheek. "Barr," he said. "You wouldn't be Stancil Barr's boy, would you?"

"Yes."

"Knowed him at Spindletop before he went to Mexico. You was just a buddin' peckered boy then. Had a couple of sisters, didn't you?"

Barr nodded.

"Well, how in the hell is the old wart hog? Doing all right?"

"He died last year in San Antonio."

Day shook his head sorrowfully. "I'm a son of a bitch, that's bad news. Your mama and sisters, they doing all right?"

"Doing fine."

"Well, that's something, ain't it? And I reckon you're as good a man as Stancil or you wouldn't be running this job." He nodded. "It'll be a pleasure to work with you."

"Yawl know we're going to drill in the lake, don't you?" Barr asked.

Day grinned, showing yellow teeth. "Oh, hell yes, we know that. The reason I took the job. Any old fart can drill a well on land." He turned to Watkins. "Ain't that right, Bill?"

Watkins offered a shy smile, as if he were embarrassed at being called upon to comment. He was a small man, smaller than Joe Reid, but despite his shyness there was an aura of hard masculinity about him.

"Old Bill here," Day said, "he don't look like much but he's been in places other folks couldn't throw a rock. And he always knows where his bit's at."

"Good enough," Barr said. "One thing." He took Eduardo Vigas by the arm. "This is Eduardo Vigas. He helped me build the drilling platforms, and I promised him he could roughneck on the well. Any objections?"

Day took Vigas' hand and shook it. "Best roughneck I ever had was a mescan named Torres, out of Webb County, Texas. One hell of a derrick man."

"All right," Barr said. "We'll move the rig to location as soon as you get crewed up."

K. C. Hopkins, owner, editor and star reporter of the Maracaibo *Tropical Star*, counted one hundred and four persons on the shore when the British Meridian drilling crew moved out on the lake to the platforms by water taxi. Most of the crowd were roughnecks and drillers from the Shell camps, and their hoots and jeers floated in the small boats' wakes. Joe Reid stood in the stern of the last boat in line, screaming curses at the tormentors.

Phil Carter had stayed behind, and Hopkins now moved through the crowd to him. He touched Carter's arm and the geologist wheeled angrily to face him. Hopkins threw up his hands as if to defend himself. Carter blushed. "I'm sorry," he said quickly. "I thought you were one of those baboons." He nodded at the yelling Shell men.

Hopkins laughed. "I guess they don't mean any harm, Phil." Then he added, "Nobody seems to think you've got a chance in hell of completing a well out there."

"They're wrong," Carter said firmly.

"Are you really that optimistic?"

"All of us are."

Hopkins nodded as if he were impressed by such unanimity.

"Our lawyer is in Caracas right now," Carter said. "He's going to try to get the law changed so we can drill all over our concession, not just on the kilometer line. That's how optimistic we are."

Hopkins nodded again. The crowd was dispersing. "You'll keep me up to date on your progress, won't you, Phil?"

"Of course."

"If Joe Reid will let you."

Carter flushed. "Perhaps you should ask Joe to keep you up to date."

Hopkins laughed. "Joe wouldn't give me the time of day if he had a watch in every pocket."

"Then you'll have to just make do, won't you?" Carter said primly. "Until the well comes in."

Hopkins laughed again. "Until the well comes in," he said, and walked away.

Fairbanks was indeed in Caracas. Despite the oil boom in the Maracaibo Basin, Caracas was still a sprawling, drowsy metropolis, tucked in a high mountain valley like a pearl cupped in the palm of a lovely woman. Clouds drifted down from the mountaintops as if to seal off the valley from the rest of the world. It was an enchanting remoteness . . .

Stores, for the most part, were low-slung buildings with no showcases. Wares hung from the walls and ceilings. Open-air stalls displayed everything from hardware to vegetables. The haciendas of the wealthy were scattered among the adobes of the poor. There were few automobiles and fewer streets to accommodate them.

Fairbanks found a room on Plaza Bolivar where the hero of the republic, mounted on his charger, surveyed the valley with a challenging gaze. Determined to be thrifty with the British Meridian money Joe Reid had doled out to him, he entered the city's political-business-social whirl with caution. He was swept up in welcoming arms, however—it appeared that memories of Walter Fairbanks were still fresh and warm.

He worked at his task. He received smiling promises that the Congress would certainly consider his proposal, and soon. And yes, the proposal stood a very good chance of acceptance and enactment into law. Gomez, he was assured, wouldn't put his foot down against such a reasonable proposal from the son of Walter Fairbanks.

Fairbanks was delighted with his progress and with himself. Then, at a party he was introduced to Stephen Adams, a shipping magnate. Adams found an opportunity to be alone with Fairbanks.

The man seemed ill at ease. "I say, are you sure you're doing the right thing?" Adams asked finally. "For yourself, I mean."

Fairbanks was puzzled and his face showed it.

"Oh, I see," Adams said quickly. "I'm just back from London, you know, and I have a friend on the British Meridian board of directors. He was telling me that Pan Union Oil was dickering for BM. Interested in leases BM has in the east, he said. I guess you were unaware of that."

Fairbanks was shaken to the core. Adams placed a hand on Fairbanks' arm. "Just in the dickering state, you understand."

Fairbanks nodded dumbly.

"It may never come to pass," Adams went on, "but I think you should check with someone, I really do. Does London know what you're doing here? What you're trying to accomplish?"

Fairbanks shook his head no.

"You fellows in Maracaibo are pretty much on your own, then?"

Fairbanks nodded.

"You're trying to drill in the lake, I've been told. Is that on your own, or on instructions from London?"

"On our own," Fairbanks said. And he added defensively, "It's the logical thing to do."

"Ummm. Well, you're a decent enough young fellow and I think you should scurry back to Maracaibo, I really do. No sense doing all this work for someone who may not want it done. I mean Pan Union. Who knows what they'll want? Providing, of course, that something is consummated."

"You think there will be, don't you?"

"I have no idea. Only thing, my friend on the board was very interested. I think I can safely say that."

Fairbanks scurried back to Maracaibo as Adams had suggested. He reported what he had heard to Joe Reid only.

"Oh, shit!" Reid said. "I've been with this outfit for three years now, and there's always talk of somebody taking it over. Don't worry about it."

"I'm not worried," Fairbanks snapped. "I'm concerned."

"Be what you want to be, Tom. What I want to know is what did you get for the money you spent."

Fairbanks told him what he had done, what he had been promised and how little money he had spent. Reid allowed himself a small grin. "That's good," he said with something resembling satisfaction. "Do you think I ought to start trying to pick up some more Strip leases?"

Fairbanks hesitated.

"Well?" Reid demanded.

"Maybe we ought to wait and see if we make a well," Fairbanks said.

"It'll be too late then. Every son of a bitch and his brother will be fighting for them."

Fairbanks was surprised. "You sound like you're *sure* we're going to hit."

Reid's mouth twisted in a wry grin. "Oh, hell yes. I've got the fever now. Almost as bad as Phil."

Fairbanks smiled at this admission. "All the more reason you ought to talk it over with the board by telegraph before you spend any money on leases. Let them know how strongly you feel about making a well. The board's entitled to know, if they *are* dickering with Pan Union. It could influence a decision. And it would allow them to make the decision on whether to try for new leases. Doesn't that make sense?"

Reid sneered. "You're still worried about that damn rumor."

"Just concerned, Joe. I think I've outlined a prudent course. You're accustomed to running the show on your own because you've had to. Make the board handle this one. They won't think any the less of you for it."

Reid was obviously impressed with Fairbanks' argument, but he couldn't let go completely. "All right, damn it, I'll think about it. That good enough for now?"

"Sure is. And tell me something. What does Barr think about making us a well?"

Reid made a sour face. "That son of a bitch thinks it's *his* well." Then, "Seriously, he's a hell of a driller. Old Homer Day lost a drill bit just below three hundred feet, and Barr fished it out of the hole like a whore picking a drunk's pocket. He's working everybody's ass off, including his own. I got to admit that."

Fairbanks smiled. "Maybe he'll make us all look good."

Beaming, his lips smeared with mud, Phil Carter trod gingerly across the rig floor to Grady Barr. Homer Day was drilling and the roughnecks, including Eduardo Vigas, were busy at their tasks. Barr turned around from his study of a joint of drill pipe and Carter handed him a cutting that had just been washed to the surface from the bottom of the well. Barr smelled the cutting, then touched his tongue to it.

"Tar sand!" Carter shouted above the noises of the drilling rig. "We're right on schedule."

Barr grinned at Carter's exuberance. Carter grabbed Barr's arm. "Let's go to the house and talk it over."

They clambered aboard a launch which Reid had reluctantly

rented, and Barr steered it to the short pier they had built from shore out into the lake. Perhaps a dozen men, all Americans or Europeans, were standing on the shore. "Goddamn it, there's been a new bunch here every day since we started drilling," Barr groused as he tied up the launch at the pier. "Sometimes I think you invited them."

"They come from everywhere," Carter burbled happily. "That little fellow in tropical whites—the one with the pith helmet three sizes too large—he's a geology professor from London University."

"He damned near talked me deaf yesterday," Barr said. "Let's get our talking done before you start entertaining them." He walked resolutely past the visitors, nodding but not speaking when they hailed him. Carter dallied briefly, then joined Barr in the house. They walked between two rows of cots to a high work table at the rear of the room.

Carter took a notebook from a drawer and opened it. He pointed to a column of figures. "This is what I've learned about the Shell gusher."

Barr looked at him admiringly. "How in the hell did you get that?"

Carter chuckled. "Scientists find it difficult not to confide in fellow scientists. Let's leave it at that, shall we?"

"Fair enough."

"Well now," Carter said professorially, "it's common knowledge that the original hole was only about five hundred and fifty feet deep. They abandoned it at that depth back in nineteen-eighteen. Then they resumed drilling at that depth last year." He moved his finger down the column of figures. "They encountered several tar sands between nine hundred and a thousand feet and the well blew out at fifteen hundred."

He closed the notebook and smiled triumphantly at Barr. "I had calculated that the pay sand was about a hundred feet deeper at our location, you see, and what we've just encountered proves it! They reached the tar sands at nine hundred and we've just reached them at a thousand. They reached the oil sand at fifteen hundred—when the well blew out—and we'll reach it at sixteen hundred." He added apologetically, "Pardon me if it sounds as if I'm talking down to you, old boy, but it's essential that you understand completely."

Barr poked Carter's shoulder playfully. "Hell, I learn a new word every time you open your mouth, Phil."

Carter was reminded that despite Barr's past experiences, his hard-headed approach to getting things done and his intellectual curiosity, he was still only twenty-five years old.

"What I want you to do," Carter said, "is start using heavier drilling mud when you reach fifteen hundred feet. We don't want a blowout, do we, and that heavier mud will hold down the gas pressure. You've done this before, haven't you?"

"Lots of times in Mexico. Some of them wells could flare up on you quicker'n rain."

"Good. And you're satisfied with that blowout preventer Mr. Hanlon so thoughtfully provided?"

"It works as smooth as bear grease, Phil, but there ain't none of them foolproof, to my mind."

"Well, you know the score. If we foul the lake, we lose the concession."

"If that oil's where you say it is, we ain't going to foul nothing. You can count on that, Phil."

"Then nothing can stop us, can it?"

On the first bright morning after a rainy week, Joe Reid brought Guillermo Cerro Soto across the lake for a look at the well. With them was Cerro Soto's adopted daughter. She said that she really didn't want to see the well, that she had come along simply for the trip and the sunshine, so Reid spread some blankets on the pier to make her comfortable. Men were sleeping in the hut, he explained. He woke up Grady Barr and told him he had Cerro Soto in tow. "I'll show him the well. Just don't let nobody come outside and piss in the wind. There's a girl on the pier."

When the launch headed for the well Barr washed his face, combed his hair and strolled out on the pier. The woman was sitting on the edge of the pier like a fisherman, dangling her feet into the water. She watched Barr approach and sit down near her without greeting him with word or gesture.

"I used to sit like this for hours at a time when I was a kid," Barr said, looking out over the water. "On an old bridge over a creek. I was trying to learn how to spit through my teeth like an old bootlegger named John D. McEnrue." He smiled. "He would blink his eyes and spit at the same time. He never did one without doing the other that I remember."

She said nothing. She, too, was looking out over the water.

"I'm real sorry about that night in town, in front of the Bull Wheel," Barr said. "It's good to have a chance to tell you so."

She did not acknowledge his apology. They sat in silence for perhaps five minutes, then Barr moved to get to his feet. She reached over and touched him lightly on the arm.

"Was it true what you said, that you weren't trying to strike at Hernan Robles through me?" she asked slowly.

Barr had learned his lesson. He said simply, "Yes."

"You wanted me just for myself?"

"Yes," Barr said again.

"Why did you kiss me . . . at the door of my house?"

"I don't know," Barr said evenly. "Smart aleck, I guess. And you were so pretty. You are now."

"I have had three men in my life. A boy when we were both sixteen. A husband who deserted me. And Hernan Robles. You have had many women."

"Yes," Barr said.

"And I am beautiful to you?"

"Yes," Barr said again.

She nodded, as if confirming something to herself. "My name is Christina."

"It's a pretty name," Barr said.

They both raised their heads to look toward the well. The launch was returning. As Barr got to his feet she looked up at him. "You are beautiful to me," she said. Then she looked back at the nearing launch.

Eduardo Vigas was in the launch with Reid and Cerro Soto, and only he stepped out on the pier when the launch nestled alongside. Cerro Soto smiled up at Barr. "It is going very well, Mr. Reid says. I have promised to say nothing about it."

Barr smiled in return. Vigas helped Christina into the launch and shoved it away from the pier. Cerro Soto waved goodbye. Vigas tugged at Barr's shirtsleeve as the launch roared out into the lake. Barr looked around at him.

"She's dangerous," Vigas said earnestly. "She tells everything she knows, and even more. She's what you Americans call a blabbermouth. She's flighty, Grady."

Barr grinned. "They're all dangerous in one way or another, Eddie."

Vigas shook his head. "Not the way she is."

Barr shrugged. "I'll probably never see her again, anyway."

* * *

From the Maracaibo *Tropical Star* of August 12, 1923:

> The government has granted a giant concession of 2,900,-
> 000 acres which covers the entire floor of Lake Maracaibo
> with the exception of the Kilometer Strip, according to un-
> confirmed reports from Caracas.
>
> The concession went to twenty Venezuelan citizens, ac-
> cording to the reports. The citizens were not identified, but
> it was understood that they are politicians and businessmen
> who are held in high regard by General Gomez.
>
> It also was understood that an American oil company will
> acquire the concession shortly, and plans to drill it.
>
> It has been universally accepted that drilling overwater
> would be a foolish, if not impossible, task. However, British
> Meridian is drilling in the Kilometer Strip, or appears to be.
> It is a 'tight' well, and no word of the company's progress or
> lack of it has been made public.

Joe Reid slammed a fist down on the newspaper spread out on
his desk. "I wonder where that drunken bastard Hopkins gets
such bullshit," he growled. "All he does is sit around the Bull
Wheel and swill rum."

"He didn't get *that* at the Bull Wheel," Fairbanks said. "He got
it from somebody who knows what's going on. And it fits very
nicely with the telegram from London." The telegram was a
reply to Reid's telegraphed suggestion that British Meridian try
for additional Kilometer Strip acreage since the lake drilling was
progressing so well. The reply said succinctly: CONTINUE DRILL-
ING BUT NO MORE ACREAGE. "Whoever is going to buy the lake
acreage wants ours, too," Fairbanks continued. "They'll want it
all."

"If you're so damn smart, why in hell don't they tell us what's
going on?"

"The deal's not set yet with Pan Union. They don't want to be
premature. Anyway, Joe, I'm not so smart. In fact, I'm pretty
dumb. All the time I was thinking I was doing so good in Caracas,
those slick politicians knew all about this big concession. That's
why they promised me so much."

"Well, what are we going to do, Mr. Lawyer?"

"I don't know," Fairbanks said.

Barr was doggedly writing a drilling report by lamplight when he heard the launch pull up the pier. He was surprised—it was midnight, and the launch was not due in from the drill site until daybreak. He stepped outside the hut into the bright moonlight and began walking toward the pier. The lights on the derrick shone pale in the distance.

But it was not the launch. It was a water taxi from Maracaibo, and the person who climbed up on the pier was Christina. Barr stopped when he recognized her. She came to him in steady strides. Barr could see she was wearing a simple dress of many colors, and her sandals left wakes of shiny sand. When she reached him Barr took her in his arms without a word. "Can we go in your house?" she asked.

"No, the men are sleeping."

She pulled back and looked at him. "We can go to a place I know." She held her head for Barr to kiss her. He kissed her softly, and when she tried to force her lips against his he moved his mouth away. Then he kissed her softly again.

"I know a place," she said. "I came here as a child, and later on the boy and I found it again. It is a great salt flat called La Salinas. Do you know it?"

"I've seen it, honey."

She took his arm and led him past the house and into the jungle along a path she seemed to know . . . Past the noises of Cabimas on the left . . . Into the darkness the bright moon couldn't penetrate . . . And finally they emerged onto a shimmering apron of salt, out into the moonlight again, and the salt glowed like the marble flooring of some ancient arena.

They undressed and spread their clothing to cushion their bodies. They laid down and Barr took her in his arms. "You feel so good," she said, nestling her heavy breasts against his chest. Barr kissed her breasts with long loving care, then moved slowly down her body, taking his time, kissing her stomach, touching his tongue to her navel, nipping gently below her navel, blowing his warm breath into her pubic hair.

He opened her legs and ran his tongue along the crease between her thighs and vagina, taking his time and being careful not to touch her vulva. "So good," she murmured, "so good." He licked the outer lips of her vagina slowly. "Oh, so good, so good." He began licking the inner lips. "Oh, God, so good," she murmured. "So good, so good." He thrust his stiffened tongue deep into her vagina again and again. Her body shivered. He relaxed his tongue and slid it upward until it reached her clitoris. He stroked her clitoris with his tongue, then pressed his lips against her flesh and sucked the clitoris and its surrounding tissue into his mouth. *"Jesus, Jesus, Jesus!"* she cried in Spanish. *"Jesus, Jesus, Jesus!"* Her body stiffened to begin the climb to orgasm, and Barr drew back and moved quickly to insert his penis in her.

For a long moment her flesh resisted the head. He moved it slowly, opening her vagina gradually until there was a sudden *thuck* and perhaps five inches penetrated. She became a wild thing, thrashing beneath him like a wounded bird, her very movements easing more of his penis inside and delivering her into the lunacy of orgasm.

Just as her spasm began to taper off, Barr slid the rest of his penis into her. He held her close to him, his penis deep inside her, and rocked from side to side. As she again began the climb to orgasm, he withdrew until only the head remained inside her. She reached for him franticly, sobbing in her frustration, and Barr thrust deep into her. He held her in the rhythmic rock and brought her to four shattering orgasms that came so close together they seemed as one. Barr came with her, emptying himself with sharp cries he muffled against her cheek.

"May God in heaven bless you!" she whispered in his ear.

"He has," Barr said.

For hours they lay on the salt flat, touching, kissing, holding, talking, making love while the paling moon moved slowly to the mountains. She said she had learned English at school. In Caracas. She told him of her marriage, her affair with Hernan Robles, her love for Cerro Soto. Barr said little. He let her talk, listening with patience if not interest, knowing that at some point her need to learn about him, to unravel his past to the cradle would overcome the confessional and even her need for his body.

But at five o'clock they heard a report that sounded like distant thunder. "It came from the lake," Christina said.

"It's the well," Barr said with sure instinct. "She's blowed out. Get your clothes on."

They hurried back with Christina leading the way. They went straight to the pier where Phil Carter and Bill Watkins and his roughnecks, fully awake, were waiting for the approaching launch. Carter was near tears. "They can't be below fourteen hundred feet, Grady. They simply can't be!"

"It's blowed out, wherever they are, and that's a fact. Now quit that damn sniffling." Barr was straining his eyes. "Can anybody tell if the full crew's aboard?"

"There are five men," Christina said.

"Good. That's all of them."

The launch reached the pier and Homer Day began talking as Vigas tied up. "Nobody hurt, Grady." He spat in the lake and climbed up on the pier.

"The blowout preventer?" Barr asked.

"She held up at first, then it blowed through that six-inch bleed line. That oil's shooting straight out across the water for a hundred and fifty feet, by God."

"We'll lose the concession," Carter wailed.

"We ain't going to lose a goddamned thing," Barr said. "Not if we can help it."

"What do you want us to do, Grady?" Day asked.

Barr grabbed Vigas' arm. "You and Christina get to Maracaibo in the launch. Tell Reid and Fairbanks what's happened. Tell Reid to see the Shell big shots and get a tanker over here. Tell Fairbanks to go to the Cosmos Club and see Louise Bremond. Tell her to get her women over here as quick as she can. You and Christina go to Cerro Soto. I've got to have all the canvas in Maracaibo and all the fire hose. Tell him I've *got* to have it or this whole damn lake is going to be ruined. You understand all that?"

"Yes," Vigas said.

"And big needles and twine. I almost forgot that. Needles and string that'll fit them. All right?"

"We're gone," Vigas said.

"Phil," Barr said, "we're going to have to try to stab that son of a bitch. We need a joint of six-inch pipe that's beveled on one end and has got a valve on the other. You know what I mean?"

Carter nodded.

"You got to talk Shell out of one. If they ain't got one, they got to make one. We got to have it."

The launch roared to a start and Barr turned to allow himself a wave to Christina. Then, "Bill, you and Homer take the boys and round up every oil drum on this damned coast. Beg, borrow or steal. Pay for them if you have to. And we need scrap iron. Anything at about a pound or two. Now get going."

"Grady . . ." Day said.

"It ain't nobody's fault, Homer," Barr said. He started stripping off his clothes. "Yawl go on. I've got to take a look at that son of a bitch." Naked, he dropped off the pier into the water and began wading toward the distant rig.

Chapter Five

Stretched out across the lake in a wavy single file, the Maracaibo water taxi fleet approached La Rosa pier where Grady Barr stood waiting. On the beach behind Barr were rows of empty oil drums, and roughnecks were unloading more from wagons commandeered in Cabimas. Two men were plugging the drums to make them air tight. Waiting, Barr cursed Phil Carter in a soft monotone; the geologist had not yet returned from his mission to obtain a stabbing device. Meanwhile the well was still spouting a solid stream of black oil onto the lake. Far beyond the spreading oil a Shell tanker stood at anchor.

Louise Bremond was in the first taxi. Barr had not seen her since Hernan Robles had ordered him out of the country. He had avoided her at first, even after Cerro Soto had lifted that order, to save her from trouble with Robles. And then he had got involved with the well. He had stayed away then because he had hoped to present a completed well as a trophy and proof of his more conventional abilities.

More than a dozen whores clambered up on the pier behind Louise. Like her, they were clad in colorful beach pajamas, the hookers' trademark and street attire. Other taxis laden with bolts of canvas arrived. Barr waved to his crews, and they waded into the water to unload them.

Smiling, Barr reached out for Louise, but she held him off. "Why haven't you been to see me, Grady?" she asked in a cool voice.

Barr shook his head. "Not now, Lou. I need your help. We can talk later." His tone was as level as hers.

She tossed her auburn mane. "All right. What do you need?"

He grinned. "We're going to put on the biggest sewing bee the world has ever seen. Yawl get on up there on the beach and I'll be right with you."

Homer Day called out, "Here comes Phil, Grady!"

A wagon driven by a Venezuelan emerged from the jungle near the thatched-roof house. Carter was standing unsteadily, waving a hand in triumph as the wagon rocked beneath him. Barr waved back at him, muttering, "Hot damn!" He hurried to the beach, waving a hand and calling out, "Homer! Bill!"

He went to where the women were waiting. "All right, girls, here's what we're going to do." He winked at Louise. "Them oil drums are about two feet in diameter. That means they're about six feet in circumference . . . around them. Them canvas bolts are eight feet wide, it looks like. We're going to sew them together until we've got a strip eight feet wide and a mile long or whatever turns out. Then we're going to tie weights to the bottom side of the canvas and wrap the top around them oil drums. We're going to float the drums out on the lake. The weights are going to pull the canvas down in the water. We're going to circle that oil. The canvas will hold it and keep it from spreading. Then I'm going to pump it right off the top of the water into that tanker out there. You got it?"

"Let's just do the sewing first," Louise said. "Some of these men are going to have to unroll the canvas for us."

"They'll be glad to," Barr said.

With Day and Watkins following, he went to where Carter's driver was pulling the wagon to a halt near the pier. Carter climbed down.

"They had to make us one, you see," he said apologetically. "That's why I was so long."

"It's all right," Barr said. He looked over the side of the wagon and nodded approvingly. "All right, Homer. You and Bill take Bill's crew and stab that sucker. His boys are fresher'n yours."

"Homer's tard," Watkins said. "He ain't had no sleep a tall."

"I'll tell him when he's tard, Bill."

"I ain't tard," Day said. "Let's get at it."

Carter said, "Grady, I'm sorry about it all."

"You found them an oilfield, didn't you? Your geology was off a little, but Joe Reid ain't going to complain about it." Barr gave Carter a little shove. "Go out there and look at your well. It's a good un."

Carter trotted off and someone tugged at Barr's elbow. It was Eduardo Vigas. He pointed to the pier. Resplendent in a white military uniform and white pith helmet, Cerro Soto strode on the pier toward the beach. "Christina's locked up at the mansion." Vigas said softly.

"All right. You go out to the rig with Homer and Bill and learn all you can about that operation. Now scoot."

"As you say."

Barr went to meet Cerro Soto. Cerro Soto looked around with interest at the activity, but when he stopped his gaze at Barr his face was stern and his black eyes hot.

"Can you shut that well in?" he asked curtly.

"Yes."

Cerro Soto waved a hand at the women and men sewing canvas and wrapping oil drums. "And what is this nonsense?"

"It ain't nonsense," Barr said tersely. "I aim to suck every drop of that oil off the lake."

"Tell me how."

Barr explained his plan. Cerro Soto listened closely, but his manner didn't change. When Barr finished his explanation Cerro Soto said, "When you get through here I want you to report to me at the mansion."

"Joe Reid's the manager. He can report to you."

Cerro Soto's restrained anger escaped. *Fuck* Joe Reid!" He jerked his head toward the lake. "And *fuck* that well! You do as I say or I'll have you dragged there."

"You'd better send a bunch of 'em." Barr said steadily, and turned and walked away toward the working men and women.

Luck was with them. The oil was shooting out into the lake, not toward the shore, and a steady hot wind from the Andes kept pushing it in that direction. The "stabber" Shell had constructed for them slipped snugly inside the belching flowline. Homer Day had dangled the device into the stream, and roughnecks had gently positioned it so the fluid shot into the "stabber" and through its open valve. Then the roughnecks had nudged the beveled end inside the flowline and clamped it in place. The open valve had been closed slowly; the flow was cut off and the well was under control.

But an enormous amount of oil had gushed from the ruptured well. The hookers' flying fingers stitched canvas until Phil Carter estimated there was enough for a canvas dike to encircle eight acres. The canvas was affixed to the oil drums. The iron weights were put in place. And the taxi flotilla puttered off with Barr in the lead vessel. He was bone weary and suffering from lack of sleep, but he was buoyed by a sense of accomplishing something magnificent. Behind him he could see the dike begin to take shape as the iron weights pulled the canvas below the water line.

Hours passed before the encirclement was complete. The Shell tanker crew had tied in Barr's fire hose with a pump. Barr and two helpers pushed the loose end of the hose across the dike and into the glistening oil. The pump was switched on, and oil and water began flowing through the hose and into the tanker.

To no one in particular Barr said softly, "It's working slick as goose grease."

On the shore Louise Bremond sat on an overturned oil drum, watching with a smile as a half dozen hookers besieged Joe Reid, demanding payment for their labor. One of them was waving a bloody hand in Reid's face. "Look at them fingers, you son of a bitch! Look at 'em and tell me you're not going to pay us!"

"I didn't say that," Reid protested. "I said I didn't have any money *with* me."

"You said you didn't have much in your office, too, you rat bastard! Where *do* you big shot oilmen keep your money?"

"I said . . ."

"Oh, fuck you," the hooker said wearily, turning away.

Another hooker sniffed. *"I'd* rather sew for the son a bitch than fuck him."

Carter pulled Reid away from the women. "It's getting dark, Joe. Why don't you call Grady in and let them finish up tomorrow. It's safe enough, you know."

"All right," Reid growled. "I guess it'll be all right. And get the rest of these people out of here," he said, waving a hand. "I'm going back to the office."

Barr, Carter and the crews spent the night in the shore house. By noon the next day the clean-up job was completed. Barr steered the launch across the area the oil had covered on a final inspection. "If we missed a drop, some fish swallowed it," he told Carter.

He left Homer Day in charge of completing the well, and he and Carter crossed the lake to report to Reid. Carter was bubbling with enthusiasm for the future. In his mind he saw a forest of derricks springing up in the lake. "It's going to be one of the world's great fields, Grady. You must believe that. Billions of barrels, I'm sure. Not millions, you understand, but billions!"

Barr nodded occasionally as Carter let his imagination ramble, too caught up in his dreaming to notice Barr's preoccupation. He was still talking when they tied up at the dock and headed for the BM office. "It will be up to you, Grady, to find ways to drill out in the deepest water, but surely you will do that." He slapped Barr's back. "It will be a lot of fun."

They went into the BM office. Reid, Fairbanks and two strangers turned from the big wall map. Reid was pale—the words burst out of him.

"Phil, Pan Union took over the company last Monday!"

A keening whimper came from Carter's throat.

Fairbanks stepped forward quickly and grabbed Carter's shoulders. "No . . .!" Carter wailed. Fairbanks shook him. "They did," he said harshly. Carter's eyes begged, but Fairbanks said again, "They did. They took us over and leased the entire lake floor. And Gulf took over all that was left in the Kilometer Strip."

Carter shook his head. "The whole lake," he said brokenly. Then suddenly he brightened. He stepped past Fairbanks and went to the tall, thin-faced stranger wearing a brown suit. "But you will need us, won't you." He waved a hand at Reid and Fairbanks and Barr. "We're experts, you know," he said, his face aglow. "We'll show Shell and Gulf a thing or two, won't we now," he said to the thin-faced man.

"Phil . . ." Reid said.

The thin-faced man said, "I'm Arthur Fedderson, Mr. Carter. I'm sorry, but the fact is we won't need any of you." He jerked his head at his companion. "Mr. Drury has a contract with Pan Union to do all of our work for us. And we have our own geologists."

Carter stepped back, his face flushing. "Of course."

Barr turned to Drury, a heavy-set man in khakis. "You might want to keep our drillers and roughnecks. They're good men."

"Don't need 'em," Drury said tersely. "Got my own crews."

Barr nodded, then said to Reid, "They're hooking the Christmas tree onto her now, Joe. And they ain't been paid."

Fedderson said, "We'll bring them back here and everybody can get their checks tomorrow. After one o'clock." He cleared his throat. "Now, if you'll excuse us, gentlemen, Mr. Drury and I have things to discuss.

*   *   *

The four men talked for a few minutes on the sidewalk in front of the office, then Reid left with Carter.

"But after all, Joe, we *did* show them, didn't we?" Carter said.

And Barr and Fairbanks heard Reid say, "Oh, shit!"

"I'm starved," Fairbanks said. "Why don't we go to the Blue Book and clean out their kitchen."

Barr pointed to his oil-stained clothing and boots. "Let me go get cleaned up first. I orter be there in less than an hour."

"I may be drunk by the time you get there," Fairbanks warned.

"Don't drink it all," Barr said. He waved goodbye and walked to the corner where he hoped to find a cab. But as he turned the corner he found three men standing in a line across the sidewalk directly in his path. All three were in gray police uniforms with badges. Barr stopped. He paid attention to only one man, the one in the center. He was no more than five feet tall but he looked as if he weighed three hundred pounds. There was a big smile on his flat face, and his black eyes were merry.

"Do you know me?" he asked Barr.

Barr shook his head.

"They call me the Pig."

Barr looked him up and down. "Clean you up a little and you might pass for one." As the words cleared his lips, Barr shifted his feet and struck at the fat man's face with all of his strength. His big fist landed square on the Pig's nose and mouth but, with incredible speed, the Pig had stepped back gracefully and Barr's blow lost most of its impact. Blood trickled from the Pig's nose, and there was blood on his lips, but the lips still smiled and the black eyes were still merry. He nodded his head and one of the other policemen struck Barr across the small of the back with his club. As Barr winced the third policeman clubbed him across the forehead, and Barr wilted to the sidewalk. The policeman drew back his foot to kick Barr in the ribs, but the Pig pushed him aside.

"No!"

They stood and watched as Barr struggled to his knees. Venezuelans passed them by on the street, but none stopped to watch. Barr got to his feet and faced the smiling Pig. "You have my admiration," the Pig said. "Now, will you come with us?"

Barr hit him in the face again, and this time the Pig staggered backward from the blow, but again Barr was driven to the sidewalk by the clubs of the other policemen. The Pig lifted Barr to his feet with ease and held him close to his huge body. Barr fought his way out of the hold. He stood back. "He said he'd have me drug to the mansion. Let's see you do it." He was groggy.

"This is ridiculous," the Pig said with mock gravity. "Those two are clubbing you, but you continue to hit me." He spread his hands widely. "Why?"

The hand-spreading was a signal. A policeman hit Barr in the back of the head. As Barr sagged, the Pig caught him. "Again," he said. The policeman hit Barr again. "Enough."

He waved a hand and a Studebaker a half block down the street came to them. Barr was placed in the back seat with the two policemen, and the Pig got in beside the driver—Captain Ramirez. The car pulled away.

"You should have seen him," the Pig said to Ramirez. "He knew we meant trouble for him when we stopped him so he hit me, without question or argument." He daubed his lips and nose with his shirt tail. "If he ever learns he also has a left hand to fight with, he will be formidable."

Ramirez merely grunted.

"You appreciate only money," the Pig said.

"And you a chance to show off your education," said Ramirez. "Now shut up."

They rode in silence, not to the mansion but to Christina's house. Barr had regained consciousness by that time, but he had made no move to escape. When Ramirez stopped the car, the Pig turned around to face Barr. "He is alone in the house. We were to bring you right here and no farther. Will you go in?"

"Not unless you drag me in—if you can," Barr said.

"Get out!" Ramirez said harshly.

Barr got out of the car, and Ramirez drove quickly away. Barr stood in the large driveway for a moment, looking at the house. Then he began walking in the direction of the city proper. He had lost his hat in the scuffle with the Pig, and now he tied his bandana over his head and under his chin to protect his throbbing head from the sun. He walked for more than a mile before he saw in the distance the end of the trolley line. There were several persons standing or sitting at the stop and he quickened his pace, hoping to catch the next trolley.

He heard two quick bursts from a rubber auto horn. A long, black sedan with a cloth top—to Barr it looked like the kind of car favored by American gangsters—pulled up beside him and stopped. Cerro Soto, coatless and tieless, was at the wheel.

"Get in," he said.

Barr got in the car and took the bandana off his head. Cerro Soto put the car in gear. Looking straight ahead he said, "It was the angry father, not the man, on the beach at La Rosa. When you walked away from the house I realized I could not allow the angry father to make the man repudiate his promise of safety to you."

Barr said nothing.

"Do you understand?" Cerro Soto asked.

"I ain't sure."

"I cannot renege on my promise of safety for you because of a personal matter." He glanced at Barr. "Did they hurt you?"

"Not much."

Cerro Soto looked more closely at Barr. He shook his head. "Sixteen years ago last month Cipriano Castro had me beaten and placed in chains in San Carlos prison. There is no such thing as a good beating." He paused. "When General Gomez released me fourteen months and seven days later I weighed less than a hundred pounds, and I wept in his arms."

There was a silence, then Barr said, "That's a way of apologizing to me, ain't it?"

"Of course," Cerro Soto said.

"When she came across the lake, it was just a natural thing to happen," Barr said. "I've been doing a lot of thinking about it and I figure neither one of us could help it. I didn't think about you and I didn't think about Hernan Robles neither. And I didn't think about her maybe telling you, though I guess I orter've. I reckon she'll tell Robles if she gets mad enough at me—or mad enough at him. She's that kind of woman."

"Yes," Cerro Soto agreed. "Fortunately, Robles is in Trinidad."

They rode in silence for a while. Then Cerro Soto cleared his throat. "Do you . . ." He didn't continue.

"Just as a woman," Barr said. "That's the way I feel about her. I didn't mistreat her. I think she must have told you that."

"Vividly," Cerro Soto said dryly.

They rode on. "I think it best that you not see her anymore," Cerro Soto said.

"Hernan Robles don't worry me," Barr said quickly. "He can . . ."

"For her sake," Cerro Soto broke in. "A bad marriage and even Robles haven't cured her childish romanticism. No one dies of a broken heart, but she would attempt it." He looked at Barr and

Barr nodded agreement. "Now," Cerro Soto said briskly, "where do you want to go?"

Barr told him. They rode without talking until the car reached Plaza Sucre and stopped at the hotel. "Now that all of you are fired, what are you going to do?" Cerro Soto asked. Barr looked startled. "I know about it," Cerro Soto said. "It shouldn't surprise you. Do you have any plans?"

"No, sir. Not yet." Barr fingered his bruises and grinned. "I ain't had much time for planning."

"If you can use my help, ask for it."

Barr nodded.

"Perhaps later we will talk about Eduardo Vigas."

"Yes, sir."

Barr got out of the car, stepped back, and Cerro Soto drove away.

The hotel lobby was deserted when Barr came down from cleaning up. Not even Harry Little was in sight. He stepped outside into the unaccustomed silence. Only a few older Venezuelans were on Plaza Sucre. It was as if an air raid warning had cleared the area but for those who would wait for the proof of the bombs themselves. As he walked toward the Blue Book on Plaza Baralt he saw less than a score of people on streets where hundreds normally pushed and shouted. Plaza Baralt also was practically vacant. Barr was bewildered and a bit worried, but he spoke to no one until he reached the Blue Book. Inside were two dozing drunks and a bartender.

The bartender grinned. "Which way you come from?" he asked Barr.

"International Hotel. Where the hell *is* everybody?"

The bartender poured Barr a drink. "They're all at the docks or in that neighborhood. Trying to get a look at what's left of a bunch of guys that tried to drill a well in the Perija. From what I've heard, not too many came back."

"What the hell happened to them?"

"Motilons and malaria, I guess. That's what got some Shell guys a while back." The bartender grinned again. "Motilons and malaria—sounds like a song title, don't it?"

"Yeah." Barr drank his drink. "You got a phone I can use?"

"End of the bar, but we ain't got no book. You know the number you want?"

"Cosmos Club."

The bartender laughed. "Two seven, two seven—and outside of me and you and these drunks, the gals are probably the only ones that stayed put."

Louise Bremond answered Barr's call. "I want to see you, Lou," Barr said. "It's all right from my end to come over there."

"Come on," she said flatly.

She met him at the door, opening it quickly and pushing him into a small room just inside and away from the darkened gambling layout. "Grady . . ." She stopped when she saw his bruises, and touched his face with gentle fingers. "Baby, what happened?" Alarm and concern were on her face.

Barr smiled and took her hand from his face. "You weren't going to invite me upstairs, were you?"

She tried to look stern. "I want you to tell me what happened."

"We got lots to talk about, Lou, and we're going to do it." He touched her face. "But first, honey, I want to hold you for a long time. Just lay there and hold you in my arms, and you hold me." His voice was questioning.

Her face softened and she sighed. "You son of a bitch, you may be the only man under forty who would say that to a woman and know how important it is to her."

Barr pulled her to him. "You know I mean it, Lou, don't you?"

She shook her head. "I don't know for sure, but I guess I don't care." She reached up and kissed his bruised face.

From the Maracaibo *Tropical Star* of January 7, 1924:

> The ragged remnants of SCI's Buena Suerta Expedition staggered into Maracaibo yesterday, leaving behind them in the Perija some $2 million worth of equipment and 87 dead men.
>
> Sixteen of the dead were killed by Motilons with their black palm bows and six-foot arrows. The rest died from malaria, snake and animal attacks, and a strange fever that resembled beri-beri.
>
> SCI would not release the death list, but it was learned that it contained the names of eight Americans, one Belgian and 78 Venezuelans.
>
> The well, The Buena Suerta #1, was not completed; only 2,000 feet of the planned 3,400 feet was drilled before the pullout. Left behind was the drilling rig, pipe, lumber, wire and a railroad engine and cars and enough rail to lay 17

miles of narrow guage trackage. Food and medicines had been exhausted.

SCI manager Ed Gurwell said the original party contained 20 Americans and Europeans and 150 Venezuelans.

It was more than a year ago when the party set out from Maracaibo for the Perija, the most rugged area in the country, a land of forbidding jungles, terrifying gorges. A wet and steaming land full of sickness and death. Beautiful country, it is said, but in the strange and haunting way that a tiger's face is beautiful. The mighty forests of palms and mahogany and oak are festooned with lichens and orchids. A million birds sing and rustle through them. And along the trails in the brush move the deer, the tapir, the jaguar and the python.

But more fearsome than the beasts and fevers is the Motilon Indian, a fierce and cunning savage that no man to this day has ever seen face to face, according to all the records available to this newspaper.

A great crowd was on hand when the party set out in their convoy of launches and bongoes. The convoy sailed southward along the lake shore to where Rio Santa Ana pours into the lake. They sailed the Santa Ana without trouble for a month before they reached the juncture of Rio Lora and then sailed that stream until they made a landing.

It was not until the headquarters camp was built and the tracks to the drill site laid that the Motilons struck. After that, the men drilled and worked with one hand, so to speak, and fought for their lives with the other. The Indians never raided, never exposed themselves to the pitiful weapons the party owned. But from out of the jungle and across every clearing the arrows whistled.

The shafts bounced off the drilling rig boilers without shattering. And to the Motilons the dinky railroad engine must have appeared as a snorting beast, for they attacked it with great delight, shaking the bushes as their arrows bounced off the moving engine. The engineer they ignored at first, but one train driver was among the dead.

When the Indian attacks occasionally tapered off, there was always the fevers. Toward the end there were days and weeks when not enough well men were available to perform the simplest tasks.

The payoff came when a driller sat down at night to write

his daily report. It never got written. Three long arrows rasped through the screen wiring covering a window in the drillers' quarters. One went through slats in the back of the chair in which the driller was seated. It sunk deep into his back. When he lurched to his feet the arrow hung on the slats of the chair and twisted in his body. It took the driller eight days to die.

Tracks in the soft earth near the window showed that the Indians had stalked to within 10 feet of the drillers' quarters before selecting a target. That was enough to prove to the party that it was no match for the savages. The long trip home began.

SCI placed some of the survivors in the hospital here, and the rest are being checked over in SCI camps in other areas.

The survivors brought back bales of arrows and several black palm bows. The men believe that the Indians sit down and hold the bow with their feet and then pull back on the string. The bows are too strong to shoot arrows like the American Indians shoot them, from a standing position.

The Americans and Venezuelans went into the Perija for their regular wages, it was learned.

The loss in the jungle is the last in a string of failures for SCI. The company has been operating in Venezuela since 1920, and has yet to find oil . . .

Chapter Six

Tom Fairbanks went to work for SeaCoast International—SCI—ten days after he was cut loose at British Meridian. On that morning he found a message in his hotel box from Ed Gurwell, SCI's manager in Maracaibo, asking if he would stop by the SCI office at his earliest convenience. He went there immediately, without breakfast and without reservations about accepting an offer of employment.

Gurwell, a slim, sleek-haired man in his thirties with shrewd tan eyes in a sallow face, welcomed Fairbanks into his office. He showed him to a chair. Then, without preamble, he handed Fairbanks a telegram. Fairbanks read it. IS TOM FAIRBANKS AVAILABLE FOR SCI EMPLOYMENT IN CARACAS? It was signed by Charles Cannon, president of SCI–Venezuela.

Gurwell took the telegram from Fairbanks' hand. "Are you?" he asked with an arch smile. He went behind his desk and sat down.

"I'm available," Fairbanks said. "How does it work?"

"I'll give you expense money to Caracas. When you get there, ask Cannon for twice what you were getting from British Meridian." Again the same smile. "He won't give it to you, but he'll appreciate the gesture. He may kick in a couple of extra bucks."

"I'll pay my way to Caracas," Fairbanks said. "If he doesn't kick in enough extra bucks, I won't feel indebted to him. I may want to try someone else."

"That's up to you." Gurwell got up and walked around the desk, handing Fairbanks the telegram. "This may help you get in to see Cannon quicker. His secretary is an old prick."

Fairbanks prepared to leave, and Gurwell went to the door with him. "That fellow Barr, the ex-pimp, what's *he* doing in the oil business?" Gurwell asked.

Fairbanks said coldly, "He's an ex-pimp, but he's a lot more than that. He's a damned good oilman. Pan Union made a mistake in not keeping him." He paused. "Any oil company would be making a mistake in not thinking of him in those terms."

"You're right, and I'm sorry I said it," Gurwell said. "Are you recommending him to SCI?"

"I'd recommend him to anyone, but you'd think he didn't need it after what he did in the lake."

Gurwell started to say something, then closed his mouth, obviously changing his mind. "If you see him before you leave town you might tell him to come and see me. All right?"

Fairbanks nodded. "If I see him."

Barr was not at the hotel, but Fairbanks found him in the Bull Wheel drinking beer with Pete Hanlon, the rotary rig salesman. Both men were a little high, and Hanlon greeted Fairbanks with warmth and enthusiasm, arranging a chair for him, ordering more beer, talking all the while. He shoved some papers at Fairbanks.

"Look at 'em! Orders, orders, orders! Sixteen from Shell and fourteen from Gulf, and that's just the beginning. That tough bastard at Pan Union, that Drury, he's bringing in five from Texas, but that's not going to be enough. Am I right or Amarillo?" Hanlon thrust his flushed face toward Fairbanks. "There's going to be a drilling war like you've never seen, sure as I'm a foot high. They're going to march up and down, you hear me, with Shell on the land and Gulf in the Strip and Pan Union in the lake. They'll *have* to offset each other!" He looked around at Barr and then back to Fairbanks. He winked. "A drilling war, and Peter Anthony Hanlon is going to supply the artillery!"

Barr smiled all through Hanlon's recitation, pouring beer into glasses from a heavy pitcher with a steady hand, but when Hanlon paused for breath, Barr broke in.

"Shut up a minute, Pete, and let me tell Tom about Joe and Phil." Barr grinned at Fairbanks. "Damn if Phil didn't catch on with Gulf, and Joe caught on with Shell." He nodded. "Phil's going out and study some leases Gulf got in the east, and ol' Joe's going to work right across the lake. As toolpusher."

Fairbanks whipped the telegram out of his pocket with a flourish. "They're not the only ones," he said airily. He handed the telegram to Barr. "Read that!" As Barr took the telegram from him, Fairbanks remembered Barr's difficulty in reading. "SCI wants me in Caracas," he said quickly to Hanlon. "Right, Grady?"

"Are you going?" Hanlon asked.

"Just as sure as you're a foot high," Fairbanks said, feeling exuberant now. "Just as sure as you're the best damn rotary rig salesman in the whole wide world." He reached out and plucked the telegram from Barr's hand. "And that's not all. Ed Gurwell would like the pleasure of Mr. Grady Barr's presence in his office at Mr. Grady Barr's convenience!"

Barr was grinning at Fairbanks' exuberance, but Hanlon said, "Shell and Gulf already offered him a job as driller and he turned 'em down. Even when Gulf offered him almost double wages."

Fairbanks frowned. "Why, Grady? That sounds pretty damned good to me."

"Maybe later," Barr said. He punched Hanlon in the ribs with a stiff thumb. "I couldn't sit here and drink beer before noon with Peter Anthony Hanlon if I took the first thing that came long." He poured more beer. "Don't worry, Tom. I'll pick up something pretty soon."

"Go see Gurwell. He may want you to go out east. It could be better than anything around here. Hell, you might even have to come through Caracas every once in a while."

Barr nodded. "I'll see him."

Fairbanks got up to leave. "Yawl take care. I'm going to try to get out of here by noon if I can. Hope we see each other again, somewhere, sometime."

Both men rose and Hanlon shook his hand. But Barr walked to the door with him, telling Hanlon to sit tight. On the plaza Barr was grave as he shook Fairbanks' hand. "I want you to know I appreciate what you done for me, and I'm proud of your friendship."

"You made us all look good, Grady. We're in *your* debt."

"That ain't what I mean. I mean just taking me for a friend and trusting me."

It was an awkward moment for Fairbanks, but just then Barr grinned. "You give 'em hell in Caracas, you hear, and if you ever need me for something, holler." He turned quickly and went back into the Bull Wheel.

Fairbanks stood there a moment while the crowd pushed by him, knowing he would miss Grady Barr for more reasons than he could enumerate, and he vowed to himself that some day they'd work and enjoy life together again.

Barr didn't go see Ed Gurwell that day, but later that evening as he dined with Louise Bremond in the Blue Book, Gurwell approached their table and introduced himself. Barr invited him to sit down with them.

"I was aiming to come and see you in a day or two," Barr said. "Since you've come to see me, I figure you ain't got a plain, old driller's job in mind. Something, maybe, that won't wait."

"Yes, I was wondering if you'd be interested in taking a party into the Perija. We'd like to complete the Buena Suerta well and get our equipment out of there."

"How do you know your equipment's still there? Maybe them Indians have tore it up by now."

"No," Gurwell said, "that's not the way they operate, apparently. They destroy personal belongings—paper, clothing, things like that. Even food. But they've never bothered housing and equipment even when it went unguarded for long periods. Even when they would find an untended bongo, for example, they'd ransack it but leave the boat alone. I feel sure you'll find everything there and ready to go—engine, cars, drilling rig, everything."

"But what if it ain't?"

"Then I'd expect you to do the best you could."

"You mean salvage what I could if everything's out of shape. Is that it?"

Gurwell nodded.

Louise stood up. "I've got to get back to the club, gentlemen. And Grady, you've got to be as nutty as a peach orchard boar if you let this man talk you into this." She leaned across the table and shook a finger at him. "You know what happened to the others, don't you?" She gave Gurwell a scornful glance, and was gone.

Gurwell acted as if she had never been there. "Interested?" he asked.

Barr nodded. "Some. But there was a couple of things in that newspaper story that interested me, too. One was that the party went up there for their regular wages. Was that right?"

"It was."

"Well, I ain't going to do that. I've been thinking while you was talking. I'd want three thousand a month for myself . . ."

"But . . ."

"And fifteen hundred for the drillers, and a thousand for the roughnecks and other white men, and twenty bolivars a day for the natives."

Gurwell was red-faced. "That's ridiculous!"

"Maybe, but so is getting shot in the ass with one of them six-foot arrows. If you can get a gang to go up there for less than that, more power to you."

"I damned sure will," Gurwell said. He pushed back from the table and stood up.

"Maybe you want to hear the other thing that interested me in that story," Barr said. "Might help you in getting up your party."

"Let me hear it," Gurwell said impatiently.

"It was that part that said that while the Indians was eating them up, the party fought back with what pitiful weapons they owned. What was them pitiful weapons?"

Gurwell hesitated. "Two revolvers," he said finally. "They were illegal, damn it. You know that. We're going to catch hell for it. General Gomez simply doesn't allow weapons of any kind in the country."

"Except for the military," Barr said.

"Except for the military."

"How are you going to explain it?"

"We didn't know about the guns. SCI didn't. One of the men sneaked them in."

"Who?"

Gurwell's smile was frosty. "One of the dead."

Barr laughed silently and went back to his dinner, dismissing Gurwell. Gurwell watched Barr take a bite of steak. "What would *you* require, Mr. Barr, a couple of dozen machine guns?"

Barr chewed his steak and swallowed it. He cut another bite of meat, concentrating on the job as he answered Gurwell. "It might be best that you don't know, if you decide to meet my price."

He went on eating, and Gurwell finally walked away.

Shortly before noon the next day, where the Street of the Hanging Pirate meets Plaza Baralt, while hundreds of Maracuchos watched in silence, Grady Barr met Hernan Robles in hand-to-hand combat that would have satisfied the cruelest Caesar.

Though the intersection was the city's busiest and generally the heaviest policed, there was not a law enforcement officer of any stripe to be seen on the ancient, sunlit plaza when Robles accosted Barr. Robles was coatless, and in his frilly white shirt and black trousers he was every inch a rake prepared to duel for a lady's honor. Barr was booted and his fresh khakis still wore the flatiron's mark. Robles stepped out of the crowd to face Barr and stop him. His face was twisted with anger.

"Son of a whore!" Robles hissed, and he slashed Barr across the face with the back of his hand.

Less than a dozen of the hundreds heard Robles' words or saw his flashing hand, but as if by magic a clearing was made, leaving the two men facing each other in a heavy silence. Robles lifted his hand to slash Barr again, and Barr hit him with a clubbing overhand right that drove Robles reeling across the clearing. Barr then went after him in quick strides, obviously intending to end the fight quickly, but Robles met him with a snapping left jab to the face, then threw his right fist into Barr's stomach with all of his strength.

Barr grunted and bent over. Robles stepped back, grinning, and Barr rushed him. Again Robles snapped the left into Barr's face, halting the rush. Barr tried to grab him, and Robles pushed him back with both hands and again shot the left jab to the face. The blow caught Barr going away, but Robles hit him once more with the sharp left and moved in to hit Barr a solid blow on the cheek with his right.

In the past Robles had dropped opponents with less powerful blows, but Barr only shook his head. So Robles pressed him, snapping the left again and again into Barr's face, fighting coolly now, blocking Barr's swinging blows with his hands and forearms, occasionally throwing a right hand to Barr's face or stomach, moving confidently but with some caution. He had been impressed by Barr's absorption of the heavy punch.

Barr was being humiliated. He could not fight through Robles' guard, and the left hand that thudded against his face was as the pricking, weakening lance in the grasp of the *picador*. As he moved backward he tried to brush aside the left as it reached for him, but it always slipped past to further shred his lips or hammer his nose. He stumbled on a loose paving stone and Robles drove through the opening with another powerful right that sent Barr staggering with blood gushing from his broken nose.

Robles went after him relentlessly, slashing Barr's face and pummelling his body, cursing him in dull monotone. Suddenly

Barr dug in and rammed his head at Robles' chest. The maneuver caught Robles by surprise. He instinctively bent forward, and Barr's skull clicked against Robles' chin with astonishing force.

Robles sagged, then straightened up to fight with a wild desperation as Barr smothered the blows and, in close, clubbed Robles' head with his own shocking blows that forced Robles to his knees.

Out of the crowd a dirk came flying through the air to lay glinting on the plaza near Robles' hand. Robles clutched it. He began rising to his feet with the dirk aimed at Barr's heart. Barr clubbed him on the top of the head with both hands, one blow after another, and Robles sank to the plaza.

Barr stepped back. Again Robles began to rise, still clutching the dirk, and Barr kicked him in the head, just above the left temple—the cracking of Robles' skull rang out across the plaza.

Barr stood looking at his foe for a long moment while a ragged sigh of relaxed tension swept through the crowd. Then he walked unhurriedly into the throng of spectators and disappeared down the Street of the Hanging Pirate.

Maracuchos were not surprised that police had not shown up at the fight; they knew Captain Ramirez had ordered them to stay away, giving Hernan Robles free rein to beat Grady Barr to death. Nor were they surprised at the massive manhunt Ramirez initiated when Robles was the loser. What mystified them was Barr's elusiveness, for the long day dragged by, hour after hour, without an announcement of his capture.

An announcement did not come even after nightfall when some of the off-duty military joined the search for the sport of it. By that time the hunt had spread to the oil camps across the lake and to the rancheros of the poorest Venezuelans.

Eduardo Vigas found him about eleven o'clock. He drove the Studebaker into the sweeping driveway of Christina's house, parked, then stood in front of the car while the headlights illumined him. Barr opened the front door of the house, then closed it. Vigas turned off the car's lights and approached the house. Barr let him in. He had one of the shotguns from the den in his hand.

"The old people?" Vigas asked. "The ones who work here?"

"In the cellar," Barr said. "They're all right."

Vigas moved quickly to the kitchen area, Barr behind him, and opened the trapdoor to the cellar. He went down the stairs, Barr still following. The big room was lighted by four lamps. An old couple sat at a bare table.

"Have you been frightened?" Vigas asked in Spanish.

"He put another gray hair in my head," the old woman said.

Barr grinned at her with split lips. "It just made you prettier," he said in Spanish.

She looked at his swollen face with scorn. "This one thinks a smile wipes out all sins. Ten year ago I would have pulled all the marrow out of his backbone in one hour."

"Maria . . .!" The old man was shocked at her language.

She patted his arm. "Not you, my stallion. But these golden ones carry nothing in their trousers." She made a face at Barr.

"Enough," Vigas said. "Go on to bed as if nothing has happened. Use the lights you need. This one is a friend."

"So he said," the old woman sniffed. "I told him his nose is broken and his mouth looks like a hen's ass stretched over a doorknob, but he does nothing. And his bottom teeth are loose."

"I'll take care of him," Vigas said, and he shooed them up the stairs. "Sit down," he said to Barr in English. "Ramirez will never enter this house without permission." Barr sat down, laying the shotgun across the table. "Is that loaded?" Vigas asked. Barr nodded. "I found a ton of shells in a closet in his den. All kinds, from bird-shot to double-ought buck in brass cartridges. I took down the other gun, too. It's on his desk. I loaded it, too. I figured Ramirez and his people would want to kill me."

Vigas bent over and began gently probing the lumps on Barr's face. "Did you come here thinking he would help you?"

"I figured he wouldn't let them outright kill me, that he'd see that I got a trial or something. When they told me he'd gone to Caracas, I figured I'd stay here until the hounds stopped yelping. And I hoped you'd come along.

"Let me look at your teeth," Vigas said. Barr opened his mouth and Vigas checked the looseness of his front teeth with his forefinger. Finished, he sat down at the table with Barr. "Can you breathe through your nose?" he asked. Barr nodded. "Good as ever." Vigas grunted. "It's broken, all right, but I don't know what to do about it right now. And I think your teeth will tighten up if you're careful of what you eat. Can you see all right between those purple slits?"

Barr nodded. "All I need is to clean up and rest some, Eddie. I'm a quick healer."

"Did you have to kill him?"

84

"I thought I did. He was going to kill me unless I ran, and I couldn't do that."

"Not even Cerro Soto can keep you from going to prison. He can save your life but that's all. You could kill a dozen workmen—but not a Hernan Robles."

"They ain't caught me yet, Eddie."

"They won't stop hunting you until they do," Vigas said. "They'll check every boat that leaves the lake from now on if they have to. I think you'd better stay here until Cerro Soto gets back and turn yourself into him. You'll be safe here."

"What about Christina?"

"He took her with him to Caracas."

Barr sighed deeply. "He waited too long. She'd already sprayed her poison on Robles." He stood up. "I've changed my mind, Eddie. I ain't going to wait for him to get back because I ain't going to no prison for something I don't feel bad about doing. You let me lay around here while I figure out something, and then I'll be long gone." He put a hand on Vigas' shoulder. "Fair enough?"

The younger man's stoic composure broke, but he said steadily, "Fair enough."

"My father was an army officer, a colonel," Vigas was saying the following night. "He was killed fighting for General Gomez in the revolt against Cipriano Castro. General Gomez asked Cerro Soto to take me in his care. I was just a small boy then, and my mother was dead."

"He didn't adopt you like he did Christina, huh?" Barr asked.

"He did what General Gomez asked him to do. It was enough."

The following night the Pig came to the house. Vigas had watched him park his car and make the journey to the door. "He knows you're here or he wouldn't have come," Vigas said to Barr. "I'm going to let him in."

Barr said nothing. He had his shotgun at the ready.

Vigas opened the door as the Pig raised his hand to knock. "Welcome to the house," he said in Spanish.

"You honor me," the Pig said. He saw Barr and the shotgun. "You have no need of that with me, Grady Barr." He entered the house and Vigas shut the door. "We can talk here," the Pig said. "I guessed you came here the first night, Grady Barr, so you should know I mean you no harm. I'm here to deliver a message."

"Louise Bremond?"

"No, Ed Gurwell of SeaCoast International. He asked me today to let him know if I found you first. He offered me a sum of money. He said he has a plan to save you from the prison. He wants to talk to you. I don't know what the plan is."

"I think *I* do. I think I know something about it."

"Will it work?" Vigas asked quickly.

Barr chuckled. "I'm sure it will work for him, and it might work for me."

"If you don't want to see him I'll say nothing to him," the Pig said.

"No, I guess I'd better see him. I haven't come up with anything on my own." Barr nodded. "Yeah, I'll see him. How are we going to arrange it?"

The Pig looked at Vigas. "I can bring him here after midnight."

"Do that," Vigas said. He shook hands solemnly with the Pig. "You have my gratitude in this matter."

Barr also shook the Pig's hand, but he said, "If you figured out right away that I was here, I wonder how come Ramirez didn't figure it out. You got any idea?"

The Pig nodded. "He's obsessed. He believes Louise Bremond has hidden you in some place known only to her. Others believe that also."

"Has he hurt her?"

"No, no, no. He has questioned her twice to my knowledge, and with no more than his usual surliness. She has made many friends quickly, the kind of friends who would resent her mistreatment. You can see that?"

Barr nodded.

"He thinks he can outwait her," the Pig said. "She is watched constantly, but that is all."

Vigas touched the Pig's shoulder. "Go quickly, good friend of ours, and exercise caution."

The Pig grinned at Barr. "What an educated way to tell me to be careful." He opened the door wide enough to permit his passage, and was gone.

"Like Louise Bremond, you also make friends quickly," Vigas said.

"And enemies," Barr said.

Ed Gurwell displayed no sympathy for Barr's plight. They talked by lamp light at the kitchen table; Vigas and the Pig were in Cerro Soto's den. As coolly as if he were explaining his budget to an aide, Gurwell outlined his plan. Barr would head the expedition to the Perija, for regular wages. In return, SCI would use its considerable influence with General Gomez and Cerro Soto to have Barr placed on probation when he came back. "In effect, SCI will be responsible for your future behavior in Venezuela."

Gurwell paused, waiting for Barr's answer, but Barr said nothing, so Gurwell continued. "As soon as I leave here I'll get a launch started for Rio Santa Ana. Upriver, the crew will find a clearing or make one. We'll get you out of here tomorrow night. We'll have a launch and crew ready for you. You go to the clearing and wait for the main party. You'll be in charge. Take them up there and finish that well and bring our stuff back."

"You talk like you don't expect us to strike oil."

"I don't, but the goddamned geologists do. I think the location is too high. It's too far out of the basin, but the scientists in Houston say I'm full of shit. They sat up there and punched a hole in a map and said drill it right there. And that's what I'm going to do. You go down to thirty-four hundred feet, and be damned sure to keep a log to prove it. I want to show those bastards."

"But if we do hit?"

"Cap it and move the rig to a location of your choice to drill a confirming well. There are five sites marked on a map I'll give you. Send a party back to let me know, and I'll send a whole goddamned army up there to relieve you and exploit the field."

Barr grinned. "A man could learn an awful lot from you."

Gurwell acted as if he did not see the grin or hear the words. "There will be three revolvers and ammunition on your launch. There will be another one on the launch ahead of you. I trust that you'll throw them away before you get back and say nothing about them."

Barr said, "I can see how SCI might have some influence with Gomez, but how about Cerro Soto? Robles was kin to him?"

"Robles was buried here yesterday. If Cerro Soto shed a tear, he did it in Caracas. I assumed you knew that. Young Vigas is at least a friend of yours."

"What's your story going to be?" Barr asked. "It'll have to be a cute one."

"It's cute enough. Our party found you wandering up the Rio Santa Ana. They didn't feel they could bring you back here, so they took you with them." Gurwell showed Barr his arch smile. "While you were working up there you demonstrated great leadership qualities and got rehabilitated. That's why you deserve probation—under SCI supervision, of course."

Barr shook his head. "Vigas will have to tell Cerro Soto the truth."

"Not until Cerro Soto gets back from Caracas, and he'll be there a month at least. We'll go to work on him as soon as he gets back. By the time *you* get back, I'm pretty sure he'll help us sell the story to Gomez." Gurwell made an impatient gesture. "What else can you do but trust me?"

Barr stood up. "Wait here," he said. He left the room and returned with Vigas and the Pig. Standing by the table, he told the pair of Gurwell's proposition in detail. "Now," he said, "Mr. Gurwell here may not be the man in charge when I get back. He may be in the States somewhere or China, for all I know. So I want Tom Fairbanks to know all about this deal. I want you to tell him about it, Eddie." He grinned. "It's kind of important to me."

"As you say," Vigas said.

"I resent your implication," Gurwell said coldly.

"That's too fucking bad," Barr said. He put a hand on the Pig's wide shoulder. "You watch out after Eddie, will you?"

The Pig laughed. "Let him watch out for himself. I'm going with you." He was delighted with himself. He took up a boxing stance. "Someone has to teach you to use your left hand." His fat left arm shot out quickly and his fingertips brushed Barr's forehead. "Like that!" he cried.

The launch *Musa*, Enrique Lopez at the helm, slid down the lake in darkness and at dawn entered the mouth of Rio Santa Ana. One of the four crewmen served coffee and bread rolls to Barr, the Pig and Lopez. Barr and the Pig had slipped aboard the *Musa* at the SCI dock, and the crewmen had transferred their belongings to the launch from Eduardo Vigas' Studebaker. Barr had taken the two Perez Soto shotguns onto the launch, and the crewmen had loaded wooden cases of shotgun shells in the stern. Lopez had shown Barr the three revolvers Ed Gurwell had promised him and ammunition for them.

Lopez had smiled at the shotguns. "The big stud horse Gurwell knows nothing of them, I'll bet," he said to Barr in a Spanish accent strange to the American. "He would be shitting green if he even suspected them."

"What he don't know won't hurt him," Barr had said.

They had traveled in silence after that, but now in the river mouth Lopez signaled for Barr to join him at the wheel. "I would guess they are waiting for us at Cano Norte," he said to Barr. "It is a place upstream where the river widens and the land on either side is firm, not swampy. It is far this side of Indian country. The Motilons range many miles upstream, around Rio Lora."

"Where the drilling rig is," Barr said.

"Yes," said Lopez, "where the drilling rig is." He ran a broad hand across his coffee-wet handlebar moustache. "The shotguns may save our hides. Do you have buckshot?"

"Cases of it," Barr said. "Smaller shot, too."

The Pig had joined them. "You are Colombian, eh?" he said to Lopez.

Lopez nodded. He pointed upriver. "On the other side of the Perija Ridge." He smiled. "Your Spanish is of Madrid, and Grady Barr learned his in Mexico. The crewmen are Andinos, mountain men, and their Spanish is different from that heard in Maracaibo."

"Very good," said the Pig. "You are wondering what a policeman is doing aboard your launch with a man charged with murder . . . correct?"

"I thought about it, but not very hard."

"Also very good," the Pig said.

"How far is this Cano Norte?" Barr asked.

"We should be there by noon," Lopez said.

Soon they were in a lost world. The Santa Ana became a deep coffee color, and the banks were lined with grotesque trees whose stilt roots extended upward at least twenty feet out of the water. Beyond the banks was nothing except for what seemed to be flooded tidal flats and a solid jungle mass. Alligators by the scores slithered down the mud banks and into the water.

As Barr looked at the twisted trees in wonder, a great swarm of red howler monkeys swept through them, their voices blending until the sound was of a great wind screaming in the wilderness.

On the opposite bank a tree in the jungle ahead looked as if its leaves had been dipped in blood. But at the monkey howls, hundreds of flamingos beat the air with their wings and flew away, leaving the tree the same monotonous green as all the others.

Behind the monkeys flocks of macaws descended in clouds on the wild palm trees to rip the jungle as they fought and squawked over the nuts. And in an infrequent patch of sunlight a huge boa constrictor sunned itself.

It was a show that did not end for hours, not until the launch approached Cano Norte, where the clearing extended from either bank to perhaps half a mile into the jungle.

"The launch is here," Lopez said, "but I don't see anyone."

"This fellow Jenkins is supposed to have eight natives with him," Barr said.

"Nationals!" Lopez snapped. "They don't like being called natives."

Barr said nothing. The *Musa* pulled up beside the other launch and a crewman leaped ashore to fix a line to a protruding root. Barr was the next ashore. He had a shotgun in his hand. The others followed him. The Pig also had a shotgun.

Some thirty feet inland Barr held up a hand to halt the party. Ahead of them, resting on the sand, was what appeared to be a human form. Barr motioned them forward, and the group slowly advanced on the prostrate form.

"It's Ernie Jenkins," Lopez said.

Jenkins was naked. His head had been sliced off but was resting by the body as if still joined to the shoulders. The right hand had been amputated and placed across the scrotum. But most horrible of all, Jenkins' chest had been cut open and the heart removed. It was nowhere in sight.

A crewman vomited noisily.

"He's already spoiling," Barr said. "We'll bury him right here." He pointed the shotgun straight up and fired it three times.

"What's that for?" Lopez demanded angrily. "Are you trying to bring the Indians back?"

"No, I'm letting those eight *nationals* know somebody's here—if they ain't dead or out of hearing distance. I figure we're going to need every man we can rustle up."

Lopez looked at him in angry astonishment. "Do you mean you're going on . . . after this?"

Barr ignored the question. He said to the Pig, "I don't see his clothes. Check the launch. See if that revolver is there." Then he faced Lopez squarely. "I sure as hell am going on—and so is everybody else." He turned to some crewmen. "Get shovels and bury this man." He looked back at Lopez. "Now, I don't want to hear any more about it."

90

Chapter Seven

There was no positive evidence of a Motilon presence in the Perija, but Grady Barr acted as if the expedition was in imminent danger of an Indian attack from the moment he assumed command at Cano Norte. He was ever vigilant, and he made the others vigilant by the force of his will. Some of the more intelligent in the party resented what they considered his obsessive concern for their safety, but Barr gave them little free time to allow the resentment to fester. He drove them and he drove himself toward the accomplishment of their mission.

Sixteen Americans and forty-two Venezuelans tied up at Cano Norte. That he was wanted on a murder charge did not disturb the Americans. Some had witnessed his fight with Hernan Robles and approved his actions. All of them knew he had drilled the first well in the lake. All of them had heard that he had been a pimp; this simply made him more interesting to them. And all of them appreciated his blunt statement that Ernie Jenkins had been killed by Motilons and the eight Venezuelans were missing. "I don't know where in the hell they are," he said. He satisfied their curiosity about the Pig's presence. "He wanted to come because we're friends, and I'm damned glad to have him along. He ain't looking to arrest nobody. He ain't a cop no more. And he says his real name is Ignacio Acero, and I advise you to call him that."

Barr and Acero shepherded the convoy of launches and slow-moving bongos up Rio Santa Ana and into Rio Lora to the headquarters camp, riding in long canoes paddled by Venezuelans. From time to time Barr fired loads of birdshot into the jungle on the right side of the stream and Acero did the same on the left side. It was Barr's theory that the shotguns' roars and the pelting shot would make the Motilons hesitant to attack. He and Acero had buckshot aboard the canoes for use if an attack materialized.

The abandoned headquarters camp had not been molested by the Indians, as far as Barr could tell, and he decided to let it remain abandoned. The drilling rig had been set up seventeen kilometers west of Rio Lora. When an engineer and fireman got up steam in the locomotive, Barr ordered all hands and equipment and supplies aboard for the journey to the rig. "We ain't coming back here until we complete the well," he said. "We ain't going to split up our people and supplies."

The Motilons did not attack the engine on the trip to the drill site. "If they didn't know we were on the way, they damned sure know it now," Barr told Acero. "That engine sounds like a Gulf Coast hurricane."

There was no indication that the Motilons had returned to the drill site after the attack in which the driller was killed. Still Barr and Acero marched around the perimeter of the vast clearing and fired birdshot into the jungle mass. Barr issued the revolvers, including the one Acero had found in Ernie Jenkins' launch, to four Americans who said they were familiar with the weapons. And he set the Venezuelans to work digging a deep trench around the drilling rig. "If those boogers start shooting those arrows in here, I want every son of a buck who's in the open to head for that trench," he explained. He had the windows in the driller's quarters boarded up, and the windows in the roughnecks' huts and the Venezuelans' huts also were covered. "It ain't so hot we can't stand to do without a breeze," he said. "We're going to have somebody on guard every night, but there ain't no use in inviting trouble with just screens on them windows."

The drilling rig and equipment was intact. "Those other guys just worked daylight hours and hung it up at night," Barr told the Americans. "We're going to work three eight-hour shifts and get this thing done and get our asses out of here." He took Enrique Lopez aside and told him, "There ain't too much for these nationals to do until we get ready to tear down the rig and tear up the tracks. I want you to try to keep them busy. Keep them busy doing anything you think will make it safer for us up here." He added significantly. "If you don't think you can do this, Enrique, tell me now, because I aim to keep all hands working and alive." Lopez nodded. "I can handle it."

And so their new lives began. It was dull for Barr at first—the drilling held no excitement for him. Gurwell had said the well would be dry and Barr believed him. He shared this belief with no one else, however, and the Americans worked with the enthusiasm that hunting oil in new and strange places always created among them.

Barr had spent most of the war in Mexico and had no military experience, but three or four times every day he would shout a command and all hands would scoot to the trench. Then a Venezuelan, bolder or more foolhardy than the rest, gathered some wood at the clearing's edge and fashioned some whistles with his knife. Every time a man went on guard he had a whistle, and the little instruments emitted such a piercing sound that it could be clearly heard above the noises of the drilling rig.

Day after day Barr would send the men to the trench with his whistle or a shouted command. If the Venezuelans resented the seemingly senseless drill, they did not show it. Some of the Americans grumbled when weeks passed and there was no attack. Barr let them grumble until he became irritated with it.

"Complaining about it ain't going to make it go away," he told a mass meeting, "and it ain't much of a price to pay if it saves your ass. I could tell you you've *got* to do it or I'll see that SCI docks your pay. I guess I'm tough enough for that. But I'd rather you do it because you think it's a smart thing to do." He grinned. "Or, you can say to yourself, 'old Grady's a little goofy, so I'll do it to humor him.'"

"All right, Grady," said Shorty Dow, a driller, "but if I bust my balls jumping in that fuckin' ditch, I'm going to sue you for ruining my manhood."

"Shit, Shorty," Barr said, "everybody knows you ain't come since your mama called you."

The meeting broke up with laughter and the drills continued.

Late one afternoon Acero called Barr out of the drillers' quarters. "Time to begin your lesson," he said. He set himself in the classical boxer's stance, left foot forward, left hand and arm extended out with the right hand held back to guard the chin. "You must learn to move properly and, above all, you must learn to use your left hand." With that he slapped Barr's cheek briskly with his left palm.

Barr went after him but Acero skipped nimbly out of the way. "No fists, just the open hands," he said, and again he slapped Barr soundly with his left palm.

"You fat bastard," Barr grunted.

Acero stepped inside of Barr's looping slap and jabbed the stiffened fingers of his right hand into Barr's belly. And again he slapped Barr as he moved away, blocking Barr's looping slaps with quick movements of his hands and arms, reaching out again and again with astonishing quickness to slap Barr's face.

"Enough," Acero said, and caught Barr's swinging right hand in both of his. "You look like a wild woman shitting in the snow," he said. He released Barr's hands. "Come, let me show you how to do it."

Almost every afternoon from then on, Acero taught Barr how to fight with his fists. The Venezuelans loved it, primarily because they loved seeing the fat man teach an American anything. They had a love of graceful movement, and Acero was as graceful as a bullfighter. A love of combat, too, lay just beneath the layer of servility their ignorance had produced, so when the time came when Barr responded to Acero's teaching, their afternoons were enlivened by the resounding smack of palms on cheeks as Barr earned Acero's commendation.

"I would dearly love to see you fight now with your fists, not the palms," Acero said. "With your strength and what you have learned, you would be very good, my friend."

That night he told Barr something of himself. He was born in Madrid of well-to-do parents. He had left home at eighteen, going to England on a shipload of oranges his father was selling to the London market. There he improved the English he had learned in school in Spain. He had lost his British accent while peddling fruits and vegetables in New York City. He had polished his English further while teaching the language in Puerto Rico. He had sold powdered milk in Mexico and Peru. Growing fatter year by year but no taller, he had returned to the States where he had gained employment as the chauffeur to a wealthy Italian in Tampa. The Italian loved boxing, and he owned a stable of fighters who fought in all divisions from lightweight to heavyweight.

"I started hanging out around the fighters' training quarters," Acero said, "and they made fun of me because I was so fat. I didn't take it very well, and one day I hit a middleweight named Manila Smead. I knew nothing of boxing, you understand, but it took Smead longer to subdue me than he had thought it would." He waved a hand. "It was because I could move so well for a fat man. After that, Smead took me in tow and worked out with me

94

when he could." Acero smiled deprecatingly. "I learned very well, but as Smead often told me, I couldn't punch my way out of a paper bag." He shrugged. "It's like you say about a baseball player, 'good field, no hit.'"

"How in the hell did you wind up in Maracaibo as a cop?" Barr asked.

Acero laughed. "The pay was good and the opportunity for advancement splendid."

And he would say no more.

The men bathed under oil drums which had been placed on platforms. When water from the water well was pumped into the drums it showered down on the men through perforations cut in the drums. The water well had been drilled by the first expedition.

When Barr showered, Venezuelans under neighboring drums would cast quick glances at his long, thick penis, then turn away. They were not as heavily hung as he, and neither were the Americans. The Americans, however, kidded Barr about his "horse cock," and suggested various uses for it. "He could club you to death with it," said a driller, "then pole vault out of this goddamned jungle."

As the weeks passed there was always talk of nocturnal emission—"wet dreams" the Americans called them—and masturbation. "I heard old Luther loping his mule around the camp last night," someone said at breakfast, and Luther grinned with the rest of them. "I had a wet dream last night," Shorty Dow announced, "and if I hadn't gone to sleep I'd a had another one" Such remarks brought on howls of laughter.

Barr suffered perhaps more than any of the men from the lack of women. His sleep was often fitful, as women he had known as well as women strange to him danced enticingly on the threshold of consciousness. Yet they always eluded him . . .

One night he awoke and realized he had been dreaming of Hazel Cotton, the woman who had steered him into the world of whores, pimps and square johns. He smiled in the darkness. He remembered the time in the Bull Wheel restaurant when Tom Fairbanks had been on the verge of asking him why he became a pimp. He smiled because he knew that every whore is asked by almost every trick why she became a whore. "How did you get into this, little lady?" was the standard question. And every whore had a story—the mother dying of cancer, the three chil-

dren and her their sole support, the father who raped her and
sent her out on the street. There were a thousand variations on
the basic theme of deprivation, and they were all tearjerkers
which sometimes wrung another dollar or two from the trick's
pocket.

Barr's smile became a wry grin. As much as any whore's, *his*
story was a tearjerker—and it was true. Now, in the darkness, it
played across his mind like an old movie. . . .

Grady Barr celebrated his twentieth birthday, in 1918, on a
muddy derrick floor near Punta Azul in Mexico. The messenger
from the oil camp found him there. His father, Stancil Barr, had
been badly hurt by falling pipe when the well he was drilling ten
miles away had suddenly cratered. Barr's mother and two sisters
were at his father's bedside at the camp hospital when he got
there. The camp's physician was cruelly blunt. "He'll live, but
he'll never be active again. He's crippled for life."

Stancil Barr wanted to go home, to San Antonio. World War I
had not yet reached its climax. Barr easily got a job in the Alamo
City in a smithy-garage, but his salary was hardly enough to
support the family. He planned to get to some Texas oilfield as
soon as he could; he would be able to send more money home
than he was making at the smithy-garage.

Meanwhile, he met a dark-haired girl named Velma Harkins
who worked at Jesse Elkins' drugstore. Velma stayed at the store
to clean up after Elkins left at ten o'clock. On the battered old
couch behind the prescription counter Barr and Velma made
love.

Hazel Cotton was a whore who lived and conducted her business in a row of apartments above the drugstore. Six girls helped
her bring comfort to the neighborhood's restless males.

One night Barr found the drugstore dark when he arrived.
Velma was sick. As he walked away he almost bumped into Hazel, who had stepped down on the street for a breath of fresh air.
She was a small woman with red hair, about twenty-seven at the
time. She was wearing a dark green housecoat. She had to look
up at Barr.

"Buster," she said with a grin, "does old man Elkins have any
idea of what you're doing to that Harkins girl most every night?"

Barr had seen Hazel from a distance—and knew her profession. "What do you mean?" he stammered.

Hazel laughed. "That girl provides her own cheering section, buster. You can hear her squeals for three blocks—much less upstairs. You've got my girls wondering about you."

With unaccustomed boldness Barr asked, "How about you? Are you wondering?"

She laughed again. "If I took you upstairs, I'd turn you every way but loose, buster."

She was irking Barr with the "buster." "Try me," he said.

Hazel studied a moment. "Everybody wants the madam," she said finally. "Come on, buster, you only live once."

Barr followed her upstairs. She had a one-bedroom apartment and she went straight to the bedroom. She faced Barr at the side of the bed and pulled at her housecoat. It fell to the floor and she was naked, the first totally naked woman Barr had ever seen.

"Come and get it, buster," she said huskily. "I haven't been with my man in three months."

Barr later would make a lot of money from that primitive urge that compels a man to forget everything—fame, fortune, status— to satisfy the hunger he was born with, and he would pander to it. But that night in 1918 he rushed to Hazel Cotton, tearing off his clothes. He was savage and she utterly wanton, ripping at his back and shoulders, moaning like a schoolgirl and mouthing obscenities. When it was over, she gasped. "Don't move, sweetheart."

Barr grinned down at her. "Through calling me buster?"

She nodded.

"My name's Grady. Grady Barr."

She took in a deep breath and let it out slowly. "Well, Grady Barr, we just took the edge off of it. In a little while, when that dick of yours gets hard again, I'm going to show you how to use it."

She did, all through the night . . .

Two weeks later she told him that she and the girls were moving to Dallas, that the town was opening up and she had a fix in. "Go with me," she pleaded. "You'll have enough money to take care of your folks and get your daddy an operation. Please."

Barr knew he could go to the new oilfields in northwest Texas and make a living wage. He had been taught by older boys through childhood that a man should get all the pussy he could but that a pimp was to be scorned.

"You can't make enough money in the oilfield to live on and still send enough to your folks to really help them," Hazel said, as if reading his thoughts. "And who in the hell cares what happens to them but you? Who gives a shit what Grady Barr does or doesn't do? Nobody. Besides, no one will know you in Dallas."

So he went, telling himself it was because of the money but knowing also that he was looking for something new, something exciting in a strange place, and knowing even then, at that early age, that he was proud of his sexual competence, hiding but feeling nonetheless a sense of power from his mastery over Hazel and the others, and always assuring himself that he could quit when he wanted to quit, when he got far enough ahead financially.

He took Velma Harkins with him because she begged to go along. "You'll have to work like the others," he had told her. "The others won't put up with it if you don't."

"Don't leave without me, Grady," she had said.

In Dallas the girls worked out of their small hotel as freely as if they were distributing soap samples. Velma pouted when Barr added new girls to the stable, but she didn't pack up and leave. The money came rolling in, and much of Barr's went to his mother. He moved in with Hazel, but he didn't neglect the others. He shaved in Velma's room and loved her some. He washed his hair in JoAnn's room and loved her some. He read the newspaper in Lurline's room and loved her some . . . .

"Don't worry about them," Hazel told him. "Each one of them believes in her heart that you belong to her . . . that you'll finally get rid of the others and have only her."

She was right, and Barr played it that way.

One night when Barr returned to the hotel from a movie, Velma met him in the lobby, and she was crying. "Grady! Hazel got run over right out in front of the hotel! She's dead!" She wailed, "What are we going to do?"

Grief hit him quickly and was gone. What *were* they going to do? The other girls had gathered around Velma. All were looking at him for leadership. Behind them an older pimp named Bandera was leaning against a lobby column. He wanted to see how Barr would handle the situation.

"All of you get upstairs," Barr snapped. "Right now! I'll take care of things." When they hesitated, he barked, "Now!"

They left, glad to be told what to do in the face of the crisis. Bandera grinned. "What *are* you going to do, bucko—after the burying?"

"I'm going to Houston," Barr said promptly. "It's booming and wide open. I'm going to make a million."

Bandera nodded solemnly. "Good boy. If I was ten years younger I'd go with you."

By the time he got to Houston Barr felt that he was completely mature. He had ideas and the nerve to try them out. He kept his girls off the streets. He made a pitch to every bellhop and every porter at every hotel of any status in town. And he didn't neglect cab drivers. All of them were hustlers, men who would do anything for a buck. Barr told them his girls were clean. They were well-coached and well-behaved. And Barr squared all complaints.

He prospered. He drove home to San Antonio to see his family. They were living in better quarters. His father had a patio in the sunshine. The girls were growing up healthy and attractive and his mother looked good with no financial problems to worry her. But his mother said, "You ought to be home. I worry about your sisters with no active man around the house." Barr shook his head. "You can't have it both ways. I can't make the money here you have to have."

Though he prospered, he was restless, not quite as satisfied as he might have been. He had heard someone in a bar once say that a pimp was someone prostitutes could regard as more despicable and degraded than themselves. Barr had heard that line for years, supposing that in some cases it was true, though he felt sure it was not so for him. But he thought about it often, more often than he wished, until he met Louise Bremond and bedded her.

She loved him, he knew. He didn't love her, had never experienced the emotion, but he liked her, was more than fond of her, liked her as much for her poise, her humor, her genuine interest in things outside the business as he did for her competence in bed. She was the first woman he enjoyed talking to. And she dulled the edge of his cynicism. With Louise he could laugh again, and his indictment of the world lost some of its harshness.

Velma left when Barr began spending time with Louise. There was a note on the bed: *I'll always love you, Grady, but I've got to go. You don't need me anymore.* His only emotion was anger, briefly held, and Velma was forgotten.

He accepted eagerly when he was offered the job of managing partner of the Shark's Head in Galveston. He could make more money there and he needed a new challenge. He took his girls with him and mixed them in with the girls already there.

By the time the Texas Rangers raided the brothel and padlocked it, Barr had more than eighty thousand dollars in a San Antonio bank for his mother to draw on. He closed out a much smaller account in a Galveston bank. The hot check which he would later send to Cerro Soto was drawn on this bank.

He left Galveston with few regrets, looking forward to going into business with Louise Bremond in Maracaibo, believing he could hold his own and flourish whatever the nature of the new terrain. . . .

Now, lying in the darkness in the Perija, he knew that as a pimp he had missed the company of men like Tom Fairbanks and Phil Carter and Acero and, yes, the men sleeping and working around him at this moment. Cerro Soto. Eduardo Vigas. The men who had helped him drill the well in the lake and had helped him staunch its random flow. Now, at this moment, he was proud of what he had accomplished in Venezuela. He had killed, but he could rationalize that.

And suddenly he thought of Velma Harkins again. He had dismissed her memory with ease. Now she was back in his mind, a simple girl he had brutalized, ignored and forgotten. He writhed on his cot in a spasm of shame and regret.

A single arrow heralded the Indian attack Barr had been long anticipating. It flew across the clearing from the east and shattered against the heavy mesh curtain Barr had erected around the drilling rig. A shrill whistle from the derrick floor roused the camp and the men quickly made their way to the trench. Shorty Dow and Melvin Sharp, on guard duty with the shotguns, sent a hail of birdshot into the jungle then quickly switched to buckshot. The pistol toters held their fire at Barr's command. Dow and Sharp also waited. The driller had shut down the rig machinery and rustling jungle sounds crept across the clearing's silence. It was early afternoon and the sun was bright. "Keep a lookout in every direction," Barr said loud enough to be heard around the trench.

"Grady!" Acero said softly.

About fifty feet north of the spot where Dow and Sharp had sent their shots the jungle brush was shaking. "Hold it!" Barr snapped.

A figure stumbled out of the brush, a white man naked except for his boots. He put up a hand to shield his eyes from the sun's glare, then broke into a staggering trot across the clearing toward the trench. About halfway across he stumbled and fell to the ground.

"Hold it!" Barr said again. "He's got a lot of life in him."

The man sat up facing the trench. His body was covered with cuts and bruises where the jungle had lashed him. He opened his mouth to cry out, but no sound came.

Behind him, out of the jungle, stepped a naked Indian. He held a black bow in one hand, a sheaf of arrows in the other. He moved about five feet into the clearing. Other naked Indians were coming out of the jungle, lining up beside the first Indian like soldiers lining up for inspection. All had bows and arrows.

"Twenty of 'em," said Shorty Dow. "Three of 'em's women. Leastwise, they got titties and no dicks."

For perhaps a minute the Indians stood in the loose formation, the hands holding the bows and arrows dangling by their sides. Then one stepped forward. "A woman," Shorty Dow whispered. The woman took six paces, then bent gracefully and placed her bow and arrows on the ground. As she straightened up, another Indian moved forward and stood beside her. He placed his bow and arrows on the ground. As he straightened up another Indian moved forward. This continued until all of the Indians had formed a new line with their weapons on the ground beside them.

"Give me that shotgun," Barr said to Melvin Sharp. He touched Acero's shoulder. "Go with me." Then, "Melvin, you and Larry come along and bring that poor bastard back here."

All four of them scrambled out of the trench. Barr and Acero strode past the sitting man without a glance. As they walked on, Sharp and Larry Morrow lifted the man to his feet. Barr and Acero walked to within six feet of the Indians. Barr held the shotgun at his side, but his finger was on the trigger.

The Motilons were short and squatty, women included. Their black hair looked as if a barber had placed a bowl on their heads and trimmed around it. Their faces and bodies were brown, but their cheekbones were a faint yellow; their eyes were big and black and slanted, reminding Barr of pictures of Eskimos he had seen in a school book.

The Motilons were studying Barr and Acero as they themselves were being scrutinized. One of the men stepped forward and with a quick movement slapped Acero lightly on the cheek. Acero dropped back in a fighting stance instinctively, but the

Indian moved on to stand in front of Barr. He slapped Barr lightly on the cheek. Then he moved back into formation.

"They've been watching us," Barr muttered.

"For God knows how long," Acero said softly. "I wonder what's next."

As if in answer to his question, the woman who had first laid her bow and arrows on the ground moved up in front of Barr. She was expressionless, as were all the Indians, and her black eyes were like glass, devoid of any emotion, but she looked directly at Barr's eyes. Her hands went to his shirt front. Her fingers fumbled with the unfamiliar buttons. Barr did not let his gaze falter as he said to Acero, "Take the shotgun, but keep your finger on the trigger."

Acero took the shotgun. Barr slowly lifted his hands and gently moved her hands aside. Without haste he unbuttoned his shirt and freed it from his trousers. The woman dropped her gaze to his bared chest. She ran her hand slowly over his body from neck to waistband, feeling the golden body hair with her palms and fingers. She looked up at Barr's face again, her eyes still devoid of expression.

Suddenly she removed her hand and stepped back a pace. She placed her hands on her heavy, sagging breasts, and Barr saw that the dark nipples had hardened. She took her hands from her breasts and stepped back into her place in the line.

"None of the men have body hair," Acero said, "and the women have no pubic hair." He paused. "I feel like Christopher Columbus, Grady. More than that. We're the only human beings for centuries, perhaps much longer, to see these people face to face. There is no record of them *ever* being seen face to face, not even by a Venezuelan."

"They haven't made a sound or cracked a smile," Barr said. "Do you reckon they talk to each other?"

Acero didn't reply. The woman who had caressed Barr's chest sat down in a single lithe motion and the others followed her lead like a row of falling dominoes. They sat there cross-legged, looking from Barr to Acero and back again like spectators at a tennis match.

"Hey," Barr said. "I think they want to see us going about our business. What do you think?"

Acero chuckled. "What a reversal of roles! A scientist would give years of his life to observe these beauties in their natural habitat—and they want to study us!"

"That's what they want," Barr said. "Let's get at it."

They turned and walked unhurriedly back to the trench. Shorty Dow greeted them. "Son of a bitch, Grady! Why didn't you show her your dong and they'd a made you chief of the tribe!"

Barr laughed along with the rest of them. "Not me. She's hot for you, Shorty. Said you wouldn't have to bend over to snap her titty." He held up a hand. "I think these people want to watch us work so let's get the rig running. Everybody get at something. Show off a little. I think they'll pull out in a little while."

The stranger was slumped exhausted in the trench. He raised his head to look at Barr. "Why didn't you slaughter them when you had them under your gun?" he asked. He spoke with an accent, and Acero looked at him curiously.

"I thought about it," Barr said shortly. He looked away. "A couple of you guys get him in the drillers' quarters and we'll see what we can do for him."

"They killed my friends," the stranger said as he was helped to his feet.

"They didn't kill you," Barr said. "Now, come on."

The stranger's name was Oeuvery. He and his partner, Kuhn, were Swiss engineers who with eight Venezuelans had been setting up concession markers for Shell to the northeast, near Rio Lora. Oeuvery and Kuhn had been armed with revolvers; the Venezuelans had machetes. In the early morning the party moved out to plant new markers, Kuhn in the lead. A small hill was on their right and to the left, below a slight bluff, was Rio Lora, swollen and rumbling from rains higher in the mountains.

As Kuhn passed a huge rock by the side of the trail, an arrow tore into his back, fired by an Indian hiding behind the rock. Kuhn apparently thought someone had tossed a rock at him as a signal. He wheeled around. "What's going on?" he demanded. But then he saw the far end of the arrow. "My God!" he screamed.

A volley of arrows came from the top of the hill. Oeuvrey and the Venezuelans hurled themselves off the bluff into the river. The raging river tossed them about like twigs. Oeuvrey fought against the torrent, trying to make his way to the far side of the river. He failed. A fallen tree halted his desperate attempt. He held onto it, then pulled himself up on the river bank.

Two Motilons helped him to his feet. Other Motilons came up.

They forced Oeuvrey ahead of them through the jungle. Finally, in a small clearing they stopped. Kuhn's naked body was on the ground, face up. A Motilon woman and a Motilon male knelt beside the body.

Oeuvrey could not watch, but when the job was done, he looked. Kuhn's head had been sliced off and was resting by the shoulders. His right hand had been amputated and placed on his scrotum. And his chest had been cut open and the heart removed. The woman held the bloody organ in one hand, a stone knife in the other. She began cutting small pieces off the heart and passing them around until every Indian had a bit and there was a tatter left for her. As if they were one, the Indians put the flesh in their mouths and chewed and swallowed it. Oeuvrey vomited and lost consciousness.

When he awakened, the Motilons stripped him to his boots and forced him ahead of them into the jungle. They traveled that way all day until they reached the oil camp and he was pushed out into the clearing.

"I can't fathom why they didn't kill me, too," said Oeuvrey.

"I think I can," said Barr. "They used you to get them into camp."

Oeuvrey, though skeptical, was nonetheless polite. "Perhaps."

"Get some sleep," Barr said.

He left the Swiss and went outside. Acero was waiting for him. "They haven't moved an inch, Grady." Barr looked around, first at the seated Motilons, then to his men busy at their tasks. Acero bowed as deeply as his girth would permit. "Shall we dance?" he asked with a broad grin.

Barr nodded and took off his shirt. He moved against Acero, flicking his left hand at the fat man's face, beginning the practice session that had intrigued the Motilons. They sparred until Acero grew weary. "Enough," said Acero. "You're too strong for me." He sat down on one of the benches the Venezuelans had built, and Barr joined him.

The Motilons rose to their feet. They gathered their bows and arrows. The woman raised her bow over her head and the others turned around and disappeared into the jungle. She stood there a moment, bow in the air, gazing across the clearing as if having a final look. Then she was gone.

"If I live a million years," Acero said softly.

"Set the guard up," Barr said.

Acero turned his head sharply to look at Barr. "They won't be back, Grady. They won't bother us."

Barr nodded. "Maybe. And maybe they ain't the only Indians in this neighborhood."

At ten o'clock the next morning Shorty Dow called Barr from the drillers' quarters. When Barr joined him, the usually garrulous driller seemed to have lost his tongue. Finally he knelt down and began drawing figures in the dust with a forefinger. Barr hunkered down beside him.

"Grady, we got us a dry hole," Shorty blurted. "I've been holding off telling you since breakfast. We've done gone down farther than we were supposed to." He could not hide his great disappointment.

"It's the breaks of the game, Shorty," Barr said soothingly. "We've got it all on the log, haven't we?"

"Oh, hell yes, we've got it all on the log," Shorty said, his voice bitter.

Barr stood up and lifted Shorty to his feet. "Fuck it, Shorty, it ain't the first one. Let's start clearing off this damn drill site. All right?"

Shorty grinned weakly. "Glad you're taking it so well, Grady."

Barr's guilty knowledge almost made him blush, but he said, "What the hell, Shorty."

Oeuvrey came out of the drillers' quarters. He was wearing shirt and trousers given him by Melvin Sharp. He looked around, inhaling deeply. "Good day," he sang out to Barr and Shorty. "It's great to be alive." He swung out on a tour of the working area, examining everything, muttering and chuckling to himself.

He didn't see the whistling arrow until it struck him in the chest. He spun like a top, clutching at it, before he crashed to the earth. Barr and Shorty ran to him. Behind them they heard the whistles blowing, the shotguns firing at the jungle and the rush of feet as the men made their way to the trench.

Oeuvrey was dying, and he knew it. "They've killed me," he said to Barr, his face old with pain and the presence of death. "They had their way. They meant to all the time."

Barr turned him on his side because the arrow had gone completely through his body. "You'll make it," Barr said.

Oeuvrey shook his head violently. "Please, I beg you in the name of Christ, please don't bury me up here. Don't leave me here where they can walk on me, I beg you. Take me out of here." He clutched Barr's arm at the elbow. "I beg you, don't leave me with them." He was crying. "I beg you. I beg you. I beg you."

"Don't worry, old hoss," Barr said. "We won't leave you up here."

Oeuvrey tightened his grip on Barr's elbow. "Can I believe that?"

"It's a promise," Barr said.

Oeuvrey relaxed his grip on Barr's elbow. He closed his eyes. His body shuddered violently for a moment and he was dead.

Shorty Dow shook his head. "How you going to keep such a promise, Grady? To a dying man? He'll be rotting by this evening late. You know that. So how we're going to get him out of here and back to Maracaibo?"

"I'll think of something," Barr said.

"Wait a minute!" Shorty said. "We've got some cement left. Why don't we ship him back to Maracaibo in a cement block? When they chip it off of him, he'll be as fresh as mama's milk!"

Barr grinned. "Ignacio Acero would call you a genius, Shorty."

Though the return trip was without incident, Barr and Acero rode shotgun on the launches and bongos until they reached the safety of the lake. In his concrete tomb Oeuvrey was taken into Maracaibo, and the Shell people had him buried with proper rituals in the growing American-European cemetery on the outskirts of the city. The cemetery was called Oilville.

Barr was freed from the threat of prison. SCI and Cerro Soto had done their part. In exchange for a guilty plea to a charge of manslaughter, Barr was placed on probation for five years. It was not part of the plea-bargaining procedure, but it was generally understood that SCI would be responsible for his conduct during the probationary period.

Chapter Eight

(Special to the New York *Times,* June 26, 1927, by K. C. Hopkins)

An estimated 700 persons died Thursday night when fire destroyed the village of Lagunillas, which was built on stilts over Lake Maracaibo.

Seven of the dead were identified as American oilmen. The remainder were Venezuelan men, women and children.

Lagunillas was an ancient village. The first European to see it was Alonso de Ojeda when he discovered Lake Maracaibo in 1499. It was these stilt houses that reminded the explorer of Venice and prompted him to name the country Venezuela. Gutted by the fire was a church built in 1545.

The huts were connected by walkways. The fire started in the Club Dandy, a brothel and drinking spot frequented by oilmen. The club sat near the shore on one of the main arteries leading to land.

It was reported that one of the hostesses, a Belgian beauty named Martha DeWilde, threw a lamp at the piano player, Barton McGruder. She missed, the lamp broke against the piano, and in seconds the hut of wood and straw was a mass of roaring flames.

Someone shouted 'fire,' and those who heard the cry went wild. The boardwalks connecting the huts rumbled beneath the pounding of running feet. But the flames in the Club

Dandy ate through the artery leading to shore. They also spread to neighboring huts.

There was an accumulation of oil sludge on top of the lake near the shore. A flashing timber fell into the lake and the sludge ignited with a swoosh. The fire roared through the village like an angry dragon. Giant flames leaped skyward, and in their light hundreds leaped to the lake below. For most it was a leap of death. Falling debris killed some. Others were burned alive and still others succumbed to smoke and heat and drowning. The luckiest swam to safety.

The fire burned itself out Friday morning. The wooden pilings on which the houses had stood looked like blackened stumps of trees after a forest fire.

Oil camp clinics and Maracaibo's hospital are jammed with the suffering. Many bodies may never be retrieved from the water.

The fire did not halt the drilling pace in the Lagunillas oilfield, the fifth and largest field discovered on the lake's eastern shore. It was discovered by Gulf in the Kilometer Strip acreage it controls, but Shell and Pan Union moved quickly into the area, Shell drilling on land, Pan Union drilling in the lake. There are no dry holes and the wells flow from 10,000 to 15,000 barrels of oil per day.

Living conditions for the oilmen are intolerable, and next to impossible for the Venezuelans who constitute the common labor force. The Americans live in tents on swampy land, the Venezuelans, it is said jokingly, sleep in the trees. The swampland is subsiding as the oil is sucked out of the earth, and a dike has been built to hold back the lake. Dozens of pumps are operated around the clock to pull water and slush out of the living area. After a heavy rain the oilmen are forced to take boats to make their way about.

The men eat in shifts of 45 minutes each, on a 24-hour basis. Often a man has to jump out of line, grab the dirty dishes from one who has finished eating, wash them beneath a spigot, and then get back in line.

Crews work day and night building 80,000 barrel tanks to store the oil before it is shipped out on the lake tankers. So thick is the jungle around the camps that contractors and their Venezuelan laborers work around the clock just to keep the land cleared ahead of construction.

Under such conditions it was inevitable that the oil sludge

would gather on the lake surface beneath the Lagunillas huts and become an inferno when ignited. . . .

K. C. Hopkins sat alone at his table in the far corner of the Bull Wheel. Everyone called the table Hopkins' office because he sat there while news was brought to him. Today, however, he was not being disturbed—he had what he called his "thinking cap" on. His brown homburg hat was pushed forward on his head until much of his face was covered. When he was ready to receive callers, the hat would be pushed back on his head to reveal his friendly face.

Hopkins was a tall, gaunt man. He was only thirty but his sallow, hollow cheeks were lined and grooved and his long sideburns were silver. His mouth was big and so were his teeth, which added to his emaciated appearance.

In addition to being the *Tropical Star's* owner, editor and reporter, Hopkins was a "stringer" for the New York *Times* and *Fortune* Magazine, publications that maintained a continuing interest in Venezuela and the Maracaibo Basin in particular.

Now he was sipping rum and thinking about the Lagunillas fire story he had sent the *Times.* He expected it to cause him some trouble. The oil companies would be displeased about his writing that the swampland was subsiding as the oil was being extracted and that a dike had been built to hold back the lake. The oil companies, he knew, preferred to ignore the subsidence. The companies would be even more displeased by his writing about the oil sludge that had accumulated under the Lagunillas huts and his suggestion that the sludge was responsible for many of the deaths. The companies preferred to ignore the sludge, and they likely would consider Hopkins' story an invitation to relatives of the deceased to sue them. The story could even cause a government investigation. Hopkins discounted this possibility because nothing he had written in the past had stirred interest in governmental circles in Caracas.

Several months past he had written a story for *Fortune* which said at one point that Venezuelan workers were contracting gonorrhea at an alarming rate in the oilfield brothels. He also had written that workers from the mountains near Caracas and from the Andean states were falling ill from malaria in the steaming Maracaibo Basin, and that many were dying from the fever. He had heard nothing from Caracas, nor from General Gomez in Maracay.

Gomez. Hopkins blinked his large gray eyes under the canopy of his hat brim. Perhaps no man in the western hemisphere since Montezuma, he suspected, had held such absolute power. He seldom left his ranch at Maracay, yet he seemed to know everything that was going on in even the most remote outpost of the country. He seemed to be unaware of the politicians in Caracas, yet no political action was taken without his approval and consent. He did not hesitate to employ the whip to those who annoyed him. General Gomez displayed such cold-blooded willingness to enforce his wishes on the recalcitrant few that the many could not escape the obvious implication . . .

Hopkins knew he feared Gomez. He never wrote about the dictator in stories he filed for the *Times* or *Fortune*, but because he was ashamed of his fear he occasionally mentioned Gomez in the *Tropical Star*—and not with undue reverence. It was salve on his pride. But he had ignored the student revolts in Caracas which Gomez had crushed, had ignored the imprisonments, the exilings and the hundreds of young men put to forced labor in malaria-infested areas. Gomez had been quoted in *Nuevo Diario*, an official organ which Hopkins read religiously, "Since they don't want to study, I am teaching them how to work . . ." Hopkins had flinched at such cynicism. But on that same day the *Tropical Star* had featured a story about a Rumanian circus that had set up its tents in Maracaibo for a month's run.

Hopkins did not enjoy probing too deeply into his own insecurities, but he knew it was necessary to keep himself in perspective. At times, however, his many and excellent sources burdened him with more information than he could handle, told him more than he really wanted to know. The day had long past when he felt obliged to be privy to every man's secrets. . . .

He was startled out of his thoughts by the sound of a woman's laughter. It was Louise Bremond, looking like someone's secretary in a white blouse and dark skirt with her auburn hair pulled back in a bun. With her was Grady Barr and Tom Fairbanks. They took a table near him and ordered drinks.

The woman was still as fresh-faced and attractive as she had been the day she landed at the Maracaibo docks, Hopkins thought, but she seemed more poised now, more sure of herself, and he knew from his contacts that she could hold her own with any businessman in town. The town was settling down a bit, but it would have to grow considerably more sedate before the Cosmos Club would lack for patronage. Maracaibo, he thought, was one of the few cities on earth where it did not seem improper for an oil company attorney to be drinking in a public place with a madam and an ex-pimp. Brothels and gambling joints were accepted parts of the business establishment, and their operators were accorded the respect they could command.

Barr, though, had changed. The planes of his cheeks had hardened and his nose curved markedly to the left. His chin and lips bore scars to remind him of Hernan Robles' fists. But he was still an attractive man, Hopkins thought. Indeed, perhaps the scars made him more attractive to women, and more interesting to men.

Both men were dressed in white linen suits and Fairbanks, with his dark, broad face and black eyes, could have passed easily at first glance for a Latin American merchant or politico. Fairbanks looked up and caught Hopkins watching them. He excused himself and came to Hopkins' table. "Is your office open?" he asked pleasantly.

"Have a seat," Hopkins said.

Fairbanks sat down and studied the journalist's face for a moment. "You don't like oilmen, do you, Mr. Hopkins?" he said finally.

"Oh, but you're wrong," Hopkins said. "I like oilmen very much. It's oil companies I sometimes find hard to take. Companies have a way of doing something to a man, I've noticed." He nodded to himself. "You might be a case in point, Mr. Fairbanks."

"Maybe I can dispel that notion," Fairbanks said. "Starting Monday, work will begin on every complaint you've ever made."

"How can you be so sure? Your company has no interest in the lake area. No direct concern."

Fairbanks smiled. "SCI is in the lake now, Mr. Hopkins, and SCI is a practical company. We've convinced the others to be practical."

Hopkins knew Fairbanks was telling the truth, but it was hard to believe. "How can SCI be in the lake? There's not a loose acre up for grabs, and you know it."

Fairbanks smiled. "To coin a cliche, there's more than one way to skin a cat. I assume you remember that Gulf got most of its Kilometer Strip acreage from the Cajun Syndicate."

"I do."

"But did you know that Cajun retained a one-fifth overriding royalty, twenty percent of Gulf's net profit from Strip production?"

"Jesus! And you bought the royalty from Cajun!"

"Uh huh. Something like that."

"You mean you stole the meat right off Gulf's plate?"

"Gulf never knew what hit 'em," Fairbanks said, not too smugly. "The story is yours, but I'm not to be quoted."

"You won't be. But tell me privately, did *you* pull off this deal?"

"I dreamed it up," Fairbanks said, "but the redhead over there went up to New Orleans and sewed it up."

"So *that's* where he's been."

"I don't think it will get you anywhere, but you could try to talk to him."

Hopkins laughed. "I tried to talk to him after he came back from the Perija. He said he'd give me a story if he ever had one that would benefit him, not me." He laughed again. "No, I'm satisfied with what I've got."

"Now," said Fairbanks briskly, "about the sludge on the lake at Lagunillas and elsewhere."

Hopkins braced himself. He appreciated Fairbanks giving him the Cajun story, but he wasn't going to be criticized for the fire story.

"The companies have contracted to have it cleaned up, and the crews will get at it as soon as possible," Fairbanks continued. He paused. "For practical reasons."

Hopkins relaxed and sipped his rum. His eyes were solemn. "With you, it isn't entirely for practical reasons. I've got a hunch you'd like to help those people."

Fairbanks smiled faintly. "Perhaps."

"I'll settle for that," Hopkins said, smiling.

"Tell me, Mr. Hopkins," Fairbanks said abruptly, "how would you sum up the situation in Venezuela in a sentence or two? How do *you* see it?"

Hopkins answered without hesitation. "Gomez and his family and his political pals and the army officers are getting fat and living like royalty off oil company bribes and concession payments while the people of the country are living in misery and ignorance. That's one sentence. Here's another: the oil companies are raping the country while Gomez et al spread the country's legs for them." He paused. "Can you stand another one?"

Eyes narrowed, Fairbanks nodded.

"Your father wrote the petroleum law that made a lot of it possible, and you think about that every time you go through a village where naked kids with skinny arms and legs and swollen bellies are playing in the mudholed streets."

Fairbanks was silenced for a moment by Hopkins' brutal candor. Then his face hardened, his mouth closed and his dark eyes glared at Hopkins. *"Damn* you!" he said softly but vehemently, and he got to his feet.

"For being right?" Hopkins asked.

Fairbanks turned and went back to join Barr and Louise Bremond. Seeing Fairbanks' face, Barr shot a quick curious glance at Hopkins, but the newsman had slumped back in his chair and pushed his homburg down on his face.

Hopkins found himself trembling. Never before had he openly discussed his feelings about the relationship between the oil companies and the country, and he was still surprised at the speed with which he had replied to Fairbanks' question. And he was having second thoughts about the remarks he had made about Fairbanks and his father. It was true that Walter Fairbanks had written the cruelly unfair petroleum law, Hopkins thought glumly, but it was not a very decent thing to remind his son about it so cruelly—especially when he felt certain that Tom Fairbanks was not only intelligent but also sensitive to the needs of those around him.

He was just going to have to watch his tongue, Hopkins told himself. Just as a man didn't have to know everything in the world, neither did he have to tell everything he knew. Not that he thought the oil companies would have him hurt or killed, or even have his press wrecked. But there were other ways, more subtle ways, that a newspaper could be forced out of business. And there was always Gomez and his minions. That Hopkins was an American would hardly stay their hands if they became displeased enough. If nothing else, they could spread the rumor that he was a Communist, which would certainly destroy his credibility with his American readers.

Well, to hell with it, Hopkins thought. He filled his glass from the rum bottle and pushed his hat farther down on his face. He wouldn't open his office today, not even if he were promised notice of another world war.

Grady Barr had a letter waiting for him when he returned to the hotel from the Bull Wheel. He always stayed at the hotel, though he saw Louise Bremond almost every day and spent several nights a week with her. Harry Little handed him the letter with a smile. "It's from Eduardo Vigas," he said.

"Thanks," Barr said dryly.

"I guess the first time you ever saw young Vigas was right here in this lobby," Little said. "He brought you some kind of message and you went off with him."

"That's right," Barr said.

"If you won't feel like I'm intruding, I'd like to know if young Vigas is all right—after you read the letter. If you don't mind."

Barr nodded absently and went upstairs to his room. While Barr was in Perija, Vigas had gone to the States and enrolled in the University of Texas to study petroleum engineering. Cerro Soto had been pleased. "I don't want to make too much of it, this sudden ambition," Cerro Soto had told Barr, "but I think you had something to do with it." Christina, too, was in the States, with relatives in Baltimore, Cerro Soto had told Barr. "I had to tell her you were not dead or missing. I felt I had to tell her where you were. As you can imagine, it presented her with an opportunity to play a role in a great tragedy." He had shaken his head. "I would love to hear the story with all its embellishments as she told it to her aunts and cousins. I'm sure I'm an ogre, but I couldn't guess your role."

Barr opened the letter from Vigas. He sat on the side of the bed and what he painstakingly unraveled was, he knew, a cry for help.

"Dear Grady Barr," the letter said. "I am writing you because I can say to you things I cannot say to Guillermo Cerro Soto, my patron. I do well in classes. I am learning. My professors say they are pleased with me. But the professors are the only ones who talk to me. To the students I am a *mescan*, the only one on campus. I think you know what this means.

"The school term ends in three weeks. I had intended to attend school right through the summer, but I have changed my mind. When the term ends, I am coming home where I belong.

"I ask you now to see my patron and explain to him why I cannot remain here. I came to UT because it is the best school for petroleum studies. It would have been better to have gone to school in some state where there are no *mescans* and I could have been a Venezuelan.

"If you explain all of this to my patron, he will understand and believe you, and he will forgive me for coming home and not think less of me. Please see him quickly . . ."

114

Barr sat staring at a fading pink throw rug on the bare floor, then stood up and jammed the letter in his coat pocket. He left the room, hurrying down the stairs and walking swiftly through the throng to Plaza Baralt and the telegraph office. On the pad the clerk handed him, Barr laboriously printed his message to Eduardo Vigas. It said: IF YOU COME HOME YOU ARE A MESCAN.

Barr slept. He was naked and lying flat on his back on Louise Bremond's bed. His penis, looking much like a baby's forearm and fist in its flaccid state, lay across his thigh. His face was calm and peaceful, but inside his skull was a picture of Ernie Jenkins with his head sliced off and his heart torn from his chest. The mouth spoke, saying over and over, "Find it, find it, find it," meaning the missing heart. Barr knew the Motilons had chopped up the heart and eaten it, but he kept saying, "I'll find it, I'll find it, I'll find it." And the dream went on and on.

Louise Bremond watched over Barr as he slept. She sat in a rocking chair at the side of the bed, clad in a thin blue robe. She had been crying.

Barr had not seen her tears; she had held them back until he went to sleep. Now the tears were gone. She was exhausted from their lovemaking, but she didn't want to sleep. She wanted to keep him in her sight until he woke up and left for Caracas and eastern Venezuela. Something had whispered to her that she would never see him again once he departed Maracaibo . . .

Tom Fairbanks was off for Europe on a mission whose purpose would be explained to him on his arrival, he had told her and Barr in the Bull Wheel. Barr, meantime, would take on the assignment of obtaining a giant concession for SCI in the east. "If you can handle those Caracas dandies like you handled those Cajun boys in New Orleans, you'll make our geologists the happiest guys in the country," Fairbanks had said. "They want that concession in the worst way."

Barr was eager to go. He had not been eager for the New Orleans venture, and had been doubtful that he could complete the transaction with Cajun. But Fairbanks had encouraged him, and finally had convinced him that no one else could do it better. In the end Barr had guided the negotiations through several stages to consummation, relying on all the resources he had ever learned. "It's just dealing, Lou," he had said with a grin on his return to Maracaibo. "It's a hell of a lot more money, but it's still just dealing." The SCI board of directors in Houston had also been unsure of Barr's trading abilities, but they had succumbed to the wishes of Fairbanks and their Venezuelan managers.

Barr's work had delighted them and they had accepted readily Fairbanks' recommendation that Barr make the try for the eastern concession. "You've made me look smart," Fairbanks had said, "just like you made everybody look good when you drilled the lake. Don't let me down on this one. Remember that I'm your probation officer."

So Barr was eager to test and prove himself once again. And Louise was hurt and angry that he did not attempt to conceal his eagerness. "This country's as rich as three feet up a bull's ass, Lou, and I'm going to get my share of it," he had said. But he also had been smart enough to detect her unhappiness, try as she had to hide it. "Lou," he had said earnestly, "I think more of you than any woman I ever met, and I think you know that. But I'd be lying to you if I said I loved you. I reckon I really don't know what that means. If it means not being able to get along without somebody, then I don't think it's ever going to happen to me. But don't tell me what we've got isn't pretty wonderful because it is. I like being with you. I like talking to you, drinking with you, eating with you or just sitting with you. And touching you sets me on fire and you know it. Ain't nobody I'd rather be with."

"Don't say ain't, Grady. You know you've got to stop it."

And he had laughed and kissed her and their lovemaking had begun and now she sat in grieving silence while he slept . . .

BOOK TWO

QUIRIQUIRE

Chapter Nine

East of the Maracaibo Basin, beyond the Andes which formed the basin's eastern lip, the bulk of the country lay as tantalizing as a burlesque queen, promising much but delivering nothing to the American oilmen who swarmed across it. The mighty Orinoco River, running roughly west to east, cut the country almost in half. South of the river was an area called the Guiana Highlands, a land of mystery and legend, of strange beauty and rumored wealth in gold and diamonds. It was a place for adventurers and explorers, not oilmen. Scarcely two percent of the country's population lived there, and not even General Gomez pretended to know how or why.

To the north of the river was The Plain. Here were the flat grasslands known as *llanos,* and vast jungles which seemed to have no end. From April to October torrential rains fell, the rivers overflowed and flooded great stretches of land. From October to April, the air became dry. No rain fell and the smaller rivers dried up. Even the jungles lost much of their foliage.

This was the true tropics. The rivers and lagoons were full of exotic fish; tembladores that could paralyze a bull or horse with their electrical discharges; caribes with jaws like pincers; fishes with fangs and fishes with poisonous bites.

To the north of The Plain was the Coastal Mountain Range which fronted the Caribbean and the Atlantic. These mountains and the Guiana Highlands south of the Orinoco formed a great basin; sediments had washed down from them and formed the petroleum reservoirs beneath the jungles and *llanos* of The Plain.

Scores of wells had been drilled but none had produced enough oil to grease a wagon wheel. SCI had failed. So had Shell and Gulf and newcomers like Texaco and Sinclair.

Now SCI–Venezuela was seeking acreage even farther to the east where the jungle held trees one hundred and eighty feet tall and so closely packed that sunlight never penetrated to the jungle floor. It rained ten months out of the twelve. The climate was constant, ninety by day, seventy-five by night. There was no wind, and the humidity sapped the strength of both man and beast. And always there was malaria.

It was a part of the country Gomez had never seen, preferring as he did the more salubrious climate of the Andean city of Maracay, fifty miles from Caracas, where a large military force was garrisoned. There, miles out of the city, on the shore of beautiful Lake Valencia, Gomez lived unpretentiously in a sprawling ranch house while his herds roamed and fattened on the surrounding acreage.

It was here that Grady Barr finally came in a desperate effort to obtain the concession that the SCI geologists wanted so badly.

The plump geese waddled in majestic single file along the shore of Lake Valencia. They haughtily ignored the dozen men who sat in rawhide-bottomed chairs in a semi-circle just a few feet away. At one end of the semi-circle a man said in soft Spanish, "The geese are fat and healthy. To be in good health makes them happy."

All eyes turned from the geese to the speaker. He wore a white military uniform, black patent-leather boots and a wide-brimmed Panama hat. He was in his sixties but the piratical mustache under his beaked nose showed not a fleck of gray. He was just an inch under six feet, heavy but not paunchy.

At the opposite end of the semi-circle a man rose to his feet. He took in the geese and the party of men in a wide sweep of his hand. "What a great man!" he cried in admiration. "On his shoulders lays the burden of administering a great government, yet he thinks of the welfare of a goose."

There was a general nodding of heads as the man resumed his seat. Juan Vicente Gomez did not acknowledge the extravagant compliment. He was accustomed to such eulogistic outbursts at his smallest comment. He got to his feet and strode off in the direction of his ranch house. The men trooped after him.

Barr marched fourth from the rear in the single file. This was his third day at the ranch and Gomez had not even acknowledged his presence. He had hoped to have a word with Gomez on one of the *paseos* the general conducted twice daily, but on each occasion Gomez had looked right through him. Barr had been told that no one spoke directly to Gomez unless he requested it. And no guest got a chance even to see Gomez except on the *paseos.* The guests would gather in the rear of the house at the appointed times. Gomez would appear. Without a word he would set out on his tour and the group would follow.

At first Barr had been disgusted with the fawning politicians in the party, and disgusted as well with Gomez for permitting this. And he had been angry for being made to appear ridiculous, walking around in the sun afraid to open his mouth. But then his honesty made him admit that he was like the others. He wanted something from Gomez. They walked as he walked because they wanted something or wanted to keep something or perhaps wanted to keep Gomez from doing something harmful to them.

And he had stayed on.

As they neared the house, Barr noticed that Gomez had veered in a direction that would take them past one of the many big red barns on the estate. The house, too, was large; Barr estimated that it held as many as twenty rooms. It was a two-story stucco with a red tile roof, ornate as the Mexican haciendas Barr had seen, but it was built on the lines of a Deep South mansion with great white columns rising from a long porch to hold aloft the upper story.

The man ahead of Barr stumbled but quickly regained his stride. Barr had noticed him because on two occasions he had smiled and nodded at Barr, something the others had not done. He was short and heavy in the shoulders and his white suit fit him like a glove. Barr suspected the man was foreign-born from the cast of his countenance. He had not heard him speak.

Near the barn Gomez stopped to examine a big brown steer. He turned to face the file of men. "Grady Barr!" he called out. *"Venga!"* Come!

Barr left the file and walked quickly toward Gomez. *Now's the time,* he exulted. *I'm going to make my play!*

Gomez was frowning at the steer's ear when Barr reached his side. He said angrily in Spanish, "Ticks! What can be done about them?" He looked at Barr. "What do they do about them in Texas and Mexico?"

"They cut them out of the herd and dip them," Barr said promptly in Spanish.

"Dip?"

"Yes. They dip them in some kind of medicine that kills the ticks."

"What is this medicine?"

Barr did not hesitate. "I don't know, General. I can find out."

Gomez turned away from Barr without a word and moved on toward the house. The other men drew near Barr as Gomez walked across the patio and into the house. No one spoke. Barr grinned at the men. "I'll be back in the morning," he said. "Don't let anybody get my place in line."

He strode off jauntily, cursing Gomez beneath his breath. He drove the SCI-owned Ford back to his hotel in Maracay. He knew that the others, singly and in small groups, would be following him.

He had come to Maracay after spending three months in Caracas trying to get a Gomez favorite to approach the dictator about the concession SCI wanted. He had met with more than a dozen men, but each one had insisted that Gomez would grant no more concessions for a year or two. The implication had been that the dictator was resting from his labors—or had no present need for cash.

Charles Cannon, president of SCI–Venezuela, had been upset when Barr suggested that he himself call on Gomez at his ranch. "He'll know why you're there, and he won't see you, Grady. We don't want him to get mad at us."

"Can we afford to wait a year or so? Will the SCI board in Houston let us wait?"

Cannon had shaken his head slowly. "No. Houston already asked me twice what's holding us up."

"Then I'm on my way," Barr had said.

He had learned about the *paseos* from the clerk at his hotel. "Every morning at ten, every afternoon at three," the helpful fellow had said. "There will be others there, so simply go out and mix with them. He may see all of you or none of you."

Barr had gone out to the ranch for three days. Now that Gomez had dismissed him so abruptly, he was determined to show the dictator he was a persevering man.

He parked the Ford at the hotel and walked to the telegraph office in the next block. Without saying why he wanted it, he wired Cannon asking for all available information on cattle dipping as quickly as possible. An hour later, after he had cleaned up for dinner but before he ate, he returned to the telegraph office and wired Cannon again, saying that he needed the information by nine o'clock the next morning.

He was crossing the hotel lobby on his way to the small dining area when he heard his name called. A man in a white suit was approaching him. It was a moment before Barr recognized him as the man who had marched in front of him at the ranch. The man's eyes were a bright, hard blue and his dark hair was streaked with gray. He was smiling.

He bowed slightly. "I am General Pedro Fontenot, Mr. Barr. Would you spare me a few moments of your time?"

Barr nodded. "I was just going for supper. Maybe we could eat together."

Fontenot's smile was apologetic. "I have eaten, but I will be happy to sit with you." His English was not accented as far as Barr could tell.

"I can wait to eat," Barr said. "Let's get a drink across the street."

"Fine."

The tavern was long and narrow and cooled by fans which hung from the high ceiling. The long bar was crowded with beer drinkers. Most of them were listening to a young man singing without accompaniment on top of a large round table against the far wall. Perhaps a dozen men were seated near or around the table. As Barr and Fontenot reached the bar, the young man sang in Spanish:

> Strong as the tree against the wind,
> Strong as the rock against the river,
> Strong as the mountain snow against the sun,
> So strong is the Andino!

The singer smiled and bowed to the loud applause at the tables. He was dressed in low boots, gray work trousers and a gray shirt that was open to the waist. He mopped his handsome face and bare chest with a large red hankerchief, beaming at the applause and the cries for more songs.

The bartender placed beer in front of Barr and Fontenot. Some at the bar regarded Barr and Fontenot with curiosity, but only for a moment. The young man on the table commanded their attention.

Fontenot chuckled. "An Italian immigrant singing the oldest song of the mountain men to a group of lowland sheep herders. Those at the tables."

"He looks queer to me," Barr said.

"Homosexual? Of course. And his lover, or lovers, are at the table."

"Well, we can't talk with him singing. Want to go back to the hotel—in the lobby or my room?"

The sound of laughter made them turn around. Barr had placed his hat on the bar, and the singer was pointing to Barr's golden hair and lifting his own blond locks. "Brothers!" he cried in Spanish. "There is my brother!" He leaped from the table like a dancer and skidded to a halt in front of Barr. He ogled Barr, rolling his tan eyes and pursing his lips for a kiss.

"Don't strike him," Fontenot warned softly in English. "Turn your back on him." Fontenot turned back to his beer.

Barr did as he was told. The singer, laughing with delight, reached out and tugged at Barr's shoulder.

"Let's go before I kick the dog shit out of him," Barr said. He shook off the tugging hand, put on his hat and headed for the door. The singer ran around a table and planted himself in Barr's path. "Go around him," Fontenot said. "Don't strike him."

The only sound in the tavern was the singer's laughter. The men at the bar held their places, but two men at the tables had stood up.

Barr tried to go around the singer, but the singer leaped in front of him. "Not even a goodbye kiss?" he cried, pursing his lips.

"If you don't get out of my way," Barr said in Spanish, "I'm going to kick your ass until your nose bleeds."

"He wants to play with my ass!" the singer said for all to hear. He turned quickly, bent over and wiggled his buttocks at Barr. "Take a bite, my love!" he cried.

Barr kicked him, and the singer went sprawling to the floor. Behind him Barr heard the rush of feet. Fontenot grabbed his arm. "Outside! Come on!" But Barr turned around. Two men had halted several feet away from him. One of them had a bright skinning knife in his hand. "Keep that cocksucker off my back," Barr said to Fontenot.

"If you have hurt him, you will die," said the man with the knife.

"You missed your chance," Barr said. He reached out and got a chair and raised it over his right shoulder as a weapon. "I'll stomp a mudhole in his goddamned ass if I take a notion, and I'm going to beat your goddamned brains out with this chair if you both don't get back to that table."

"Go back!" a beer drinker said to the two men. "He *wants* to kill you!"

The men looked at Barr without fear, but the one without a knife turned and headed toward the table.

"I won't wait," Barr said to the man with the knife.

Behind Barr the singer shouted, "Go back, Felipe! Go back!" He was crying and his voice was shrill. "Please, Felipe!"

Barr abruptly put down the chair, wheeled and headed for the door, nudging Fontenot ahead of him, passing by the still prostrate singer. Barr led the way across the street and into the hotel lobby. The two men sat down facing each other across a small writing table.

Fontenot exhaled sharply. "I thought you were going to crown him with that chair."

"A while back I would have," Barr said. He smiled faintly. "Maybe I'm mellowing." Then, "What do you want to talk about?"

"I know what you want, and you must know who I am."

"You're the president of the state of Monagas, and I want a concession that covers your whole state."

Fontenot nodded.

"I didn't come to see you because the politicians in Caracas say you're on Gomez' shit list. High on it."

Fontenot nodded again. He pulled back his cuffs. Old scars circled his wrists, marks of dungeon chains. His blue eyes were slightly mocking. "I sinned, and I spent four years in prison for it. Now I come here four times a year to do penance. I spend a week. He never speaks to me. When I get back home in Maturin, there will be a list of instructions and probably a number of questions he wants me to answer. It's a little game we play."

"Why does he play it, General?"

"Because he respects my judgment on matters of state, and my presence on the paseos demonstrates my servility." The blue eyes were mocking again. "If we both die natural deaths, I will outlive him."

"That must be a good job you've got or you'd sneak out of the country. You could do it easy."

"And miss being a pall bearer? Never."

Barr chuckled. "Have it your way, General."

"I can help you and you can help me," Fontenot said, his eyes no longer mocking. "I can tell you that he already has granted the concession to Alfredo Munoz, a nephew. Munoz hasn't yet filed with the Minister of Development. At this time he is with a woman in Valencia. You can go there and deal with him. It's a short distance from here and the road is good."

"How do you know this?"

"He boasted of it last week to my wife. She's visiting her sister in Valencia. It's the first time Gomez has favored Munoz."

"I wonder why he did it this time?"

"Who knows?"

Barr shook his head. "They told me in Caracas that Gomez wouldn't grant *any* concessions for a year or two. That's why I came out here—to talk him into it."

Fontenot smiled. "They lied to you. It's an old habit, hard to break. They knew, or suspected, he would grant the next one to Munoz. As it turned out, it was the one you want."

Barr was thoughtful. "Say all this is true . . . about Munoz and where he is and so on. I wonder why he told your wife, or why he would tell anybody before he filed."

Fontenot laughed. "Munoz has women everywhere. It's a widow in Valencia. But he lusts after my wife, and she is an enchantress. She could win all his secrets with a smile."

"He could have been bragging a lie," Barr said. "That's when men lie the best, it seems to me."

Fontenot closed his eyes and shook his head. "You simply have to believe me. My wife would know his lie as she knows his truth."

Barr nodded. "All right. Now what do you want from me?"

Fontenot said, "I'm putting my life in your hands, Mr. Barr. I want you to deliver ten thousand dollars, in my name, to someone in Caracas. I think what I have told you about Munoz is worth more than that to your company."

"Is politics mixed up in this?"

Fontenot hesitated, then said, "In a way. This person has escaped from a labor camp and is hiding in Caracas. He needs the money to get out of the country."

Barr frowned. "I don't think you've been plumb fair with me, General. They tell me Gomez knows it every time a bird shits. Won't he learn about that ruckus across the street and this little meeting of ours?"

Fontenot sighed. "Perhaps."

126

"And he might tie your friend getting out of the country to this little meeting of ours?"

Fontenot didn't answer.

"He might do it even if your friend gets the money somewhere else," Barr said flatly. "Me and my company would be up shit creek—without a paddle."

Fontenot closed his eyes and rubbed a big hand across his face. "If you won't help, please don't betray me."

"I don't know why I let myself talk to you in the first place," Barr went on. "You told me who you was, and I knew then you were on his shit list. I've probably already screwed myself with him. The company, too."

Fontenot stood up. Defeat made him look older and his eyes held tears. "I'm sorry, Mr. Barr." He turned and walked across the lobby and out of the hotel.

Barr sat at the table, staring across the lobby for perhaps five minutes. Finally, he got up and went into the dining room. He waved aside the menu the waiter held out. "Your choice," Barr said absently. The waiter returned with a *hallaca,* a cornmeal pie filled with chicken, pork, onions, garlic, capers, olives, almonds and sliced eggs boiled in a plantain leaf. Barr took several tentative bites of the steaming dish, then attacked it ravenously. He left the dining room with his hunger—and his worry—somewhat dissipated.

In the lobby waiting for him stood the singer and the man with the skinning knife. "I am here to apologize," said the singer. He looked young and repentant.

"So am I," said the man with the skinning knife.

The singer said quickly, "I acted badly. I know it. Please forgive me."

Barr looked directly into the singer's tan eyes. "I'm over being mad. All right?"

"I'll remember you," the singer said.

"I'll remember both of you," Barr said, "for more reasons than you'll ever know." He walked past them to the stairs that led to his room.

The information from Charles Cannon in Caracas arrived the next morning while Barr drank coffee in the dining room. The clerk brought it to him and waited patiently as Barr slowly read the long message. "Is there a reply?" he asked politely when Barr had finished.

"Not at this time," Barr said and tipped the clerk. He read the message again. Cannon had been thorough. The dipping process was explained in detail, and in the name of SCI he offered to import from the States whatever quantity of the tick eradicator was needed and have it delivered to any point in the republic. Barr smiled. Cannon had not mentioned Gomez, but he had made his point.

Barr drove to the ranch, arriving in time to join the paseo. Gomez did not even glance at him as the tour began, and neither did Fontenot. The day was bright and crisp and Gomez led the tour at a good pace, breathing the air in deeply from time to time. Several politicians followed his example, exhaling loudly so that Gomez would be aware of it. Barr was in his customary place in the file, fourth from the rear. Gomez led them to the lake shore then swung toward the red barns without pausing at the waiting rawhide-bottomed chairs.

On Gomez went, around the barns and past the grazing cattle, heading into the home stretch. At that point Barr broke ranks. He strode to the head of the line and then drew even with Gomez. Gomez appeared not to notice him. They walked side by side for several strides, then Barr held out the message in front of Gomez where he could not fail to see it. "The dipping information," Barr said. Gomez took it without looking at Barr. Barr dropped back to his place in line. Gomez walked on with the message in his hand. He crossed the patio and entered the house.

Barr's action had shocked the politicians, even Fontenot. As they gathered on the patio, some of them looked at Barr as if they had not seen him before. Finally one could not contain himself. "What did you hand him?"

Barr looked solemn. "A declaration of war." He doffed his hat to them and went to his car in the parking lot. He drove to his hotel and went to his room to pack. He had hoped that Gomez would invite him into the house for a talk, but he was not overly disappointed. He had delivered the dipping information as promised. That could help him and the company in the future. And somewhere in Valencia was Alfredo Munoz with a concession grant. If trouble developed because of his meeting with General Pedro Fontenot, he would handle it the best he could.

Two soldiers in forest green uniforms and khaki leggings and wearing automatic pistols on their hips were in the lobby when Barr descended from his room. One of them wore an officer's insignia. Barr set his bag down.

128

"Come with us," the officer said in English. "The clerk will tend to your bag."

They escorted Barr outside and into a black Buick. Barr sat in the front seat by the soldier and the officer lolled in the back seat. As the car was driven away from the hotel the officer said, "Have you no curiosity, man?"

Barr said pleasantly, "I think I can hold it. It don't make sense to ask too many questions of a man with a gun."

The officer laughed. "Gather your wits, then. You may need them."

"Thank you," Barr said drily, and the officer laughed again.

The soldier drove to the Gomez ranch and parked the car. "Did you think you were being taken to the garrison prison?" the officer asked as they walked to the house.

"No," Barr said. "I asked General Gomez to send yawl for me. I told him I was tired of driving."

The officer missed a stride, then laughed again. "You're a droll fellow, Mr. Barr."

A man in white trousers and a long white jacket opened the back door. "We'll be out here," the officer said. The man led Barr down a hall and into a large recreation room with three pool tables and a bar. "I will interpret for you," the man said. "The general speaks no English."

"Yo hablo el Espanol," Barr said.

The man smiled. "His may be a bit more ceremonial than yours."

"I'll get his drift," Barr said.

The man nodded and showed Barr the way to a sun-filled room where Gomez was stretched out on a leather couch, the only article of furniture in the room. But Barr seemed not to see it, or Gomez. From the bare floor to the ceiling the walls were lined with shelves holding hundreds of dolls, all the same size but wearing military uniforms of varying cuts and colors, an army and navy of black, brown, white and yellow men.

"Their virtue is silence," Gomez said. He sat up and motioned for Barr to be seated on the floor. "A representative of every nation with a military force," Gomez continued. "I make them myself."

Barr sat down on the floor, still looking around at the dolls, but Gomez brought him to sharp attention. "Listen to me," he said coldly. "I will speak without interruption. You came here uninvited. It was bad form. You should have known better, whether you came because of pressure from your superiors or because of your own impatience. There are certain ways to do certain things."

Barr reddened. Gomez' dark eyes had a Mongolian slant, reminding Barr of the Motilons.

"And then there was the affair at the tavern and your conversation with the esteemed president of Monagas state," Gomez said. "He is a wise man, but he is a fool in two matters, his wife and his son, and I suffer the fool to profit from his good sense. The son reads Communist literature and leads students against the barracks in Caracas. Now he is hiding when he is not being hunted. For one of his temperament, being in hiding is punishment. Do you understand?"

Barr nodded.

"I won't ask if Fontenot begged your help for the son, or if he offered you something in return. If he asked, I assume you refused. I have been told that you are a bold and resourceful young man, and I believe it. I do know something of you. Now I tell you that I have granted the concession you want to Alfredo Munoz. Remember the name if you don't know it. Find him before the others find him and deal with him. Do you wish to say something?"

Barr grinned. "Nothing but thank you, and I've enjoyed meeting you."

Gomez nodded. "You also are artful. I will let Charles Cannon know how much tick solution I will need and when I will need it."

Gomez fell back on the couch, stretched out and closed his eyes. Barr got to his feet and left the room. The man in white was in the recreation room, shooting pool at one of the tables. When he saw Barr enter the room, he placed his cue in a rack and escorted Barr to the back door. "It's a shame the general wasn't in the humor for pool," the man said. "He shoots a good stick." He smiled. "That's an American expression, isn't it?"

"It sure is," Barr said, smiling. He went out on the patio. The officer and the soldier were sitting at a table under a large umbrella. Barr went to them, still smiling. "I'm ready to go back to town, gentlemen."

"Well," said the officer, "you look like a man who has been promised a full belly and a warm bed and a bright future."

"Uh huh. And all it cost me was a piece of my ass."

* * *

The Valencia police chief had been charming. Barr had explained that he was seeking the wife of Pedro Fontenot, president of Monagas state, but had misplaced the card bearing the name and address of the relative she was visiting. The chief had the information Barr sought; the newspaper had carried news of the lady's visitation. He had asked if he could perhaps escort Mr. Barr to the home of Senorita Elvira Obregon, and when Barr refused told him that the directions on the card would be perfect.

The house sat in a cul-de-sac off the Street of Singing Birds. Barr followed a winding path that cut through beds of flowers alive with colors and shades to reach the entrance. Two lamps glowed at the doorway. He pressed a doorbell and heard its silver tinkle inside the house. A woman in black and white and with a tiny white cap on her dark hair opened the door and looked at him with questioning eyes. Inside someone was playing an instrument whose sound Barr did not recognize.

"Senora Fontenot," Barr said. "Can I see her? My name is Grady Barr."

"She is expecting you," the maid said. "Please come in."

Barr followed her inside, hat in hand. The room he entered was large and high-ceilinged, warm with growing plants and polished furniture and lighted by an enormous chandelier. At the far side from Barr glass doors were open on a patio. The music was coming from there, and he could see a woman in a sleeveless white gown sitting before a golden harp, teasing the music from it with caressing fingers. Another woman sat watching her play. The patio lights were gently illuminating, bathing the tableau and causing the sequins in the watching woman's otherwise subdued mauve gown to twinkle.

"Let her finish," Barr said softly to the maid.

But their presence had distracted the harpist. Her hands fell to her lap and she turned her head to see them. Noticing this, the other woman rose and came to meet Barr. The maid left the room. The woman appeared to be about forty years old, a handsome woman with a commanding presence. Sorrow had brushed beneath her eyes and tightened her lip corners, but otherwise her face was as smooth as a girl's. A streak of gray an inch wide ran through her hair from her forehead to the black bun at the nape of her neck. The gown had not been designed to be revealing, but it could not blur the line of her breasts and the caliper hips. Her complexion was ivory with a few drops of blood stirred in it.

"I am Elvira Obregon," she said. "My sister has asked me to welcome you into my home. I do so." Her face was expressionless, and her dark eyes examined Barr without curiosity. She ducked her head slightly. "I leave you with her." She walked past Barr and up a spiral staircase to the second floor.

Barr watched her climb the stairs, hoping to catch a glimpse of her legs but being unable to move his gaze from her swaying buttocks. Meantime, the harpist had left the patio and was at hand. Her soft laugh brought Barr's attention to her. "She would be near to fainting if she knew you had looked at her like that," she said in English.

Barr flushed, and the harpist laughed again. "Most men prefer to look at me," she said, "but perhaps because I am ten years younger. What do you think, Mr. Barr?"

She was a reduced image of the older woman, but beautiful where the sister was handsome, with a face shaped for laughter and untouched by any grief. Her blue eyes were roguishly alive. The hair was solid black. Her tongue wet her lips and white teeth as she waited for Barr's reply.

"Back home they'd call you saucy," Barr said, "and I reckon it's hard to see anybody else if you're around." His face was solemn. "I never saw a prettier woman than you, Mrs. Fontenot."

"How nice!" she said, and Barr thought she seemed inordinately pleased. But she also seemed satisfied with the impression she had created. "I'm a flirt, Mr. Barr, not a seductress. I like attention, but I have never been unfaithful to my husband." She took Barr's arm. "Let's have our talk." She was now a serious woman prepared for a serious discussion. She moved them to the patio, found a chair for Barr and sat near him on a couch of soft leather.

"My husband called me on the telephone," she said. "He said you probably would try to find me, that you certainly would try to locate Alfredo Munoz . . . even if you did not agree to help his son."

"He didn't say it was his son," Barr said.

"By a previous marriage. But would it have made any difference?"

"No, I guess it wouldn't have."

"But still you expect me to point you to Alfredo."

"I *want* you to," Barr said earnestly. "You know my company wants that concession, and I think your husband orter want us to have it. We haven't found any oil down here like Shell and Gulf have, and we'll spend a lot more money than they will in trying

132

to find it. The money will be spent in your state. I think your husband wants to help his people, and the money will do it. It'll be good for him, too, running a rich state instead of a poor one."

She looked at him keenly for a moment, then put her gaze on the carpet. "Our father came here from Ireland," she said. "O'Brien, Obregon. He made a fortune, but he also became part of the country. He became a Venezuelan, in his heart and in his actions." She looked up at Barr. "You Americans don't do that. You come and go."

"The companies don't come and go," Barr said. "The life of most of the concessions don't give out until the nineteen-sixties. They'll be here that long at least, and I figure there'll be extensions after that. I figure they'll be here from now on." Barr smiled. "We'll make our headquarters in Maturin, and you'll have a lot of men to flirt with."

She laughed. *"Touche!* And God knows there are none there now!" She quickly sobered. "All right, Mr. Barr, I'll tell you where to find Alfredo Munoz. My husband told me to use my own judgment if you came here."

"Help me more than that," Barr said. "Can you tell him that it's important to you for me to get the concession? Important to the state of Monagas?"

She made a mouth and her eyes were roguish. "What did my husband say about me? Tell me!"

"He said you could make Munoz tell you all of his secrets."

"Without compromising myself, of course."

"I don't know what that means," Barr said.

"Without giving myself to him."

"I wouldn't want you to do that if you didn't want to, and I reckon your husband wouldn't want it either."

"I'm sorry," she said ruefully. "I was playing with you. But yes, I'll talk to Alfredo. I'll ask him here for a drink."

Barr sighed and grinned at her. "I could stand a drink of brandy myself, Mrs. Fontenot."

"Teresa," she said. "Isn't that a lovely name?"

Alfredo Munoz gazed with impartial lust at the three women at the dining table—his woman, Maria Torres, Teresa Fontenot and Elvira Obregon. He raised his wine glass. "My God," he said. "What a feast for the eyes!"

Maria Torres tittered. Teresa Fontenot was bemused. But Elvira Obregon made no effort to hide her disgust.

"We are fortunate, my friend," he said to Grady Barr at the other end of the table. "Such lovely women!"

"Agreed," Barr said, lifting his glass.

Munoz was built like an Italian tenor, all chest and belly, and a purple vein in his hooked nose throbbed with each heartbeat. His white suit was soiled, his black hair uncombed. He had drank four brandies on arrival and now had ignored the food for the wine. "I am a natural man," he had told Barr over his third brandy. His tiny mistress seldom let her sparkling eyes stray from him.

"I have told Elvira it is not too late for her to get a man," Munoz said. "She spent the past fifteen years of her life caring for her father, who may not have appreciated it." He waved a hand at Teresa. "Look at her. She married to get out of this prison. Elvira should have left him to the nurses and the doctors. God knows he could afford them." He drank from his glass. He looked around the table. "Am I talking too much?" he asked.

"Not enough to drive me from my own table," Elvira Obregon said. "You are disgusting as always, Alfredo, but you are an interesting specimen so I tolerate you."

The telephone rang and Teresa left the table to answer it. When she returned she was subdued. She sat down at the table without looking at anyone.

Barr spoke. "I spent some time with your uncle today," he said to Munoz. "He told me he had granted you the Monagas concession. He told me to find you and buy it from you. He told me you were in Valencia."

Munoz was sober. "Did he mention Maria's name?"

"No. He said you were here and that Mrs. Fontenot could help me find you," Barr lied.

"He must know about Maria," Munoz said with conviction. He looked at his mistress, then back to Barr. "He didn't mention her?"

"No," Barr said. "He just said you wanted to make a quick deal for reasons of your own."

"You have talked too much about Paris," Munoz said to his mistress, though his tone was not accusatory.

"It's not against the law to go to Paris, is it?" Barr said. "People do it every day."

"He didn't mention Maria? Are you sure?"

Barr shook his head. "He just wanted us to make a deal as quick as we could. He wants my company in Monagas, and I figure he wants you to have the money. That's all I can see."

Munoz was cunning. "You can speak for your company?"

"I can, and we'll pay the going rate."

"Can you leave for Caracas right away. I must file first with the ministry."

"I'm waiting for you," Barr said.

"I'll take Maria home," Munoz said. "Will you ride with me?"

"Pick me up here," Barr said. "I haven't finished my dinner."

"Were you lying to him?" Teresa Fontenot asked. "Did General Gomez tell you Alfredo had the concession?"

"He told me," Barr said. "He didn't tell me Munoz was in this town or anywhere, but he let me know he wanted me to find him. So I lied some. I didn't know what you were going to do when you came back from the phone. I figured you'd talked to your husband and he'd found out I met with Gomez. But I didn't mention your husband's name or anything like that to Gomez. I couldn't be sure what you were going to say, so I spoke up." He paused. "I figure everything worked out, don't you?"

"Don't talk to me like a *llanero,* a cowboy," she said tartly. "You're a devious man—and don't tell me you don't know what that means!"

"Hush, Teresa!" Elvira Obregon said. "Everyone got what he wanted. Look at me and hold your tongue. Am I right?"

"Do you want me to leave the table, sister?"

"No," Elvira said with sudden weariness. She got up from the table and walked to the bottom of the stairs. "Ride with Alfredo, Mr. Barr. I'll have your car driven back to Caracas, to your office." She went up the stairs.

"She acts like my mother acted," Teresa said. "You promise there will be many new men in Maturin?"

"I do," Barr said gravely. "All of them handsome and rich and healthy as armadillos."

Chapter
Ten

From the Maracaibo *Tropical Star* of September 27, 1928:

Representatives of the world's largest oil companies met in Scotland early this month to fix world oil prices and divide up world markets, this newspaper learned today.

On hand were officials from SCI, Shell and Anglo-Iranian Oil Company, owned 51 percent by the British government. Anglo-Iranian found the first oil in the Middle East, in what was Persia. Now a group of companies has found oil in neighboring Iraq, and other countries in that area are being explored.

For years Shell and SCI have tried to drive each other out of various world markets, but the current oil glut prompted the peace move. The United States, Canada and Mexico have surpluses of production, as do Venezuela and several other Latin American countries. The Far East also has a surplus, and Russia is now selling its oil on the world markets.

Now the three companies have carved the world into trading zones with each company obliged to honor the others' trade territory, this newspaper was told.

In addition, the companies agreed to sell all oil, wherever it is produced, at U. S. prices, the highest in the world. Since most U. S. oil is shipped out of the Texas Gulf Coast, all of the world's oil will be sold at the Gulf Coast price.

Further, the companies agreed to slap a phony shipping

charge on all oil. Wherever the oil is produced and shipped from, consumers will be charged as if the oil was shipped from the Gulf Coast.

The high price and the phony shipping charge is called the 'Gulf Plus System' by the oil officials.

Companies operating in Venezuela pay the government about eight cents per barrel for the country's crude. Middle East governments are paid about the same. Now that oil will be sold for the high Gulf Coast price, plus the phony shipping charge, in Europe and elsewhere.

The move comes at a time when independent producers in Texas and other U. S. oil states are pressing the U.S. Congress for a tariff on oil imports, claiming that imports are supplanting not supplementing domestic production.

Sources in the States say the Congress is receptive to the independents' arguments, and the tariff most likely will be imposed.

In other oil news, Thomas Walter Fairbanks has been named a vice-president for SCI–Venezuela. He attended the Scotland meeting, but has been unavailable for comment. Earlier it was reported that Edward P. Gurwell, who runs the Maracaibo office, also was promoted to vice president. . . .

There was a large stack of the newspapers on Charles Cannon's desk. Cannon, Fairbanks and Gurwell had read Hopkins' story and were waiting for Grady Barr to wade through it. All were sitting around a large table in Cannon's Caracas office. Adding to Cannon's irritation with the story was Barr's presence; Cannon could not understand why Fairbanks had insisted on Barr's presence at the meeting.

Barr finished his reading and tossed the newspaper on the table. "Glad to see you guys got promoted," he said.

"For pity's sake!" Cannon almost whispered. He said to Fairbanks, "Since you were the only person from Venezuela at the big meeting, I think I should ask you how Hopkins got that information."

"Not from me," Fairbanks said curtly. "Houston knows how he got it. There were dozens of reporters sucking around the castle where we were meeting, and somebody from Anglo-Iranian— somebody trying to kiss ass—gave the details to a reporter from the London *Globe*. The Globe didn't print the story. The reporter got mad and sent the information to his old friend and fellow newshound in Maracaibo. The reporter's been fired, but I can't seem to get a lot of satisfaction out of that."

"My people rounded up every copy they could lay their hands on," Gurwell said. "If a single copy got here to Caracas, I don't know how. What can we do about that drunken bastard?"

"Nothing," Fairbanks said.

"He wouldn't have printed this kind of story five or six months ago," Gurwell said. "Seems like now he's doing his best to fuck everybody up."

Cannon winced at Gurwell's language. He said, "Well, I guess we'll have to do our best to play it down if the word gets around, and hope no one gets too excited about it."

Fairbanks nodded agreement, but his dissatisfaction was plain. He said to Barr, "I haven't had a chance to tell you what a fine job you did in getting the concession, Grady. Everybody was pleased. It may mean a lot to the company."

"I congratulated him," Cannon said quickly. "A fine job."

Fairbanks pushed one of the newspapers with a forefinger. "What do you see in all of this, Grady? Have you got any ideas of what we can do—if anything?"

"I was just thinking that if I was the head man of Pan Union this story would be making my ass want a pinch of snuff, Tom."

"Pan Union?" Cannon said. "They're not involved in this."

"They are if Congress passes that tariff he wrote about," Barr said calmly. "SCI and Shell have all these foreign markets everywhere on the globe. Pan Union ain't got none. They got all this oil here and in Mexico, and the only place they've got to unload it is in the States. And they've got a lot of oil in California and Texas. They'd have to get rid of that first, if there was a tariff. If they can't sell this lake oil and mescan oil in the States, then they probably can't sell it at all."

"But you can't possibly believe Congress will vote to impose that tariff," Cannon insisted.

"It ain't what I think, Charley, it's what Pan Union thinks," Barr said.

"But SCI will fight against a tariff. So will Shell."

"Tell me why," Barr said. "Shell don't *have* to sell this Maracaibo Basin oil in the States. They could sell it somewhere else. SCI wouldn't have to sell it in the States if they owned Pan Union's lake and mescan oil. They got more markets than Shell, and they got plenty of production in the states."

138

"He's right as a fox!" Gurwell put in. "If Congress passes that tariff, Pan Union's tankers will be rusting from here to Vera Cruz. All they've got to do is *think* there's going to be a tariff and we could pluck 'em right off the vine. Is that what you're getting at, Grady?"

"I think so," Barr said dryly.

Gurwell's eyes were fairly gleaming. "Something else, Grady. The price of Texas oil is bound to rise with a tariff, and you can see what that would mean. We could sell this lake oil in Europe and Asia at a higher price, the Texas Gulf price." He laughed. "Plus that phony shipping charge! Bring on the tariff—I'll vote for it!"

"For pity's sake," Cannon said. "Can't we keep this on a businesslike basis?"

"I'm sorry, Charley," Gurwell said with no apology in his voice. "I think this subject is too hot to discuss with Houston by phone or cable. Don't you think Tom ought to hustle up there and lay it out to the board?"

"I'd like to take Grady with me," Fairbanks said.

Cannon shook his head. "No," he said firmly, "I want Grady to get our eastern drilling program started right away."

"You're going to make him manager in the east?" Fairbanks asked.

"I had that in mind," Cannon said a bit tartly.

"Great!" Fairbanks said. He grabbed Barr's hand and shook it. "I'll pay for one drink and a cheap snack."

Cannon said hastily, "I'll send your promotion into Houston tomorrow, Grady."

Gurwell laughed. "Good old Charley."

The geologist Cannon had sent out to stake a location for a well in the Monagas concession Barr had obtained was only twenty-five years old. His name was Ralph Lytel. He was a New Yorker, a graduate of Cornell University who had worked for the Bureau of Economic Geology of Texas, his only employer before SCI–Venezuela.

Comparing his tools for a geological investigation with those used in the States would have been like comparing a crooked stick with a tractor-drawn gang plow. Without benefit of seismic instruments, the best method he found for taking dip and strike observations for mapping structures was to dig pits in the earth. Many of the pits were as much as one hundred feet deep. They were dug by Venezuelans with picks and shovels and the dirt was lifted out in buckets. Notches were cut in the sides of the pits to serve as footholds and handholds.

Lytel would climb down into the pit, using a flashlight to study the earth. Many times the temperature was one hundred and twenty degrees at the surface.

He did most of his reconaissance work on mule back. In wet weather he rode through jungles where the mud and slime were belly-deep on his mount. He saw the mule's neck so covered with mosquitos that he couldn't put a finger down without crushing one.

He got a Ford from somewhere, without Cannon's knowledge or consent. When he ran out of oil, he poked goat grease and coconut oil into the oil intake until he could find something better. No one ever found out where he obtained gasoline. At times he hired Venezuelans to help him lower the Ford over bluffs with ropes. And once he guided the Ford down a mountain ledge while Venezuelans played out a rope behind him.

Meanwhile, Grady Barr went to Port-of-Spain, Trinidad, which was to serve as the jumping off place into eastern Venezuela. With him were two truck and tractor drivers, Frank and Harry Husting. According to plan, they were to proceed to Maturin with three schooner-loads of equipment. Drillers, engineers and other technicians were to converge on Port-of-Spain from wherever Cannon hired them and would follow Barr's party in.

But once the schooners had sailed across the Gulf of Paria and had entered Rio San Juan, Barr decided to make his way to Maturin overland. He and the Husting brothers cut their way through jungle swamps to a settlement called La Pica, which lay on a broad savanna. Here they got mules and rode into Maturin, an ancient city with a population of about one thousand people. It was an agricultural center where hides, cotton, coffee, tobacco and sugar were shipped to the outside world. And General Pedro Fontenot's seventy-five soldiers were garrisoned nearby to maintain law and order in the entire state of Monagas.

Barr stopped first at the garrison. He explained his presence in the area to the commandant and pointed to his mud-caked boots and travel-stained clothing. "Me and my friends would like to clean up a bit before we go on into town," Barr said. "I don't want my friend General Fontenot to see us like this." He grinned. "Or Mrs. Fontenot, either."

The commandant rolled his eyes. "Or her sister, my friend! A more mature version of the General's lady, visiting from Valencia." He cocked his head. "Perhaps you know her also."

"I met her in Valencia," Barr said, "and I agree with you a hundred percent."

"But she has too many years for you, my friend." The commandant patted his chest. "I am perfect for her, don't you think?"

"I think you'd make a good match," Barr said as if he meant it.

"Then perhaps you can tell the General of your stop here. In her presence you could describe me in such a way as to make me interesting to her."

Barr nodded. "I'll make it the first order of business."

"But, my friend, I must tell you that all three are in Caripito. The General went there two days ago to sit in judgment on some thieves. The ladies went with him. I sent along a small detachment. Perhaps he left word for you at the mansion. He was expecting you?"

"He didn't know the exact day I'd be here."

"Well, he'll be back in several days. Meanwhile, you and your friends can stay here, if you wish."

"Thank you, but we'd better go on in. I've got to set up a headquarters somewhere."

"Very well. Clean yourselves and go. And don't forget your promise of help."

"A promise made is a debt unpaid. That's what my old friend Bandera used to say."

"Delightful!" said the commandant.

Barr entered Maturin freshly bathed and shaved and wearing a spotless white linen suit. The Husting brothers were similarly dressed and all three were riding fresh mules. They left the mules at a livery stable and made their way to the central plaza.

It was mid-afternoon, and the town slept. There were less than a dozen persons moving about the plaza and each of them looked as if he or she was hunting for a place to rest. The low-slung stucco building reminded the men of a cowtown of the old American West. "It sure as hell ain't like Maracaibo," said Frank Husting.

Barr had spotted the presidential mansion. It was a two-story stone structure, identifiable from a couple of similar buildings on the plaza because of the yellow-blue-red flag with its arc of seven stars which flew from a pole above it, and because of a soldier slouched at parade rest in front of it, armed with a rifle.

"You guys get the lay of the land," Barr said. "I'm going to the mansion and see what's what."

The soldier listened sullenly as Barr explained who he was and what he wanted. "You can't go in," he said.

"My friend Colonel Morillo told me there might be some instructions for me here," Barr said, smiling. "Barr, Grady Barr."

The soldier snapped to attention at his commandant's name. "I will get my lieutenant," he said crisply. He went through the open door and into the mansion. Presently a young officer appeared in the doorway. "I'm sorry I can't invite you in," he said apologetically. "With the General and the ladies away, we are taking the opportunity to paint the lower floor." He smiled. "But I have word for you. The General has arranged for you to lease the residence directly across the plaza. In many ways it is much like the mansion. You can get the key at the cafe next door."

"When will the General be back?"

The lieutenant shrugged. "A day or two, perhaps three. But you can call on me if you need help. I am always here or nearby."

Barr thanked him and crossed the plaza to the cafe. The Husting brothers were drinking beer at a long counter. They were the only customers. A young black woman in a plain brown dress was behind the counter. "Hey, Grady, listen to her talk," Frank Husting said. "Say something, honey," he said to the woman.

The woman smiled. "Have a seat, sir, and I will bring you a beer."

"Hear that!" Frank said. "She sounds just like some of those Englishmen Shell brings over here."

"I'm from Trinidad," she said as Barr chose a stool. "I'm surprised you didn't hear my kind of English on the docks. It is the general language of the island."

"I never heard any niggers talk," Frank said, laughing. "All they did was sing. Ain't that right, Harry?"

"Shut up a minute, Frank," said Barr. "Are there many people from Trinidad around here, in this part of Venezuela?" he asked the woman.

She shook her head. "I'm the only *colored* person in town."

"Why is that?" Barr asked. "It's easy enough to get here from there."

"Easy, yes, but General Gomez forbids it. He doesn't like colored people, for one thing, and there isn't any work here for

142

colored men. There is hardly enough for the Venezuelans. She shrugged. "In any event, it's illegal."

"But you're here."

"I'm a woman, if you haven't noticed, and Mr. Morales got permission from General Fontenot to bring me here to teach his children English. He owns this cafe. General Fontenot wouldn't have allowed it if Mr. Morales had wanted a man as a teacher. But it is still illegal. General Fontenot took a chance."

"You're not afraid of being deported? If Gomez hears about you being here?"

"Who'd go to the trouble to tell him? You?"

Barr laughed. "Not me, baby. I like your spunk. Have you got a key for me . . . Grady Barr?"

She took a key from under the counter and gave it to Barr. "I'm the best cook in town, Mr. Barr. You can try the other places, but I think you'll come back here."

"I'll bet you're right," Barr said. He waved a hand at the Husting brothers and left the cafe. He unlocked the building next door and was immediately pleased at what he found. He entered a room so large there was only space for two small rooms on either side of it. The three rooms would be all the office space he needed. Upstairs he found four bedrooms and two bathrooms with large tubs, and in each bedroom two army cots had been set up.

Barr went back to the cafe. He gave Frank the key. "You boys get our gear at the stable and put it upstairs. We can spend the night there. I'm going to window shop a little."

On the sidewalk Frank said, "That girl's right pretty for a nigger, ain't she?"

Barr said, "If you're hoping to get some of that pussy, you'd better quit saying nigger. She don't like it."

"Well, she *is* a nigger."

"Have it your way," Barr said.

The equipment poured in, and so did the engineers who were to divide the concession into drilling parcels.

Barr cursed and fumed over the fragile telegraph line that ran from Maturin to the mountainous seacoast and then on to Caracas and Maracay and Maracaibo. Houston headquarters had sent him an old cable tool drilling rig instead of the new rotary. And the three drillers who came in with the first rig spoke no Spanish. The Venezuelans in the east were not the quick-learning workers that were found in the lake region. But Barr's complaints did him no good. He was told in effect to "Shut up and drill."

He was not the only unhappy man in the party. Lytel, the geologist, had found what he considered an ideal drilling location just southeast of the jungle village of Quiriquire. The SCI geologists told him to forget it. They ordered him to stake a location for the first well on a barren mesa rising out of the *llano* about twenty miles northwest of Maturin. The Venezuelans called the huge mesa Perro Seco, which in Spanish means Dry Dog.

Barr put the engineers to work building a road to Perro Seco. A camp site was cleared and the derrick was constructed of timbers brought in from the States.

At that point Barr met with General Fontenot in private and told him he wanted to bring in a dozen Negroes from Trinidad.

Fontenot threw up his hands. "Good God! Do you want us both flayed?"

"You've been complaining that you're short of farm workers because we pay five bolivars a day and they can't make but a few centimos a day on the farms. Well, they can't speak English, either. We're getting ready to start drilling, and our drillers can't speak Spanish. Somebody is going to get killed sure as hell with them nationals stumbling all over the rig floor. You don't want that, and I don't either. They didn't send me any American roughnecks out here like they have in the Maracaibo Basin. That waitress across the street, that Madile Horn, she says all the Negroes in Trinidad speak English."

Fontenot smiled patronizingly. "But you know it's impossible, my friend. There is an absolute ban against it."

"I saw plenty of Negroes in Caracas," Barr said.

Fontenot nodded. "They came in before Gomez took over. They came from all the islands of the West Indies and were assimilated into the population. But Gomez said there would be no more. He welcomes all immigrants but blacks and orientals. It was written into law."

"They'd be working way to hell and gone away from anybody," Barr persisted. "Nobody would know they're here."

Fontenot shook his head.

"How about Madile Horn? She hasn't been here but two years."

"Ah, Grady. That's not like you. I did a small favor for a good citizen."

"That's all I'm asking."

144

Fontenot closed his eyes and shook his head.

"I could have done it without discussing it with you," Barr said, "but I wouldn't do something like that to a friend. You might not ever have knowed it."

"Give up, Grady," Fontenot pleaded.

"We'd be solving problems, yours and mine. These land owners are going to be getting pretty loud pretty soon if all their people go to work for us. If they holler loud enough, Gomez might hear about it . . . and I don't think he'd like it. And I don't think he'd like it if it takes us the rest of our lives to drill a few wells." Barr paused. "Maybe we orter talk to him about it."

"You're a hard man, Grady," Fontenot said soberly. "You know we can't call on Gomez on this."

"He might appreciate it. He ain't the kind to let his feelings about those people interfere with his good sense."

"I don't want to know about it when you bring them in," Fontenot said with resignation. "I don't want to hear a damned thing about it. And I don't want them showing their faces around here. Is that clear?"

Barr nodded. "I understand that a smuggler called Rico brings rum in from Trinidad. Rum and other things. I'll get hold of him."

"You understand that from Madile Horn. My sentries say you spend quite a bit of time in the cafe at night. Is that wise, my friend?"

"No, it ain't and from now on I'll do my coffee drinking in the daytime."

Fontenot changed the subject. "Teresa complains that you don't attend our parties often enough."

Barr grinned. "She ain't going to be satisfied until she's broken every heart in Venezuela." He nodded. "I'll be around soon. How's Elvira?"

"She's going home Saturday, but she'll be back in June." Fontenot cleared his throat. "An interesting woman."

"She's as much woman as I ever saw in my life," Barr said with an earnestness that surprised Fontenot.

The Trinidadians made good roughnecks. Their lilting English was pleasant on the ears. Drillers, upon being threatened by Barr, learned to say Negro instead of nigger. But everything that could go wrong on a well went wrong at Perro Seco. The cable tool rig was not designed for the loose sands and shales of eastern Venezuela, and more than two months passed before the well reached six hundred feet. Then a shoe joint was lost in the hole. It took days to drill it up. Cement wouldn't set, the hole wouldn't drill straight, water kept breaking in.

Barr spent little time in Maturin. He was at the drilling rig most of the time, driving the men and driving himself. He was heartened when five new rigs arrived and all were rotaries. He imported the roughneck crews to man them without consulting Fontenot, and roads were built to sites selected by the geologists in Caracas. They had again ignored Ralph Lytel, and the young geologist resigned in disgust and left the country. Barr knew him only through copies of reports Lytel sent to Caracas, but he regretted Lytel's resignation. He had enjoyed the young geologist's enthusiasm for locations he liked and his steaming criticism of locations he considered of no value. His letter of resignation carried the phrase, "You people want to drill out on the llano where life is easy but there is no oil instead of in the jungle where life is hard but the oil is waiting."

But Barr had little time to think about Lytel and his departure. He was always on the move, traveling from one drill site to another, giving instructions here, issuing orders there, pitching in to help when his expertise was needed. And he always returned to Perro Seco.

The drillers reported a show of gas at 2,084 feet. Barr drove out from Maturin. The drillers confessed they weren't sure about the gas show and blamed their report on their hopes for one. At 2,292 feet the hole began to cave. Barr took over the drilling, cursing the cable tool rig and the men who had sent it to him. He managed to drill down to 2,315 feet and then could drill no farther.

"Plug the son of a bitch," he ordered bitterly.

Fifteen months had passed since drilling commenced, fifteen months of anxious waiting in Caracas and in Houston by men who had set their hopes on the well.

Back in Maturin Barr composed a four-word telegram to Caracas: PERRO SECO ES SECO. Dry dog is dry!

146

Chapter
Eleven

(Special to the New York *Times,* May 2, 1932, by K. C. Hopkins)

SeaCoast International Petroleum Corporation has gained control of the most valuable crude oil properties in the Western Hemisphere by purchasing Lake Maracaibo and Mexican concessions held by Pan Union Oil & Transport Corporation for $140,452,292.11, some $50,000,000 in cash, the remainder in SCI stock, this reporter has learned.

It was the largest deal in the history of the oil industry. It was learned that Pan Union was ready to sell the concessions because of fear of a United States tariff on imported crude and refined products. Imposition of the tariff is expected within a month. It will provide for a duty of 21 cents a barrel on crude and $1.05 a barrel on gasoline.

The tariff is not expected to harm SCI at all since the Venezuelan and Mexican oil can be marketed in Europe and elsewhere. Pan Union has no foreign markets and all of its crude and refined products were sold in the United States. In the deal Pan Union apparently did the best it could to pull itself out of an untenable position. For SCI, it was the best spent money in its corporate history.

It was learned that Thomas Walter Fairbanks, vice-president of SCI-Venezuela, led negotiations for SCI, and Robert Henry Howard, Pan Union board chairman, headed the team representing the seller. The deal was consummated in Houston, Texas.

But things were not going well in eastern Venezuela. Barr had drilled thirteen dry holes in a row. He was restless, irritable. It did not matter that living conditions in the wild had improved, nor that the engineers had succeeded in laying out a primitive road between Quiriquire and Caripito, a village on the San Juan. It did not matter that boats could now unload at the Caripito dock and supplies could be hauled directly to Quiriquire, eliminating the necessity of poling supplies by *alijo* down the Guarapiche to Maturin and then making the long overland haul to the oil camps. But what did matter was that Charles Cannon in Caracas and the SCI brass in Houston appeared not to be overly worried about the dusters—or that a new resident geologist staked drill sites exactly where Caracas ordered apparently without discussion or argument.

His name was Rod Macon. He was a tall, wide-shouldered, powerful man in his thirties, friendly, talkative, obviously proud of his sleek black hair and trim moustache, obviously certain that he was, as Frank Husting said, "God's gift to women." A bully lurked in his big gray-green eyes.

"You fret too fucking much," he said to Barr. "Let's go to Maturin and have some fun. You can play cards with the general and I'll screw his old lady." They were talking in Macon's tent.

"Not today," Barr said, forcing a grin. "But I do want to talk to you about something, Rod."

"Fire away."

"I've been going over the stuff from those Caracas geologists, and they say that this area we're drilling in now is a big anticline."

"Right."

"They say that the oil sands dip away from the crest of this anticline to the east and the west, but that the real good sand is to the west, back toward the llano."

"Correct."

"Do you remember Ralph Lytel, the guy that came out here first and really studied this country?"

Macon dropped his patronizing air. "I remember him," he said shortly.

"Well, he said this structure was a monocline. He said those thin, no-good sands to the west hold a little oil that migrated from the east. He said the real oil play would be to the east, in the jungle."

Macon stood up. "Ralph Lytel wouldn't know a monocline

148

from a mongoose," he said with cold scorn. "If you think we're going to drill in there, you're blowing smoke up your ass."

Barr kept his seat. "What would it hurt to try?" he asked calmly. "Everything else we've touched has turned to shit. We've got two wells drilling right now that are going to be as dry as a popcorn fart."

Macon was angry. "You're in charge of drilling operations and so on out here, Grady, but Caracas says where we drill unless I recommend a change. And I'm damn sure not going to recommend that fucking jungle."

Barr stood up. "All right, Rod. Keep your shirt on." He nodded his head. "I thank you for your time."

Barr walked outside into the sunlight. He could see the jungle in the far distance. Where the llano ended and the jungle began was called *La Boca de la Bruja* by the Venezuelans, The Mouth of the Witch. But Barr knew that the road Lytel's crew had cut to his favored drill site had not yet been taken over by the jungle. Some of the crude huts they had built were still standing.

Barr drove his Ford over the rough road to Maturin. On the outskirts of town he passed an airstrip engineers were constructing to receive the shiny Ford Tri-motor airplane the company had purchased to fly its executives about the country. Why Cannon felt justified in building a strip at Maturin was more than Barr could fathom. "They've got more confidence in that damn llano than I have," he muttered to himself.

He parked on the plaza and gained entry to the presidential mansion. The Fontenots were entertaining Colonel Morillo, the garrison commandant. Morillo was profuse in his greeting of Barr, showing off his eloquence for the ladies and cutting a fine figure in his fresh uniform. Barr was his finest friend, he declared, a stranger for less than a moment when he rode into the fort astride a dirty mule, himself only a trifle cleaner, needing assistance which was readily given, for who could forego aiding such a splendid fellow?

It was Morillo who was such a splendid fellow, Barr avowed, a defender of his state, a man among men, and knowing him was the pride of Barr's life.

"Now will you both sit down," Teresa said, laughing.

"And you are as pretty as a flamingo," Barr said.

"My, my," said Fontentot.

Elvira Obregon said nothing. They had been drinking at a large round table in the upstairs living room. Barr filled a glass

149

with brandy from a sidebar and joined them. Before he sipped his drink he said to Elvira, "It's a pleasure to see you again."

"Thank you," she said gravely.

"What brings you to town?" Fontenot asked.

"I've got a problem, and I need some help," Barr said.

Fontenot shook his head. "May the lord have mercy."

"Shut up, Pedro," Teresa said.

"It will be of benefit to you, too, General," Barr said.

"Spare me," Fontenot said, rubbing his brow.

"I mean it, General." Barr explained his problem: he believed the oil was to the east, in the jungle, but he would have to go against orders to find it. "These dry holes don't do a thing for your economy, General. Let me find that oil and things will boom. You can see that."

"But what can I do?"

"Keep Rod Macon out of my hair long enough for me to get the equipment in place and start drilling. Invite him to a party and keep him drunk." He looked over at Colonel Morillo. "Arrest him and keep him in the garrison." He looked back at Fontenot. "Something, General, to get him out of the way for four or five days."

Teresa's laugh was a trill. "I told you the first time I met you that you were a devious man. And you are!"

"I took the trouble to find out what that means," Barr said. "I don't think I'm devious for the sake of being devious. I'm not always devious."

Elvira spoke. "Do what he asks. He may fail. The jungle may hold no oil. But as he says, they have found none elsewhere. And certainly it would help the economy if he succeeds." She paused. "Rod Macon is a beast." Her lips curled in a slight smile of satisfaction at her last remark.

"How regal!" Morillo breathed.

"It's a wonderful idea, Pedro," Teresa said.

Fontenot threw up his hands. "I ask the father of us all if ever a man was so oppressed!"

"Then you'll do it?" Barr asked.

Fontenot said wearily, "I have no choice."

"A toast to the General's courage and wisdom!" Morillo cried.

Fontenot laughed. "Anything is an excuse for a toast, eh, Colonel." He turned to Barr. "Drill your well. We'll take care of Rod Macon."

* * *

The road Ralph Lytel's crews had cut into the jungle was too rugged for the trucks, and the equipment was taken in by the mules. Barr had chosen two drillers for the job at hand, Buddy Calvert and Mike Phipps. Ten Trinidadians were in the party.

"I was looking for a job when I got this one," Calvert said when Barr warned him that they could all get in trouble by drilling the well. "I'm tired of dry holes. If you think there's something out here, that's good enough for me." Phipps seconded Calvert's sentiments with a nod.

Barr watched the setting up of the rig as if his life depended on its proper functioning. He was on hand when Calvert spudded in, and studied cores from the well, sniffing at them and tasting them with his tongue, as he had seen geologists do for a smell or taste of oil or gas.

The Fontenots had somehow kept Macon in Maturin for five days, long enough for Barr to get the equipment into the jungle site. On his return he went about his business, apparently unaware of what had transpired in his absence. As the days passed, Barr stole time away from other well sites to sneak into the jungle where Calvert and Phipps were steadily sending the drill down into the earth.

But on the day the bit reached fifteen hundred feet, Macon rode into the clearing. Astride another mule was a stranger to Barr, a graying, pale-faced man with a curved pipe in his mouth. Barr clambered off the rig floor and went to them.

Without dismounting, the stranger reached into a pocket, took out an envelope, handed it to Barr. "I'm Fred Hubbard from Caracas," he said. "I'm the company's chief geologist."

Barr nodded and opened the envelope. It contained a message from Charles Cannon ordering him to stop drilling the well. It accused him of overstepping his authority, and hinted darkly that Barr was through.

Barr ignored Macon, who had sat silently all the while. "I'm fifteen hundred feet down," Barr said to Hubbard.

"Shut 'er down," Hubbard said.

"Why don't you get down and come take a look at it," Barr said. "Like I said, I'm fifteen hundred feet down."

Macon spoke. "If anybody gets off a mule, it'll be me, you son of a bitch. You heard the man. Shut 'er down!"

Barr continued to ignore Macon. "I'm aiming to drill this well, Mr. Hubbard. I'll appreciate any advice you can give me about how it looks right now."

Macon slid off his mule. Calvert, Phipps and the Trinidadians had gathered by the side of the rig and Barr heard a Negro laugh nervously. Macon stood in front of Barr, between Barr and Hubbard. "Somebody bent your nose and scarred you up a little, but I don't think he did a good enough job," Macon said with easy confidence.

"The man who did it is dead," Barr said, and again the Negro laughed.

"Then he must have . . ." Macon said no more because Barr's left hand flashed out and struck him square in the mouth. Macon's head jerked backward, and again Barr's left fist struck his face. When Macon lifted his fists to protect his face, Barr pivoted and drove his right hand into Macon's body. The blow bent Macon's upper body forward, and Barr threw a left hook that caught Macon flush on the jaw. Macon stumbled back against Hubbard's mule.

The mule shied away from Macon. "Kill the cocksucker, Grady!" Calvert shouted. The big man reeled. He was groggy, helpless, out of control. Every dry hole, every frustration, had been in Barr's punches, and now they propelled him after Macon. But Macon retreated unsteadily. Holding out his hands for Barr to stop, he scuttled away from Barr's advance.

Barr halted, and his big fists uncurled. He turned to look up at Hubbard. "Will you look at the well, Mr. Hubbard?"

"No," Hubbard said around his pipe. He jerked at the reins and wheeled his mule around. He kicked the mule in the sides and the animal headed out of the clearing.

Macon had managed to mount his mule. Slumped forward, his face bloody, he reined his mule after Hubbard's. Barr watched them enter the jungle road, then he went back to the rig. Calvert jerked a thumb toward the grinning Negroes. "They'll be singing a song about it before night, you wait and see."

"If they are, it'll be while they're working," Barr said.

The well came in quietly, under control. Barr, Calvert and Phipps stood on the rig floor and marveled at it. It was one of the finest wells any had ever seen. On the first test it produced 1,006 barrels of good crude in fifteen hours. There was very little mud in the oil and only three percent water.

Two days later they tested it again, for five hours. It flowed 361 barrels with the same pressure as the first test. This time there was no mud and no water.

152

"We ain't going to crow about this," Barr said. "We're going to be unconcerned, just like it happens every day out here." He grinned. "Like old Bandera used to say, we're going to be *non-shay-lont.*"

He sent a brief message over the wire to Cannon that a well had come in and appeared to be a good one. Without waiting for orders, he set a crew to clearing another jungle area for a drill site. Macon had spent most of his time after the fight in his tent, and Barr had not disturbed him.

Three days after Barr wired Caracas about the well, Cannon walked into Barr's field office tent. It was late afternoon, and Cannon obviously was weary from the plane flight from Caracas to Maturin and the rough journey to Quiriquire. But he didn't even take off his hat.

"Let's take a look at that well, Grady," he said.

They rode to the well in silence. Cannon inspected it solemnly while Barr watched in surprised admiration. When Cannon was through, he motioned for Barr to join him and they walked to the mules. Cannon took a small notebook from his coat pocket and opened it. "For your information, Grady, the string of dry holes from west to east that led to this well cost the company forty-six million, two hundred and fifty thousand dollars, give or take a dollar or two." He put the notebook away. "This well justifies the money we've spent, in my mind, and it justifies us spending some more."

Barr said nothing.

Cannon glanced at his watch, looked at the sun. "It's a little late, and you may not have time today, but first thing in the morning get somebody to start laying a pipeline to the Caripito docks."

Barr nodded.

They rode back to camp. Neither mentioned Cannon's scathing message to Barr. The next morning Barr drove Cannon to the Maturin air strip. As they stood by the plane, Cannon said, "Grady, I know a lot of people think I'm just a fuddy-duddy. Maybe I am. I'm a company man, through and through. I go by the book. It's ingrained in me. I couldn't do what you did. I can't admire you for it, but sometimes I wish there was a little of you in me. If there was a little of me in you, you might be better off for it." He stuck out his hand and Barr shook it.

"Charley, send me a new geologist out here, will you?" Barr said.

Cannon studied Barr's face. "Rod Macon was doing his job, Grady."

"He's going to have to do it somewhere else. I want somebody like Ralph Lytel." Barr paused. "Charley," he said earnestly, "there's oil all over this part of the country, and I don't just mean in Monagas. We've got a good start on everybody out here—Gulf, Shell, everybody. I want somebody who'll get off his ass and help me find it."

"I think you've got a big field right here," Cannon said. "It's going to take a lot of work defining its limits and exploiting it. Macon can help you do that."

Barr shook his head. "I ain't mad at him, if that's what you think. But he ain't going to be any good to himself out here. Everybody knows I whipped his butt, and he ain't the kind that can laugh it off and say what the hell. He's sitting in his tent dying a little bit every day, Charley, so you'd be doing him a favor, too. He might be a good company man somewhere else."

"A good company man, huh?" Cannon laughed. "All right, Grady. I'll find you a maverick."

Barr moved out boldly. After Quiriquire 1, the first well, the wells came in like champagne corks popping on New Year's Eve. Almost every well was a fine producer, some of them flowing more than eight thousand barrels a day. The docks at Caripito were busy as tankers loaded the crude for delivery at refineries around the world. The road from Quiriquire to the docks was paved to handle the growing traffic on it.

The geologist Cannon sent Barr was indeed a maverick, brilliant, ebullient and impulsive. For Steve Boosie, everything he saw of consequence was the greatest he had ever seen. He was a tow-headed wisp of thirty with laughing blue eyes and ears that sometimes seemed to flap when he strode across a clearing. "He could take off and fly in a high wind," a driller remarked.

On their first meeting Barr told Boosie that he had been staking locations in Quiriquire by the seat of his pants or wherever he liked the way the land laid. "There's another geologist coming out next week, and I'll give that chore to him. What I want you to do is cut your wolf loose and get out there and find us a new field or two. We've got this whole state under concession."

"I saw a couple of interesting structures from the airplane," Boosie said. "Looked like a peanut from the air."

"Think you can find it again?"

"Do geese fly south?"

"I wonder how come nobody else ever mentioned them?"

Boosie shrugged. "It was my first airplane ride and I didn't want to miss anything."

"When you want to start?"

"Right now!"

"Need for me to get you anything to get you started?"

Boosie shook his head. "I'll find what I need."

"Going to be fun, huh?"

Boosie laughed. "I'll be in touch with you."

"Do that," Barr said.

Barr didn't see Boosie for two months. Then Boosie stormed into Barr's office, eyes flashing and talking a mile a minute. The "peanut" he had found to be two separate and distinct structures. Fine prospects, he exclaimed—two great oilfields, no doubt about it.

"Let's drink a cup of coffee first, before we get started digging," Barr said. "All right?"

Boosie laughed. "All right, but I'm not kidding about how good they look."

"I know you're not," Barr said.

The bit subsequently found oil on both structures. Drillers, however, lumped them together and called the area Goober Field. Barr registered the area under that title. A pipeline was built across the llano and crude from Goober Field was pumped to the Caripito docks.

On Boosie's recommendation and at Barr's insistence, the company obtained a concession to the west in Falcon State, and only four miles from where the Caribbean lapped the coast, drillers found a field that yielded the highest gravity oil in the entire country.

Again on Boosie's recommendation, and with Barr fighting both Caracas and Houston for permission, crews were sent far to the east of Quiriquire to where the mighty Orinoco fanned out in countless tributaries that poured into the sea through treacherous swamps and marshes. Tides and the extreme thickness of soft silt made the setting up of derricks and boiler stations an almost impossible engineering project, but the men got the job accomplished and brought in another field.

Barr was busier than ever. He directed operations from his Maturin headquarters. Because it now was necessary for him to handle many reports, Cannon sent him a male secretary, a recent

Yale graduate. "I ain't going to make no bones about it," Barr told his new employee. "I ain't always sure of what I read, and writing is a hell of a chore. When I ain't sure of what I'm reading, I'm going to call on you for help. In the reports from here, I'll tell you what I want to say and you write them up."

As far as Barr could tell, the serious young man did as he was told. And there was never a hint that Barr's lack of education made the slightest difference in their relationship. But to Barr it was a kind of bondage that he couldn't tolerate. He said as much one evening while visiting the Fontenots . . .

Elvira Obregon was back in town on one of her periodic visits from Valencia. She brought Barr a dictionary from her living quarters, and showed him the guide to pronunciation in the front of the book. "I've had this since my school days," she said. "Study this section and learn the symbols, and you will be on the way to an education in your language." She smiled. "Your Spanish is better than your English."

"And it ain't much good, either," Barr said, grinning.

Later she gave him some books to read, and told him the names of some he could order from the States. After that almost every ship that landed at Caripito unloaded several books for Barr. And more and more Barr found himself talking only to Elvira when he strolled across the plaza to the mansion where the door was always open to him. These were the occasions when the Fontenots had something else to do or were entertaining someone they felt Barr would not care to meet.

On one such evening Elvira's hand touched Barr's as she bent over his shoulder to turn a page. She quickly withdrew her hand. Barr turned to face her. The very touch of her hand made him feel as if someone had caressed his penis. Now he saw naked longing for him in her eyes. He stood up and took her in his arms, wanting to crush her in his hold. But he held back and kissed her gently. Her mouth, sweet and smoky, opened, and for a moment they kissed in the wildest passion. Then she pushed him away. She was gasping, shaking her head. She seemed on the verge of hysteria, and Barr moved to touch her, to calm her. She turned away from his outstretched hand and went to the couch. Barr realized that he too was trembling, that his penis was erect and clearly outlined in his trousers. He sat down on the couch, away from her.

Minutes passed, and neither spoke. Barr was prepared to grant her the lead. Finally she spoke. "I was forty when I first saw you in Valencia," she said softly. "I was much older than you. Now more years have passed. Only a desire for a woman, any woman, would make you want me."

"I want you more than I ever wanted any woman," Barr said as softly as she had spoken. He made no move to her. "I've wanted you for a long time," he went on in the same soft tone.

She shook her head, but not in negation of his words. "I think about you," she said. "When I go home to Valencia you go with me in my mind. And so I always come back to see you with my eyes. Helping you with your English has been the greatest pleasure of my life because I have been near you, talked to you, listened to you, watched you move and laugh. And I am ashamed of it all, ashamed of myself. I am ashamed for several reasons, I suppose, but mostly because I have so many more years than you."

"That means nothing, Elvira."

"And I do more than think about you," she said as if Barr had not spoken. "I have never been with a man, but I lie in bed and think of making love with you, and sometimes I want so badly to have you there that I make love to myself . . . and I still want you."

She looked directly at him now. Her face was troubled. "I think I love you, Grady. I must love you if all these things happen."

He moved toward her, but she held out a hand to halt him. "When my hand touched yours, before we kissed, I felt like you had put your hand between my legs."

"Don't you know it had the same affect on me, Elvira?" Barr moved toward her again, and again she stopped him. "I don't know anything about love," he said, "but I've never felt this way about a woman in my life."

She stood up quickly and faced him. "Not here, Grady. Not now."

"But where?"

Her smile was shy. "Where I have dreamed of it happening. Some place where we are completely alone. And in the sunshine, Grady. Is that foolish? In the sunshine and with no one for miles around?"

"It's not foolish," Barr said.

It seemed to take forever for him to penetrate her. She winced at his gentle probing, and once when he heard her sob in pain he tried to withdraw, but she clutched at him with savage strength and pulled him back. "Hurt me, but I must have you! I must!"

He had driven across the savanna to the broad mesa that stood four hundred feet higher than the surrounding countryside, to Perro Seco where he had first tried and failed to find oil. They could see to the horizon in every direction. It was as if they were alone in the world with not even an animal to distract them, or a flying bird. He had spread the blankets and sheets on the soft grass. She had undressed without a word and carefully stacked her clothing. Naked, she had been the most beautiful woman he had ever seen. She had watched him undress. By the time he had loved her until her vagina was wet and steamy the sun had their bodies glistening with perspiration.

She screamed when the tip of his penis finally entered her, but held him fast and urged him on with soft cries. He took his time, gaining inch by inch, and with every gain she suffered a spasm of pain. But as he knew would happen, and as she must have sensed, the pain began to diminish. Slowly, gently, he moved his penis inside her.

He had expected it to take another long while before pleasure surmounted the pain, but he was wrong. Suddenly she pulled him to her with surprising strength. She tried to lift her hips from the sheet, and her pelvis dug into him. "Yes, Grady! Yes! Yes! Yes!"

Many women over the years had told Barr they did not favor prolonged bouts of intercourse, that they preferred shorter bouts of greater intensity and more of them. But Elvira Obregon seemed to have no satiation point and the final orgasm of that first congress was as stormy as her first. For Barr it was like a football game in which she did all the scoring. The few times he neared a climax she destroyed his rhythm by falling limp from an orgasm of her own. Before he could regain his stride, she was off in a world of her own, reaching for and always achieving the ecstasy she had discovered. And on and on it went.

At her first slight sign of weakness, Barr withdrew. He laughed as he held her and caressed her, telling her she had worn him out. But he was tender and loving with her also, and she wriggled in his arms in appreciation.

Later, when they were drinking and washing themselves with water Barr had brought in jugs, she said, "Grady, is there any woman more carnal than a recent virgin?"

"Carnal?"

She laughed. "You'll have to look it up in your dictionary . . . and I know you will!"

Later she insisted on washing Barr's penis. It stiffened immediately. She bent it back against his stomach. "My God, Grady, did all of that go inside me?" she asked in wonder.

"Almost," Barr said.

"I want it all," she whispered. "Now!"

It was as if the first coupling had not occurred. In losing her virginity she seemed to have gained instant competence, and the unreasoning wanton had somehow become a premiere courtesan. Not that her orgasms were fewer or less shaking, but now she was aware of Barr, aware that he should receive as well as give. She moved her body to meet his, in keeping with his, as if they were performing before an audience of sexual critics, as if she and Barr had been created to do nothing else.

Barr had known no more than five women who could exercise the *constrictor cunni* without conscious, dedicated effort. But at one point Elvira's vagina closed on his penis like fingers, and she milked him as a goat is milked. She forced his body still during this maneuver. While he lay motionless and silent, she moaned with each contraction, increasing the pressure and frequency until she climaxed in a frenzy of effort and Barr ejaculated with an animal cry.

They coupled once more before they headed for Maturin at dusk. About ten miles from their destination she unbuttoned his trousers and kissed and fondled him as Barr drove along the rough road. Two miles farther on, Barr put her in the back seat and they made love again.

The day on the llano set a pattern for them. As the weeks and months passed Barr was only dimly aware that he was neglecting his affairs as he and the woman sought a sexual gratification beyond human reach. At times he would seek the intelligent, compassionate woman he knew she was, but he could never find her in the haze of lust. And she obviously was incapable of finding him. He wanted to talk to her, eat with her, read with her—to enjoy her totally. But they had no time for anything but satisfaction of the great hunger they held for each other's flesh. There were times when Barr felt as if he could never come another drop, but her touch would inflame him and they would be at each other again as if they had never left the llano. When Elvira said she loved him, he knew she now meant simply that she loved to fuck him. And they always found the time for it, and a place.

Ed Gurwell, who had forced Barr into the Perija, shook him out of the haze. He slouched into Barr's office one morning, and jerked a thumb at the secretary. "Take a tour around the plaza, young fellow," he said pleasantly, "or maybe three or four. I want to talk to your boss." He sat down across the desk from Barr and took off his hat. "Charley Cannon sent me out here, Grady."

"I figured it wasn't social," Barr said.

"Fairbanks was in Caracas for a few days, and he wanted to come out, but Cannon said I'd better do it," Gurwell said easily.

"Get on with it, Ed."

Gurwell nodded. "Remember the message from Cannon that Gulf was drilling a tight well over in the next state near El Gato? He wanted you to keep your ear to the ground."

"I remember."

"Did you hear anything, with your ear to the ground?"

"Don't get sassy, Ed."

"No, you're the one who won't get sassy. I'm out here to fire you. But you don't have to answer the question. I'll do it. When Charley didn't hear from you after a reminder message, he sneaked his chauffeur down there to work as a roughneck. When the drillers got excited over a core, the chauffeur pinched off a chunk when no one was watching and he ran to Charley with it. Our geologist said it was rich with light oil. Are you with me?"

Barr nodded.

"So there we were with three or four days start over Gulf, and we already knew most of the area close to the well was national reserves. Nobody, but nobody, had rights to them. So Charley hurried over to see Miguel Serna, the minister who's the old man's favorite of the moment. Charley handed him a check for five million and Miguel grabbed it like a bandit. All he had to do, Miguel told Charley, was clear it with the old man, and there'd be no problem with that. So there we were, ahead of Gulf and everybody else, with the reserves practically in our hands.

"I can guess," Barr said. "The old man said no dice."

"Exactly. Can you guess why, Grady?"

"Something to do with me, I'd say. Bringing in those people from Trinidad, probably."

"Shit! He knew about the niggers as soon as they went to work. The honcho in every state is on the wire to him every day, buddy, and he knows as much about you as if you lived in his coat pocket.

160

If you don't think Fontenot told him about the niggers, you're crazy as hell. No," Gurwell went on, "it wasn't that. He passed the word through Miguel that he was disappointed in you. Said you had shown a weakness he hadn't expected you to have. Said he'd rather somebody else had the concession instead of us. His implication, my friend, was that you were out here wallowing around in pussy and letting everything else go to hell. Charley couldn't deny that you hadn't been up to snuff for quite a spell."

"I can't believe Fontenot told him something like that," Barr said.

Gurwell laughed sourly. "Because she's his sister-in-law? He was looking out after his own ass, Grady."

"I wonder why he didn't say something to me?"

Gurwell laughed again. "He told me an hour ago that you and the lady were running around here like a couple of dogs. He said he knew it wouldn't do any good to talk to either of you, so he didn't try. And he wouldn't let his wife."

Barr sat lost in thought.

"The company is growing fast out here, Grady," Gurwell said. "What happened to your idea of building a permanent headquarters in Caripito? It made sense to me. All you needed was to push Charley a little. And the refinery you talked about. Caripito is a perfect place for one, in my mind. You could have pushed it through." A grievous tone had come into Gurwell's voice. "I used to read your reports and think how much sense you were making about a lot of things, damn it."

Barr smiled faintly. "Don't take it personally, Ed."

"But I am. Charley's not going to be down here much longer. They'll call him to the SCI board pretty soon, I think, and he deserves it. And I think I deserve his chair. You're not my favorite person on this old earth, but I was counting on bringing you into Caracas to help me."

"Admitting that I fucked up, it seems to me that I pulled off enough coups in the past for Charley to give me a chance to show I can straighten up. Not out here, of course, but there are other places."

Gurwell shook his head. "Charley's worried about Gomez. He thinks the old man expects him to fire you. He thinks he'd resent it if you stayed with us in any capacity, and he'd take it out on the company. Charley won't chance that, and you can't hardly blame him."

"You say you talked to Fontenot this morning. Was she there?"

"She's on her way home." Malice crept into Gurwell's eyes. "You'll have to do without the farewell piece of ass, I'm afraid."

Barr stood up and began assembling papers on his desk. "Where are you going to head for, Grady? Going to follow the lady to Valencia? Going back to the madam in Maracaibo?"

Barr's hands trembled under his restraint. "You've got a nasty mouth, Ed. If you weren't right about so many things you said, and if I didn't feel so goddamned low down right now, I think I'd slap the shit out of you. Now let me get out of here."

Gurwell flushed. "I'm sorry, Grady. That was pretty thick. Where *are* you going?"

Barr grinned. "I think I'm going to try to play some pool with a guy who's supposed to shoot a pretty good stick."

The hotel room was the same one he had stayed in when he first came to Maracay to make the paseo with General Gomez in a try for the eastern concession. He had been bold and eager then, and optimistic. Tonight, lying on the bed in the darkness, blowing smoke rings at the ceiling, he was more subdued than he had ever been in his life. He had not smoked since his mother had asked him to quit when he was seventeen. He had not missed tobacco, but tonight he had bought two packs of Wings in the lobby shop. He was chain-smoking them, as if to make up for the years of abstinence.

If, as Ed Gurwell had said, he had been wallowing in pussy in Maturin, tonight he was adrift on a sea of shame and misery. He thought of Elvira, and of how humiliating it must have been for her when Fontenot let her know he was aware of her conduct. Had she left the mansion of her own accord, he wondered, or had Fontenot sent her home? If she had regained her senses as Barr had done in Gurwell's presence, was her pride broken or even destroyed? What *had* the humiliation done to her? Was she in bed at home at this moment hiding in the darkness, thinking of him with hatred and disgust, looking back with revulsion at every unbridled moment they had spent together? Would she ever regain the serenity, the poise, that had so impressed him when first he met her? The taste of his shame was as bitter in his mouth as the taste of the tobacco.

Barr extinguished a cigarette and lit another one. He had come to Maracay with the half-formed idea of trying to talk to Gomez. It had been in his mind to try to explain to the old man what had occurred, that he was sorry that it had happened and that it damned well would never happen again. He wanted Gomez to believe that. He believed every story he had ever heard about the general's tyranny. But it somehow seemed important that Gomez still believe that Grady Barr was the man he had always been. And Barr knew that the only way to convince Gomez would be to show him by act and deed . . .

He became aware of a growing noise in the plaza below his window; it had crept into his consciousness slowly, like a gathering storm. And now that he was fully alert to it, he heard shouts that seemed to come nearer as they grew in volume. Lights from below created shadows on his ceiling.

He got up and went to the window. The plaza was full of people, as if a national holiday had been declared and orders issued that a ritual be observed. Some carried torches though the plaza was well-lit. The sound that reached Barr's ears was like the humming of a great swarm of bees or the passage of a flock of birds large enough to hide the sun.

He put on his clothes and went to the lobby. Perhaps a dozen persons were there, all looking out the big windows onto the plaza. Barr headed for the door. A tall, flaxen-haired man in a pale blue suit grabbed his arm. "I wouldn't go out there if I were you," he said with a definite British accent.

Barr shook off of the stranger's hand. "And why not?" he asked.

"General Gomez died about an hour ago, and they're just now hearing about it."

"You mean we've got a revolution?"

"No, not that. Actually, it's more like a hysterical release of emotions, if you see what I mean. These people have been living under oppression, you know. The top's just blown off. There are no leaders, or anything like that. But they could turn nasty very easily. So far no soldiers have shown up."

"I heard them hollering something," Barr said.

The Englishman nodded. "Death to Gomecistas. That's why I stopped you. That might include foreigners, you know."

The door opened and three men entered the lobby. They were part of the mob, and one of them had a forbidden pistol in his hand. Of those in the lobby, Barr and the Englishman were nearest the door. The three men glanced around the lobby, then centered their attention on Barr and the Englishman.

"Gomecista?" the man with the pistol asked Barr.

"A friend of the people," Barr said quickly in Spanish. "Death to Gomecistas!"

"You lie," said the man with the pistol. And he shot Barr in the chest. He turned and shot the Englishman in the abdomen. "Suffer in hell!" he shouted. He turned the pistol on the hotel clerk. "Die!" But the pistol failed to fire. The man threw it at the clerk. "Die!" he shouted again, and all three men wheeled and went out the door to the plaza. "Sweet mother of God!" the clerk said.

Barr and the Englishman were both on the lobby floor. Barr was silent, but the Englishman said in a calm voice, "Somebody help us, please. Our friend may be dead already, but I could use a helping hand."

Barr opened his eyes in a hospital room. He was flat on his back on a high bed. And someone was snoring.

He turned his head slowly. A nurse was asleep in a straight chair against the wall. A short, bald man in a doctor's white jacket came into the room. A stethoscope hung from his neck. He shot quick glances about the room as if he suspected someone was hiding in a corner to steal his patient. He stopped short when he saw that Barr's eyes were open.

He came to Barr's side, lifted Barr's hand and felt for his pulse. Barr lifted his other hand for inspection. It was thin and pale. He raised the hand to his face and brushed his palm across a heavy beard. The nurse snored on.

"Wake her up," Barr said crankily in Spanish. "She sounds like a lost freight train." His voice was a hoarse whisper.

"Well, Lazarus has returned," the doctor said. He continued his examination, listening to Barr's heartbeat with the stethoscope, thumbing back his eyelids, running his hands over the heavy bandages that swathed Barr's chest. He stepped back. He took a pellet from his pocket, pitched it in the air and caught it. "A souvenir, Mr. Barr." He placed the pellet on the night table. "Alicia helped me save your life." He cocked his head and said with mock humility, "That's pretty good work for a couple of Venezuelans, isn't it?"

"Don't belittle yourself to me," Barr croaked. "I thank you, and I'll pay the going rate on Americans."

The doctor laughed, showing stained teeth. "Your friend said you were as tough as a cactus-eating burro."

"What friend?"

But the doctor turned away and shook the nurse's shoulder. She woke up with a start. "He's all right," the doctor said soothingly. "He just came around." The nurse stood up and stared at

164

Barr. She was in her fifties with a lined face and sorrowful eyes. She closed her eyes. "Thank God, doctor!"

"He had nothing to do with it," the doctor said. "Get the man some food, then see that he rests. I'll be back later in the evening."

"What friend?" Barr croaked.

But the doctor was ushering the nurse out of the room. "A lot of broth, Alicia," he said.

Barr tried to sit up, but Ed Gurwell pushed him back down on the bed and held him. "She's all right, I said!" he whispered furiously. "Goddamn it, you want me to get the doctor to knock you out? I told you she's all right!"

Barr relaxed. "Where is she?" he asked, not quite believing.

"Curacao. She went there a week before it happened."

"Don't shit me, Ed," Barr warned. "What's in Curacao?"

"She was vacationing." Then, true to form, he added, "She made the trip with a big Dutchman she's been shacking up with."

He had told Barr that while the mobs did little in Maracay and less in eastern Venezuela, they had run wild in Caracas and Maracaibo, burning and looting and killing. Two sides of Plaza Sucre had been put to the torch; the Cosmos Club had burned to the ground. Louise Bremond was all right.

"Does she know about me?" Barr asked.

Gurwell shrugged. "I haven't any idea. What I know is what I got from our people in Maracaibo. I'll tell you one thing . . ."

"What the fuck was Cerro Soto and all those troops doing all that time? They had all the weapons, for Christ's sake."

Gurwell said easily, "They pulled Cerro Soto out of his car and threw him into the city incinerator. Captain Ramirez, too. And a few other Gomecistas before the troops got around to quietening things down."

"Jesus! I wonder if Eddie Vigas knows about it."

"I don't know. I'd think so. Last I heard he was working for Pure Oil in East Texas. Don't you ever hear from him?"

Barr shook his head. Then, "How did you know I was here, Ed?"

Gurwell laughed. "According to the doctor, you told your life story a thousand times while you were delirious. You mentioned me a few times."

Barr's pale face reddened. Gurwell laughed again. "I was flattered enough to come to see you."

"Why are you here, Ed?"

Gurwell nodded as if communicating with himself. "You've got sense, Grady, and you've got more guts than a slaughterhouse. I want you to suck up those guts and go back east and take over again. All right?"

"You mean with the old man dead I'm not a leper any more?"

Gurwell nodded. "That, and my belief that you won't go chasing pussy through the boondocks any more. That you'll be discreet when you do knock off a piece."

Barr said nothing. "You'll have to take a lot of shit," Gurwell said. "You'll have to make your peace with General Fontenot. And for what I've got in mind, you'll have to use that charm on the chief of every state in the east. You'll have to get to know them well, make them like you, but still let them know that the oil companies are running things as always."

The doctor came into the room just as Barr asked Gurwell, "Who's taking over the government?"

"The minister of war," Gurwell said.

"Another Andino," the doctor said with a trace of bitterness. "Another Andino in a long line of Andinos, and may God have mercy on us all for a little while longer."

Chapter Twelve

The heir to the Gomez dictatorship was General Eleazar Lopez Contreras, "elected" president in 1936 by the Gomez cabinet of which he had been a member as minister of war and the navy. He had every intention of perpetuating the dictatorship, but the outbreaks of violence following Gomez's death prompted him to make some changes in government. The changes were cosmetic, and temporary.

Exiles were welcomed home. Freedom of the press was granted. Political parties were allowed to form. Labor unions were permitted to organize. And, Lopez Contreras announced, he would "sow the petroleum." By this he meant that government income from oil would be used to promote agriculture and other industries.

He apparently failed to understand that he had become the leader of a new Venezuela. No longer was it a simple pastoral country. Citizens had streamed to the cities and particularly to the oil camps, giving birth to a new working class. They were ready to listen to the bright young returned exiles who made speeches to them and sought to educate them in the press and with hundreds of thousands of pamphlets.

Lopez Contreras reacted swiftly. Freedom of the press was revoked by executive decree. The workers reacted; a general strike broke out. Troops fired into workers. Mobs rioted and looted in the cities. Sharecroppers attacked landlords. Lopez Contreras made promises that he would liberalize his regime, and the strike ended.

There had been no violence in far eastern Venezuela where

Grady Barr had resumed his managership of Cajun Petroleum Corporation's holding. But when the strike ended, workers returned to Cajun installations to find the gates locked against them. A group of them marched on Barr's office in Caripito for an explanation. He refused to talk to them. "Pick you a spokesman, and then the rest of you get the hell out of here," Barr said.

The spokesman was a sober man in his forties. Barr knew him as a good roughneck. "We have no quarrel with the company, at present," the spokesman said. "The strike was against the government."

"What do you mean, at present?" Barr asked.

"You must know that we will have to talk about wages and living conditions some day," the spokesman said.

"With a strike?"

"This strike was against the government," the spokesman repeated.

"Maybe," Barr said, "but it hurt the company anyway. Now I'm going to strike for a while. I'll let you know when I feel like going back to work."

So, while other fields hummed with activity, Cajun installations in the east were silent. Days passed. "I'm not ready yet," Barr would say when the spokesman would come and stand silently in the office doorway. The spokesman would go away.

General Fontenot came up from Maturin. "I don't understand this, Grady," he said. "Those men are having to go out into the jungles to get food for their families. Doesn't that mean anything to you?"

"It does," Barr said.

"Merchants in every town in the state are angry. They're calling on me and sending wires to the President. It can't go on."

"Let me handle it, Pedro," Barr said.

"I'm trying to help you out of a bad situation."

"Let me handle it."

On the tenth day Lopez Contreras sent Barr a wire ordering him to open the gates. Barr ignored it.

Fontenot returned. "I'm appalled, Grady. How can you ignore a presidential order?"

"It's against my principles to let anybody else run the company's business," Barr said. "Let me handle this."

On the fifteenth day the spokesman stood in the doorway. He spoke quickly to prevent Barr from again saying he was not yet ready. "We are starving," he said simply. "Our children and women are suffering. Please, open the gates and let us work."

"I'm not responsible for your hunger," Barr said evenly. "The men from the west who came here to talk you into striking, they are responsible for your hunger. And they still are in Caripito." Barr paused. "As you know."

The spokesman stared at Barr with unblinking eyes. He got to his feet slowly and departed without a word. The next morning he was at Barr's office waiting when Barr arrived. They met at the steps. "They are gone," the spokesman said.

"Did they go willingly?"

"You know they didn't. Like Gomez, you know everything that happens. They talked against having to leave, and some of the men got desperate. They beat them out of town."

"I'm ready to go back to work," Barr said.

As the airplane approached Caracas, Barr could see from his window the devastation the sharecroppers had wrought. Fields had been put to the torch. Fences were torn down. Barns were collapsed. Cattle lay bloating in the pastures.

The destruction in Caracas itself was not as obvious. It was scattered throughout the city, and by now the city boasted a population of 250,000, and oil revenues had financed a construction program that was giving shape to the magic cosmopolis Caracas would someday become.

The company's original quarters had been in a small building on Plaza Espana. The purchase of Pan Union and the formation of Cajun Petroleum Corporation had forced a move to a larger, two-story building, complete with patio and three great palm trees. And now a German contractor was planning for the company what would be the most modern and imposing structure in the city.

Charles Cannon was waiting impatiently when Barr arrived at Cannon's office. "Come on," Cannon said, "we've got a date at Miraflores Palace." As they walked across the patio, Cannon said, "I hope to God you've got the right answers to his questions, Grady. I let you play your hand without interfering, and I kept Houston off your back."

"I know it, Charley, and I appreciate it."

The palace grounds were beautiful with great rows and beds of flowers. Carved in the palace wall were the words Columbus had used in his letter to the rulers of Spain to describe the virtues of the new land he had discovered. Barr wanted to look at the legend but Cannon hurried him on. They went through three offices with as many officious male secretaries before they were ushered into the presence of General Lopez Contreras.

It was a spacious office, dominated by a full-length painting of Gomez in military uniform hanging on the rear wall. It was furnished with a soldier's simplicity; only a small globe decorated Lopez Contreras' desk. The general was standing behind the desk, and he asked Cannon and Barr to be seated in front of it. He was a slender man of medium height with a plain and uninteresting face, marked chiefly by a mustache which struggled for flamboyance but did not quite make it. But then he spoke, and the required facial movements brought his face alive with strength and subtle charm. "I'm happy to welcome you both," he said in Spanish. He sat down, smoothing his uniform with both hands as he made himself comfortable.

"We're happy to be here," Cannon said, and Barr nodded agreement.

"If you will pardon me, sir," Lopez Contreras said to Cannon, "I shall address myself to your representative in the east." He looked at Barr with hard eyes. "Why was a presidential order ignored? I understand it was your decision."

"It was, Excellency," Barr said without a hint of an apology. "I kept the gates closed because I was certain I knew more about the situation than you did. There were seven union organizers from the lake area in Caripito. I kept the gates closed until the men were ready to run the organizers out of town. They drove them out." He paused. "I let the workers go hungry, but I taught them a lesson. There will be another strike called before the year is out. It will be well planned. The workers will be prepared to stay off their jobs for a long time. But my people won't strike. The workers will strike in the lake area and elsewhere, but my people won't. They won't go hungry again."

Lopez Contreras pursed his lips in skepticism, then said with a hint of anger, "You speak as if the government is in some kind of partnership with the oil companies."

"It is," Barr said flatly, "and we may as well recognize it. The government allowed the unions to form without discussing it with the companies, the ones most concerned. The companies have no plans to recognize the unions, as I understand it."

Lopez Contreras was holding back his anger, but it edged

170

around the corners of his thin mouth. "And who will meet their demands when they make them?"

"It is something to be discussed at the proper time," Barr said, as if unaware of the general's restraint. "In the meantime, I think I should bring up something that must be discussed as quickly as possible, something that will increase revenues to both the government and companies."

Lopez Contreras glanced at Cannon's impassive face, then looked back at Barr. "And what is that?" he asked with faint sarcasm.

"We have to dredge out that sand bar between Lake Maracaibo and the open sea," Barr said. "Stop all this hop, skip and jump with the lake tankers and let the ocean-going tankers come in and get the crude. It should have been done long ago."

Lopez Contreras stared at Barr as if he had not understood him. He stood up quickly and faced Cannon. "And what is your opinion of all of this?" he demanded.

Like Barr, Cannon appeared unaware of the general's agitation. He spread his hands. "It makes sense to me, Excellency. We know why General Gomez let that sand bar stay, but he was fearful of many things. Things you disregard . . . as you should."

Lopez Contreras was lost. He knew the ball had been taken away from him. He wanted to get back to the subject of Barr's lockout, but he couldn't do it gracefully, and so he compromised. "Very well, sir," he said to Cannon. "I will want a complete report on the dredging and its rewards, if any, to the republic. Before the month is out. I assume other companies involved will want to participate in the report. See to that. It will then be discussed with the cabinet." He paused. "Then I will let you know my answer. Understood?"

"Understood," Cannon said agreeably, and he stood up. Barr also got to his feet.

"And I'll want reports on any union activity that comes to your attention," he said brusquely. "Weekly reports. Understood?"

"Yes, Excellency," Cannon said.

"Very well," Lopez Contreras said, dismissing them. He turned away as if heavier affairs of state were calling him. He had restored himself.

Cannon had waited until they reached his office before he said anything. He plopped down in his chair and exhaled noisily. "Whew! That was mighty rough, Grady."

Barr lit one of Cannon's cigarettes and put his feet on Cannon's desk. "He's not Gomez, is he?" he said smugly.

"But you didn't know it."

"I knew he wasn't sure of himself when he picked on me. Gomez would have chewed your ass for letting me make such an important decision." Barr chuckled. "You really came in there and made things jell, Charley."

"Yep, we made a good team." Cannon lit a cigarette. "That was a hell of a thing about the dredging. The way you switched to it."

"It's been in my craw since I first got here," Barr said.

"It's been in everybody's craw. How much do you think a job like that will cost?"

"Us or the government?"

Cannon laughed. "Maybe we ought to share it."

"Maybe, if the cost to the companies isn't too much . . . if you let him think he forced it on us."

Cannon laughed again. "You're a son of a gun, Grady." He shuffled some papers on his desk. "Couple of things you might want to see." One was a copy of the Maracaibo *Tropical Star.* Under a column heading WHO'S DOING WHAT was an item marked with a red pencil. It said: "Miss Louise Bremond is re-building the Cosmos Club on the same spot on Plaza Sucre. She has taken a partner in the venture, Sidney Andrau."

"Thought you might want to know she's all right, Grady," Cannon said.

Barr nodded his thanks. He began reading the second offering, an in-house report prepared on Cajun stationery. It said: "Eduardo Vigas has been appointed inspector general of a technical group which will work under the Minister of Fomento. Job will be to see that all wells are properly spaced, wells drilled correctly, safety rules enforced. Vigas is son of late Colonel Hector Vigas, ward of late General Cerro Soto. Received his BA, Petroleum Engineering, from University of Texas, MA from University of Oklahoma. Worked for Sinclair in West Texas Division, Pure in the East Texas field. Houston office investigation team says he is brilliant, hard-working. Stayed to himself. Not friendly but not unfriendly, if you get what I mean. Showed no interest in politics. Did not apply for new assignment; was asked to take it while here to settle Cerro Soto estate. Suggest we find someone who knows Vigas well to ascertain his intentions and attitudes."

"You know him pretty well, don't you, Grady?" Cannon asked.

Barr nodded.

172

Cannon took another sheet of paper from his desk and slid it across the desk. It was another memo. It said: "This may be important, Charley. One of our younger engineers was at University of Texas with Vigas. Only knew of him. Said Vigas was a loner. Said someone put him up for membership in engineering fraternity and Vigas was voted down. Not because of grades or class standing but for other reasons. Our man says it could have been because he was a loner, but more likely because he was an alien, if you get what I mean. Vigas seemed to take it all right."

Barr put the memo on the desk. "They treated him like he was a mescan," he said softly, not looking at Cannon.

"Of course," said Cannon, a Texan himself. "But he seemed to take it all right, according to that memo."

"He would. He'd never let them know how much it hurt. But I'll tell you, he'll never forget it. That's for *damn* sure."

"But he stayed up there and worked. That doesn't sound like he's full of hate. He may have never come back here if Cerro Soto hadn't been killed. The minister asked him to take the job."

"He stayed up there to learn, Charley. He took this job because he thought he was ready for it."

"You know I respect your opinion, Grady, but what can he really do to us? Assuming he doesn't like us? Nag us is about all he can do, isn't it?"

Barr nodded. "At the present. As long as Lopez Contreras sits in Miraflores Palace."

"That's five years, according to the law. And he's sure to hand pick another Andino to succeed him."

"I know," Barr said.

Cannon leaned across his desk. "See him, Grady," he said urgently. "Hang around town a few days and take his pulse."

Barr shook his head. "He'll find me. He may figure he owes me something."

"Does he?" Cannon asked eagerly.

"No, but he'll want to see me anyway." Barr stood up. "Let me handle it, Charley. All right?"

"All right," Cannon said reluctantly. "Are you going back east today?"

"I may take an extra day getting there," Barr said. "Damn it, I keep missing Tom Fairbanks. Even when he came to see me in the hospital at Maracay I was out of my head. When is he due back here again?"

Cannon shrugged. "He's on the go all the time. Around the world. I think he's in the Middle East right now." He nodded judiciously. "He'll be the head of that foreign producing department within five years. I'd bet on it."

Barr looked directly at Cannon. "How long am I going to have to be discreet in my sex life before you give me that vice-presidency he vacated, Charley?"

Cannon said bluntly, "Don't push me, Grady."

"Is anyone in the running with me? You owe me that much."

"You know there isn't."

Barr nodded. "Fair enough." He went to the door. "You'll hear from me about Vigas."

As Barr had predicted, Venezuelan oil workers struck while the memory of the general strike against the government was only six months old. Before the strike the workers asked that the companies recognize the unions as fact. The companies refused. The workers asked for better wages and living conditions. The companies shook their heads. The strike lasted seventy-nine days before Lopez Contreras ordered the workers to return to their jobs, but Barr's workers had not been absent from their labors for as much as a single day. Memories of Barr's lock-out and their near starvation were still strong in their minds.

Prodded by Lopez Contreras, the companies agreed to make some concessions. There was a pay increase of twenty-eight cents per day. An additional twenty-eight cents per day was given as a housing allowance to those who did not have company housing. And the companies agreed to provide cold drinking water in the work areas.

K. C. Hopkins wrote an article about the settlement for *Fortune* magazine of such virulence that the editors refused to publish it. Later on, however, the editors dispatched a man named Clarence Horn to survey the situation. Horn wrote:

> The oil companies use 20,500 Venezuelans as staff employees and workers. About 17,000 of them work in the prolific oil zone of Maracaibo, where a heavy scum of oil on the lake waters discourages their bathing to refresh themselves from the heat. The rest work in the oil camps of Quiriquire and Caripito, carved out of the jungle.
>
> The Labor Law obliges the companies to give housing to the workers, with a space of 4.5 square meters per family

member. Also, they must supply water, sanitary facilities and light. Compared with what the ordinary peon has in Venezuela, this may seem like heaven.

However, in terms of civilized living conditions, it is nothing. The minimum oil wage is Bs. 8 ($2.25) daily, plus housing and services. But the cost of living is so high in Venezuela that this scarcely provides for food, clothing and entertainment.

If the worker prefers to pay for his own housing, he will get Bs. 9 daily as a minimum. In the Lake Maracaibo areas this means that he will live in a shack built out over the lake waters, into which he is likely to fall when drunk. To bathe, he will have the lake, if he takes care to first scrape off the scum of oil on its waters.

He must buy water to drink. His food consists of corn, bananas, brown sugar, black beans and rice for which he must pay Bs. 5 or 6 daily. The rent will cost more or less Bs. 12 for a room.

He will have no money left by the end of the month when he is likely to have contracted a venereal disease. The company doctor will treat him for this without charge. . . .

Tom Fairbanks read the *Fortune* article in his hotel room in London. He had been on a tour of Middle East oilfields and was waiting for a ship for the States. Living conditions for Venezuelan oil workers, he knew, were not much better than the day when he flatly told K. C. Hopkins that they would be improved for "practical" reasons. There was always something, it seemed, to prevent the companies from getting on with the task. Malaria had been vanquished with quinine and oil spraying, and that was about the only plus Fairbanks could tote up. The sludge had been cleared from the lake, but it had returned. Dispensaries had been set up, but they were inadequate.

He remembered sitting in the Bull Wheel with Hopkins and hearing Hopkins tell him that the oil companies were raping Venezuela. Hopkins had added, "Your father wrote the petroleum law that made a lot of it possible, and you think about that every time you go through a village where naked kids with skinny arms and legs and swollen bellies are playing in the mud-holed streets." Fairbanks had been furious at Hopkins' statement, but he knew that it held more than a kernel of truth.

175

The situation was much the same in the Middle East, Fairbanks mused, with the American and European oil company employees being well taken care of and the natives—"nationals"—being left to their own devices. Boards of directors were not inclined to fret over "humanitarian" whims that cut into profits for themselves and their shareholders.

But Fairbanks was disturbed. He had developed a genuine liking for the Venezuelan people. He had grown up with paternalism, and he did not like it. His family's ranch had been established in 1867, and generations of Mexican-Americans had lived their lives without setting foot off of it. The ranch fed them, clothed them, and provided shelter and even entertainment. It was a benevolent paternalism, but it was, he felt, deadening to the spirit. "They're contented," Fairbanks had heard his grandfather say many times, and later his father had used the same phrase. The families *were* contented, but in the same way as the cattle they tended. In all of them was a basic fear that to leave the ranch would be to face perils no man could conquer.

But the oil companies and the privileged clique had made no pretense at paternalism, Fairbanks mused. "Let 'em sleep in the trees if they don't like it," an SCI board member had grunted when Fairbanks had suggested better housing for Venezuelan workers in newer oilfields. The words could have fallen as easily from the lips of a Gomecista. But Fairbanks felt that the Venezuelan oil workers didn't want paternalism of any kind. He had seen ambition among them, an eagerness to try new tasks, an occasional flash of intelligence that bespoke something approaching genius. He recalled an engineer pointing to a Venezuelan foreman and saying, "That son of a bitch got down on his knees on the ground and drew a picture of a blowout preventer and explained it to his crew a hell of a lot better than I could ever do."

If we don't change our ways, they'll make us do it some day, Fairbanks thought in his London hotel room. From what he had read in Company memos, and from what he had deduced, the seventy-nine-day strike had not been a traditional worker–company contest. A patriotic movement had developed in support of the workers, one which saw many Venezuelan industrialists and businessmen unite with intellectuals and students in support of the workers. It was patriotic in the sense that it made clear that the enemy was a foreigner—the oil companies—and the enemy's collaborator was the Lopez Contreras dictatorship. The way Fairbanks viewed it, the support had amounted to a national plebiscite backing the oil workers. They asked for so little, he thought—and wondered what they would demand the next time . . .

Barr's secretary said a Mr. Fontenot wanted to see him, and Barr assumed the General was paying him a surprise visit. But the man waiting for him in the reception room was a younger edition of Pedro Fontenot, short but not squatty, with enormous black eyes in a tan face and dark hair brushed straight back from a high forehead. He appeared to be several years younger than Barr. He was well dressed in a black suit, white shirt and black tie. He ignored Barr's extended hand. He said in Spanish, "I am Roberto Fontenot. I stopped by here to see the man the workers did not strike against."

Barr said nothing. His face was impassive.

"I wanted to see this man who starved out the workers in the first strike," Fontenot continued. He spoke deliberately, but his eyes were unfriendly as he studied Barr as if memorizing his every feature. "I wanted to know him if our paths cross in the future."

Barr nodded as if he understood completely. "Have you been visiting your father?"

"I have no reason to visit him."

"Well, don't be so stiff-necked about it," Barr said easily. "I happened to have liked my own father, but I understand not everyone does. Now," he said crisply, "you've had your look. Is there anything else on your mind?"

"I'm satisfied," Fontenot said curtly. He nodded at Barr's secretary and turned and went out the door. Barr went to a window and watched him get into a waiting taxi. "I wonder where these revolutionaries get their taxi fares if they aren't talking to their fathers," he said over his shoulder to his secretary. The secretary laughed.

Barr went back to his office and sat down. He knew quite a bit about Roberto Fontenot, as he did about most of the political and labor activists. Fontenot had studied under the noted Latin American novelist and teacher Romulo Gallegos at the Liceo Caracas, and he had entered law school at Caracas' Central University. His studies had been cut short when he was arrested for participating in what Gomez had considered a revolutionary movement. While many of his comrades had been exiled, Fontenot and others had been sent to labor camps where they built roads under the threat of soldiers' rifles.

He had escaped from the chain gang and had hidden out in Caracas. General Fontenot had asked Barr to help his son get out of the country, and Barr had refused. The younger Fontenot had stayed under cover for years until the death of Gomez. He had come out of hiding to join the returned exiles in forming political parties and organizing unions. Now he was one of the leaders of *Accion Democratica*—Democratic Action.

Barr now knew that the son would have refused any help he thought was initiated by his father. To him, General Fontenot was just another Gomecista, despite the General's imprisonment by Gomez. He had, after all, returned to rule Monagas state once he was freed by his master. The General seldom mentioned his son, but Barr believed he loved him and suffered because he thought the younger man despised him.

He's smart and he's tough, Barr thought. He didn't let my manner turn him off. He came to say what he had to say and then got the hell out of here. We'll damn well be hearing from him in the future.

Barr well knew where the revolutionaries, as he called them, got their taxi fare. Union dues, of course. But many of them had slept between clean sheets and ate good food in homes in Caracas and Maracaibo during the seventy-nine-day strike, sponsored by merchants and industrialists who supported their movement and loathed the dictatorship. They're being financed by the same people now, Barr thought. That's why that son of a bitch can rent a taxi in Caripito and ride out here to my office to stick his tongue out at me. That's why they can afford to run for office in state and city elections. And they'll probably win some, too. But I know what the workers need, he thought, and I'll see that they get it, but I'll do it because I want to, not because somebody says I have to do it . . .

And the revolutionaries won some—too many for Lopez Contreras. He made harsh speeches against them, calling them Communists. His newspapers inveighed against them. And finally he ordered the political parties disbanded. Almost fifty political leaders were sent into exile in chains.

Barr happened to be in Caracas when the manacled men were placed in trucks to be taken to a seaport and shoved aboard the ship *Flanders*. He studied every man that was loaded up, and

Roberto Fontenot was not among them. Barr later learned that Fontenot and some others had escaped the dragnet and had gone underground. Well, Barr thought, who will pay their taxi fare now?

Chapter Thirteen

Tubbagut Timpson leaned against the cookshack and watched the five figures coming toward him in the shimmering morning sunlight. He had been watching them for ten minutes or more. They moved slowly. He had first noticed them when they broke clear of the heavy brush a half a mile away. He knew they were not from the drilling camp. All of the workers were at the drill site, down a hill to the east several hundred yards.

There was something wrong with one of them. He walked with a tight, mincing stride—like an American woman, Timpson thought. And he stumbled repeatedly on the rough ground. Timpson stuck his head in the cookshack window. "One of you get down to the rig and get Grady Barr!" he snapped. "Tell him to hurry!"

One of the cooks took off on the run. The five figures halted; they had seen the racing cook, Timpson figured. They sat down on the ground. Timpson rolled a Bull Durham cigarette and lit it. He was the camp boss, but he was willing to let Grady Barr deal with this. Timpson knew he was taking a chance on getting his butt chewed out, for Barr was as fractious about this well as Timpson had ever seen him. He had been hovering over it like a mother hen since the well was spudded in, frowning and barking orders.

Barr came around the corner of the cookshack. "What the purple-starred hell is going on, Tubbagut?" he asked, obviously irritated by the summons.

Timpson pointed to the five figures. They had risen to their feet at Barr's arrival at the cookshack. "They came out of that brush, Grady. You don't see no strangers wandering around in this country very damn often, do you?"

"No, you don't." Barr touched Timpsons shoulder. "Well, let's get it over with." They began walking toward the five figures. As they neared them, they saw five ragged, bearded men. One of the men held up a hand in greeting. "Fierce looking bastards, ain't they?" Timpson said. Four of the men had blood-stained rags wrapped around their feet. The fifth—the one who had walked in such a peculiar manner—was wearing a woman's high-heeled shoes. "Goddamn, Grady, they look plumb starved to death!"

"Who are you?" Barr asked the man who had held up his hand. The man shook his head that he didn't understand. Barr repeated the question in Spanish. Again the man shook his head, but he rattled off a string of sentences and looked at Barr inquiringly.

"I think that's French," Barr said to Timpson. "Run down to the . . ." He stopped. "Send somebody down to the rig to get the Coonass. I think he might be able to talk to them." The Coonass was Henry Thibodeaux, a Cajun from South Louisiana. "I think they need more food than medicine. Got any food ready?"

"Plenty," Timpson said.

"Food," said the man who had held up his hand, as if the word were part of a universal language. And he shoveled imaginary food into his mouth with both hands. Forgotten were the jungle sores, the weariness, the bloody feet. Bright-eyed, the others bobbed their heads, and the man with the woman's shoes chirped like a bird.

Barr led them to the cookshack. Timpson sent a runner for the Coonass. Cooks ladled huge bowls of steaming stew and placed long loaves of bread on a long wooden table. The men ate, breaking the loaves with their hands, spooning the hot stew into their mouths, rolling their eyes in ecstasy, talking around mouths full of food, gesturing with the bread to emphasize a point. They emptied their bowls and cooks refilled them from the cauldron. More loaves were placed on the table. Coffee was served in large white mugs. Again the stew disappeared and ready hands refilled the bowls.

"They're going to get sick," Barr said.

"Who gives a shit," Timpson said. "Let 'em enjoy it now."

The Coonass arrived. He stared at the eating men whose whiskers were wet with stew juice. "They're on their third bowls," Timpson said. "Jesus!" said the Coonass. "Where in the hell did they come from?"

"I hope you can find out," Barr said. "I think they're French."

The men cleaned out their bowls with bread. They looked at each other and smiled. The leader—the one who had held up his hand to greet Barr—sipped his coffee and belched with contentment. The others laughed as if they were all alone.

"They're French, all right," Coonass said. He began speaking French to the men. The leader frowned, struggling to understand, knowing he was hearing familiar sounds, then beginning to grasp the variation on his language. The others nodded their heads as they too began to catch on to Coonass' brand of Louisiana French. Then the leader responded. Now it was Coonass' time to be bewildered but, like the Frenchman, he began to understand. He cocked his head to listen, his face strained with concentration. He shook his head from time to time as if what he was hearing was almost beyond belief.

"Shiiiiiit!" Coonass said. When the leader paused, he turned to Barr. "He says they escaped from Devil's Island, Grady!"

"Let me hear it all," Barr said.

The men, Coonass related, had made their escape from the notorious French penal colony by canoe to French Guiana. Living like beasts because there was a price on their heads, they had traversed French Guiana, Dutch Guiana, British Guiana, and on through eastern Venezuela until they had spied the oil camp. They'd had enough; they had decided to stop even though they risked being turned over to the authorities.

The leader broke in. He talked, pointing around the kitchen. Coonass said, "He says he was a famous cook, a chef, at the most famous place in Paris, a restaurant called Pierre's. Says he can cook anything, says he hasn't forgotten anything about cooking."

"Why was he on Devil's Island?"

"Murder."

"Maybe. I don't think they send famous chefs to that kind of prison."

The leader grasped Barr's implication if not the words. He slit his throat with his forefinger. "Pierre!" Nodding, he spoke again.

Coonass laughed. "Says he killed Pierre, the restaurant owner, who was more famous than he was. Says he cut his throat with a bread knife."

"And I think he enjoyed it," Barr said. "What about the one in the woman's shoes?"

182

Coonass questioned the leader, and the leader spoke. "He says he stole them off a back porch in a town about a hundred kilometers back. Sounds like Caripito."

Suddenly the shack began to shake. Cups and bowls slid off the table. Pots and pans banged against walls. The men grabbed the table for support.

"Earthquake!" Timpson shouted. "Get outside!"

But Barr was already on the move. He was out of the cook shack and running across the clearing. The earth stopped shaking, but still Barr ran. He reached the crest of the hill and paused, looking down the slope to the drill site. The workers had deserted the rig and were standing in ones and twos about fifty yards away.

And then the well blew out.

So powerful was the first surge of oil and gas that it blew hundreds of feet of the four-inch drill pipe completely out of the hole. As Barr watched, the pipe sailed high over the crown block, spouting oil as it soared, and some of it crashed back down through the derrick, threading and twisting through the girts like spaghetti.

Rocks came hurtling out of the eight-inch casing, tearing the rig to pieces. Barr did not move; the men below had raced away from their positions to put even more distance between themselves and the wild well. Timpson, Coonass, the Frenchmen and the Venezuelan kitchen staff had pulled up beside Barr. The man who had worn the woman's shoes was barefooted now. The well had cleansed itself of rocks and trash and was spouting a gaseous crude oil alone. It was a majestic sight, Barr thought, that spume of oil rising high in the sky on the broad savanna. The Frenchmen were entranced. "Son of a bitch!" Timpson whispered in awe.

There was a great *whooosh*—and the oil spume burst into a mass of boiling flames and twisting black smoke. "A rock sparked it!" Timpson said.

Barr headed down the slope. The others trooped behind him. Heat from the fire radiated so that no one could get nearer than five hundred feet to it. One of the drillers, Ike Harris, came to meet Barr. He spat tobacco juice and wiped his mouth on the back of his hand. "I've seen a pretty good few of these, Grady, and this one here ain't gonna crater and it ain't gonna bridge over below the casing. That's my opinion." He waited for Barr's judgment.

"I think you're right," Barr said.

"You might have to call the Kinley brothers down here from

Houston," Harris suggested. "Floyd flew down here and put out a fire in the lake a couple of years ago."

"All he did was whipstock a directional well to the producing sand and pump it full of mud," Barr said. "We can do that ourselves, but goddamn, it'll take a long time."

"Shore will," Harris agreed.

Barr made up his mind. "Send some men to Caripito, Ike. Tell them to get everything we'll need to drill a directional well. And get some heavy mud, the heaviest in the warehouse." He shook his head. "Shit!" he said disgustedly.

Coonass had come up. With him was the barefooted Frenchman. Coonass was tentative. "Maybe you ought to hear this, Grady." He jerked his head at the barefooted Frenchman. "He says there's going to be another quake pretty soon. Damn soon, as a matter of fact."

"Wait a minute, Ike," Barr said to Harris.

"I'm telling you what he said," Coonass said. "He uses big words, Grady. He says a quake like the one we had . . ." He looked at the Frenchman. "There'll be an aftershock exactly half as strong in twenty or thirty minutes. That's what he says. And he says there'll be another aftershock behind that one, about half as strong, in forty minutes or an hour." Coonass shook his head vigorously. "He's a professor or something. Name's Aubert. Louis Aubert."

"Go on," Barr said. "He'd be popping his buttons to speak English, if he had any buttons on that shirt."

"Says this aftershock probably will shut off the fire. Probably seal it off at the bottom. Says he's seen it happen in Sumatra, wherever the hell that is."

Barr was as eager as a bird dog. "And that second aftershock? What about it?"

"Well, he says it could open it up again. Start the well flowing again. Says you ought to put a device on the well real quick if it shuts off. I guess he means like a Christmas tree, a connection." Coonass grinned. "I guess we'd have sense enough to do that, wouldn't we?"

"I think so," Barr said dryly. Then to Harris: "Hurry, Ike. Get that connection assembled. We can't use the derrick so we'll use that truck to mount it. Rig a boom on the truck's A-frame. I want to be ready to dangle the connection over that casing when she shuts off. Scoot!"

"But there probably ain't no threads on that casing, Grady. Not with the fire and all them rocks that came out of there."

"Get at it, goddamn it! There'll be threads. Get everybody moving! We haven't got much time."

Harris hurried away, shouting orders. Barr looked at the professor. The Frenchman was small and scrawny in his tattered clothing, and his beard and hair were nearly white. His sunken gray eyes watched Barr patiently as if he were awaiting judgment from yet another magistrate.

"Tell him if he's right, I'll buy him enough shoes to last him all his life," Barr said to Coonass. "Then ask him why he was on the island. Did he kill somebody, too?"

Coonass spoke and the Frenchman replied. Coonass turned grinning to Barr. "He says he was a forger and a counterfeiter. Says he worked on scientific papers, but says don't let that scare you. Says he's right about aftershocks." Coonass slapped the Frenchman's frail shoulder. "Says he knows about all kinds of engineering." The Frenchman nodded in silent affirmation. Coonass added, "He's kind of scared of you, Grady."

Barr nodded. "Tell him if the fire goes out, if the well shuts off, I want to cool everything off with water hoses. Ask him if that's all right."

Aubert wagged his head vigorously at the question, speaking rapidly and using his hands to illustrate his point. "Don't hose down the pipe," Coonass said. "He says it'll make it contract. Says cool off everything else, but wait as long as you can before you douse the casing. Says it'll crack if you don't."

Aubert spoke again. Coonass translated. "Says it's about time. Says everybody ought to sit down on the ground. Says it won't be near as bad as the quake, but it's safer to sit down."

Barr yelled, "Everything ready to go, Ike?"

"Yo!"

"Then everybody sit down! Right now!"

Seconds later the aftershock came, surprising even if expected, stronger than Barr had anticipated, strong enough to shake loose parts of the damaged derrick and inch equipment along the ground. But all eyes were on the whirlpool of flames and smoke above the casing's mouth. To Barr it seemed as if suddenly the casing had moved from beneath the flames, that the fire was burning by itself with no source of fuel, and just as suddenly it appeared as if it had been sucked down the casing by the devil himself.

Cessation of the roaring sound of the burning oil and gas created a silence that was quickly filled by shouts of excited men. Barr was on his feet before the final tremor. "Get it watered down, Coonass. Tell them how to do it."

While the area was being hosed down, Ike Harris showed Barr a long face. "There still ain't gonna be no threads on that casing to screw onto," he said dolefully.

"I'll bet five bucks you're wrong," Barr said. "After this, I feel as lucky as a shithouse rat."

Harris shook his head and walked away. The threads were there. Barr let the casing cool until Aubert said time was short. The shut-off device was affixed to the casing, going on smoothly.

"Now let 'er rip," Barr said happily. "If this next aftershock shakes things loose below, we've got her shut in. If it doesn't, all we have to do is go back in the hole and drill through the bridge and bring her in properly."

"I didn't call that bet," Harris said. "You know that, Grady."

But Barr had turned away, lost in thought. He called to Coonass and led the way to Aubert, who was still sitting on the ground. "Ask him how widespread the quake was. Maybe he knows." Barr could not hide his anxiety as Coonass questioned and Aubert replied.

"He says we just got the tail-end, Grady. Says he don't know where it centered, but he thinks it was a long ways from here."

Barr nodded slowly. "I was afraid of that."

Epicenter of the quake was in the Pacific Ocean about ten miles off the shores of Ecuador. More than thirty thousand persons lost their lives in that coastal province, and dozens of towns and villages were leveled. The main thrust of the quake followed a giant fault that cut across the country and through southern Colombia and southeastern Venezuela. Fortunately, the Colombian and Venezuelan areas were sparsely settled and deaths were few and damage slight.

At the wildcat well site Barr had worried that Maturin and Caripito had been badly shaken, but only weak tremors were felt there. Wells in some fields increased their output by as much as twenty percent because of the quake . . .

The quake brought to eastern Venezuela Eduardo Vigas, chief technical inspector for the Ministry of Mines and Hydrocarbons. On a bright morning he appeared unannounced in Caripito only to learn that Barr was himself making an inspection tour of the

Quiriquire field. Vigas drove to the field. He was directed to an area where Barr was having his look at a new well. Barr was alone and on foot when Vigas spied him. Vigas parked his car and hurried to catch up with Barr. As he drew near, Barr began climbing up on the rig floor of a well that was being drilled.

Vigas could hear the driller cursing as he manhandled a fishing tool. He heard Barr ask, "What's the matter, Willie? You sound like a bear with a sore ass."

"This tool ain't no good, Grady. It won't work."

Barr was wearing a white suit, but he took the greasy tool from the driller. His big hands moved as quickly as a magician's. He handed the tool back to the driller. "You just weren't holding your mouth right, Willie." He jerked a rag from Willie's back pocket and wiped his hands.

As he turned to come down off the rig floor, Barr saw Vigas looking up at him. Vigas was grinning. Barr was slow to recognize him. Finally he said tentatively, "Eddie? Eddie Vigas?"

Vigas nodded, still grinning broadly.

Barr grunted. "You took your own sweet time in getting out this way," he said sourly. He climbed down from the rig floor and faced Vigas. Vigas still did not speak, but his grin was radiant. "Shit!" Barr said disgustedly, then he took quick strides and threw his arms around Vigas and held him like a brother.

They talked away the afternoon in Barr's bungalow at Caripito, stripped to the waist and drinking Dutch beer from Barr's new electric refrigerator. Vigas could hardly believe Barr's books, his new command of English, his study of written Spanish and the ranging interests the books had created. Barr was impressed with Vigas' hard-won poise, his certitude born of work and study, his maturity. They laughed about the French fugitives, and Barr explained that the chef, Marcel Revere, was making gourmet meals in the mess hall from routine supplies the camp was furnished. "Professor" Louis Aubert was working with the camp engineers in designing some new installations and the other three Frenchmen were working as roughnecks and had been welcomed into the Venezuelan community.

Christina, Vigas said, was married to an American naval officer and living in Virginia. She had two children, a boy and a girl, and appeared to be quite happy. He spoke of Cerro Soto, and both grieved while Vigas tried to explain that Cerro Soto was a good man who died because of his loyalty to an evil one. "I couldn't blame the mob," Vigas said. "He was a symbol of the dictator to them, and they were just hitting out in every direction." Barr nodded gravely that he understood.

When the strong Dutch beer finally took hold, Barr broke a lifelong rule and told of his affair with Elvira Obregon, his firing, the shooting in Maracay, his rehiring. And something reminded him of the Perija, and he described his wonder at meeting the Motilons, seeing it at this later date as the rare, momentous occurrence it was.

But Vigas wanted to talk about *his* women. He had freely awarded his virginity to a long-haired Austin waitress who loved to wrap her blonde tresses around his penis. In Norman, Oklahoma, while obtaining his master's degree, he had spent many an evening with a college librarian who boasted that her Cherokee blood was untainted and that chieftains dangled from every branch of her family tree. And there had been a schoolteacher in Midland and a widow in Longview. "All of them wanted to marry me," he bragged, putting aside an empty beer bottle and opening a full one. "They didn't care if I looked like a mescan."

As for inspecting Cajun's eastern fields, he said it wasn't necessary. Grady Barr knew how to drill a well the way a well should be drilled, and Vigas knew that Barr would jump all over a careless worker. Barr wouldn't fuck up a fragile reservoir by overdrilling, Vigas said, the way some of those bastards appeared willing to do in the Maracaibo Basin. He had six assistants who were kept busy, too. And his assistants, they were all treated like mescans, just like all the other Venezuelans. Busy, busy, Vigas was always busy with his inspections because it was so necessary.

To keep Vigas from brooding, Barr asked lightly, "And what do you do for amusement, Eddie?"

"I keep track of things," Vigas said. His smile was sly. "I keep records on production, for one thing. On refining. On exports and imports. Things like that."

"But other people in the ministry do that, don't they?"

The sly smile. "Sure. A bureau. But they take the companies' word for everything."

Barr had not expected such a reply to his question. From Vigas' manner, Barr felt sure the companies' figures and Vigas' figures didn't correspond. And Vigas wasn't keeping track of things to be amused. There had to be a strong reason for a man to expend the effort such work demanded. Politics? Barr wondered.

"Lopez Contreras will probably give you a bonus for that overtime work, Eddie. I hear that he's relaxing a little."

"Because he has to," Vigas said grimly.

"I hear that some of the exiles are trickling back in," Barr said "and some of the underground men have surfaced. Somebody told me, I don't remember who, that the political parties are forming up again, and he's not doing anything to stop them."

"He can't afford to," Vigas said in the same grim voice. "Hitler and Mussolini are seeing to that. They're showing the world what a dictatorship is. He doesn't want to be compared with them."

"That makes sense," Barr said, then added casually, "This Roberto Fontenot, the general's son, you must have known him at the Liceo Caracas. Didn't you tell me you went to school there?"

"I knew him," Vigas said. "I thought he was a wild-eyed rebel and he thought I was a believer in the divine right of kings." He was getting drunk. "We both were wrong."

"How?" Barr asked.

"We just were. Both of us."

"Do you ever get a chance to see him, Eddie?"

"No!" Vigas said too quickly and too vehemently, and Barr knew that he had lied.

With a sudden movement, Vigas thrust his beer bottle aside. He leaned across the table and grasped Barr's wrist. "Listen, Grady," he said urgently, "why in the hell don't both of us get out of this damn country. Go to the States. Go for ourselves." He squeezed the wrist tighter. "We'd make a hell of a team, Grady, you and me. We'd show them how to find that oil. Pick up some leases and drill hell out of 'em!" He shook Barr's wrist. "You and me, Grady! Let's do it!" He shook Barr's wrist again, then slumped forward on the table. He released his hold on Barr, and passed out.

Barr put him to bed in the spare bedroom. He returned to the kitchen, got a bottle of beer from the refrigerator and sat back at the table. He's keeping records for Fontenot, Barr told himself, and God knows what else he's doing. He doesn't like *all* he's doing, that's why he talked so strong about getting out. But that was drunk talk. He'll stay—you couldn't run him off with a cannon.

He's not a born conspirator like most of the brainy ones in this country, Barr thought as he sipped his beer. He hates the necessary deception. He's being paid by Lopez Contreras' government, but he's doing his hardest work for the opposition. Barr drank again, slowly and thoughtfully, sorting out what he considered to be Vigas' true feeling, arriving at a conclusion as he sat the near empty bottle on the table: Vigas was not so much against the government and for the opposition as he was against what he considered the white-man oil companies, and since the government was in league with the oil companies then he must help the opposition. It has little or nothing to do with patriotism, Barr conceded to himself; it is a personal vendetta.

Barr had agreed with Charles Cannon that Vigas could do no more than nag the companies over regulatory matters as long as Lopez Contreras sat in Miraflores Palace and his successor was another greedy Andino. Now Barr was not so sure. Of late his spies had been telling him that Fontenot and others were already moving freely about the country, promising to visit every village and town and city in every state, preaching one basic sermon: the companies were taking the oil out of the country and selling it at a great profit in which the Venezuelans were not sharing. "It's the first genuine political campaign in the country's history," one of his spies told Barr, "and the people are listening." Another said, "They also are saying that what oil revenue the government is getting is not being spent wisely and for the betterment of the people." Another warned, "The companies have not recognized them, but the unions are growing stronger."

Barr got up and went to the doorway to look in at the sleeping Vigas. He was still sprawled across the bedspread as Barr had placed him. Barr felt a flash of pity for the younger man, mistreated and unhappy in the States, unhappy at home where he served two masters to further a revenge that might never come to pass. Barr was more than merely grateful for Vigas' help in the past; he was fond of him. Standing in the doorway, Barr decided that he would keep his thoughts on Vigas to himself and not expose him to covert attack by Charles Cannon or direct action by the government. But he wouldn't let Vigas damage the company, either. He couldn't allow that. If the time came when Vigas established himself as a positive threat, Barr would do what was necessary to deflate him. He hoped the time would never come . . .

It was too late to visit the mess hall, so Barr dined on cheese and olives and smoked fish from his refrigerator and brewed a pot of coffee. He turned away from a novel he was eager to read to instead study the Spanish grammar he had recently acquired.

Elvira had taught him how to study, and for that he would be forever grateful. He studied until eleven o'clock. Vigas had not awakened by that time, so Barr went to bed himself.

Vigas woke him up at six in the morning, singing out at Barr's bedroom door, "Wake up, Jake, day's a'breakin', coffee's in the pot and the hoe cake's bakin'!" Vigas laughed at the slow-wakening Barr. "There was a landlady in West Texas who used to wake up a whole boarding house with that," he chortled.

"I hope you told her to kiss your ass," Barr grumbled. He sat up on the side of the bed and rubbed a hand across his face. "I hope you're not shitting me about the coffee."

"Do you want it before or after you clean up?"

"Both," Barr said.

They breakfasted on pork chops and eggs in the mess hall. There Vigas made his only reference to the night before. "It doesn't take much to make me drunk," he said sheepishly. "I hope I didn't talk your arm off."

Barr said gravely, "Just bragging about your women. You hadn't completed the list when you decided to go to sleep."

Impulsively, Vigas reached across the table and touched Barr's arm. "Grady," he said earnestly, "let's don't ever lose sight of each other."

Touched, Barr said, "We're friends for life, Eddie."

By noon Barr had brought Vigas up to date on the operations in all of Cajun's eastern fields, and by two o'clock Vigas was on his way back to Caracas. He had taken Barr's word on conditions in the fields in lieu of a week-long inspection. No, Barr told himself, changing his mind, that's not it. He already knew what was going on out here. Somebody out here is keeping records for him, somebody he trusts.

He told his secretary to bring him the personnel files, and he locked his door for an afternoon of study.

Barr had said that he knew the needs of the Venezuelan workers and that he would see that those needs were satisfied, but that he would do so because he wanted to, not because somebody said he had to do it. When the Earthquake field showed every sign of becoming the largest and best field in eastern Venezuela, Barr reported to Cannon in Caracas:

"Last Monday Earthquake 12 was started up with an entire Venezuelan crew, running one tour only, and progress has been quite good. A second Venezuelan crew was added on Friday. It is too early to judge definitely how the experiment will turn out, but I am convinced that with more experience the Venezuelans will make satisfactory drillers. . . ."

A brick hospital was built at Quiriquire, modern in every respect. Barr reported: "Dr. Leoni and his staff of technicians have performed twenty-six major operations and sixty minor ones in the eight months the hospital has been open. It is my plan to open the hospital to all Venezuelans in the area whether or not they are company employees. Last week saw the opening of the first aid station in Caripito, with a Venezuelan physician in charge, and it will be a complete dispensary by year's end. Doctors are also stationed at Cumarebo and Maturin. . . ."

Again he wrote: "The 100th new house for employees was completed Tuesday, and the others are right on schedule. They are equipped with modern sanitary facilities and are on drained streets. As you know, the first Venezuelans who moved into these houses almost destroyed them because they did not understand the proper function of the toilets and other facilities. To prevent recurrence of such incidents, classes are being conducted for prospective tenants. . . .

"At the suggestion of Eric Seybold, my new assistant, an Industrial Relations Office has been opened to hear worker complaints and problems. Schools to promote safety and better understanding of intricate equipment have been established, also at Seybold's suggestion.

Seybold occasionally sent in reports to Caracas when Barr was busy in the fields. While Barr generally approved the reports, one infuriated him. It said: "The Venezuelan mess hall in Caripito was closed Wednesday and all monthly employees, foreign and national, began eating together in the main dining room. The operation has started off nicely, and it appears the new arrangement will prove entirely practicable. . . ." Seybold should have stopped there, but he added: "The reaction of the Venezuelan staff to the consolidation of the two mess halls has been very favorable, and we believe any claim of discrimination or differentiation between the foreign and national staff in this connection, which might have been made previously, has now finally been eliminated. . . ."

In his coldest voice, Barr told Seybold, "Those two mess halls weren't consolidated to satisfy a son of a bitch outside the officers of this company. Not to erase any claim of discrimination. Not to kiss some union organizer's ass, or some government big shot. I did it because I thought it needed being done—*and because I wanted to!*"

During the building program Barr initiated there were certain structures which seemed to be erected by shadows in the villages near the various producing fields. Barr appeared to be unaware of them, and they were never mentioned in his reports. The buildings were all similar in size and design.

The first one sprang up at Mata Blanca when Elena Garza came to the village looking for a place to rent. She couldn't find one, but she found a lot of American oilmen who remembered her from other oilfields or had heard about her. In the days that followed, Ray Soupstone, Cajun's warehouse boss, noticed that every time a toolpusher ordered cement he always asked for a couple of extra sacks, "just in case." So it was that Soupstone was not surprised one day to see a new building going up on the outskirts of the village though no workmen were on the job. That night he investigated and found Cajun employees laboring at the site under the direction of Skinny Morris, a Cajun engineer. Soupstone pitched in and helped. Soon Elena Garza had a shiny new cantina. And shortly thereafter she stocked the place with nine young women, brought into the country by Rico the rum smuggler, who had brought in Barr's Trinidadian roughnecks. Rico was accommodating enough to supply the ten other cantinas that mushroomed near the other fields.

Barr during this period was not celibate, but he was discreet. At separate times three women of Caripito were part of his life. So much so that a wit remarked with admiration in a Caripito cantina: "Rico the smuggler has brought in so many condoms for that son of a bitch that if you tied 'em end to end you could make a slingshot that would shoot a rock to the North Pole!"

Barr was inspecting the new Josephine field in the state of Anzoategue when he received a radio message that he had a visitor in Caripito. The radio communications system was new, a company-government project that could not have been installed in the days of Gomez. Gomez had been content with the single galvanized wire that stretched across the country; to him, radio was a Communist device.

Even on the air waves the chief clerk could not keep the excitement out of his voice. "It's Mr. Craig! He wants you back here right away!" John Henry Craig was chairman of the board of SeaCoast International and the most powerful figure in the world of oil. "Anybody with him?" Barr asked. "No, he's by himself, Mr. Barr." "I'm on the way," Barr said.

Barr was nervous on the flight back to Caripito. He had never met or been in communication with any high-ranking SCI official, much less the board chairman. He had seen newspaper photographs of Craig; he was a huge man, tall and heavy with a jowly, moon-shaped face and thinning gray hair, strongly resembling ex-President Herbert Hoover, a close friend of Craig's. Barr had heard the legends of Craig's boldness, his resourcefulness, his ability to sway government leaders. Now he was going to meet him face to face, and he hadn't the vaguest idea of why Craig was in eastern Venezuela. Why hadn't he been briefed on what to expect from Craig? And why was Craig alone? Where was his usual entourage? Fuck it, Barr finally told himself; I'll find out in due time . . .

Craig was not waiting in the reception room but in Barr's office, seated behind Barr's desk and reading one of Barr's books, *You Can't Do Business With Hitler.* He closed the book and stood up at Barr's entry. His big belly rumbled as he straightened up. He patted it fondly and smiled engagingly at Barr. "Your clerk brought me some food from the mess hall that was as fine as I ever ate. And he told me how you obtained your chief cook. Quite a good yarn." He offered Barr a massive hand, which Barr shook. "I'll continue to use your chair, if you don't mind," he said, and he sat back down in Barr's chair. Barr took the visitor's seat in front of the desk.

Despite his disarming manner, Craig's pale blue eyes were cold. "They tell me you used to be a pimp," Craig said. "Do you find that background useful in the oil business?"

"I do." Barr showed no surprise at the question.

"There are several members of the board who wouldn't grant you that."

"Is that why I'm still a manager and not a vice-president?"

"I expect so." Craig changed the subject abruptly. "I'm here to inspect the fields and the facilities. I want you to ignore me and continue on with your normal duties. I can take care of myself. Your assistant assured me that you would be happy to let me use your spare bedroom, and I assumed he was correct. He had my luggage moved in."

"He did just right," Barr said.

Craig stood up. "Very well. I will begin at once."

Barr stood up. "If you're going to begin your inspection in this

194

area, I'd like for you to eat with me in my bungalow about seven. The mess hall serves at six, but that's a little early for me."

Craig smiled. "What's the martini situation?"

"Five-thirty, in my kitchen," Barr said promptly. "In the field, you're on your own."

"I'll manage," Craig said. He squeezed around the desk, got his Stetson from a rack and left the office.

He was at Barr's house when Barr reached there at five o'clock. Barr heard him being noisy in the shower. He came out of the shower and heard Barr moving around in the kitchen. "Don't bruise the gin!" he said loudly. "I won't!" Barr sang back. He stirred a pitcher of martinis. He turned from his work when he heard Craig come into the room.

Barr saw a huge globe of a belly rising up to wide shoulders and three chins. For the first time, he really looked at Craig's face. It was a pink moon with a small baby's mouth, a button nose and the pale blue eyes, big and round beneath heavy white brows. The thinning gray hair was sleeked back. Small, neat ears completed the picture. But the eyes were the man; cold, hard and eternally questioning. The golden dressing gown draped on Craig's massive frame could have carpeted a bedroom floor. His bare legs were larger than Barr's thighs, and his slippers looked like picnic baskets.

"Quite a sight, I imagine," he said pleasantly. "I hope you don't mind this attire."

"Not at all," Barr said. He poured drinks while Craig got seated at the round table. When Barr sat down Craig lifted his glass and said, "May our enemies be confounded." Barr clicked his glass against Craig's and said, "For the rest of their days." Craig sipped his drink. "Ah, it has the proper sting. Not too much vermouth." He sat the glass down as Barr took a sip from his.

In his abrupt manner, Craig said, "Cannon says you're pressing him to enlarge the refinery here. What's the urgency?"

"There's a war coming on. We might not be able to get the necessary steel and equipment if we don't get it pretty soon."

"Then you don't believe Mr. Hitler, that he simply wants what he considers his?"

"No, I don't."

"And the British?"

"They're arming, trying to catch up. Somewhere along the line, I have no idea where, Hitler will put them in a position where they have to fight. He may even do it by mistake."

195

"And the United States?"

Barr shook his head. "I don't know. I think Roosevelt will want to help England, if she's attacked, but who knows how the American people will feel about it."

Craig nodded. "I wonder what a war would do to the oil business?" he mused.

Barr drank, content to accept the question as rhetorical.

Craig shrugged his wide shoulders. "Well, we shall see, if you are on target." He drained his glass. Barr got the pitcher from the refrigerator, drained his glass, then refilled them both. As he put the pitcher away, Craig asked, "Have you heard about Texaco's little problem?"

"Down here?" Barr asked.

"No, no. Mr. Roosevelt finally learned that Texaco had diverted shipments of oil from Belgium to Franco in violation of the neutrality laws." Craig smiled. "He slapped their wrist. Not much else he could do with the revolution over and Franco the winner."

"I'm sure he can be tougher than that," Barr said. "Germany and Italy are stockpiling, and everybody's supplying them. But if war comes to Europe, I suspect that Roosevelt would like to see those supplies cut off."

"Does that disturb you, everybody supplying Germany and Italy at the moment?"

Barr said evenly, "Nothing disturbs me but my own shortcomings."

Craig closed his eyes for a moment. "Laudable," he murmured. Then, "What if SCI was doing business with Germany, something besides selling her oil, something not exactly secretive but, shall we say, unpublicized."

"If it has something to do with Germany's war potential, I'd say publicize it immediately and try to get out of it. If my opinion was asked."

"But, ah . . . it may not be that easy."

"Easier now than later," Barr said flatly. "If there is a war, and I think there will be, and if the United States gets in it, and I think they will, any unpublicized dealings will damn sure get publicized somehow. History proves that."

"You don't mind speaking your mind, do you?" Craig said mildly.

"I assumed you wanted me to." Barr killed his drink. "They

196

won't bring our food until I order it. Do you think we can stand another martini or two?"

Craig smiled. "By all means! I was hoping you'd suggest it."

Barr stirred another pitcher of martinis and poured drinks. Craig said, "You're not completely awed by this surprise visit by the chairman of the board, are you? You're not diffident in the slightest."

Barr grinned. "Like you suggested this afternoon, I've always got another trade to fall back on . . . for a few more years." The grin disappeared. "I think I've learned a lot in the past ten or fifteen years. I think I've grown a lot. I like to think I can be at ease in a Caripito pool hall or Miraflores Palace." He paused. "And I think I've done a damned good job for Cajun." He poured fresh drinks. "I'm not afraid to drink with you because I know how to drink, and I'm pretty sure you do, too. I've fouled up once since I've been with the company. It didn't have anything to do with excessive drinking, as I'm sure you know. But I learned my lesson." He drank from his glass. "Now I've said everything I'm going to say in that regard, so let's have another drink and then eat supper. Tomorrow you can go out and inspect to your heart's content."

Craig held out his empty glass for Barr to fill. "Speaking of women," he said, gazing at his brimming glass, "I met a remarkable woman when I was in my late twenties." He looked up at Barr. "Do you mind this?"

"I want to hear it," Barr said, though he was more than a little surprised at Craig's sudden change of tone.

"She wasn't a 'loose woman.' She came from what was called a good family in those days."

Barr nodded.

"Of course I was a lot slimmer in those days," Craig said, smiling.

Barr nodded.

"Well, to get to the point, while we were making love—I was on top of her—she reached around and under her leg and gently squeezed my balls." Craig paused, waiting for Barr's nod.

Barr nodded.

"Well, that was it. We both climaxed immediately after that. I think it was the high point of my sex life."

"I can understand that," Barr said gravely.

"I mean . . . it was so unexpected," Craig said, remembering.

"It came as a complete surprise." Almost shyly he added, "We were never together again. I was on the move a lot in those days."

Barr nodded, waiting.

"I've thought about it often," Craig said. "I've wondered if she were accustomed to doing that. If she had done it before . . . with someone else . . ."

"I don't believe so," Barr said promptly. "It was an impulsive thing, something she suddenly wanted to do because she was enjoying herself so much. You said she was a nice girl, didn't you?"

"She came from a good family," Craig said. "She didn't have a bad reputation."

"Then I'm sure I'm right," Barr said with finality. "It was an impulsive, passionate gesture. She probably never did it again in her life, even with her husband, if she had one."

"I had that feeling myself about it," Craig said. "I said I've wondered about it, and that's true, but I felt all along it was like you said."

"You were just doing a good job on her and she couldn't help it," Barr said.

Craig nodded. Then abruptly, "Well, shall we see what your chef has prepared for us?" He was bright, ready for food. A ghost had been laid.

Craig was up at five the next morning. He spoke briefly with Barr before going to the mess hall for breakfast at six. By seven he was on his way to Goober field, riding in the back seat of a vehicle he selected at the motor pool and driven by the motor pool manager whom he ordered behind the wheel.

Barr kept track of him by radio in the days that followed, but he made no effort to influence the inspection in his favor. Craig obviously knew his business, according to the radio reports. In the more remote camps where mules were still the conventional mode of transportation, only the sturdiest animals were capable of bearing his bulk. "The mules are afraid he's going to eat 'em," one superintendent chuckled to Barr over the radio. "If he stays an extra day, you're going to have to send me some extra rations."

Craig had said that he intended to spend at least three weeks on the inspection tour, but he returned to Caripito in the middle of the third week. He explained that he wanted to give Quiri-quire field a more thorough examination, and would spend the remaining days at that chore. Barr welcomed him with martinis and a promise of a good supper.

Craig was pleasant, but he went to his room right after eating. And he was up at five the next morning on his rounds. Barr did not hear from him during the day, but Craig was back at the bungalow and ready for martinis at five-fifteen. He looked tired and spoke little. He toyed with an excellent casserole of sauteed veal and shrimp cooked with asparagus, cheese and chablis. He excused himself and went to his bedroom shortly afterwards.

Barr went to bed about ten o'clock, but woke up about three in the morning. At first he thought the casserole had upset his stomach, but then he heard a noise in his room. Suddenly his light clicked on. Barefooted, in rumpled polka dot pajamas, Craig stood in the center of the room glaring at him.

"Wake up, Grady!" the old man said peevishly.

Barr sat up on the side of the bed.

"I'm tired of this damned foolishness," Craig growled. "As of right now you're the president of Cajun, and I want you to be in Caracas by the first of next month." He turned to leave the room without waiting for a word from Barr. At the door he tossed back over his shoulder, "Get some sleep. I'm getting the hell out of this damned country in the morning."

"Wait a minute!" Barr said.

Craig stopped and turned around. "Charley Cannon's moving up to the SCI board," he said.

"I figured that, but what about Ed Gurwell? He outranks me."

"We'll transfer him to Colombia or the Middle East."

"No! Don't do that. Let me keep him and give him a fat raise. I'll need him for a year or so."

Craig's smile was frosty. "A good thought." He left the room.

Barr rummaged around in his night table drawers until he found a crumpled package containing three cigarettes, badly bent. He took his time lighting one, savoring the moment, savoring the first deep drag, savoring Craig's words, thinking suddenly, absurdly, of the malicious grin on the face of the tall, big-hatted Texas Ranger as he padlocked the door of the Shark's Head in Galveston so long ago, thinking immediately then of Gomez and wishing against his will that the dictator could come back long enough to see Barr sitting behind his president's desk in Caracas.

He lit another cigarette from the butt of the first, grinning inwardly, knowing full well that his knowledge, skill, hard work and dedication to duty were no more important to gaining the presidency of Cajun Petroleum Corporation than his solemn explanation of why the girl from the good family had done what she had done to John Henry Craig.

BOOK THREE

CARACAS

Chapter Fourteen

World War II began in Europe, and the British blockade shut off the flow of Venezuelan oil to Germany and Italy. Production slowed down in every field. Grady Barr spent most of 1940 hunting—and finding—new outlets for Cajun's oil in neighboring South American countries. Shell and Gulf followed his lead. The sag in production was halted. The next year, the U.S. government bought huge quantities of Venezuelan oil to supplement American oil shipments to the British, and by year's end the Venezuelan companies had chalked up a new production record.

But the Japanese bombing of Pearl Harbor ended the boom. Venezuela broke off relations with the Axis powers, and the Caribbean became a hunting ground for Nazi submarines. If the Germans could cut off the supply of oil from the Maracaibo Basin, they would be striking a major blow at the Allies.

On the night of February 14, 1942, torpedoes destroyed seven ocean tankers, fully laden, within sight of the Venezuelan shore. And the next day in Caracas Barr got a frantic call from Cajun's marine superintendent in Maracaibo. "Mr. Barr! They've got a tanker afire at Aruba and now they're shelling the refinery!"

"I just got the word from Ward Hawkins at the refinery," Barr said, "and all he can do is hunker down and take it. The Venezuelan troops are shooting rifles at them." Barr was calm.

"Yes," said the superintendent, "but there's something else." His voice was freighted with fear and worry. "Thirty-two lake tankers cleared the bar this morning for Aruba. They're in the Gulf of Venezuela right now."

"Can you stop them?"

"We don't have radio communications with the fleet," the superintendent said, and in his voice was the undertone of an ancient grievance. "We never have had."

"Gulf's got one of those amphibian airplanes," Barr said. "Get hold . . ."

"Not any more, Mr. Barr. They flew it back to the States."

"Is there *any* aircraft at Maracaibo?"

"Not that I know of." The superintendent was on Barr's thinking line. "How about the military, Mr. Barr?"

"No, the tanker crews wouldn't know what the hell was happening. They'd probably think there was a revolution going on."

"Uh huh, and they'd probably zigzag to hell and back."

"We'll do it from here, Shilstone. Keep in touch with my office."

Barr called the airport and told the Cajun superintendent what was going on and what he wanted to do. The only plane available, the superintendent said, was a BC-40 Taylorcraft. "It's so damned slow we might have to get out and push it, Mr. Barr." Barr told him to get it ready.

He sent out a call for every map case in the Cajun building. Secretaries were put to work writing a brief message: "Subs ahead. Turn around." The messages were stuffed in the map cases and loaded into Barr's Cadillac. Barr, riding in the front seat with his chauffeur, got them to the airport. They were placed aboard the plane, a two-seater with the pilot and passenger sitting side by side. Two Cajun pilots were ready to make the flight.

But Barr shucked his coat and loosened his tie. "No, Horace," he told one of the pilots. "I wouldn't miss this to see Peter walk the water." He overrode all protests and climbed aboard the plane. He grinned at the pilot. "Drive carefully, Jojo. You've got precious cargo aboard."

Once airborne, Jojo said, "Bored, Mr. Barr?" His tone was noncommittal, and he looked straight ahead.

Barr glanced at him. Finally he said, "Exactly. I was bored stiff."

"Well, hang on to your ass because this crate has to strain every gut to do a hundred." Jojo didn't speak again on the flight over the mountains, flatlands and finally the Gulf of Venezuela. Barr was so wrapped up in the urgency of their mission that he was slow to realize that Jojo resented a non-flyer, president of the company or not, accompanying him on a dangerous assignment where a second pilot's knowledge and skills could mean the difference between success and failure, perhaps life and death. Jojo broke his silence when they spied the long line of tankers ahead of them. He reached behind him and got a pair of goggles. He handed them to Barr. "You'll need these when I open a window for you to throw out of." Barr put on the goggles.

Crews of the tankers began coming out on deck when Jojo flew over them. The plane was a bright yellow, Cajun's corporate color, and Cajun's name was emblazoned in black on both sides. Many of the crewmen waved. Jojo flew out ahead of the tankers, then turned the plane around.

"I'm going to make a pass from one end to the other," he said. "Drop as many as you can."

Barr lowered his window slowly, but still the howling wind sucked at him. He gathered up all the map cases his left arm would hold against his body.

"Here we go!" Jojo shouted, and he took the plane down in a shallow dive. He leveled off not more than fifty feet above the tankers. The wind tore the first case out of Barr's right hand as he stuck it outside the window to drop it. Thereafter he made no attempt to aim, but simply got the cases through the window as best he could. Jojo completed the run, then banked the plane to fly back. Barr rolled up his window.

"Not a hit," Jojo said, but his tone was not accusatory.

The cases had missed the tankers by a wide margin, some as much as a hundred yards. The crews were paying no attention to the cases, but it was obvious they were cheering Jojo and Barr, and were waiting for them to make another run. "Why don't somebody net one of 'em aboard, the silly bastards," Jojo muttered.

"They won't do that," Barr said. "As far as they know, the cases are empty. They probably think we're a couple of drunks. We've got to lay one on the deck."

"Well, let's do it then."

Jojo made adjustments for the wind, then made another pass. This time Barr could see the cases as the wind carried them toward the tankers, but even with Jojo maneuvering the plane at Barr's hand signals every case overshot the mark. Though he had reasoned why the sailors ignored the cases in the water, Barr cursed them in a dull monotone. "You'd think at least the captains would be curious, goddamn it!" Meanwhile he was cleaning out his trouser's pockets, placing the contents on the floor. He began sneaking out of his trousers. Jojo watched him suspiciously.

Barr tied each trouser leg around a map case. "This ought to make somebody pay attention. I'm going to drop this when you're level with the third tanker, Jojo. Hope to Christ I hit *something!*"

"You're thinking they'll net those britches if they see the cases tied to 'em?"

"That's what I'm thinking. I don't want to have to jump out of this goddamned plane to make them wake up!"

"Here we go," Jojo said, and Barr lowered his window, trousers in hand. Just before the plane drew even with the third tanker, Barr tossed out trousers and cases. Jojo, as well as Barr, could see them buffeted and whirled by the wind. Jojo banked the plane almost immediately and both of them saw the trousers land almost amidship of the third tanker. "Pray!" Jojo said. They saw a seaman grab the trousers and take them to someone else, probably the captain. "Pray!" Jojo said again as he flew in a taut circle around the third tanker. Barr was silent, but suddenly he heard his stomach rumble from the tension, and he thought with a small smile of John Henry Craig. "By God!" Jojo said. The captain—if that's who he was—had opened a map case and was reading the message. He waved a hand and disappeared into the wheelhouse. "He's spreading the word," Jojo said.

And indeed he had. He came back on deck, and at the same instant the lead tanker began circling to return to Lake Maracaibo. The captain waved at the plane in acknowledgement and appreciation.

"Wait and see," Jojo said. "I won't be able to buy a drink in Maracaibo if there's a tankerman in the joint. Not for a long time."

"I just hope you've got an extra pair of pants in the hangar," Barr said.

"Even the president might buy me a drink," Jojo said.

"He may at that," Barr said.

Jojo's lean face flushed. "I didn't mean you, Mr. Barr. I was talking about the president of the country."

"I know," Barr said. "The president of Cajun is going to buy you a half a dozen drinks—providing you come up with that pair of pants."

Jojo grinned. "We had us a time, didn't we, Mr. Barr?"

"We sure as hell did!"

206

* * *

The president of the country was General Isaias Medina, selected by Lopez Contreras as his successor and rubber-stamped by the Congress. Reluctantly, Lopez Contreras had passed over the reins in deference to a rag-tag Constitution which limited the presidency to five years without immediate succession. Medina was an Andino, to be sure, but he lacked Gomez' brutal, arrogant certitude and he had more than his share of Lopez Contreras' wishy-washiness. At times it seemed as if his chief concern was to resist the insistent tutelage of Lopez Contreras; when Medina appeared to be wavering on an issue, Lopez Contreras would announce that the moths had not yet eaten his uniform, that he was prepared to don it if necessary and march on Caracas from his Andean estate. Medina was also under a low-key but constant assault from Roberto Fontenot, who traveled the country spreading his brand of liberalism. And another foe, a secret one, stood waiting in the wings.

Meanwhile, the giant companies left Grady Barr and his counterparts to deal with Medina. They had problems at home and in the new oil province of the Middle East. Great new fields had been discovered in Kuwait and Saudi Arabia in 1938, joining the early fields found in Iran, Iraq and Bahrain Island. The fields could not be exploited, however, with the war going on. And so daily prayers went up from Houston, New York, Los Angeles, Pittsburgh and London that British troops would deny the spoils to the Axis powers.

In the States SCI was accused of treason by a senator who had led an investigation of SCI's pre-Pearl Harbor business dealings with German companies. And Texaco supplied oil to Germany after the war began in Europe and before Pearl Harbor, and also financed a German initiative aimed at dissuading America from supplying Britain with arms. The public somehow soon forgot these transgressions; the oil companies went their way while governments went theirs. To be sure, they called on each other when necessity demanded it, but even then they were secretive and suspicious, each ready to knife the other in the name of profit or national security.

Barr had not anticipated that the "map-case bombing" of the tankers would generate public interest, but he had not reckoned with the need for heroes both in the States and Venezuela. The U.S. was still reeling from the assault on Pearl Harbor, and anything that smacked of striking back at the foe was caught and held greedily as proof of the American spirit. The Venezuelans themselves had not had a hero since Simon Bolivar had torn the country from the clutches of Spain. The story was printed on the front pages of newspapers on both continents, with Barr's doffing of his trousers to turn the ships around to safety the chief "human interest" angle.

At an interview session, Barr saw among the reporters a tall woman with long brown hair, carelessly combed. The other reporters, all male, had trouble concentrating on the business at hand—the woman's breasts seemed to occupy all the free space in Barr's office. She wore a brown skirt with a plain white blouse that seemed ready to burst open. Her otherwise slender figure accentuated what was described in a whisper as her "chest muscles."

Barr had always had a secret smile for men who declared themselves to be obsessed with a woman's breasts. But noting the trim legs, the slim waist, the graceful neck, Barr decided quickly that in this case he might not permit prejudice to guide him—if she were imaginative and intelligent. But the woman didn't ask a single question. She listened to the others and wrote busily in a notebook when Barr replied. When she glanced up, however, Barr saw that she had hazel eyes, a warm generous mouth, and a wide brow just this side of being noble. Her brown shoes, he noted, were scuffed, and her left stocking had a wide runner. Barr doubted that the other men in the room were aware of the hair, the shoes, the stockings, so taken were they with her magnificent bosom. She's a mess, he thought, but who the hell gives a damn . . . Hunger for her warmed his loins.

Barr put on a show for her, a charming show with a touch of sarcasm here, a bit of self-deprecation there, an embracing act that plainly implied that all present were in league to give readers exactly what they wanted.

While the men were basking in the glow Barr had created, the woman spoke, her voice as harsh as a clanging gate. "Now that we've saved the fleet, Mr. Barr, perhaps you can tell us when the oil companies are going to share more of their wealth with the Venezuelan treasury."

The other reporters forgot her bosom momentarily. Obviously some of them considered her question an intrusion, a violation of the rules of the game. But Barr shot her a smile as bright as a press flashbulb. "It's a big industry, ma'am, and I can't speak for everyone." Then he waved his hands as if he were shooing away chickens. "You people have deadlines, and I have work to do. Thank you for coming by." His secretary passed them out the door like a butler checking departing guests for stolen silverware. The woman was the last to leave. Barr thought of her occasionally during the afternoon but finally lost her under his mountain of work.

But when Barr was leaving the office building at the end of the day she was in the lobby, seated comfortably on one of the ornate benches. If he walked quickly, Barr knew he could have avoided her, and instinct told him to do so. But he wanted badly to know why she had asked such a question. That, and his love of excitement, guided him to stand in front of her.

She looked up at him. Her pale face was dusted with tiny freckles, and her upper lip bore the slightest hint of a blonde mustache. Barr noticed that her fingernails were clean and well-shaped as she smoothed her skirt with both hands. He could see her pen and notebook where she had jammed them in her bag.

"I'd like a scotch and soda," she said. Her manner was straight-forward, but she had softened her voice.

Barr reached out a hand and helped her to her feet. "Get your bag," he said.

Emiliano's was crowded with soft-speaking drinkers, but the host found a booth in the rear for Barr and the woman. As the host left with their drink order, the woman settled into the seat in such a way that her breasts extended over the table. "They're real," she said.

Barr's brows lifted. "I never doubted it."

"I just wanted to get them out of the way as a topic of conversation."

"Fine. What's your name and who do you work for?"

"Naomi Boxer. The Caracas *Daily Star.*"

Barr's brows lifted again. The *Daily Star* was a new publication, the city's only English language newspaper, founded by K. C. Hopkins. It was an ambitious project. Barr smiled. "Old K.C. must have made more money and drunk less rum in Maracaibo than I thought he did. Are you his star reporter?"

She smiled. "He says I am." Her teeth were clean and straight.

A waiter brought the drinks. Barr waited for her to sip from her glass, then said bluntly, "Why did you ask me about oil revenue to the government? At such a time?"

"Did I upset you?"

"No. Are you working now or is this a social meeting?"

"You had them eating out of your hand," she said with faint contempt. "I just wanted to bring you down a peg or two. You were showing off like a peacock."

Barr laughed.

"No, I'm not working now," she said. "Anything we say is off the record."

"Good. I thought perhaps old K. C. was going to mount a crusade against the oil companies. Is there any danger of that?"

"Not that I know of. I told you, I just *had* to say something to break the spell. It was the first thing I thought of."

"I wonder why it was . . . the first thing you thought of?"

She looked at him with surprise. "My God! It's about all you hear on the streets. Why don't you come down out of that crackerbox you stay in and find out what people are saying? You'll never read it in the newspapers. Medina sees to that."

"Not even the *Daily Star?*"

She flushed.

"I'm sorry, Naomi," Barr said. His voice was gentle, but he added: "I can't help feeling that you may have pushed at K. C. Tried to get him interested." It was a question.

"He's not interested," she said sullenly.

Barr clicked his glass against hers. "Then tell me why we're having this social meeting." It was a challenge. "Do you hope to take me down another peg or two?"

Her smile was rueful. "Sometimes I'm not very bright."

"Nobody's bright on just one drink," Barr said. He signaled the waiter for refills. With the waiter gone, he said, "I gather this isn't a prelude to seduction, so you'll have to satisfy my curiosity."

"I wanted to satisfy *my* curiosity," she said. "I wanted to know why Eduardo Vigas always takes up for you."

Barr made a face. "Somebody has been saying something bad about me?"

She nodded. "Like locking out workers several years ago. They were starving."

"And not recognizing the unions?"

"Yes, and other things."

"And Eddie takes up for me, huh? That sounds like Eddie."

"He's a fine man," she said with some force, as if she had to defend Vigas.

"He is. Are you his girl?"

210

"Yes."

"Don't be defensive about it, honey. It's an insult to him. We agree he's a fine man. Does he know you're satisfying your curiosity about me?"

"He's in Maracaibo, but I wouldn't mind him knowing it. I'll tell him when he gets back."

The waiter served the fresh drinks. "Tell me about yourself," Barr said. "How you met Eddie."

She laughed, as if he had proposed a game to play. "You first. You're of age . . . why haven't you married?"

Barr looked solemn. "I reckon I orter think about it, ma'am. Marriage has many pains, but celibacy has no pleasures."

She laughed with delight. "Samuel Johnson. *Rasselas.* How dare you!" She shook her head. "And what do you know about celibacy? Emily Loring says you're an absolute tomcat."

"Emily Loring speaks with a forked tongue," Barr said gravely. Emily Loring was the wife of the British consul. "Speak up. What of Naomi Boxer?

She spoke up. Born in Little Rock. Studied journalism and Spanish at the University of Missouri. Honor graduate. Joined staff of Memphis *Commercial-Appeal.* Married Jerome Weingart, a photographer for *Life* Magazine whom she met while both were covering a story in Nashville. Joined her husband on the *Life* staff. Happy times, happy times . . . Tears formed in her hazel eyes. Weingart had gone down with a troop ship ferrying Canadians to England when German submarines had ambushed a convoy. *Life* had sent her to a Berlitz school for a Spanish brush-up, then had shipped her to Rio, Buenos Aires and Caracas to cover the South American viewpoint of the war. Pearl Harbor had caught her in Caracas. *Life* wanted her to return to the States, but by then she had met Vigas. She had asked K. C. Hopkins for a job, and got it. *Life* had accepted her resignation.

By now they were on their fourth drink. "Jerome," she said. "He was a fine young man. My first and only man." Her smile was wry as she touched her breasts lightly. "These kept me pure, do you believe that?"

"How?"

"When any man acted like he liked me, or showed some kind of interest in me, I always thought it was because of them. They were almost this big when I was thirteen."

"I'm sure they're gorgeous," Barr said, meaning it.

She nodded. "They are." She pushed aside her empty glass.

"Now, I think we ought to eat, because I want you to go somewhere with me."

"Are you going to marry Eddie, Naomi?"

"He's asked me. But I haven't slept with him, if that's what
you're asking."

"Why did you marry Jerome? Why did you think he was serious?"

She smiled. "He said he had two sisters at home with bigger tits
than mine."

Barr had left the tavern in good spirits, the glow from the
drinks not yet completely killed by the food they had eaten. But
now he was annoyed; Naomi was steering them in the direction
of the Nuevo Circo, the Caracas bullring, the largest gathering
place in the country. He stopped at a street corner and took her
by the arm. "I'm not going to let you drag me to listen to political
speeches," he said. "I've got people who go to such things. I'll
have a report on my desk in the morning of every word that's said
tonight."

She shook free of his hold. Under the street lamp her eyes were
more yellow than gray, and they glinted with anger. "You *are*
going. Reading speeches is one thing. You're going to *hear* them.
You're going to watch the people. You're going to find out what's
really going on in this country!"

Barr shook his head. "I already know."

She put her anger aside. She said earnestly, "You're American.
You've got every freedom in the world back home in our country. But you've got freedom here, too. Americans and Europeans
act like this is *their* country, and the Venezuelans are just here
to do the dirty work for them. Don't you see what I mean? This
is their country, but they don't have as much freedom in it as a
foreigner. How can you not care about something like that? How
can *any* American not get angry about it?"

"I'll go," Barr said. "Just don't stomp your foot at me."

She took his arm possessively and smiled at him. "Thank you,"
she said demurely, and they both laughed.

They sat among the people, on the side of the ring farthest
away from the section reserved for the news media. Barr had
never seen such a large gathering before. Every space was filled.
It was not a noisy crowd, but there was a constant murmur, which

212

Barr likened to the purr of a mighty creature capable of a sudden shift to anger and great violence. It made him uneasy.

Attention was focused on a high platform in the center of the ring. It looked like a boxing ring without ropes. It stood so high above the ground that Barr could see several figures moving around under it.

Then the stadium lights were dimmed and four spotlights bathed the platform with brilliance. The crowd grew silent. A trapdoor opened, and a man with a microphone scrambled up on the platform. He closed the trapdoor and took his time in adjusting the long leg of the microphone to what he considered the proper height. The crowd waited.

The man was Roberto Fontenot, dressed in a black suit, white shirt and black tie as he had been dressed when he called on Barr at Caripito. He pivoted slowly, looking in every direction around the ring, then came back to the microphone.

He began to speak, his voice carrying to the farthest reaches of the bull ring. It was not an oration; he spoke calmly, slowly, talking as one human being to another on a subject of mutual interest.

He was not preaching revolution, he said. His party, still not officially recognized, would not sanction any move to overthrow the government of President Medina. "God knows, we have seen more than enough blood on our plazas in our lifetimes."

He paused, as if waiting for the crowd to continue for him. Tension built. Finally he resumed speaking. "We preach simple things," he said. "We demand nothing. Instead, we ask the return of sovereignty to the people, a simple request. We ask for direct elections of the president and all congressmen by a universal secret vote." A small wave of the hand. "A thing to be cherished because it is the cornerstone of political liberty.

"Again," he said, "I want to stress that I am not thinking in terms of gunpowder. We have smelled it too many times in our lifetimes. And I don't want anyone to think that I would ask the unions, still not officially recognized, to take any steps to interrupt production in the oilfields. We are proud to send our oil to the aid of those fighting against totalitarianism. That is an undisputed fact."

But he had a few things he wanted to say about the government and the oil industry. They had been said before, he granted, but they bore repeating. And if the crowd would stay with him while he rambled, he might come up with a new idea or two on the subject.

Take Mexico, for example. Everyone knew, of course, that Mexico had nationalized the oil industry in 1938 because its leaders had been unhappy with its share of oil income in comparison with the companies' share. But did you know that the companies were paying Mexico thirty-eight cents a barrel before nationalization? Imagine that! Thirty-eight cents a barrel! But Mexico's leaders thought their country was being short-changed. A small laugh, a friendly chuckle. "Our government, as you all know, gets less than ten cents a barrel for its share of the country's oil. Seven or eight cents is closer to the mark."

Not that he was suggesting a nationalization policy for Venezuela, he was quick to say. Not at all. Venezuela needed the oil companies at the present time. Everyone knew that. And perhaps some of those present remembered what happened to Mexico for nationalizing the oil industry. The companies simply refused to buy Mexican oil. A boycott. "Let them *drink* their oil, the companies said." The Mexican economy was devastated.

So we are not suggesting nationalization, he said. We are simply asking for a larger share of the oil dollar for Venezuela. The price of crude oil keeps rising. The companies' profits keep increasing. And Venezuela keeps on getting her ten cents a barrel or less.

He didn't want to carp, he said. But it was worth noting that last year the country had produced oil valued at more than $172 million. A lot of oil, a lot of millions. The companies kept $151 million and gave the government $21 million. The figures, he wanted it understood, came from the government. The chuckle. There were other figures floating around Caracas indicating that the companies got even more and the government got even less. The chuckle. Unofficial figures.

Not to appear greedy, but the country certainly could stand an increase in oil income. To build schools, for one thing. Fifty-six out of every one hundred adults were illiterate. More than 800,-000 children were eligible for schooling but only 280,000 were enrolled. Why? Because there were no schools for the remainder to attend. So, if the country was ever going to have the doctors and engineers and other professionals it needed it must build schools to educate them.

The country needed hospitals and clinics and dozens of other things. Everybody present knew that, so he wouldn't continue

214

with it. Indeed, he thought that he had said everything he wanted to say. His party was asking for two simple things, two things well within the power of the Medina government to supply. "We are asking for the right to vote on a secret ballot and an increase to the government in oil income."

An apology. There *was* one more thing. Since he had mentioned all those unofficial figures, he may as well say what they were. Last year the country had produced oil valued at more than $230 million, according to the unofficial figures. The companies kept about $207 million and gave the country $23 million. Unofficially. "You may want to write them in your mind."

He was through. He did not wait for applause but took his microphone and disappeared down the trap door. Barr was reminded of the fire and smoke that vanished so abruptly at the wildcat well in Earthquake field.

There was no applause. The crowd rose as one man and began making way toward the exits. Zombies, Barr thought. He has them spellbound. He followed Naomi in the shuffling throng.

Outside, she pinched his arm and said, "What do you think?"

"I think I ought to get a taxi and take you home," Barr said.

"I can get home by myself. I want to know what you think about the meeting."

"It was nice. Now, let me get that taxi."

She stared at him. "You're incredible! Do you know that?"

"Listen, Naomi. I'm not going to stand out here and talk politics and business. I'll buy us a drink or take you home or wherever you want to go. I'd rather buy the drink."

"*Nice!* The meeting was *nice!* Boy, you *are* a Neanderthal."

Barr grinned. "Is that Eddie's word for me?"

She nodded. "Poor Eddie. He thinks there's hope for you."

"And you don't?"

"He couldn't be wronger," she said flatly.

Barr put on a sad face. "And I was growing so fond of you, Naomi."

"Humph!" She jabbed his chest with a forefinger. "Let me tell you something, wise guy. Fontenot draws this kind of crowd at every stop he makes, and he goes to every town of any size in the country." She jabbed him again. "The people are behind him."

Her stance, the angry cock of the head, the jabbing forefinger, all reminded Barr of Louise Bremond. Laughing, he caught Naomi's hand. "You're going to stab me to death with that damned finger!" Still laughing, he pulled her to him and held her cheek against his chest. He rested his chin on the top of her head. "Naomi," he said chidingly, "you know I was impressed with the meeting, with Fontenot. Anybody would have been. And I know something of his strength. What else do you want me to say? That I'm going to turn my company over to him? That I'm going to boot Medina's ass out of Miraflores and install Fontenot as Roberto the First?"

She tried to pull away, but Barr held her cheek firmly against his chest. And old man passing by, a straggler from the mob, grunted, *"Bravo, hombre,"* and Barr said *"Gracias, viejo."*

"He thinks I'm going to bed with you," Naomi said.

"Naomi Boxer, Great Liberal, takes Arch Conservative to bed to woo him away from his worn-out creed and lead him onto the path of righteousness," Barr intoned. "Regrets that she has only one fair body to give to the cause."

Naomi giggled and pulled away from him. "I think there may be hope for you after all, Grady Barr." She walked a few steps away from him. Over her shoulder she said, "I don't want you ever to hold me in your arms again. Okay?"

"I can't if I don't see you," Barr said.

"I think I'd better let you send me home," she said.

Barr went to the curb and beckoned the lead cab from a short rank a half a block down the street. She joined him at the curb. "Thank you for being with me," Barr said, "and say hello to Eddie for me." He opened the cab door. She started to get in, but paused to look at Barr. "May I call you at your office? Some time?"

"I wish you would," Barr said.

She got in, gave the driver her address, and Barr handed the driver money through the window. The cab pulled away from the curb and was caught up in traffic.

Barr walked back to Emiliano's and had a nightcap before taking a taxi to his apartment. He was grim and thoughtful as he prepared for bed, and he lay awake for more than an hour while Roberto Fontenot crowded Naomi Boxer out of his mind. He's a dangerous son of a bitch, Barr told himself. He says he's not preaching revolution, but if he keeps on like he's doing, the people will revolt anyway. They'll take it away from him. They'll sweep out Miraflores and sweep him in even if he says he doesn't want it. But he wants it.

He says he's not preaching nationalization, but Vigas is his advisor, and Vigas wants it, and he'll get it with Fontenot in power. Vigas, he thought, I've been underestimating him, but I won't any more. And I damned sure won't make that mistake with Fontenot.

Chapter Fifteen

Barr was busy. The refinery on Aruba was repaired and placed back in operation. The U.S. government sent submarine chasers to escort lake tankers across the Gulf of Venezuela to the refinery and to Shell's installation on Curacao. Other sub chasers were made available to escort convoys of ocean-going tankers to refineries on the U.S. Atlantic seaboard. Now and then Barr gave thanks that Lopez Contreras had reneged on the proposal to dredge the sand bar between the lake and the gulf, and that Charley Cannon, Barr's predecessor, had not pressed the issue. Had the sand bar been dredged, submarines could have entered the lake with impunity and reduced the entire basin to rubble . . .

Cajun engineers had wrought miracles in the lake. When Barr drilled the first lake well he had fashioned tree trunks into pilings for his foundation. Over the years the engineers had devised steel and concrete pilings and eventually had created a drilling barge, an over-water drilling system that made it easier and cheaper to drill on the lake than on the land.

Steel was needed to manufacture the barges and as reinforcement in construction of concrete pilings, and steel was in short supply. Barr went on a junk-collecting rampage, and a junk pile became a treasure chest. Every piece of scrap metal was rounded up. Barr even went so far as to tear out the railroad trackage between La Salina and Lagunillas. Many a toast was drunk to the old landmark by men who had ridden through the swampy jungle on the tracks in the twenties.

But always, Roberto Fontenot lived in a corner of Barr's mind.

Barr studied every Fontenot speech, kept a record of his travels, learned all he could about the people with whom Fontenot consorted.

And he compiled a list of Cajun and other company social accomplishments. Barr had led the way in Eastern Venezuela with the construction of good worker housing, hospitals, clinics, mess halls and other facilities; and Cajun, Shell and Gulf had followed his lead in the Maracaibo Basin. Nowhere on earth, he was convinced, were there oil camps with better accouterments. And certainly all of the companies were moving toward the day when every job on a drilling rig would be performed by a Venezuelan.

Meanwhile, Barr was seeing Naomi Boxer about one evening a week. She would call him at his office and he would meet her after work. They would have several drinks in a tavern, then go their separate ways. At their third meeting, Barr teased her. "What about Eddie? Does he know we're meeting like this?"

"I make my own way and do as I please," she said shortly.

"But I see him from time to time in the course of business," Barr said. "We have lunch together."

"What he doesn't know won't hurt him." She obviously didn't like the subject.

But Barr persisted. "He'd be jealous if he found it out from someone else."

She pushed her drink aside and leaned over the table. "Grady, when you put your arms around me at the bull ring, I told you never to do it again. I meant it. But you know I enjoy being with you, and I think you enjoy being with me. I don't want to stop seeing you, and I don't intend to . . . if you feel the same way."

"You mean what you feel for Eddie is something else?"

"That's what I mean." She said it flatly, laying it out on the table for Barr to accept or reject. When Barr didn't speak, she changed the subject, talking about a new book she had just read, asking him about his progress in reading Spanish. Barr was soon caught up in her enthusiastic interest.

They had an unspoken agreement not to discuss Roberto Fontenot and Venezuelan oil and politics. She was always interested in what Barr was reading at the moment. He told her about his experiences as a youth in the Mexican oilfields. She described people and events she had "covered" in her journalistic career. When they talked of present-day Caracas, it was gossipy talk about the people in the news. And they talked about the war.

"Wouldn't you like to be in the fighting?" she asked.

"No. I wouldn't have tried to avoid it, if I had been in the States, but I'm not going to go running home to enlist." He grinned. "Besides, I'm over the draft age."

"I'd like to go fight," she said.

"Why not? Look what you've got to hide behind."

She warned him off the subject of her breasts with a cold eye, then warmed to a discussion of how bad the mail delivery had become . . .

Barr continued to be sexually active, discreetly so, but never by word or gesture did he make a pass at Naomi. He was content simply to be with her, and she was obviously happy in his presence. It was the first time in his life that Barr had drunk, eaten and talked at length with a woman he was not bedding. He recognized this as an oddity, but gave it no significance.

But he did realize that she was becoming more important to him, was "growing on him," as they said in Texas. He caught himself waiting a bit anxiously for her calls. And he would think of her at odd times, remembering something she had said, remembering the way she had looked when she said it, and he would warm to the recalled moment.

He had told himself from the beginning that he would not approach her sexually despite the provocative bosom and what he believed was a passionate nature. He tried on occasion to imagine her in bed with Vigas, but he had found it impossible to do so. Vigas, he thought, would never nudge her toward his bed, and she would not invite him to hers unless he had the ring in his hand.

But Barr awoke one night from a dream in which Naomi had coupled with him in unrestrained passion. He was trembling, and as he became fully awake he was filled with a longing for her presence as powerful as the aching want for her naked body. He couldn't go back to sleep.

That evening he met her in a small, gaily-painted restaurant that clung like a flower to the north wall of the Caracas valley. As they lifted their first drinks in a toast, a cloud eased by their window, obscuring for a fleecy moment the lights of the city below. Naomi cried out in delight, and Barr hungered to capture her like that and join his mouth to her smiling lips.

Impulsively, he reached out and touched her wrist. She turned from the window to see why he had attracted her attention, and she read on his face what was in his heart. She recoiled as if his hand was on fire. "Don't be a fool!" She spoke so sharply that several persons in the restaurant looked in their direction. Barr was unaware of the looks. His face was pale and his throat worked on unspoken words.

She got up from the table and walked stiff-legged toward the exit. Barr put money on the table and followed her. He caught up with her on the long verandah. She was lifting a hand to summon a cab, but Barr grabbed her arm and turned her to face him.

"Don't you say it," she warned. "I won't hear it." She was coldly angry. "I want a taxi, and I want to go home. You've spoiled everything." She walked away from him, signaling a cab when she reached the top of the steps.

Barr let her go, standing in the same spot until she entered the cab and was driven out of sight down the mountainside.

She didn't call, and he told himself he was glad of it. He was prepared to be busy if she did, or so he told himself. He was honest enough to admit that he was suffering as much from a badly bruised ego as from a broken heart, if such a thing there was.

At times he hated her for rejecting him so out of hand. Then he would be angry for placing himself in a position to be rejected. At times he would feel ashamed for being so weak. He would wish with all of his heart that the memory of the rejection could be erased from her mind as well as his. *Shit,* he would tell himself, *she's already forgotten it!* And he would hate her for being so shallow. He catalogued her faults like a penitent reciting his sins, but found no absolution in it.

He tried to hate Vigas but couldn't manage it. So he avoided him as much as possible, seeing Vigas only when it was necessary to the conduct of his business. Vigas was always friendly and full of humor on these rare occasions, and Barr couldn't help but respond in the same fashion. But later he would picture Vigas kissing and caressing the breasts Barr had never seen, and bitterness would sear his stomach.

An article in the Accion Democratica's weekly newspaper jerked him to attention and set him on the road to healing. An international commission had ruled that Mexico should pay $25 million to the oil companies whose concessions had been nationalized in 1938 instead of the $250 million asked by the companies. The commission also had decided that Mexico had the moral and legal right to take over the assets of the concessionary companies.

The story also said that the U.S. government had opened a credit of $40 million to the Mexican government to help stabilize the Mexican currency. The U.S. also had agreed to buy six million ounces of Mexican silver annually, and the Export-Import Bank had loaned Mexico $30 million for public works projects.

And there was a brief editorial: "See what Mexico has obtained. On the other hand, Venezuela continues with contracts signed under General Gomez, drawn up according to laws which were written by lawyers of the oil companies. We are not asking for the immediate nationalization of the oil industry but for measures which will strengthen our economy and our fiscal position. We ask, simply, for an increase of our part of the oil income to the degree that justice and equity indicate. . . ."

Barr telephoned his counterpart at Shell and asked him if he had seen the articles. The Shell man said he had read them.

"How long do you think Medina can stand up under this kind of bombardment?" Barr asked.

The Shell man was calm. "Those people have been spouting that shit for years, if I may quote our good friend at Gulf. He called about half an hour ago."

"He's not worried, then?"

"Not particularly, Grady. Do I take it that you are?"

"Some, for several reasons. With the cutback in production, I'd guess the treasury is bare. Medina has stopped all public works projects as far as I can see. Hell, he's even selling some of those confiscated German and Italian ships to get money to pay the military and his bureaucrats."

"That's not news, Grady."

"Soaking us would be a fast way to get new money."

"The economic picture will brighten soon enough, if you will allow me to use such language," the Shell man said. "They tell me from London that the submarine menace is on the wane. Let the sea lanes get fairly clear, old boy, and we'll be going at top speed. We'll have the beloved president as fat as Jack Bolton's goose."

Barr laughed. "Who is Jack Bolton?"

The Shell man chuckled. "Mercy, I have no idea. Some Irishman, I presume."

"What do you hear of Lopez Contreras? Anything?"

"Still in the mountain fastness. You know he only makes an

appearance on Christmas, or is it his saint's day?" The Shell man chuckled again.

Barr laughed with him, and got off the line. He called his Gulf counterpart and told him of his conversation with the Shell man. "You're not as complacent as he is, are you?" Barr asked.

"No, but I'm not as worried as you appear to be."

"I'm not worried," Barr said irritably, "but I don't see a hell of a lot to rejoice about."

"Do you know something I don't know?"

"No, I guess not."

"Well, I'll see you at lunch Thursday," the Gulf man said, and he hung up.

Barr left his desk and paced the floor. He went into the reception office and bummed a cigarette from his secretary. He returned to his office and stood at the big window, staring with unseeing eyes at the traffic below him, coughing but continuing to smoke the cigarette. He wheeled from the window abruptly and walked restlessly to the reception office door. His secretary, a pretty young Venezuelan girl, reached for her cigarette package to offer him another cigarette.

"No, not that," Barr said. He smiled and went back to his desk. He sat in thought, ignoring the paperwork on his desk that needed his attention. Finally he telephoned the Senate Office Building on his straight line and asked for the office of Senator Filemon Vela. He told the Senator's secretary who he was, and presently Vela came on the line. "We've never met, Mr. Barr."

"That's right, Senator, but I wonder if you could spare me a half hour or so . . . at your earliest convenience."

"Who could refuse a hero, a man who saved Venezuelan lives with his airplane bravery?" The voice was deep and harsh, the voice of an old man.

Barr laughed. "It wasn't that much, Senator, but I thank you just the same."

"Lunch tomorrow, Mr. Barr. In these austere times I eat at my desk. I'll have a sandwich for you, if you like."

"I was thinking of something more private," Barr said.

Vela chuckled. "Do you wish to make a small conspiracy, Mr. Barr?"

"Exactly," Barr said, but he laughed to show he didn't mean it.

"Do you play checkers, Mr. Barr?"

"I know how. I haven't played in a long, long time."

"A beautiful American woman taught me the game. Now, do you know Miranda Park?"

"I know where it is. Yes, sir."

"I will meet you there at noon tomorrow, and I'll bring the checker board. No one will pay attention to two men playing checkers. Now let me tell you where I'll be waiting for you."

No one would have guessed that Filemon Vela was anything but a public servant. He was of standard height, standard weight, he had the standard stoop to his shoulders, his white mane flowed outward from his nape, his handsome face was clawed by dissipation, his brown eyes were knowing and merry. Distinguishing him from the run of public servants was his dress—black suit, white boiled shirt, black string tie.

"It's your move," he said to Barr.

Barr moved a checker. They were seated at a concrete table under tall trees away from the beaten paths. Barr at first had thought the Senator was a bit gaudily dressed for the park, but no one appeared to pay them the slightest attention. "You're a pragmatic man, Senator, or so I have been led to believe by my people," Barr said.

Vela shrugged and moved a checker.

"And you have the ear of the President."

"Both ears," Vela said, smiling as he moved a checker. "But why bother with me? A man in your position can talk to him anytime."

"Let me put forth something," Barr said, moving a checker. "First, you must understand that he has left us alone, the oil companies, and we have left him alone. For good reasons, political reasons."

Vela nodded and moved a checker.

"I think the President could be described as a liberal autocrat."

Vela nodded. "The political dungeons are empty."

Barr moved a checker. "I speak boldly now, Senator. I think the President wants to change the petroleum law, but doesn't want it to appear that he was forced into it by Roberto Fontenot and Accion Democratica."

The old eyes studied Barr. "What do you fear, Mr. Barr? We are both pragmatic men."

"Above all, nationalization," Barr said. "It would be a disaster for the country and the oil companies."

224

Lids closed over the old eyes. "And you think Fontenot could force him that far?"

"No. But he has to be an absolute idiot if he doesn't know that Fontenot has driven public opinion in that direction. The people may decide to take matters into their own hands."

Vela jumped two of Barr's checkers. "If there was an election tomorrow in which all of the people could vote, Fontenot would beat him ten to one. I have told him that. I have told him that if things continue as they are he will not be able to select his successor and have him approved without bloodshed." Vela shrugged. "Of course you know how bad tidings are received by an indecisive leader." He waited for Barr to jump two of his checkers and he jumped three of Barr's. "Do you have a benign alternative to the calamities we see approaching?"

"Perhaps," Barr said.

"It's not only that he thinks Fontenot would get credit if he proposed a new petroleum law," Vela said. "He also thinks the oil companies would fight him tooth and nail, and the arguing could go on forever. For him it is a terrible dilemma."

Barr spread a big hand over the checker board, stopping the play. "He could suck the wind right out of Fontenot's sails, if he held his mouth right, Senator. He could tell the Congress that his administration *already* was drawing up a new petroleum law that would assure the state a greater share of oil profits. Then he could stump the country with the same message." Barr paused. "As a patriot, Fontenot would have to applaud him, and I think Fontenot *is* a patriot. Even if Fontenot went around saying he forced Medina's hand, it wouldn't have much weight. After all, Medina is in power, and he would be doing something, acting and not merely talking about it."

Vela said soberly, "You have given this much thought?"

"Maybe not enough, but we may not have much time, either." Barr raised his hand and moved a checker aimlessly. "I'll help him with the law so he can be assured of a substantial increase in taxes and royalty payments. If he wants my help, you understand. He'll have to talk to all of us in the long run. I think I can give him ideas in advance to use as a framework."

Vela lifted his head in surprise. "Do you mean you haven't discussed this with the other companies?"

Barr grinned. "Why don't we let Medina's speech be a surprise to them?"

"But they'll be furious. They'll fight him."

Barr shook his head. "I can handle them. In any event, they can't *stay* furious if I don't."

"But . . ."

"There's something he can offer the companies to soften the blow, Senator. He can agree to extend the life of the concessions we have for another forty years. Nobody can complain about that, and it's something the companies really want. They're due to expire in sixty-five."

Vela smiled. "You *are* pragmatic, my friend. Nothing else?"

Barr grinned. "I think he ought to grant some new concessions. Lopez Contreras stopped it in a fit of pique. New concessions mean new oilfields, maybe, and new fields mean more money to the government—especially under the kind of law I'm thinking about."

"You said a substantial increase in taxes and royalty payments. How substantial?"

"I don't know right now, but I'll get my people to work on it right away. But I'll tell you this now, Senator. It'll be substantial enough so that he won't have to feel ashamed of it when it comes out before the public. I guarantee that."

Vela nodded. "I think I'll suggest to him that none of the terms of the law be made public until he presents it to the Congress. That way no one can snipe at it while it's being put together."

"Good idea. Do you expect it to be approved quickly?"

Vela smiled. "With the customary minor modifications."

Barr looked down at the checker board. "You were beating me pretty badly, Senator."

"It's an old man's game."

"Do you see anything wrong with our plan?"

"I'll talk to him in the morning."

"And you'll let me know?"

Vela nodded. "We *do* have us a small conspiracy, don't we?"

"It looks like it," Barr said, and he placed his palm on top of Vela's weathered hand.

Back in his office, Barr was filled with sudden misgivings. Had he been too hasty? he wondered. Was he exaggerating the danger Roberto Fontenot posed? No, he told himself. He had seen the man mesmerize the crowd at the bull ring. Fontenot had spoken in language they all could understand. It was the same wherever he went; the people sat silently and absorbed every nuance of his speech. When he said he wasn't preaching national-

226

ization of the oil industry he actually *was* preaching it; the constant reiteration was pounding the subject deep into the mind of the people.

It's better to give up a little now and forestall having it all taken away, Barr thought. Helping Medina is the only sensible move to make. And actually we'll be helping ourselves in a more obvious way when we get a time-extension on our concessions and get some new ones to boot. In a sense, we won't be giving up a damned thing, he thought.

Did he do wrong in not discussing his plan with the other companies? he asked himself, and wasn't completely sure. But it probably would take months to make the stubborn bastards see the light, and by then it might be too late. He had told Vela that he could handle the other companies, and by God he would.

He would have to get someone he could trust to help him draw up a new law for Medina. Someone who would keep his mouth shut. Several someones, in fact.

He smiled and picked up his telephone and told the operator to call the SeaCoast International office in Houston and get Tom Fairbanks on the line. He got up and paced the floor, whistling softly, until the phone rang and the operator told him that Fairbanks was ready to talk.

"Grady! I've been thinking about you. I'm going to be down there in a couple of months."

"Make that a couple of days, Tom. Can you do it?"

"Something wrong?"

"I need you, old friend. The sooner the better. I can't explain on the phone."

"Grady, does it have anything to do with a subject you've been writing about in your reports?"

"I didn't know anybody had been reading them," Barr said tartly.

"They've been read, I assure you. But I didn't get to them until last week. Friday, in fact. Has there been a new development?"

"Major."

"I'll have to tell the powers-that-be about this, Grady. I can't dash out of here without *some* kind of explanation."

"Tell them. They know I don't jump at shadows."

"So do I. I'll be there as quick as I can get there."

"Thanks, Tom. It'll be great to see you."

"You too, my friend."

Barr hung up the receiver and sat staring at the window. He smiled. He hadn't thought about Naomi Boxer all day.

But thinking about her now produced a stab of pain in his stomach. He got up from his desk to bum a cigarette from his secretary, but a sudden thought put him back in his chair. Vigas. He'd have to warn Vela about him. There would be hell to pave if Vigas ever got the slightest hint that Barr was involved in a Medina decision.

He would protect Vigas every way he could, he told himself, but he would be goddamned if he was going to let Vigas hurt the company . . .

Barr had stepped out of the shower and was fixing a scotch and soda at his bar when the telephone rang. He put the receiver to his ear. "Grady?" It was Naomi Boxer.

"Yes, honey."

"Would you like to get together for a while . . . talk some?"

"Not tonight, Naomi. I have plans I can't change."

"Tomorrow night, then?"

"No, baby. It's not a good idea."

"I'm sorry, Grady, but . . ."

Barr interrupted her. "No explanations, baby. None needed. Let's just leave it that way. Now I've got to run."

"Are you so angry, Grady?"

"Not anymore. I *do* have to rush, Naomi."

"Grady . . ."

"Good night, Naomi." Barr put the receiver in its cradle and repeated softly, "Good night, Naomi." He completed mixing his drink and sat on a barstool sipping it. "That's the one who got away," he said aloud, grinning foolishly at himself in the bar mirror.

He killed the drink in swift swallows, mixed another. "Careful," he said to his mirror image. "Don't ever drink for a reason. Drink because you like it." He liked what he had said, so he smiled. He killed the drink and mixed another. He sang softly, "She's got a pair of tits just like Jack Dempsey's mitts, say boys, that's where my money goes!" He hummed as he drank, using the sips to punctuate the music breaks, and he mixed another. "She's got a head of hair just like a grizzly bear, say boys, that's where my money goes!"

The telephone rang again. Cursing softly, he got the receiver, prepared to be tougher with Naomi and, this time, thoroughly understood. But it was Ed Gurwell, calling from Maracaibo.

"We had a little trouble at Cabimas tonight, Grady."

"Anybody hurt?"

"Nobody or nothing. Everything's all right now."

"What happened?"

"Fontenot made a little speech, and when it was over about ten or twelve of his listeners tried to climb our fence. They were going to tear up something, the way I hear it."

"But they didn't."

"No. The local AD guy got to them. Told them Fontenot wouldn't like it. They settled down right away. Everybody went home or at least got out of the area."

"Ed, answer me this: if Fontenot snapped his fingers and said sic 'em, what would happen?"

"Shit. They'd tear up the whole fucking country. You know that."

"All right. What if they *thought* he said it?"

"Same damned thing."

"Could he stop them, once they got started?"

"I don't think so, Grady. Do you?"

"No, I don't. Come over tomorrow, Ed. Come prepared to stay a while. Maybe a couple of weeks. Can you get clear?"

"What's on your mind?"

"I'll tell you when I see you."

"All right, Grady."

"Good night, Ed."

Chapter
Sixteen

Senator Filemon Vela called on Barr's straight-line telephone shortly before noon. "Have no fear," he said. "I am calling from a safe place."

"Of course," Barr said. He jerked his head at Ed Gurwell, who was in Barr's office, to let him know Vela was on the line.

"He is a strange man," Vela said. "I spoke. He had never been so surprised in his life, I'm certain, but when I was done he said he had been contemplating such an action for some time and was working on a speech he intends to make within a week or ten days. He said it without batting an eye."

"Do you believe him?"

"Who knows, but perhaps it is better this way."

"Uh huh. What else did he have to say?"

"Oh, he's perfectly willing to have your help. Secretly, as you suggested. I'm to be the go-between." Vela chuckled. "At my age."

"What about extending the life of the concessions, and new ones, Senator?"

"You'll have no trouble there, from the way he reacted. When can I expect something from you?"

"I'm working on it," Barr said. "He doesn't need anything from me for his speech, does he? He's just going to talk generalities, isn't he?"

"That's correct. By the way, he said he may have a surprise for you."

"A surprise?"

230

"He wouldn't say what it would be, but he was amused by thinking of it."

"That worries me a little," Barr said.

"Oh, no! Not that kind of surprise."

"Well, we'll see, won't we. I'll be in touch."

"Very well."

Barr hung up the receiver and told Gurwell what Vela had said. Gurwell laughed. "That sly bastard. He may be planning to steal our socks, Grady."

"I don't think so." Barr was thoughtful as he reached over the desk and dug Gurwell's cigarettes out of his shirt pocket. He flipped a cigarette from the package and put it in his mouth. "Anyway, Ed, I've got a few other ideas up my sleeve. I'll tell you about them later." Gurwell flashed his lighter and lit Barr's cigarette. "When are you going to start buying cigarettes instead of bumming them?" Barr shook his head. "It's a nasty habit, and I don't want to get it." Gurwell laughed. "The habit's all you've got."

Tom Fairbanks arrived from Houston the next day. His happiness at seeing Barr vanished after five minutes. He was shocked and outraged at what Barr was telling him, and didn't even let Barr finish his explanation.

"Why in the hell didn't you talk to somebody *before* you passed the word to Medina?" he demanded angrily. "How in the hell could you make a move of this magnitude on your own, without approval? What makes you think the board would want you to make such a move?" All of a sudden Fairbanks was the chief of SCI's Foreign Producing Department wanting answers. "Are out of your goddamned mind, Grady?"

It had been a long time since anyone had raised their voice to Barr, and Fairbanks never had before. Barr was embarrassed and angry. "Before you talk to me like I was a schoolboy, I think you ought to hear me out. I might not look so goddamned foolish then."

Fairbanks was tight-lipped. "Tell it."

"Give me a cigarette, Ed," Barr said to Gurwell who was sitting in on the session. Gurwell tossed his package of cigarettes to Barr and slid his lighter across the desk. Barr lit up, taking his time, cooling off, giving Fairbanks time to cool off. He told it from the beginning, repeating points he had already related to give Fairbanks the complete picture.

"Still, you probably pushed him into it," Fairbanks said.

Barr nodded. "Medina saying he was going to do it anyway doesn't take the curse off me, if that's what it is. I did what I thought was right. I did it before I told Ed anything about it, but he agrees it was the thing to do. He's seen and heard and sensed everything I have. Ed's not a fool, and I'm not either." He grinned. "Hell, Tom, I really think it was a damned smart move."

Fairbanks didn't smile, as Barr had hoped he would. He turned in his chair and faced the window. His face was bleak. "Why did you get me down here, Grady?" he asked quietly.

Barr glanced at Gurwell, who shrugged. Barr said, "Who else has sense enough to help us write the new law, see that it's done properly? You're the only one, Tom."

Fairbanks turned back to face Barr. "My father wrote Gomez' petroleum law. Did you know that?"

"I guess I'd heard it, Tom. Maybe you told me. But I'd forgotten about it. What difference does it make?

Fairbanks turned his gaze back to the window without answering. Barr winked at Gurwell. "Ed, why don't you go check on that new eocene well. We ought to know how it's doing."

"I was just thinking about doing that. I'll let you know what I find out." Gurwell left the office. Barr lit another cigarette. He smoked, waiting patiently for Fairbanks to speak. Finally Fairbanks said, "I'm not going to help you, Grady."

"All right, old friend," Barr said easily. "Want to tell me why?"

Fairbanks swung around. "It's a terrible law, Grady. Terrible for this country, for these people. I'm ashamed my father wrote it." His smile was bitter. "That's the first time I ever admitted that . . . that I'm ashamed of something my father did."

"Come on, Tom, don't talk like that."

"I've started something, Grady. Let me finish it. I'm talking to you like I've just had a revelation, but it's something that's been growing on me for years. I've been pushing it to the back of my mind, and I guess I would have kept on pushing it there if I hadn't come down here. Grady, what I'm saying is that just about everybody who has a hand in running the oil business is amoral—completely and totally amoral."

"That's bullshit, and you know it."

"No, but I don't expect you to think otherwise. I'll tell you why. Take the Venezuelans. You don't like them and you don't dislike them. You've got no feeling about them one way or another. And

232

you've spent a big chunk of your life here. I think that's tragic, Grady. It might be better if you despised them."

"This new law is going to be a decided improvement over the old one," Barr said. "Wouldn't it be a good thing to have a hand in writing it?"

"You mean I could make amends for my father's sins?"

"Something like that. I wish you'd help me."

Fairbanks shook his head. "No, and for a good reason. You *have* to do this thing, and you're not going to give them a single penny more than you have to. And even then the board will think it's too much. You know you would have never given a new law a thought if you hadn't been forced into it."

Barr stood up. "All right, Tom, forget the fucking law. Can you stay down here a while and just visit with me?"

Fairbanks stood up. "Not this time, Grady. I might cramp your style. I'm going back to Houston and tell the board what's doing, that I think you did the smart thing." He laughed. "Fifteen minutes ago I was chewing at your ass like I was chairman of the board and right now I'm thinking seriously of telling the board they're going to have to do without me from now on." He looked rueful. "Like I said, Grady, it's been building in me a long time."

"You'll never do that," Barr said confidently. "You're an oilman through and through. Forget this damn law. I'll handle it."

Fairbanks shook his head. "It's like a boil that's come to a head finally. It's been eating at me and poisoning my system, and now it's time to lance it." He smiled. "I think I'll go to the ranch and sing to the cows."

Barr strode around his desk and put his hands on Fairbanks' shoulders. Then they were hugging. When they let go, Fairbanks said, "I know men aren't supposed to say things like this to each other, but I love you, Grady."

Barr's blue eyes were misty. "I love you, Tom."

Fairbanks grunted something Barr didn't understand, then spun around and left the office. Barr went back to his chair and lit a cigarette. He sat there smoking and thinking until the package was empty and he could hear his employees leaving the building for the day.

From the Caracas *Daily Star,* March 19, 1943, by Naomi Boxer:

President Isaias Medina today announced that his administration intends to draw up a new petroleum law which will assure the state of a "greater and more just participation in the wealth of its sub-soil."

Speaking before both houses of Congress the President said the government would work to change, "in accordance with our laws and in a search for equity, a situation that has to be changed in favor of the Venezuelan nation. We shall see that Venezuela obtains from the production of its natural wealth that part which should correspond to it in all justice, and that the industries which are the logical consequences of the production of these resources have their location, movement and expansion in Venezuela."

The President did not divulge any details of the proposed new law, but said he would have it ready for Congressional review "as soon as possible."

The announcement was greeted with enthusiastic applause by the Congress.

Spokesmen for the oil companies operating in the country declined comment on the announcement, saying they wanted first to study the full text.

Ed Gurwell laughed. "Not a mention of Fontenot in a single one of them." Copies of all the Caracas daily newspapers were spread all over Barr's desk. Barr leaned over and with his pencil underlined the words—*and that the industries which are a logical consequence of the production of these resources have their location, movement and expansion in Venezuela.* He tapped the paper with the pencil. "That's the little surprise Vela told me Medina had for us. No more refineries on foreign islands like Aruba and Curacao."

"Can we live with that?" Gurwell asked.

"I think so."

"A big refinery on the mainland will be a target for any son of a bitch with a homemade bomb. That's why we built on the islands in the first place. That and fear of revolutions."

"It might be something to give up in favor of something better," Barr said. "We'll see when we all get down to the nut-cuttin'."

Five minutes after Medina's speech, Barr had heard from the Shell man, and directly after that the Gulf man. "Preposterous!" the Shell man had said. "Ridiculous!" the Gulf man had fumed. Barr had agreed with both. "He'll have a fight on his hands," the Shell man had warned. "He can't get away with this," the Gulf man had declared. Barr had again agreed on both counts, but he also had cautioned them. "Let's sit tight and keep our mouths shut until he calls for us to meet with him. He can't do anything without us. We want to maintain a solid front on this." "Oh, indeed!" said the Shell man. "Yeah," said the Gulf man.

Barr had not heard from them since the newspaper had hit the streets but he expected to before the day was out. His clerks had reported that people were buying the newspaper eagerly but Barr knew they always did that when the President made a major address. The clerks would get a better idea of public response to Medina's statements tonight, when the cafes were full and the beer was running freely.

"Are you surprised he didn't say anything about more pay and benefits for the workers?" Gurwell asked.

"Not really. He doesn't think in those terms. It'll come up later, I'm sure."

"And?"

"Oh, we'll have to go along, if it's halfway reasonable."

Gurwell shifted in his chair. "You know, Grady, you don't seem very concerned about all this, about what we may have to give up."

"I'm concerned, my friend, but if we can get our concessions extended for another forty years, it will more than make up for what we may have to surrender. That's the real plum, and if we can get some new ones, we'll be shittin' in high cotton."

Gurwell looked skeptical. "We've got more land under concession right now than we can say grace over."

"You're missing the point," Barr said. "If you have to give up a barrel of oil to Medina, you stay even by producing an extra barrel. You need acreage to do that. And think! Every company in the country has turned back acreage we didn't drill quickly enough to satisfy the law. But that's not wildcat acreage, by God. We've drilled around all of it enough to know it's likely to be productive. Why, hell, Ed, we're just getting started in this country."

"Okay, but I hope you can sell that concept to your blood brothers. And get them to keep still while you negotiate. That son of a bitch from Gulf could fuck up a two-car funeral."

Barr laughed, then said soberly, "I don't care how loud and stubborn they are if they know when to shut up and concede. I'm going to do my share of arguing, but I'm going to grant graciously what I no longer have the power to withhold. An Englishman once said that, and I hope Mr. Shell remembers it."

Barr absently took a cigarette from Gurwell's shirt pocket, lit it with Gurwell's lighter, then began pacing the floor. "Listen, Ed," he said without looking at Gurwell, as if he were talking to himself. "This war is going to last a pretty good while, but the United States—the Allies—are going to win it because they've got the oil and the manufacturing ability. But mainly the oil. Most of it is coming from the States right now. The East Texas field can produce a hundred million barrels a year all by itself. The States is still the biggest producer, but we're right behind them. The Shell man was right about one thing: it'll take a while, but they'll clear out those submarines. And when they do we'll have a market for every barrel we can deliver."

Gurwell moved restlessly in his chair. Barr waved a hand at him and continued. "When the war's over, every man and woman in America is going to want a new car right off the assembly line. They'll be tired of driving the old ones." He stopped pacing and faced Gurwell. "I'll bet you, Ed, there are folks in the States right now that wish the auto makers would quit making tanks and planes and get back to making cars." He went back to pacing. "So demand will stay up, Ed. That's why we need those new concessions. To take care of the war and to be ready when it's all over for all those new automobiles. I think . . ."

Barr's straight-line telephone rang. The caller was Senator Vela. "He wants to make haste, my friend," Vela said. He chuckled. "I suspect for political reasons. In any event, he wants only two things to be paramount in our initial discussions—taxes and royalty payments."

"Well, they're the heart of the matter," Barr said. "Does he have any ideas on the subjects? After all, he said he had been contemplating such a law for some time."

Vela chuckled again. "Apparently he hasn't been dozing in his office as I had thought. He's got what he calls facts and figures spread all over creation. Material he obtained from the Ministry of Production. Yes, he has some ideas. He wants us to meet and compare figures. I assume that he thinks yours will be considerably lower than his."

Barr was silent, thinking. Vela said, "I do believe, my friend, that the figures you and I arrive at will be the figures on which he will stand. Why, I don't know. Perhaps it is because he knows I am so intelligent." He chuckled again. "And so loyal."

"Don't low-rate yourself," Barr said. "He couldn't have picked a better man to handle this business."

"But *you* picked me," Vela said, laughing.

"Well, I must be pretty smart myself, Senator."

"You are. When shall we meet?"

"Soon. I'll be in touch with you."

"My friend!" Vela said before Barr could hang up. "Your Spanish . . . you could have conversed with Cervantes. I must say it."

Barr was immensely pleased. "I had good teachers, Senator, and some day I may tell you about them."

Roberto Fontenot did not laud Medina's speech and proposed plan of action as Barr had speculated, but neither did he launch an attack. Medina, indeed, had sucked the wind out of his sails, at least partially. In his first public speech after the President's announcement Fontenot said he hoped for an increase "to the limit required by strict justice" in the nation's participation in oil income; the transfer to Venezuela of the refineries; a reduction of the "absurd" exemption from customs duties for the concessionaires; and guarantees for the social and economic improvements of all those who worked for the companies. "These are the bases for a new and significant oil policy."

The Shell man told Barr over the telephone, "Our Mr. Fontenot seems almost euphoric. You are aware of course that only the hardiest of souls turned up for his address?"

Barr said he was.

"Yes, our Mr. Fontenot may have dreamed up this nonsense, but the beloved President has plucked it right away from him. You do think he will be reasonable, don't you? It will be folly if he doesn't. We're prepared to dig in our heels, you know, as I'm sure you are."

"Oh, I think he'll be reasonable," Barr said.

"I've heard it said that he wants an even split of the profits. Have you heard that?"

"No."

"It's out of the question, of course." The Shell man laughed. "Oil company figures are so confusing to the layman that it would be hard for one to tell just what one *was* getting."

"Are you suggesting that we imply he's getting an even split even if he isn't?"

"It's a thought, now isn't it?"

"It's a place to wind up, not a place to begin discussion," Barr said, "but we'll never get in that position."

"Of course not. Still, I wish he would summon us into the presence. London is harassing me unmercifully. Even suggested I take some kind of unilateral action." He laughed to show he didn't take the suggestion seriously.

"The same thing is happening with me," Barr lied. "I guess it is with everyone."

"Well, preserve the solid front!"

"Righto!" Barr said.

The Shell man laughed and got off the line. Barr sat at his desk, reflecting on the conversation and wanting a cigarette. The Shell man had been *too* relaxed, so different in manner than he had been when Medina had spoken to Congress. Then he had been bubbling with anger, and so had the Gulf man. Barr was tempted to call the Gulf man, but caution stayed his hand.

He stared unhappily at the mound of reports and other papers on his desk, all of which he resented . . . He sensed that something was occurring in connection with the new petroleum law to which he was not privy. He leaned back in his chair, closed his eyes and laced his fingers across his stomach.

The laced fingers reminded him that he was developing a small paunch, that he weighed about ten pounds more than he would like to weigh, that his face, while still slim with its features well-defined was heavier, with a suggestion of sagging at the jowls. He unlaced his fingers, vowing to cut down on his eating and to begin taking exercise. He solaced himself with the thought that his vigor was undiminished and his virility, if anything, more goatish than ever. And he still had his hair . . .

His secretary buzzed him to say that he had a four o'clock meeting with the geological department. Barr exhaled slowly and got to his feet. He was going to have to make a decision: Should Cajun settle for positive miocene production in a new area of the lake or make a try for deeper, probably non-existent, eocene production? He smiled to himself. Anyone who knew him would assume he would go for the eocene.

And why not? he thought. It was higher quality crude, thus more profitable.

Barr cooked his own dinner that evening. He had broken a date with a pretty young woman from the Canadian consulate because he wanted to be alone. The young woman had been

238

upset; this was the night on which she had planned to finally succumb to Barr's blandishments. It was also the night on which Barr had planned to have her flat on her back within thirty minutes after dinner.

He cooked carelessly but well, his thoughts more on the various ramifications of the proposed petroleum law than on the meal. Sipping a scotch and soda as he worked, he produced a three-egg omelette enfolding sauteed onions and salami and crumbled bacon. He smiled with satisfaction when the concoction slid easily out of the pan onto a big plate. He ate the lot with toast and black coffee. Afterwards, he searched his apartment like an alcoholic hunting a lost bottle until he found two cigarettes among some papers on his bedroom desk. He smoked them extravagantly with more coffee, promising they would be the last.

He was listening to the war news on his radio when the telephone rang. It was the operator with a long distance call from Tom Fairbanks in Houston.

"You haven't left yet?" Barr asked.

"At the end of the month, Grady."

"Tom, I let you leave here too soon. You've been in my mind ever since."

"No, it was the thing to do. I've got a letter in the mail to you. But that's not why I'm calling. I saw John Henry Craig at a party tonight. In the Empire Room at the Rice Hotel. You remember it?"

"I know about it. I was more familiar with the Aragon Ballroom."

Fairbanks laughed. "I picked up a lovely girl there one night."

"What did John Henry have to say?"

"He said I should call you. It seems that Sinclair and Texaco and your blood brother at Gulf and some others have called on the State Department for help. And your other blood brother has called on the British Foreign Office."

Barr whistled softly.

"There's more, Grady. It seems that after an exchange of cables and so forth that the State Department is going to handle it for all concerned."

"They told John Henry this?"

"Somebody at State did. They had to. After all, you're number one down there."

"What do they have in mind?"

239

"A delegation to call on Medina. A couple of diplomatic experts who double in economics and the global view."

"What's their pitch, Tom? I don't understand."

"The stick and the carrot, according to John Henry. There's a war on. If you can't put this thing off for a few years, don't be greedy. The allied world is watching you and will remember what you did when the world is free again. We need you now, but you'll need us later. That sort of thing. Your future is bright if you'll just be sensible in the present."

"Shit!"

"That's what I told John Henry. Do you mean you hadn't heard a word about this?

"Just an inkling," Barr said. "Just an inkling."

"Will it interfere with your plans? That's what John Henry wants to know."

"It will if I don't think of something."

Fairbanks laughed. "I remember Louise. She always used to say, 'Grady'll think of something!' "

"What did John Henry say about your quitting dear old SCI?"

"That's in the letter I've written you. Come to see me when you can and I'll teach you how to make a steer."

Barr shuddered over the phone. "I'd never be able to castrate man or beast."

Fairbanks laughed and hung up.

Barr cursed and poured a cup of coffee. No wonder the fucking Shell man was so relaxed; he thought the burden would be lifted from his shoulders by British and American government intervention. The son of a bitch hadn't grasped yet what a threat Roberto Fontenot posed. Neither had the Gulf man and the others. Barr knew that with one speech about the Yankee Colossus and Perfidious Albion, Fontenot could nullify the progress Medina had made. Before any new petroleum law could be formulated, Fontenot would be shouting that it should be stamped "Made in Washington-London!"

Barr's counterparts still saw Medina as the bastard, not understanding that his proposal was the act of a man who had found himself in a political current that was hurrying him toward a precipice. They were determined to maintain the status quo, Barr thought, and Fontenot already had shot the living shit out of it.

Barr pushed his coffee cup aside. One thing was certain: If the diplomats convinced Medina, by threats or promises or both, that

240

he should postpone action or accept a token increase in oil revenue, he would end up his term in bloodshed and violence. And Fontenot would pick up the pieces.

And the next step would be nationalization . . .

Barr paced his living room carpet for more than an hour, stopping only momentarily when a thought struck him. Finally he went to his writing desk. With the aid of his Spanish dictionary he wrote a six-page memorandum, describing the situation as he saw it and suggesting a course of action. It was near midnight when he wrote the last word and sealed the pages in an envelope.

Despite the lateness of the hour, he telephoned Senator Vela at his residence.

"I will be putting something in your mailbox shortly," Barr said, in English. "It should be read tonight, and acted on as soon as possible, if all hands agree. Tomorrow would be best."

"Thank you," Vela said, and hung up.

Chapter
Seventeen

From the Caracas *Daily Star,* April 14, 1943, by Naomi Boxer:

A British-American mission en route to Caracas will be welcomed but will not be needed in the formulation of a new Venezuelan petroleum law, President Isaias Medina said today.

The President told a Miraflores press conference that he had been informed that the mission's economic experts planned to "sit in on" forthcoming meetings between the administration and oil company representatives.

"The war has damaged the Venezuelan economy terribly, and we welcome any advice our visitors may give us on how to alleviate our woes," the President said. "But the drawing up and the enactment of a new petroleum law is our affair only. My administration, and my administration only, will decide what kind of bill to present to Congress. We need no outside help. Any attempts to push such help on us will be regarded as interference in our governmental process, and so properly resented."

Asked if the foreign oil companies had requested that the mission be sent here, the President said he didn't know.

Oil company representatives professed to know nothing of the mission. Said the Shell representative, "It's news to me."

Barr had taken Naomi Boxer's call to Cajun and he had told her he knew nothing about the mission. Her voice had set off the familiar stomach pangs, but he was happy to note they were not as sharp as they had once been. Nor did they last as long. She had been all business, and so had Barr.

But after she had written her story and the newspaper had hit the streets, she called him back.

"Do you still not want to see me, Grady?"

Barr said, "I'll make you a proposition. You tell Eddie that we've had a drink together now and then and that you want to continue doing it. You do that, and I'll be happy to take up where we left off. I mean, forgetting our last little session."

"I've told him."

"Lordy! What did he say?"

"He said for me to stop it. He said he would trust you with his life but not his woman." She laughed. "He knows you, I'd say."

"What did you tell him?"

She laughed again. "I told him I would. Stop seeing you, I mean."

Now Barr laughed. "Why, you little liar! I'm surprised at you. What else have you been lying about?"

"Oh, a lot of things," she said airily. Barr's laughter had made her gay. "Whaddayasay, wise guy? Gonna buy me a drink?"

"I've decided you're too young for me," Barr said with mock seriousness. "I've realized I should have been ashamed running around with you."

"I'm twenty-nine!"

"All right, you old hag. Where can I call you about five o'clock?"

"I'll be at the office."

But at four o'clock Barr received a call from Teresa Fontenot at Maturin. The General had suffered a massive heart attack during lunch. He was in the hospital, and had just regained consciousness. "He wants to see you, Grady, but you must hurry," she said calmly.

"What do the doctors say?"

"Mumbo jumbo. But I know he is dying."

"Can I bring someone with me . . . a specialist?"

"Everything is being done," she said a bit impatiently.

"Does Roberto know about it?"

"He is here, Grady. Please hurry."

"I'm on the way," Barr said.

* * *

243

General Pedro Fontenot died fifteen minutes before Barr reached the hospital. Colonel Morillo, the post commandant, had formed an honor guard on the hospital lawn by the time Barr arrived. Teresa was waiting for him in a waiting room.

Barr knew she was several years older than he was, in her late forties, but she was as beautiful as ever. Her body was trim and not a single line or wrinkle had broken through the loveliness of her beige face. But Barr read grief and desolation in the blue eyes. "My lover is gone, Grady," she said, and Barr thought he had never heard such sadness in a human voice.

He could say nothing, so he held her there, lending her what strength he could, waiting for her composure to break. But she didn't cry. Finally he asked, "Where is Roberto?"

"He's still with the General. In the room."

Barr released her. "Wait here for me." He walked into a long corridor. Several doors away attendants were standing outside a room beside a rolling bed. They were waiting to carry away the dead man. Without speaking to them Barr opened the door and peered inside.

Fontenot sat in a chair beside his father's bed, holding a lifeless hand tightly in both of his. He turned to face the sound of the opening door. Tears were still fresh on his cheeks. He was slow to recognize Barr, but when he did he turned back to gaze at the dead man's face. Barr walked in and stood at the foot of the bed. The General's face was serene, as if he were contemplating a fine dinner or a taste of rich brandy.

"Goodbye, General," Barr said softly to his old friend.

The son looked up at Barr. His face tightened in beginning anger, but Barr shook his head. "Not now. Not here. Teresa needs you now. Let them take your father."

With that, he left the room and returned to Teresa. She was sitting on a couch, flanked by two women. The women were well-dressed, obviously of some station. They looked up at Barr with undisguised curiosity. Perhaps they believe I'm her favorite lover, Barr thought, smiling inwardly, enjoying the irony of the outrageous flirt who, to his knowledge, had slept with no man but her husband. Her reputation, he thought, outran her fidelity.

"I think you should go home, Teresa," Barr said. "I'll see to things here. I'll come over later."

She rose obediently, and the women stood up with her. Barr nodded at her. "I'll be with Roberto."

* * *

244

The two men stood beside Barr's company automobile on the hospital parking area. The body had been taken to a funeral home for quick embalmment. Burial would be the next day in the military cemetery. Fontenot had not yet spoken to Barr. He had left the hospital at Barr's side like a man in a trance. Now Barr sought to break the spell.

"Well, he outlived Gomez, that's for certain," Barr said easily.

Fontenot questioned him with his eyes.

"The first time I ever saw him he wanted two things very badly. One was to be a pallbearer at Gomez' funeral. He wanted very much to outlive the old scoundrel. Your father wasn't much at hating, but I think he detested Gomez."

"But he worked for him," Fontenot said. "And for Lopez Contreras. And Medina."

"Yes. He knew he couldn't overcome them, so he stayed on to do the best he could for the people of his state. He feared what would happen if he weren't there."

Fontenot could not hide his skepticism. "You said there were two things he wanted . . ."

"You may know the second one," Barr said. "He wanted to help you get out of the country to safety when you were hiding from Gomez' hunters." He hurried on. "He offered me a great trade secret, a very valuable one, if I would finance your escape."

"And you must have turned him down."

Barr smiled faintly. "I must have."

"I didn't know anything about it," Fontenot said.

"I'm not surprised. You never gave him much of a chance to talk to you. By the way, how did you get here so fast?"

"I was in Agua Pura," Fontenot said. "It's only forty miles to the south."

"Cajun built the road you traveled on," Barr said. "And this hospital here, where they tried to save your father's life."

Fontenot flushed. "Cajun could damned well afford it!" He swung away from Barr angrily. "Some day we'll discuss such things at the proper time and place."

Barr was instantly contrite. "I'm sorry, genuinely sorry. I want you to forgive me."

But Fontenot was striding toward his car. Barr took a step after him, but thought better of it. Fontenot had heard his apology and plea for forgiveness. Barr got in his car, cursing himself for his error in manners and in judgment. Fontenot already had considered him an enemy; now he would think of Barr as a tasteless one.

General Pedro Fontenot was buried with full military honors, and his mourners spread like a huge oil spill across the brown sea of the llano. Every shop in Maturin had shut its doors in his memory. Barr had ordered that all Cajun employees who wished to attend the services be given the day off with pay. Father Gonzalez, his voice as sonorous as a cathedral organ, eased the General into heaven, asking God to grant mercy to "this good man who enjoyed life and strove to see that his fellow man did likewise."

Roberto Fontenot wept openly, as did many of the townfolk. Barr's eyes were misty. Pablo Morales, the cafe owner, forcibly restrained Teresa when she attempted to climb on the casket as it was being lowered into the ground. A moment later she was in control, and her eyes were dry. Colonel Morillo, graying now and a bit more portly, snapped a command, the shots rang out, and chunks of earth began raining down on the casket. The contingent of officials from Caracas began milling toward the widow to say their goodbyes; the President had been forced to stay in the capital city to greet the arriving diplomatic mission from the States. The widow said she understood the gravity of his task.

The night before, in the mansion, Barr had asked Teresa about Elvira Obregon. "Is she staying away because of me, Teresa?"

Teresa had looked at him with astonishment. "You haven't heard from her? In all this time?

Barr had shaken his head. Teresa had taken him aside. "She's living in Florida. She's been there . . . I don't know how long. Long before Pearl Harbor. And you didn't know?"

Barr had shaken his head again. Teresa's smile was sad. "I'm going there to live with her, Grady."

"But . . ."

"I can't stay here. Not without my lover."

"Roberto . . ."

"Doesn't need me . . . a stepmother. But Grady, listen. He will be a great man in this country some day. The General said it often, and I say it now. Be his friend."

"If I can, Teresa."

Then someone came up to take her away on a matter of importance . . .

Now, with the honor guard's rifle shots still ringing in his ears, he rode back to the mansion from the cemetery with Teresa at

246

his side. Roberto Fontenot rode in the front with the limousine driver. He had made the choice of seat.

Barr whispered to Teresa, "You'll be the most beautiful widow in Florida . . . in the States."

She squeezed his arm gratefully. "Only the General understood me, Grady. You were next. It has been good, my friend, having you know me so well." She turned to look at him. "You are a fine man. A *real* man, like my lover."

Barr was touched by the depth of her affection for him. In a steady voice he said, "Will you call me when you come to Caracas to catch your plane?"

She squeezed his arm that she would. "Grady, you must marry. You must find yourself a good woman, one not as beautiful as I am, but a beautiful one. You deserve her."

Barr laughed. Fontenot turned in his seat at her words. He was smiling—it was the first time Barr had seen him smile—and it electrified his somber, Chopinesque beauty. "Teresa! If you would only stay here. Life will be better for you here, I assure you."

Only a stepmother, Barr thought, could turn aside such a plea from such a man. And Teresa did. "You're a charmer, like your father, Roberto, but who knows what I will find in the good old *You Ess Aye?* Perhaps another man who can come close to your father." She smiled archly. "I can always come back, and who knows, it may be as the stepmother of the president!" She turned to Barr. "Is that not right, Grady?"

Fontenot laughed. "Don't pin him down on that one."

The driver pulled up before the mansion. "My plane's waiting for me," Barr said. They all got out of the limousine. Teresa kissed Barr's cheek. "I will see you soon," she said.

Barr put out his hand and Fontenot shook it briefly. "Maybe neither one of us is an ogre," Barr said, looking directly at Fontenot's eyes."

Fontenot nodded, his face solemn. "Maybe."

Barr turned and touched Teresa's hand. "Until Caracas," he said, then left them and went to his car where the driver was waiting to take him to the Cajun plane. As he settled back in his seat Barr suddenly realized that he had not called Naomi before he left Caracas as he had promised he would do. He had not thought of her since receiving Teresa's call that the General was dying.

* * *

Ed Gurwell was waiting for him when Barr got back to his office. The mission, he said, consisted of two economists-statesmen—he called them "hustlers"—various aides and assistants, and folks just along for the ride. They were getting the red carpet treatment at the Casa del Sol hotel. One of the economists had called earlier in the day from the hotel.

"He seemed kind of pissed off that you weren't here," Gurwell said. "I told him you'd call when you got in."

Barr leaned back in his chair and lifted the receiver of his straight-line telephone. "I think it's time to talk to Senator Vela, don't you?"

"Anything to get the show on the road. But don't you think you ought to talk to the visitors first? I said you'd call when you got in."

Barr grinned. "They'll find me if they want me."

Senator Vela's brown eyes were glowing with triumph as he and Barr spread the checker board on the park table. "The President *still* hasn't talked to them about anything of consequence," he chortled. "He welcomed them to the palace, of course, but almost immediately he turned them over to his aides. He said that something had come up that needed his personal attention." He laughed again. "He may never really sit down and talk with them!"

Barr was sharing the old man's joy. Medina had greeted the mission on its arrival in Caracas, Vela told him, but had spoken only briefly with the economists before his aides tucked them away in Casa del Sol. That had been while Barr was still in Maturin. Later in the day Medina had politely denied a request for a meeting, claiming that he had already scheduled a meeting with a senatorial group. He had suggested that the visitors come to the palace the next day. "That was this morning, of course," Vela said, "and as I told you, he once again gave them short shrift."

"Were any of my brothers in attendance this morning?" Barr asked.

"Oh, no. That would have been too much. That would have been an admission of complicity. Do you mean to tell me that you haven't spoken to any of them?"

"I've been 'out' or 'in conference' to everybody, Senator. Economists *and* blood brothers."

Vela moved a checker. "Well, then, shall we get about our business? Taxes and royalties."

"How does he see it, Senator?"

"He would like a twenty percent increase in land taxes, and he would like to raise the royalty payments to twenty percent."

Barr whistled softly. "He and the companies will be fighting over that 'til kingdom come."

"I said as much. What did you have in mind?"

Barr said promptly, "A ten percent tax increase and a jump in royalty payments to twelve percent."

Vela shrugged. "That will only make him angry."

"It would put a lot of money at his disposal."

"It doesn't *sound* like enough, my friend. He didn't start it, but there is talk that the increase should be enough to assure the state of an even split with the companies. Have you heard this?"

"Talk is cheap. What sounds good to you?"

"Like you, I think it best for the country and all involved that we get this thing over and done with. He has established himself as the man in charge. He spoke confidently before the Congress and pushed aside Fontenot to some extent. Now he has put the Americans and British in their places with his treatment of the mission. He is contented with himself. We should allow him to stay that way."

"So you say what?"

"I say a fifteen percent increase in land taxes and a jump in royalty payments to about seventeen percent." Vela moved a checker. "I have read enough of the material his aides have been studying to make me believe those figures are good ones. Do you find them incompatible?"

Barr was thinking, calculating and weighing more than the figures in reaching a decision he hoped would satisfy all parties. Vela broke in on his thoughts. "I have heard, my friend, but not from the President, that your parent company simply writes off your taxes on its American tax bill. In other words, the American taxpayer pays your Venezuelan taxes. Is that correct?"

"It's not that simple, but in effect, it's true," Barr said.

Vela shrugged. "Then I think you can well accept my tax figure, don't you?"

Barr grinned. "It's the principle of the thing, Senator."

"Pah! You are taught to give up nothing. You must overcome your teaching to become a good negotiator." He moved a checker. "Then my fifteen percent tax increase is acceptable?"

"Acceptable," Barr said.

Vela laughed. "How strange it is! Here we are, two men, one

elderly, the other approaching middle age, sitting in a park for children over a foolish game, deciding what could very well be the future of a nation!"

Barr laughed with him. "It couldn't be in better hands!"

"Oh ho! You think so? Then how do you feel about the royalty payments?"

"I suggest sixteen and two-thirds percent. It's an oil figure, one the companies are familiar with. Saving that one-third of a percent will be important to them. And it will look good to the public."

"And to the President," Vela said. "I accept it."

"Of course," Barr said quickly, "this is contingent on present concessions being extended another forty-five years and others being made available."

"That is well understood, my friend."

Barr smiled. "It's a pleasure to do business with a man of your caliber, Senator."

The old man's gaze dropped to the checker board. "I wish to God all problems could be resolved so easily," he said solemnly.

"Yes," Barr said. "But there are other details to be worked out."

"We will leave those to the others." Vela smiled. "After all, they must have something to chew on."

The Grand Ballroom of Casa del Sol was sparkling with chandeliers and bejeweled women as Barr arrived. Long tables with starched white coverings held mountains of cold boiled shrimp, oysters on the half shell, plump game birds, smoking roasts of beef and pork and a dozen kinds of delicacies. Waiters pushed through those standing to carry drinks to tables; others sought their refreshments from seven bars placed at strategic spots around the room.

Comfortable in his attractive lightweight tuxedo, Barr moved down an aisle to reach one of the bars. Scotch and soda in hand, he surveyed the great room. The government's reception for the economic mission had attracted the cream of Caracas society, leaders of the Senate and the Chamber of Deputies, and the staffs of the various consulates based in the city. Conversations in a half dozen languages floated across the tables.

Medina had continued his sneaky way with the economists. He had arrived to greet them and members of the mission, and had promptly disappeared once the amenities were over, leaving his cabinet officers to play host. Barr had followed his example; he had shaken hands with the economists, smiled at some of the aides, then made his way to the bar. He had made up his mind to let his blood brothers explain Medina's words and actions; he would be friendly, nothing more.

That afternoon, on the telephone, he had told the Shell man, "I didn't ask those people down, and I suggest you get them out of here. I don't believe Medina will talk to us until they're gone."

"It looks that way," the Shell man had said. "But how does one go about getting rid of someone who has been sent to help one? Really . . ."

"One bloody well tells them to get the hell out of the country," Barr had said brutally. "One bloody well tells his home office to expedite it. One lets all concerned know that they're holding up the game and making it rougher, most likely. That's what one does."

Tonight the Shell man and the Gulf man and other oil big-wigs were drinking with the economists at a corner table. Other members of the mission apparently were mixing in the crowd.

Lazing his way among the crowd of bodies, Barr sipped his drink with enjoyment. He saw several women with whom he had spent tumultuous evenings, and several others whom he had marked down for later encounters. The young woman from the Canadian consulate was surrounded by a group of interested men. Barr changed directions; he had lost interest in her since the night when he had broken the date with her.

He turned to go back to the bar. Facing him was an unattractive Chinese woman in a cocktail gown of shimmering blue silk. She had a drink in each hand. She smiled. "The waiters are too slow," she said in American English. Barr pushed back against someone to allow her to pass. "If you are looking for a place to sit down," she said, "you might join two lonely ladies."

"Let me get a drink, and I'll find you," Barr said.

He got his drink and found them. The Chinese woman's companion was an attractive American, and Barr immediately was gallant, demanding to know their secret for remaining unmolested among so many free males. "You've cast a spell on them," he said accusingly, "or they would be fighting to sit with you."

The Chinese woman smiled knowingly; she knew she was ugly, that her face was pocked by ancient acne scars, that her body was a thin rectangle in the expensive gown. The American was accustomed to such flattery. "You're getting a seat because you're the only redhead in the place," she said with a smile.

"Golden-haired," said the Chinese woman.

Barr sat down, and introduced himself. The Chinese woman was Mary Soo, a native of San Francisco, a resident of Caracas for the past seven years. That was enough about her, she seemed to say, as she sipped her drink and waved her free hand at her companion.

"I'm Arlene Bowie," the American said. "I'm from Houston and Washington, D.C." She smiled impishly. "We knew who you were before Mary picked you up. I've been appointed to find out why you've been avoiding Edgar Plumb and Max Harrell. You've got them upset." Plumb and Harrell were the economists.

"Medina's got them upset, not me," Barr said. "You're with the mission, then?"

She laughed. "Not officially. My brother does things for the State Department and he wangled the trip for me. Mary and I are old friends from way back, and I wanted to visit with her."

"God save the American taxpayers," Barr said.

"I'm one myself," Arlene said dryly. "A pretty good one, I might add. Do you ever get to the States?"

"Once every year until the war started," Barr said. "My mother and sisters live in San Antonio. Her name is Margaret Barr—you might call her when you're in Houston again."

She nodded. "I may do that. Now tell me why you've ignored the two gentlemen."

"I didn't ask them down here," Barr said shortly.

She made a face. "Somebody's got a burr under their saddle. Is that why you were so easy to pick up? This is a big party."

Barr grinned. He liked her gibing humor. She was somewhere between good-looking and plain—"a pretty woman," Barr's mother would have called her. Barr guessed her age at about forty, and he wondered if Bowie was her family or married name. Her hair was shoulder-length and shiny brown, her merry eyes a darker shade. Her full lips were quick to smile, her teeth clean and straight. Laughter and time had cut creases in her cheeks, and three shallow furrows ran across her forehead. Barr couldn't judge her body size from across the table, but he suspected she was a bit on the plump side. There was nothing wrong with her breasts, however, as far as he could tell; they posed prettily in the low-cut pale green cocktail dress.

She had waited patiently while Barr inspected her. Now she

waggled her glass. "If you hadn't followed Mary, we had an alternate plan to capture you. We're supposed to make you feel ashamed of the way you've been acting about the mission. Are you ashamed?"

"Terribly," Barr said.

"Enough to try to save the day?"

Barr laughed. "Not that much."

She nodded gravely. "I figured that. Now answer my other question or I'll hold you in contempt of court. Are you always so easy to pick up?" This time she seemed to be serious.

Mary Soo got up in a lithe motion and left the table before either of them could make a move or say a word to stop her. Embarrassment colored Arlene's cheeks. "Oh, God! Now I see what I was doing!"

Barr nodded. "You were really asking me, 'Why did you let such an unattractive woman pick you up?' That's why I tried to let it pass."

"And I had to keep harping on it. Damn! Damn! Damn!"

"Do you want to try and patch it up with her?"

She shook her head. "I'll wait until I've figured out what to say."

"A drink will help."

She showed him the impish smile. "Food would be better." She leaned forward, confiding a secret. "I'm dying to get to those shrimp!" But then she shook her head so violently that her hair whipped across her face. "No. I've got to talk to Mary." She picked up her jeweled bag and smiled wryly at Barr. "I've already worked my jaws enough, wouldn't you say?"

She stood up and Barr got to his feet. "Are you going to try to bring her back?" he asked.

"I don't believe she'll want to. The scene of the crime and so forth."

Barr nodded. He saw now that Arlene was sturdy, not plump, and her movements were more graceful than her build would suggest. He went to her and took her arm. "Let me go with you to the lobby," he said. She smiled her appreciation. They made their way through the crowd.

In the lobby she faced him and held out her hand. Barr took it. "I like you. Do you think we can see each other again while I'm here?" she asked.

"I was about to ask you," Barr said. He released her hand. "Are you married, Arlene?"

"Divorced . . . about five years ago. You?"

"Haven't tried it yet. Are you staying here at the hotel?"

She nodded. "Room eighty-four."

"I'll call you tomorrow," Barr said.

He watched her cross the lobby. Their speech had been stilted, their hand-holding awkward, but Barr continued to gaze across the lobby after she had left. And then he saw her coming back, walking swiftly toward him, and her face reflected her happiness in finding him still standing where she had left him. But when she reached him, the awkwardness returned. She blushed and turned her head as if to hide her confusion. Barr reached out and took her hands. She faced him then, and determination was painted on her face.

"Tell me," she said. "Why *did* you let her pick you up?"

"Because I wanted to see where her path led," Barr said. "It's my nature, I guess. I think I sensed something interesting at the end of the road."

Naomi Boxer called Barr's apartment as he was preparing for bed. He explained quickly that he had failed to phone her because of his hurried trip to General Fontenot's bedside. "And it's been a whirlwind since then," he said.

"Is it too late for a drink?" she asked.

"Yes, it is," he said. "You're out of my system now, Naomi, and I want to leave it that way. And I don't want you to have to lie to Eddie."

"You don't have to be so frank about it."

"We Barrs are noted for our candor," he said, and hung up the receiver.

Chapter Eighteen

When Barr came out of an engineering meeting at 11 o'clock there were two messages on his desk. One was from the Shell man. Snubbed by Medina and goosed by the oil companies, the mission was departing Venezuela at three o'clock. Barr smiled and read the other message. It was from Arlene Bowie; she wanted him to call her at her hotel. Barr used his straight-line telephone.

Arlene was breathless when she came on the line. "Hold it," Barr said. "I know you're leaving at three."

"We've hardly got time to pack," she said.

"I want to see you, even if it's just for ten minutes. Can you manage that?"

She didn't answer immediately, and Barr said, "It's important to me, Arlene."

"Me, too," she said softly. "Listen, I'm not a daytime drinker, but we can have a quick glass of wine in the lobby bar, if that's all right with you."

"When? I can be there in ten minutes."

"Now. I'll meet you there."

She was sitting in a booth with two glasses of wine on the table when Barr arrived. One man drank in solitary comfort at the bar; the tables and other booths were empty. The bartender was whistling softly as he polished glasses. Arlene looked fresh and youthful in a beige skirt and jacket, and there was a touch of yellow at her throat. As Barr sat down across from her, she inclined her head in a bird-like gesture toward the bartender.

"That song he's whistling . . . it sounds like a real hillbilly tearjerker."

Barr nodded. "It's sad, all right."

"Do you know it?" she asked eagerly. "Sing it to me."

Barr looked dubious.

"Go ahead!" she urged.

Barr grinned. "What the hell." He listened to the bartender whistle for a moment, then sang softly, *Your love was sweet torment, even though it was heaven-sent, and my heart was torn to pieces when you went away. . . .* Barr sipped his wine quickly. "That's a pretty fair translation. The rest is just about the same." He was looking at his wine glass. Her hand reached out and took it from him. He looked at her.

She placed his glass beside hers. "Grady, this may sound silly . . . my asking you this. But do you have any feeling for me? You know what I mean." Now *she* looked at the wine glasses.

"I wish you didn't have to go," Barr said. "I wish you could stay a little longer." He grimaced. "Oh hell, we sound so goddamned juvenile!" He got up suddenly, took her hands and lifted her to her feet. Then he pulled her to him and kissed her. When he moved his lips from hers he held her cheek to cheek. "I want you to write me. I want you to come back, if you can. I'll come to see you as soon as I can. I want to be with you every chance I can get." He kissed her again, and she clung to him.

She looked up at him with an impish, conspiratorial smile on her face. "Does it make any difference that I've got all the money in Houston except a little loose change?"

"Not at all," Barr said gravely. "I deserve every penny of it."

She raised her brows.

"Bandera used to say, 'Never let a woman keep her money long enough to think it belongs to her.'"

"Bandera?"

"Uh huh. And old business associate . . . back when I was young."

"What kind of business associate?"

Barr smiled. "I'll tell you when the time comes."

He was kissing her again when a member of the mission came into the bar looking for her.

Barr had been back in his office less than an hour when Arlene Bowie called him from the airport. "Something is wrong with the plane," she said happily. "They have to work on it. So I decided to call you. Is it all right?"

"How long before they fix the plane?" Barr asked.

"They said about an hour. Why? Can you come here?"

"Get someone to point out the Cajun hangar to you. It's not far from where you are. I'll meet you at the hangar office. He heard her intake of breath before she hung up.

Barr sped to the airport in the company limousine. When he drove up to the Cajun hangar he saw the superintendent talking with the pilots and mechanics by the tail of a Cajun plane. They ignored him as he went to the office. Arlene was sitting on the superintendent's desk, drinking coffee from a heavy mug. She smiled at Barr. "The nice man fixed me a cup of coffee, then said he was going to make himself scarce for a while."

"Put that damned cup down and come here," Barr said.

She went into his arms and Barr kissed her. "I started missing you two minutes after I left you," he said.

She tilted her head back. "Grady, do you believe in love at first sight?"

"I don't know, Arlene but I believe in this." He kissed her again. "When I left you at the hotel, I felt like I had a hole in my chest, like a cannon ball had gone through me."

She snuggled against his shoulder. "Me, too."

Barr knew he had never driven so far so fast to see a woman whom he had no immediate prospect of bedding, and he almost said so.

She tilted her head back from his shoulder, and Barr could see how serious she was. "You're a fine looking man—and you know it," she said. "You're the president of a big oil company. I'd say you make about a hundred and fifty thousand dollars a year, with stock options and bonuses. When you retire your retirement pay by itself will be enough to take care of several families. And by the time you retire you'll probably be making two hundred and fifty thousand. Correct?"

Barr grinned. "Close enough. And the stock options will be better, the bonuses bigger, and the retirement pay enough to take care of a few more families. So I'm not interested in you because of your money." And he kissed her, holding her close to him.

There was a knock on the door. Barr released her and went to the door. The superintendent stood outside. "The lady's plane is ready, Mr. Barr."

"Thank you, Curtis," Barr said.

The superintendent went back to the pilots and mechanics. Escorting Arlene to her plane, Barr said, "I come out about even on the more obvious plusses and minusses, but I'm pure in heart and I do unto others and so forth. And I don't slurp my coffee."

She did not reply to his banter, but walked along beside him in silence. Barr kept his mouth shut. Other passengers were going aboard the plane, and Arlene halted near the bottom of the loading ramp. Barr took notebook and pencil from his pocket and wrote hurriedly. He tore out a sheet and handed it to her. "That's my home phone number," he said.

She put the sheet in her bag. "I'll write you first," she said. Then looking directly into his eyes, she said, "I can't kiss you here."

"Just knowing you want to is almost enough," Barr said.

She went up the ramp and onto the plane. Barr turned and strode at a normal pace to his limousine at the Cajun hangar. He quickly drove away, without waiting for the plane to take off.

With the mission gone, the haggling between Medina's "experts" and the oil companies began. As Barr told Gurwell, "I'm up to my ass in intrigue." He had to act as if he did not know that the major objectives of both sides already had been decided in Miranda Park over Senator Vela's checker board. He fought as fiercely as his blood brothers, made concessions as reluctantly, dreamed up new areas for dispute. And all the while he was steering both sides to the agreement he had made with Vela.

Out in the streets and countryside, Medina suddenly drew support from a strange quarter . . . The Venezuelan Communist Party, small but vocal, came uninvited to his side. Medina had been their enemy because he was supplying oil to the Allies; the Communists had been pacifists because the Soviet Union had a nonaggression pact with the Axis. But now Hitler had invaded Russia, and any leader who supported the Allies was sacrosanct.

The Communists, crying "With Medina Against The Reaction," jumped on the dictator's bandwagon and proceeded to attack Roberto Fontenot and his Accion Democratica. Medina appeared to be quite happy with this support, something Barr couldn't understand.

"The war won't last forever," he told Senator Vela at one of their secret meetings. "When it's over, they'll be right back at his

258

throat. If he would denounce them now, say he didn't want their support, he might go a long way toward destroying them."

Vela shrugged. "I told him he was only sharpening Lopez Contrera's sabre with such a union. But, my friend, he is enjoying too much the Communist attacks on Roberto Fontenot. He cannot hear the rumbling in the barracks above the shouting of the bolsheviks."

But Fontenot fought back. Yes, he told great throngs of oil workers, the country should send its oil without interruption to the war fronts, as the Communists said. Yes, as the Communists said, the country should guard against fifth columnists. But also, while this was being done, the workers should receive a greater share of the profits the oil companies were making.

As time passed Fontenot also began voicing concern about the secrecy with which the government–oil companies negotiations were being conducted. "There is a heavy veil of mystery over the talks that is bound to arouse suspicion among some Venezuelans," he said almost sadly. "Are we not entitled to know what progress is being made, if any, toward President Medina's announced goals?"

Medina lifted the "heavy veil of mystery" at an extraordinary session of the Congress. The petroleum bill was not distributed to the lawmakers until the day they met to consider it, June 13, 1943. In the Chamber of Deputies there were a few who wondered aloud if the bill as written protected the national interest. There was no discussion in the Senate. The bill became law.

Barr's strategy had paid off. Medina was a happy hero. Fontenot was muted. And the companies gained more than Barr had bargained for—a continuation of the exemption from import taxes, and a guarantee of their legal titles to concessions.

Barr had another iron in the fire. He wrote to John Henry Craig and the SCI board, "The tax increase, of course, can be written off SCI's U.S. tax bill. But I've been wondering about the increase in royalty payments. As you know, our royalty payments jumped from 7 1/2 to 16 2/3 percent. To my knowledge, this marks the first time royalty payments have been increased in any country where SCI has had concessions.

"Could SCI, and perhaps the other companies as well, approach the U.S. Treasury Department with an argument—or an appeal—that the royalty payments increase be regarded as a tax increase and thus deductible from the SCI tax bill?

"A good lobbyist could think of several persuasive arguments

—there's a war on, you know—and I believe the Treasury Department could do this without Congressional approval. Or knowledge, for that matter."

Craigs's reply was quick and to the point. "I didn't know that anyone other than a board chairman was capable of such sophistry," he wrote. "It is a grand idea, Grady, but I fear that it is before its time. SCI and the entire industry is still in bad odor in some government circles, and the Treasury Department is one of them. However, it is something to think about when the war is over. At that time, I believe it can be implemented easily, particularly in the Middle East, if things shape up there as I believe they will. I will discuss this with you in detail at our next meeting."

In one area, however, Barr had been outvoted by his blood brothers. Government negotiators had failed to bring up wage increases for oil workers in the discussions. In a meeting of blood brothers only, Barr had suggested that a small pay hike be initiated. "Nothing doing," said the Gulf man. "If they don't bring it up, we don't bring it up."

"Fontenot will scream his lungs out if they don't get *something*,"Barr argued, "and we'll have to go through this shit again about recognizing the unions."

"We can stop that," the Sinclair man said confidently. "The first union leader who raises his voice about recognition is going to be fired or transferred. So will any others."

Barr nodded. "That might work." And so he had given in. The law was passed with no provisions for pay hikes or union recognition . . .

But the oversight was brought home forcefully to Barr. He was eating supper one night at La Tuna field mess hall, seated at a table with the camp superintendent and the resident geologist. About twenty Americans and sixty Venezuelans were at their meal. The mess hall was not segregated, but the Americans sat in one area, the Venezuelans in another—both groups wanted it that way.

Suddenly the clatter of cutlery and the hum of voices ceased, and Barr looked up from his plate. A black man in a gray suit and gray hat had entered the large room and was heading for Barr's table. He looked from side to side as he walked along, smiling widely at the silence his entry had produced. He stopped in front of Barr's table. "Do you remember me, Mr. Barr?" he asked.

Barr stood up to look at the smiling man. Barr loved expensive

260

clothes, and his suits were cut by a French tailor on Calle Rico. This man's suit was as expensive and well-fitted as his own. The brim of the Negro's Borsalino was pulled down all around in the style of American and French gangsters. The black face was somehow familiar to Barr, but he couldn't pin it in place. He shook his head slowly.

"A long time ago, Mr. Barr."

Barr shook his head again.

The man laughed. "Quiriquire, Mr. Barr! I helped you drill Q one. Where you cleaned that big man's plow."

"I'll be a son of a bitch!" Barr said. He stuck his out his hand and the man shook it. "Jimmy Endicott, Mr. Barr," the man said, releasing Barr's hand and taking off his hat with a flourish. Barr motioned for him to sit down. The camp superintendent got up from the table, nodded at Endicott and slapped Barr's shoulder. "Yawl will want to talk," he said pleasantly. The geologist also rose, and the two men left Barr alone with Endicott. Conversations and eating at the other tables resumed. Barr pushed his dishes aside.

"I wondered why you didn't go ahead and knock him out," Endicott said. "You had him on the way. I understand you sent one guy to his maker in Maracaibo."

Barr said, "Somewhere between Maracaibo and Quiriquire, I guess I lost my killer instinct."

"I disagree," Endicott said, and he was no longer smiling. "You just transferred it to Cajun. The company's got the killer instinct, and you supplied it."

Barr said calmly, "I was looking forward to a friendly conversation."

"This can be friendly."

"Then you'd better fucking well back off a little bit."

Endicott smiled. "Let's both try to do better."

"All right. You can start by telling me what happened to that lilting, sing-song English of yours. You sound as American as Uncle Sam."

"It's a long story," Endicott warned.

"But a good one, I'll bet. Tell it."

It *was* a good story. When Barr had phased out the Trinidadians in the east to be replaced by all-Venezuelan drilling crews, he had given each one a bonus and free passage back to Trinidad. Endicott took the bonus, but he didn't go home. He had grown to love the oilfields. "I had learned a lot more than anybody gave

261

me credit for." He roamed the country, doing farm work mostly, hunting for a way back into the oil business. In Caracas he met some people who were as much impressed by his glibness as by his oilfield knowledge.

"They handed me some money, put me on a freighter, and told me to go to the States and get smart," Endicott said. "I didn't ask where the money came from. I just went."

The mess hall was empty now except for the two men and the cooks and their helpers. Endicott lit a cigarette with hands as big as Barr's own. Barr accepted a cigarette, explaining that he didn't smoke but that one would be fine at the moment. Endicott continued his story.

Arrangements had been made for him to attend a small college in the eastern part of the States where he studied economics and business management. "They didn't even ask for things like high school transcripts," Endicott explained. In the summer he worked in an Illinois oilfield, also arranged by his sponsors. "They didn't let niggers work in the Texas and Louisiana and Oklahoma fields, you know."

He had returned to Venezuela three months ago, jumping ship without so much as a goodbye wave. He grinned. "I'm a labor organizer, if you haven't guessed."

"A well-dressed one, too," Barr said drily.

Endicott laughed. "I get mine. My people like to see me look good." He sobered. "But they're not doing very well are they?"

Barr didn't reply.

"The average oilfield worker gets about eleven bolivars a day now—about three dollars and ten cents in American money. That's a bit better than the eight bolivars he used to get, but this year the price of pork has gone up fifty-three percent. Rice has gone up a hundred and twenty-six percent. Potatoes, a hundred and forty percent, and flour a hundred and eighty percent." He grinned. "I know all this because I'm a financial whiz, like I told you."

Barr said nothing.

"Of course the oil workers get some fringe benefits," Endicott went on, "but they're still close to starvation. And it's much worse for non-oil workers. They average about two bucks a day in Caracas and a lot less than that everywhere else. And, of course, no fringe benefits. That's pretty sad, isn't it?"

Endicott was speaking in a confident manner, one man reciting facts to another. He appeared to be friendly enough; a half smile played on mouth as he talked. But Barr sensed a powerful undercurrent in his speech which he interpreted as menace. He became aware that the Venezuelan kitchen crew had stopped its work, as if anticipating something unusual. A sudden tension ran from Barr's stomach to his throat.

Endicott nodded. "You don't seem to want to answer any of my questions, Mr. Barr. Why is that?"

"I think you'd better leave," Barr said.

"Oh, no. We've got things to discuss, man to man. Or do you dislike talking on equal terms to a nigger? Is that it? Don't you know there's no racial discrimination in this country?"

Barr stood up.

Endicott said, "Back at Q one you were a lot younger and a lot tougher and a hell of a fighter. But you've got a little soft now, sitting around on your ass in Caracas and eating that good food and drinking that good booze." He poked himself in the chest with a thick forefinger. "I'm younger than you, and I'm wider and thicker than you, and I think I'm stronger than you. Do you think you can clean my plow like you did that guy's back at Q one?"

"I'm puzzled by this," Barr said. "What can you possibly gain by starting trouble with me? For yourself, or for your union, or for anybody or anything? I don't get it."

"You're just scared," Endicott said lazily, "that's why you're so dense. When you attack me, that kitchen crew is going to see it, and that's the way they're going to tell it—that you started it and this poor old darky had to defend himself. And when I clean *your* plow, why I'm going to be the big man of the labor movement. Not even President Medina can fault me for trying to keep a big shot like you from killing me." He waved a hand in the direction of the door. "Don't try to run, Mr. Barr. I might decide to kill you instead of just cleaning your plow." He took a switchblade from his pocket, flicked it open and laid it carelessly on the table. He smiled. "I don't think I'll need that, but it's always good to have something handy."

"There's more to all this bullshit than what you've said, Endicott," Barr said. "Cleaning my plow, or killing me, may make you a union big shot, all right. But something else is in your craw."

Endicott's eyes got mean. "You paid me a dollar a day at Q one, a dollar for a ten-hour day, and you drove us like a team of mules. And after you cleaned that big man's plow, one of the drillers,

Calvert was his name, he pointed at us niggers and said we'd be singing a song about the fight before nightfall. And you, you son of a bitch, you said if we did make up a song and sing it, it would be while we were working. Do you remember that? We weren't even dirt to you. Work, work, work—for a dollar a day. That's what we meant to you."

"So you mean to kill me," Barr said softly.

"If I have to," Endicott said. "You don't deserve to live, but beating you to a pulp might be enough." He was smiling again. "I'll make my points either way."

"Stand up," Barr said.

Endicott laughed. "You don't have to be in such a hurry. You might want to take off your coat and loosen your tie. We don't want to get blood on that good-looking coat."

Barr took a step back and began taking off his coat. Endicott began getting to his feet, taking his time, his relaxed manner and patronizing smile expressing his contempt for Barr's prowess. He moved his hand closer to the switchblade.

As Barr removed his coat his hand brushed across the tops of several pencils he carried in an inner pocket. He tossed the coat on the table and in the same movement swung back to face Endicott. Endicott had not fully risen—too late he saw the pencil in Barr's hand. Too late, he lifted his hands to ward off the pencil that Barr drove solidly into his left eye.

Endicott's scream was not human. He fought at the pencil, lunging toward Barr with the switchblade now in his hand. Barr kicked him, cracking his left knee cap. Endicott lurched sideways, and Barr kicked his other leg. Endicott crashed to the mess hall floor, thrashing and keening. He was on his back. He had loosened the pencil, but it still was in his eye. He tried to get to his feet but his legs wouldn't support him.

The Venezuelan kitchen crew had moved out into the mess hall proper to watch the fight. They stared at Barr as if he were one of their ancient demons. Endicott had quit moving. He appeared to be unconscious.

Barr was trembling. He looked down at Endicott, but he felt no sense of triumph. A sudden impulse made him move toward Endicott to help him in any way he could.

But one of the Venezuelans coughed, and Barr stopped and looked at them. They had been prepared to witness Barr's humiliation, to see him terribly wounded or killed, and to lie about it afterward. Now they gazed at him with dumb hatred, and Barr knew that any attempt to aid Endicott would not endear him to them but rather make him a weakling in their eyes. They were cruel to their personal enemies, and expected cruelty in return.

Still shaken, Barr got his coat and put it on. Then, certain that they were still watching him, he stooped over and yanked the pencil from Endicott's eye. He wiped the pencil on a table napkin and looked squarely at the Venezuelans.

"No use wasting a good pencil," he said in Spanish, and he put the pencil back in his pocket.

He went to the Venezuelans. "Go get the superintendent," he told one of them. "Tell him to hurry." He turned to another. "This is a new field ... do you have a doctor yet?" The man shook his head. "There is a man at the clinic." "Get him," Barr said. He told the chief cook, "We need a light truck to take him to the hospital at Maturin. We need blankets and sheets and pillows. Can you do all that?" The chief cook nodded. "Get at it," Barr said. The cook scurried off. "All right," Barr said, "the rest of you get back to work until I need you." The men moved back into the kitchen area.

The superintendent rushed in, panting heavily. The clinician, a Venezuelan, was right behind him. Barr pointed at Endicott. "He's got an eye injury, a broken kneecap and maybe a concussion. I've ordered a light truck to take him to the Maturin hospital." He said to the clinician, "I want you to ride in the back with him and try to keep him comfortable."

The clinician went to Endicott's side. "What happened, Grady?" the superintendent, Alvah Falk, asked.

"I'll tell you after we get the show on the road," Barr said.

The clinician had knelt down by Endicott, touching his fingers to Endicott's carotid artery as he had been taught in the Maturin hospital. He looked up toward Barr and Falk. "He's dead," the clinician said.

"We can bury him here," Falk said. "We can do it right now."

"No, Alvah. His grave would be a constant reminder to your people here. We'll take him on to Maturin." Barr slapped Falk's shoulder. "I'll give you the whole story after they get him loaded up."

General Valmore Morillo poured brandy for Barr and wine for himself. He had moved from the barracks into the mansion at

Maturin after General Fontenot's death and Teresa Fontenot's departure for the States. They sat in the upstairs living room where Barr had spent many happy hours with the Fontenots, with Elvira Obregon, and with Morillo when he was a colonel.

"You are most fortunate he did not survive, my friend," Morillo said. "In my experience, there are two kinds of men. One, if he is cut in a fight, will walk around a city to avoid passing his knifer on the street. The other, every time he touches his scar will dream of revenge, and some day he will have it. Your Trinidadian was one of the latter. Had he survived you would have spent the rest of your days looking over your shoulder."

"I think you're right," Barr said.

"Officially, he attacked you, you defended yourself, death resulted. No more."

"I don't like the idea of the word drifting back to Caracas and Maracaibo," Barr said. "I'll make a report to President Medina, if you think that's wise, but I've got an idea I'd like to try." Barr grinned. "It'll give you a chance to show what an eloquent soldier you are, old friend."

Morillo rolled his eyes. "What military man could resist that?"

From the Caracas *Daily Star* of August 2, 1943:

> Grady Stancil Barr, president of Cajun Petroleum Corporation, killed a man who assaulted him at Cajun's La Tuna oil camp in southern Monagas, according to General Valmore Morillo, the state's acting president.
>
> "The man attacked Mr. Barr in the camp mess hall and, in defending himself, Mr. Barr killed him," General Morillo said. "The man carried no identification papers. However, my investigation has revealed that he was a Trinidadian who recently entered this country illegally. Mr. Barr said the man gave no reason for attacking him. My investigation, of course, is proceeding but I have found no evidence to this point that Mr. Barr is guilty of any wrongdoing."
>
> General Morillo said no one claimed the body, and the man was buried in the Maturin cemetery."
>
> Police records show that Barr pleaded guilty to a charge of manslaughter in Maracaibo in 1926 and received a five-year probationary sentence, General Morillo said.

Ed Gurwell shoved the newspapers around Barr's desk and

gave Barr a cigarette. "What about Houston, Grady?"

"I gave them the whole kit and caboodle," Barr said. "They're checking out where he went to college and who in the hell hired him in Illinois. And we're checking him out here."

Gurwell pointed to the newspapers on the desk. "Was that last paragraph necessary?"

"Better Morillo saying it than them digging it out and making a bigger spread of it. At least that's the way I figured it." Barr blew smoke at Gurwell. "The last time I killed somebody, you chased my ass into the Perija, you rotten bastard. Remember?"

Gurwell laughed. "Made a man of you, too." And then Gurwell couldn't help adding, "One of these days you're going to have to tell me how it feels to kill somebody."

Barr said evenly, "One of these days you're going to find your ass transferred to Antarctica, and you'll never know why." He began stacking the newspapers in a neat pile.

"I'm sorry, Grady," Gurwell said.

"I know. You always are. You can't help being snotty, just like I can't help killing people."

"Come on, Grady," Gurwell pleaded. "Give me a break."

Barr looked up at him and grinned. "Oh shit, Ed, forget it. Let's lock up and go get a drink." His grin got wider. "Unless your wife won't like it, you staying out after working hours."

"Fuck you, too," Gurwell said. "I want a glass of beer and a double shot of cheap bourbon."

Arlene Bowie's first letter had taken a long time to reach Barr, and he read it four times before he examined his other mail. After he returned from a meeting with his pipeline division managers, he read it again, leaning back in his office chair with his feet on his desk.

Dear Grady,

I want you to tell me all about Bandera, your former business associate, some time, but I already know his occupation because of what I have learned about you. I told my brother about you when I got back here to Washington. He took it upon himself to find out what he could about you. As I told you, he's with the State Department and he has very good sources of information. By the way, his name is Harley Bowie, and he's a wonderful man, Grady.

His conclusion was that a man who started out like you did

and became what you've become is worth knowing, and he wants to meet you. I think you know that I wouldn't care if you had been a triple axe-murderer. He told me you had killed a man in Maracaibo long ago in a fight over a woman, and there was a paragraph in the Washington *Post* yesterday that you had killed a man in a place called Maturin. I don't care about that either. I'm just so happy that *you* didn't get hurt. I know that what I have just written makes me sound like a fool, but I also know the Grady Barr I met at the reception and kissed in the hotel and at the airport is a fine and sensitive man. That's the way it is, and I can't help it.

It seems like I have known you forever, Grady, and I think about you when I wake up every morning and before I go to sleep at night.

I am tempted to write you about my marriage to Maco Stephens, and about my divorce, but I would rather talk to you about them. Do you mind waiting?

And I have a daughter, Grady. Her name is Millicent, her father liked that because it started with an M, and she is a wonderful girl, young woman I should say because she is nineteen. I have talked with her about you, and I guess I have to say she is withholding judgment. Could you send me a picture? One where you are as handsome as you were in your tuxedo at the reception. Or as manly as you were at the hotel bar. I want her to see you before she meets you.

I have written a lot here without saying that you walked into my heart, Grady, and I guess you are there to stay. Write me, please, and tell me that it is the same with you.

To Barr's great surprise, the next day he received a brief letter from Roberto Fontenot. It said: "James Endicott was sent to the States by a group of patriotic businessmen who were unhappy with the Gomez–Lopez Contreras dictatorships. They were not and are not Communists. Endicott, on his return, placed his personal ambition above the legitimate demands of the labor movement. We have learned that he was collecting money from the workers on the pretext that it was being sent to Washington to aid in the war effort. In his Maracaibo living quarters was found more than Bs. 40,000 and a number of valuable personal items.

"We are assuming that he attacked you, though we have heard to the contrary. In any event, he was not representative of the

268

Venezuelan labor movement, and you need not expect any reprisal for his death.

"Teresa mentions you in her letters from Florida, and always with affection and regard."

Chapter Nineteen

Barr began sending to and receiving from Arlene Bowie what amounted to love letters. She was in his mind, as he assumed he was in hers. But this could not sedate the restlessness in him, and he made no excuses for it. He liked women. He liked being alone with them. And if it came to pass, as it often did, that he wound up in bed with them, he enjoyed it to the fullest. To his credit, his early years had not conditioned him to the double standard. He had no way of knowing how Arlene was conducting herself sexually, but he did not let it trouble him. He believed, or so he told himself, that if they ever had a life together he would be a faithful lover. Meanwhile, he would do as he pleased, and he suspected she would do likewise. He remembered one of Bandera's sayings: *If a woman is in your bed, she's there because she wants to be. If she wanted to be somewhere else, in another bed, she'd find a way to get there.* It made sense to Barr . . .

Meanwhile, President Medina had lived up to his part of the new petroleum law with a vengeance. He initiated a huge concession-granting program, and did it so quietly that some companies were already drilling new acreage before the news became public. The established companies grabbed off the cream, but there was still rich land left for newcomers. Atlantic Refining joined Cajun, Shell, Gulf and Sinclair in the lake area, and so did Standard of California, now wealthy beyond dreams of avarice from its successes in the Middle East. Phillips, Socony and Texaco grabbed footholds in the east where Gulf had found a half dozen new producing areas.

Roberto Fontenot regained his voice. "In a matter of months," he thundered, "President Medina has given to the international oil cartel more Venezuelan land than was given away in all of the thirty-two years under the governments of Gomez and Lopez Contreras! In the early days it could have been argued that the risk factor was high because the oil potential was unknown. But now there is no excuse. Everyone knows the tremendous value of our oil wealth, yet it has been carelessly tossed into the maw of greed with little concern for our country's future. Almost all of the area of the nation with petroleum potential is in foreign hands!"

The Allies had almost completely cleared the submarines from the seas, and in 1944 and 1945 Venezuelan oil production soared to record highs. Congratulatory telegrams from SCI in Houston became routine for Barr.

But oil and politics were a persistently indissoluble mixture in Venezuela. Medina's term was coming to an end, and he "leaked" a story to the news media that set the country awash with rumors. He had chosen as his successor, so the story went, an obscure Andino generally regarded as a fool.

"If this is true," Fontenot shouted, "I beg him to reconsider. Now is the time for him to choose a man of honor, a man of integrity, a man worthy to lead this great nation."

Barr met with Senator Vela in Miranda Park. "Why can't the stupid son of a bitch just once in his life do something right?" Barr grumbled. "What we need is a good solid conservative who will maintain the status quo with the companies and do something for the people."

Vela shook his head sadly. "It is worse than you think, my friend. I have it on the best authority that Lopez Contreras is preparing to move against him. Already it is being bandied about on the streets. The people are preparing for blood on the plazas."

Barr was thoughtful. "Do you really believe we are going to have another civil war?"

"There is no doubt in my mind. And there is no telling how long it will last or how many will die."

Barr said positively, "The side that starts losing will try to destroy the oilfields, Senator."

"I'm not so sure of that, no. But a civil war can reduce the flow of oil to a mere trickle, my friend. The fields will be forgotten once the fighting starts. It may take you years to recoup."

Barr lit a cigarette, his first of the day. "Think back with me, Senator. One day out here we were talking about Medina accepting help from the Communists. You said something like . . . like that Medina couldn't hear the rumbles in the barracks above the bullshit of the commies . . . or something like that."

Vela nodded.

"Is there discontent in the barracks?"

"That is what I hear."

"Certainly they don't favor Lopez Contreras over Medina, do they?"

Vela laughed. "Lopez Contreras did nothing for the younger officers. He was notorious for ignoring them. But Medina is an Andino also, my friend. He has done no more for them. In the military, Andinos look out for other Andinos only."

Barr put a hand on Vela's wrist. "Would you be endangering yourself if you tried to find out just how unhappy some of the younger officers might be? I wouldn't want you to do anything too risky, old friend of mine."

Vela shrugged. "Let me see."

"Not if it's dangerous for you."

Vela smiled. "I think I see what is in your mind. Perhaps we will have us another small conspiracy."

"There's something else," Barr said. "Do you think Roberto Fontenot would honor the petroleum law if he somehow came to power? Would he let the new concessions stand?"

Vela said gravely, "We are friends, you and I. I believe with all of my heart that he would let stand the portions *you* have honored. But we both know the treasury has not received the so-called even split that Medina talked about. Medina may not know this, but you can be assured that Fontenot knows what the figures should be down to the last centimo." Vela held up a hand. "I am not faulting you and your blood brothers. You did not *promise* an even split. But Medina assumed it, and you did nothing to correct his assumption." The old man sighed. "It was the one thing I did which I did not like about our work together. Forgive me, but it is true."

It was a long moment before Barr spoke. "I think you know I love you, old friend of mine. I admire and respect you, but I also love you. And I tell you now, I would rather lose an arm than lose your regard for me. In some way, I will fix things. That is my promise to my old friend."

There were tears in Vela's eyes. "Let us talk of other things. You are thinking of young officers on whose shoulders Fontenot would ride to power?"

"It's a thought."

Vela shook his head. "They would have to believe as he does. In the universal vote, constitutional reform, the best for the people."

"There may be some," Barr said. "There may be many. Fontenot is not against a good professional military. I'll bet on that."

Vela nodded. "It could be that they could satisfy one another. But remember this. Fontenot and his party would have to be the boss. He would have it no other way, wouldn't you agree?"

"He's smart enough and tough enough to see to that," Barr said with conviction. "Find out what you can."

They met a week later, and Vela was laughing quietly when Barr sat down at the table. "We are either geniuses or poor fools," the old man said. "They already have a vast plot, and hundreds of officers located in key posts are pledged to it." He laughed again. "They have a name for their group—the Patriotic Military Union." He fumbled a slip of paper from his coat pocket and handed it to Barr. "Read that, my friend. It is their manifesto."

Barr read. "It is time to put an end to the incompetence, the dishonesty and the bad faith which characterize our government. These times we live in places an historic responsibility on the shoulders of the youth of the world. We have faith in democracy. We propose to have a government based on the universal and direct vote of the Venezuelan citizenry, a constitutional reform which will truly represent the national will, and the establishment of a truly professional army. . . ."

Barr waved the paper. "Fontenot could have written this." He read the rest of the manifesto. "How did you come by this?"

Vela hesitated.

Barr said, "I ask for one reason only, old friend. If you obtained it easily, then surely others must have seen it. Perhaps even Medina."

The old man shook his head. "Only seven men have seen it. The ringleaders." He sighed. "Forgive me my language, but one of them is a gross tub of shit, a major who longs for my granddaughter. Had I not casually asked him about unrest in the barracks he would have told me anyway." Vela smiled wryly. "He wants to save my life, you see, to prove his love for my young darling. Medina and his most trusted friends are to be killed and, of course, I am in that number. He suggested I go to my place in Puerto Cabello and stay there until all the trouble is over."

"That's not a bad idea," Barr said. "But I'll tell you now, my friend, Fontenot won't go along with killing Medina or anybody else. There may be some killing in the streets, but Fontenot won't go along with cold-blooded executions."

"They may not need Fontenot."

"The hell they don't! Ninety percent of the people think he's the reincarnation of Simon Bolivar, and you know it. If they team up with Fontenot and his party, they'll have Medina and Lopez Contreras by the balls. You know I'm right."

Vela smiled. "And there'll be no protracted civil war and the oilfields will go right on producing." He nodded. "I admire your allegiance to your company, and I'm grateful that what appears to be good for your company also appears to be good for my country."

"Bless us all," said Barr, grinning.

"But how will we get them together?" Vela asked.

"I can handle that," Barr said. "You just convince your tub of shit how much his group needs Fontenot and Accion Democratica."

The old man smiled. "How wise we are."

It was late evening, and the wind blowing across the remote section of beach had a bite in it. Eduardo Vigas, wearing a blue windbreaker, shivered slightly as he trudged along the dark strip of sand.

In a few months this waterfront would be covered with sunbathers and bright umbrellas, and the waves would throw back the shouts of children and the clashing music from a thousand radios. But now Vigas had the beach to himself, and he was as alone as if he walked the sands of a distant star.

He halted in a spot where a great greenish rock had been deposited on the beach in some long-ago upheaval of the earth's crust. He had been seeking the rock; now he looked impatiently at his wristwatch. He was startled by the crunch of shoes on the graveled shoulder of the road on the rising, landward side of the beach. Grady Barr was looking down at him from the top of the sharp incline. Barr began picking his way sure-footedly down the incline. "Don't look so sulky, Eddie," he said as he approached Vigas. "I didn't ask you out here just for the hell of it." He took Vigas' arm. "Let's walk, Eddie."

But after several yards Barr stopped. "Are you mad at me, Eddie?" he asked.

Vigas looked toward the sea, his face unfriendly.

Barr said, "I didn't make a pass at your girl, Eddie, if that's what you're hot about. She'll tell you that. And I ought not to *have* to tell you that. You ought to know that the woman loves you. She damned well made it plain enough to me."

"She's gone," Vigas said, still looking at the sea. "She didn't say goodbye or kiss my ass or a fucking thing."

Barr took his shoulder and pulled Vigas to face him. "For Christ's sake, Eddie, I didn't have anything to do with it! Don't you know that? The woman told me she loved you. That was enough for me."

"I didn't even fuck her," Vigas said, as if Barr were not present. "I treated her like a queen."

"When did she leave, and where did she go?"

"Three days ago, and she told K. C. Hopkins she was going home. Back to the States. I think she'd been planning it for weeks. I wouldn't have even known about it if I hadn't got to worrying about her and called Hopkins."

Vigas sat down on the cool sand. Barr sat down beside him. "She was a good woman," Vigas said. "I wanted to marry her. You know, she'd come all over herself when I touched her down there, but she'd never let me put it in."

"Do you want to know how I see it?" Barr asked. And he thought of the night when he had soothed John Henry Craig. "I think she truly loved you, Eddie, but I think she never could get her husband out of her mind. Loving you was somehow betraying him, dead or not. Some women are like that. They feel they have to remain faithful to a dead husband, and particularly one who died like hers did. He's a hero to her, Eddie. She couldn't help getting hot pants, but she could stop it there. She felt like she had to. And she felt the same way about marriage. I may be wrong, but I think I'm right."

"It's not easy, getting her out of my mind," Vigas said.

"I know," Barr said, remembering that just the thought of her had once been enough to make his stomach churn. "But you'll get over it, Eddie,"

Vigas tried to grin. "I missed out on some fantastic pussy, is that the way to look at it?"

"Exactly," Barr said, "but the town's full of it."

"I think you're full of shit, but to hell with it. What the hell did you get me out here for?"

Barr said evenly, "We're going to prevent a civil war." He

275

explained the situation . . . the impending struggle between Lopez Contreras and Medina that could go on for months, devastate the country and leave thousands dead . . .

"Anybody can see that coming," Vigas said.

Barr told him about the organization of young officers who stood ready to take over the Medina government and pull Lopez Contreras' teeth. "They need the people behind them, Eddie, and the people in this case are Roberto Fontenot and Accion Democratica. Together they could neutralize Medina and Lopez Contreras in a matter of hours."

"Where do I fit in all this conniving?" Vigas asked.

"Don't try to shit me, Eddie. I've known for years that you're working with Fontenot, supplying him information and God knows what else."

Vigas stood up, and Barr got to his feet immediately. "Listen, Eddie. I never told anybody what I knew. If I had, your ass would be rotting in one of these stinking prisons, and you know it. So I don't want to argue about it. I want you to tell Fontenot that the officers will go along with his political ideas and let him and his party run the show. I want you to get them together before this fucking country explodes. I mean in a hurry, before Lopez Contreras marches on Caracas."

"But how can I do that, Grady? How will I explain to him that I know all this shit? How can *I* get everybody together?"

"First thing in the morning you go by and see Senator Filemon Vela. You know him?"

"I've seen him around."

"Tell him I sent you. He'll take it from there. He knows the officers."

"But . . ."

"For Christ's sake, Eddie! Use your mind. You and Vela can work things out. You've been double-dealing ever since you came back from the States. You must have learned something."

"And you're to be left out of it—right?"

Barr grinned. "I've got no business interfering in the affairs of this country. I'm a foreigner." The grin disappeared. "Can you see how important it is, Eddie?"

Vigas nodded.

"Then get to it."

Vigas smiled. "As you say."

Roberto Fontenot, some thought, inadvertently alerted Medina to the plot that was developed by Accion Democratica and the young officers. In a rousing speech in the Nuevo Circo Fontenot declared: "There are those who say that our party's proposal for a national candidate, not a Medina bootlicker, is the same as a peaceful *coup d'etat*. That is a perfect example of the government's insolent disdain toward public opinion. . . ."

They were bold words, and a threat was implied. By the morning of October 18, 1945, Medina had learned of the plot. He ordered the arrest of various officers and issued orders placing troops in combat readiness. But he was too late, and the plot was too well organized. The fighting from west to east lasted only thirty-six hours. More than four hundred soldiers, police and civilians were slain. A junta composed of four civilians and three army officers took command of a country whose citizens were almost one hundred percent behind them. It was a political first.

President of the junta was Roberto Fontenot.

Medina, Lopez Contreras and a dozen others were sent into exile. Senator Filemon Vela was allowed to retire to his estate at Puerto Cabello. His 'tub of shit,' Major Marcos Perez Jimenez, was not given a position of importance in the new government, though he had been one of the original seven military plotters. "It is an oversight they will soon have cause to regret, in my opinion," Senator Vela wrote in a letter to Grady Barr. "It may have been smarter to have shot him."

Fontenot made clear his party's position in no uncertain terms. "We did not enter the government like a poor relative using the servants' door. We are not a party made up of literary dilettantes or romantic adventurers. The key positions where the political, economic, and social policies of the nation are determined must be in our hands. We are not interested in just having ministries. We want to put a program of national salvation into effect."

Such a program was instituted.

He also promised a secret, universal ballot in an election in which he would not be a candidate, and he again delivered.

But before this he dealt with Grady Barr and his blood brothers. "We have no idea at present of nationalizing the oil industry," he told them, "but I must tell you that it is in our future plans." He let them digest that. "Now," he said, "we want you to know that we recognize the validity of the petroleum law passed under Medina and the concessions granted under it." He smiled. "That should allow you to relax for a moment."

He was speaking to them in a large room in Miraflores Palace, a room whose walls were now empty of pictures or decorations and whose floor was now bare of carpet, as if to emphasize the austerity of the new regime . . . Or perhaps, Barr thought, to compare it with the wealth of the companies represented there.

"There are various interpretations of the new petroleum law," Fontenot said, "and I assure you now that the government's interpretation will prevail. We intend to have a true fifty-fifty law. I want to state clearly once and for all that when the taxes and royalties paid to the government do not equal the net earnings of the companies, the companies will be obligated to make up the difference. I believe that everyone here can understand that.

"Because it has not been fully understood this past year, the Cajun Petroleum Corporation, for example, owes the Venezuelan treasury about nineteen million dollars. Shell owes almost that much. Others owe smaller amounts. I am not being arbitrary in this regard. We have the figures to support our position. Will anyone here dispute them? If you dispute them successfully, we will withdraw our claim and settle on your figures." He sought Barr in the group. "Mr. Barr. What have you to say, sir? Would you argue the point, knowing that we all are dealing with each other in good faith?"

Barr stood up. "The actual figure is nineteen million, one hundred and twelve thousand, three hundred and sixteen dollars and twenty-one cents. Damned if I know if we can afford it, but we'll pay it."

Fontenot laughed. "I have heard it said that SCI shareholders bless you every night before they go to sleep."

Barr bowed slightly in appreciation. Then he said, "You have said you and your people would recognize the validity of the new petroleum law, and we think you should. But tell me, sir, do you have anything else in mind? Other laws dealing with our business, other plans?"

Fontenot nodded. "Yes. For example, we would like to see the Venezuelan oil worker receive the same wages as his North American counterpart. Will we fight over that, gentlemen?"

Barr answered bluntly. "We probably will. I had decided before your party came to power that the time had come to recognize the union as the collective bargaining agent for the workers. I intend to do that, and I expect the other companies will follow suit. But I intend to deal with the union representatives, not the government. We've all been so wrapped up in our

278

own affairs that we've hardly noticed that the war is over. Demand for oil is still strong, and I think it will stay that way for a few years. But after that demand is going to fall. Most of that demand will be supplied with less expensive oil from the Middle East. That means we're going to have to cut back on production. And it means a lot of workers are going to be laid off. When I talk about layoffs and hard times, I want to do it with the men who will suffer from it, not with a group of politicians whose bellies will always be full."

"Anything else, Mr. Barr?"

"Yes. From now on, I don't want to be told what my company will do. I want things *discussed* with me. My company is a corporate citizen of this country. We've been here a long time. When we came here, there wasn't as much as an earth auger to dig a posthole. We've made a contribution to this country, and we have no reason to expect to be treated like a bastard at a family reunion."

"Anything else?"

"Yes. One more thing. My company didn't ask the State Department or the British Foreign Office to send people down here when the law was being drawn up. I didn't want that kind of help." He paused.

"But now you are talking nationalization, something you said time and time again in every village in the country that you had no idea of initiating. Nationalization would be a disaster for Venezuela, but it also would be a disaster for my company. And if the time ever comes when I think your government is seriously considering such a step, I'll call on every agency of the United States government for help."

"Gunboat diplomacy, Mr. Barr? That's out of fashion."

"Call it what you will," Barr said, and he sat down.

Fontenot looked coolly around the room. "Does anyone else have any remarks?"

There were no replies.

"Then this meeting is adjourned," Fontenot said.

Eduardo Vigas, looking handsome in a white suit and smoking a long cigar, sat at Barr's desk and said mildly, "You talked pretty tough to our leader this morning, I understand."

"It was as much for you as it was for him, old buddy," Barr said.

Vigas raised his brows. "How's that?"

"Because you're the one who's changing his mind about nationalization," Barr said. "I know you want it, Eddie, and I know *why* you want it. But you'll never get it as long as I'm around. I know how they treated you in Texas . . . like a fucking mescan. I know they black-balled you from that engineering society you wanted to be in so badly." Barr lifted a hand to keep Vigas from interrupting. "I know you hate every American oil company in this country because of the way you were treated. But I don't want to see you destroy the industry and bring harm to your country because of that hate. Can you see that?"

Vigas smiled faintly. "The same old song, Grady. Nationalization is a crime against reason, against home, God and mother, and against Grady Barr's Cajun Petroleum Corporation."

"It *is* a crime against reason," Barr said.

"And so you'll fight it all the way."

Barr smiled. "Tooth and nail, *amigo.*"

Vigas stood up. "From now on, Grady, if I were you, I'd see to it that everything Cajun does is exactly up to snuff. No foul-ups of any kind." He paused. "Now, you've said many times that we couldn't nationalize the oil business because we couldn't run it, didn't know how to. You're right—for the time being. But it's going to happen, and get this straight: *It's going to happen in every oil-producing country in the world!*" He ground out his cigar in Barr's tray. "I'm going to do my best to see to that."

"You'll have your work cut out for you, Eddie."

"Oh, I don't know. You gave in pretty damned quick when he hit you with that nineteen million he said you owed."

Barr smiled. "I was keeping a promise to an old friend, Eddie. If it hadn't been for that, a solemn promise, I sure as hell would have haggled over that nineteen million with him until I got goddamned good and ready to holler 'calf rope.' " Barr lit a cigarette. "Please sit down, Eddie. We've both said things that needed saying, or I guess they did. But we've been friends a long time, and I can't forget things you did for me."

"No, I think I like it better the way it is right now," Vigas said. "You run your business, and I'll run mine, and let's just keep it that way. I think we're about even on who owes who." He turned and left the office.

Barr sighed, lit a cigarette, then put it out immediately. The night before Arlene had called him from Houston; Washington was no longer exciting with the war over, and she had in any case been homesick for months.

"What would you say if I told you I wanted to get married?" she had asked.

"Why, I'd say you ought to go ahead and do it."

"It takes two to wed."

"Got any prospects?"

"One."

"Have you asked him yet?"

"I'm asking him now. How about it?"

"Christ! I'll have to buy a new suit."

"Grady," she had said, her voice throbbing with excitement, "Why don't I fly down there this weekend?"

Barr had wanted to be flippant, but now he found he couldn't. Suddenly he had wanted to see her with a surprising urgency.

"Well?" she had asked.

"I'm going to marry you in Houston," Barr said. "I want your daughter there, and my mother. Your brother, too, if he wants to come."

"When, Grady? When?"

"Simmer down."

"When?"

"Just as soon as I clear up a few matters here. Less than two weeks, I'd say."

"Grady!"

He *wanted* to get married, wanted to *be* married—and he wanted to be married to Arlene. It was, as his mother would have said, time for him to get married. Now he felt that marriage with Arlene had been almost inevitable since the first day he met her.

She had begun to cry, and Barr said soothing, loving words to her, words he had never before said to any woman, words that came from a spring of tenderness he had not suspected flowed inside his heart.

Chapter Twenty

Barr laid his hands palms up on the crude table. "These hands are tender now," he said, "but they have been coarse with labor. They have grabbed oilfield iron many times, for many years. So I speak to you as a man whose back has ached and whose head has drooped with weariness."

Leonel Castillo had left a job as driller for Gulf to become chief of the oil workers union. Today he wore his best suit—his only suit—to negotiate with Barr. He was short and squatty and his oiled hair was combed straight back from a high forehead. His green tie appeared to be choking him. He showed Barr his palms. "My hands are getting smooth," he said. "I was a boy of fourteen years, selling water on the streets of Maracaibo, when I saw you kill Hernan Robles on Plaza Sucre. Now you have killed another."

"That's true," Barr said.

Castillo shrugged. "Who knows? You may have done the world a favor."

They were sitting in the little hut in Cabimas that served as Castillo's office. A ceiling fan, stirring the humid air, was a mark of his rank; with the exception of his office only the whorehouses had ceiling fans.

"You locked out the workers at Quiriquire after the death of Gomez," Castillo said flatly.

"I did," Barr said.

"Now you are here in Cabimas to bargain with me instead of bargaining with me and with government officials in Caracas. Why is that?"

"The government is not the president of the oil workers union.

Leonel Castillo is. Who knows what is best for the workers, Leonel Castillo or some official sitting on a soft chair at Miraflores?"

"It is said that you have told Roberto Fontenot and others that Venezuelans couldn't run the oil business by themselves."

"I told him that. I say it to you. There is more to the oil business than drilling a hole in the ground. Venezuelans can do ninety percent of the work of my company. Ten percent they cannot do. By the time they learned that ten percent, if they had to learn it by themselves, their children would be starving and Venezuela would be a desert." Barr paused. "Listen to me, Leonel. You are a driller. A good one. But are you a geologist? A petroleum engineer? A shipper of oil? A seller of oil?" Barr shook his head. "There are many other things you are not, Leonel. And remember, even if you produce oil, you have to sell it. If no one will buy it, you have to drink it. We're oilmen, and we know that."

Castillo changed the subject. "The average worker now gets eleven bolivars a day. It has been said that Roberto Fontenot will see that he gets eighteen."

"Are you the union chief, or is Roberto Fontenot?" Barr asked. "Is he to tell the unions when to eat and when to sleep and when to take a shit?" He shook his head. "Fontenot is a politician. He says what sounds good. You know eighteen bolivars is too much. If world demand for oil drops off, and I'm sure it will, we could keep only a few workers on the payroll at eighteen bolivars. We could keep many more on the payroll if the pay was not too high—say fourteen bolivars. There would be fewer workers laid off—and fewer unhappy with their leader."

Castillo banged the table with a big fist. "Fourteen bolivars for two years, then sixteen for three years. After that, eighteen bolivars for the lowest paid worker in the industry."

"And after that?" Barr asked dryly.

"We bargain year by year," Castillo said.

Barr grinned. "You're a scoundrel, Leonel. Your term of office is five years. You're already running for re-election when you talk about eighteen bolivars in the sixth year. You're shutting off any opposition right now."

Castillo grinned back at Barr. "I have learned much from reading the history of the United States. Do we have the backbone of a deal?"

"No strikes?"

"No strikes." Castillo held up a warning finger. "But the contract remains valid even if the government falls. That must be agreed."

Barr squinted at him. "Do you think the government could fall? Really?"

Castillo shrugged. "Who knows? Roberto Fontenot was too kind. He exiled less than a dozen or so. There are hundreds left who will spend day and night plotting against him."

"But the military is behind him," Barr said.

Castillo grunted. "The military! The military is a weather vane." Then, "My people will have to vote on these matters."

"They'll do as you suggest."

"The other companies . . . will they follow your lead?"

"They'll have to. I can convince them of that."

Castillo smiled for the first time. "If I get this contract approved and signed without help from the government, it will make me look like a smart man, a smart union leader. You worked on my vanity, Mr. Barr. And on my ambition."

Barr grinned. "Yes, but it's still a good contract."

"But what if I had said no. That I thought Roberto Fontenot ought to be involved. What then?"

"We'd be fighting over every centimo until hell freezes over. And you'd look like a *stupid* union leader."

Castillo nodded. "So I thought."

Barr smiled warmly. "I wish you would hurry on this matter, sir. I want to go to the States and get married."

"Oh! Congratulations!" Castillo reached across the table and grabbed Barr's shoulders in powerful hands. He said soberly, "I have always wished that I could have gone with you into the Perija."

"There is no man I would rather have had," Barr said.

From the Caracas *Daily Star* of November 20, 1945:

> The Venezuelan Oil Workers Union has signed a contract with Cajun Petroleum Corporation which will substantially increase the workers' incomes, it was announced today by Leonel Castillo, union president.
>
> Pay for the average Cajun worker will be hiked to Bs. 14 daily immediately, Castillo said. After two years, the basic wage will be raised to Bs. 16, and three years later the lowest paid Cajun workers will receive Bs. 18 daily.
>
> The contract signing marked the first time in Venezuelan

oil history that an oil company recognized the union as a collective bargaining agent for the workers.

Negotiator for Cajun was Grady Stancil Barr, company president.

"It is a historic day for the Venezuelan oil worker," Castillo said. "It is to be hoped that workers in other industries, other jobs, will be able to use this contract as a pattern."

Castillo stressed that the government was not involved in the negotiations.

Barr said the other companies operating in Venezuela have indicated they intend to sign similar contracts with the union. Asked why Cajun took the lead in dealing with the union, Barr said, "Our company had been considering such a move for a long time. Now, with the war over, it seemed to us that the time to act had come. We were in no way competing with the other companies to be first."

Asked why the government was not involved in negotiations, Barr said, "I assume the workers had complete faith in Leonel Castillo's ability to represent them. Certainly they have no complaint, for he conducted their affairs with skill and with boldness. In any event, the negotiations were not a concern of the administration. The administration gets its millions from the oil companies from taxes and royalty payments. The workers get their bolivars from the sweat of their brows and from the sharpness of their minds. It is only proper that they should deal for themselves."

Castillo is in his first year of a five-year term as union president.

Barr flew out of Venezuela, leaving Ed Gurwell to run the company and face the wrath of his blood brothers. "Just treat them in your usual snotty manner," Barr told Gurwell. "Ask them how they'd like it if they had to start paying eighteen bolivars tomorrow. That's what Fontenot would have made them swallow."

Barr's flight took him to Montego Bay, Havana, New Orleans and Houston. He was going through customs when he started getting cold feet about the marriage. Then he heard her calling his name. She was running to meet him, her face glowing with happiness. The crowd parted for her, smiling at her delight, and Barr took her in his arms and kissed her. Behind him he heard a gruff voice say, "Why don't you rent a room, buddy?"

Barr released Arlene and spun around. His fists were clenched and a hot retort was on his lips, but smiling at him was Tom Fairbanks. And standing beside Fairbanks was Barr's mother, slim and elegant in a mink jacket and a saucy brown hat riding her gray curls. Barr started for her, but she held out a warning hand. "Don't you mess me up, Grady Barr! It took me four hours to get this pretty!"

As Barr looked at her he thought of the hundreds of times he had seen this woman bent over a tin tub washing dirty overalls. Now she read his thoughts . . . She had seen her son seventeen times since he had gone to Venezuela in 1923, and he had made her life comfortable even before that. She had lived well, thanks to her son, but like him she was now remembering the hard years. She went to him and kissed his cheek, murmuring, "I'm happy for you, Grady, and I'm proud of you."

"As the best man of this mismatch, I want some attention," Fairbanks said. "Let's get out of here and let these other people conduct their business."

In a small library off the master bedroom, Barr stood thumbing idly through a *Time* magazine. Wearing a dressing gown of pale blue, he was waiting for Arlene to join him on their nuptial night.

The ceremony at the South Main Baptist Church had been brief and simple. Arlene's brother, Harley Bowie, had flown in from Washington, and her daughter Millicent had come down from Southern Methodist University in Dallas. Less than a dozen of Arlene's Houston friends had attended the ceremony, and Barr had invited only John Henry Craig and Charles Cannon from SCI.

The reception had been held in Arlene's mansion in River Oaks. Harley Bowie had explained to Barr over glasses of champagne that the deceased Harley Bowie, Senior had made so much money in the import-export business he couldn't count it all. "It was embarrassing," Bowie said with a smile. "Arlene and I decided to let others run the business while we simply sat back and spent the money." He was a lanky, brown-haired man of Barr's age. "Occasionally somebody in government hires me to consult with them on matters I know nothing about, so I charge them outrageous fees." He was married and had three children. "My wife doesn't like Arlene, so she didn't come. I think it just as well that you know that now, don't you?"

"Of course," Barr said.

Millicent, Arlene's daughter, was a plain, pudgy girl with mousy hair who looked younger than her nineteen years. She seldom spoke but hung on every word Barr uttered, and he flattered himself that she was taken with him. As the reception neared its end, she suddenly grasped Barr's hand and said, "May I come to Caracas at the Christmas holidays?"

Barr put his arm around her shoulders. "If you don't, I'll come up here and get you," he said. He poured her a glass of champagne and talked to her about Caracas until she emptied her glass.

Finally it was over. Fairbanks was to fly Margaret Barr back to San Antonio in his plane and then continue on to Sombrero Ranch farther south. Harley Bowie was in a hurry to get back to Washington. Only Millicent seemed reluctant to leave, but she had to get back to school, and she was traveling as far as Dallas with Harley Bowie. Eventually the caterers cleared up and departed.

And now Barr waited for Arlene, his wife.

Her dressing gown was also blue. A tentative smile was on her face when Barr tossed aside the magazine and took her in his arms. He could feel her trembling against his chest, and was astute enough to realize she was trembling not from passion but from nervous fear. He sat down in an overstuffed chair and pulled her down on his lap. He said nothing, but simply held her face against his neck. She started to say something, but Barr put a hand gently on her mouth, then withdrew it. She snuggled against him, still trembling. When the trembling finally ceased, half an hour had passed, and she was asleep.

Carefully, Barr got to his feet and placed her on the giant bed in the bedroom. She slept as if she had been drugged.

Barr made himself comfortable in the overstuffed chair. He watched her sleep, thinking of her, and then his thoughts wandered back to Caracas and recent events . . .

He had not contested Roberto Fontenot over the nineteen million dollars because he had promised Filemon Vela that he would right a wrong. He had sought out Leonel Castillo and contracted with the union because he wanted to demonstrate to Fontenot that the oil companies still had muscles, and he knew he could get a better deal for the company in direct negotiations with Castillo. But there was something else, also. He had tried to put Endicott out of his mind, but the figures the Negro had spouted at him had, for the first time, taken root in his mind. He had heard the figures before; Fontenot had recited them regularly, and Barr had regarded them as political rhetoric. But Endicott, in his offhand way, had made them real. Barr had told himself that it simply was good business to keep his work force well fed, and it was. But he knew in his heart that he had dealt more quickly with Castillo than was prudent—Endicott had made the workers' hunger palpable . . .

He went to sleep in the chair and slept until six in the morning. Arlene was still asleep. Barr cleaned up in the bathroom, made coffee, and took coffee, cream and sugar to Arlene's bedside. The sound from his placing the tray on the bed table awakened her, and she looked up at his smiling face. She was flushed with embarrassment, but before she could speak, Barr said, "Don't say a word before you have a sip of coffee. It's bad luck. I'll go get mine."

When he returned with his coffee she was sitting on the side of the bed. He kicked a chair up near the bed table and sat down. "Grady . . ."

"Let me tell you something," Barr said. "There's no law, and nothing in the marriage vows, that says *when* you have to make love. What happened last night was nothing to be embarrassed about. You'll know when you're ready, and I'll know it too. You were worn out and nervous and a little bit afraid." He smiled. "It probably would have been terrible."

"I love you, Grady," she said, not looking at him, her voice sounding as if she were trying to explain something and apologize at the same time.

He took the cup from her hand and lifted her to her feet. He pulled her close to him. "Sweetheart, you're my woman," he said gently.

She pulled her head back and looked at him. She smiled. "Well, you'd better let go of me before I commit a small nuisance on the carpet. It's either pee or drown, Grady Barr."

At breakfast she said, "You said you didn't care about what happened between Maco Stephens and me, Grady, but I have to tell you. I should have told you long ago."

"If it will make you feel better," Barr said.

When Millicent was six years old, she told him, she and Maco Stephens stopped having sex. "He just didn't want it, Grady." Later she found out he was getting it elsewhere, and that went on for years. "He asked *me* for the divorce, Grady. That's what you have to know. Not that I had done anything wrong. He had found someone he wanted to live with, and I let him go."

Barr nodded.

"So I haven't been with anyone for thirteen years, Grady. Do you understand that?"

Barr chewed his eggs and nodded.

"That's not the worst, Grady."

Barr wiped his lips with his napkin. "I know, darling. We always save the worst for last. What was it? Did he say he thought you were a lesbian?"

Arlene blushed.

"What was it?" Barr insisted.

"He said that after Millicent was born . . ."

"Yes, darling."

"He said that after Millicent was born that being with me was like raising the shade and throwing his thing out the window." She spoke in a rush, anxious to get the words said and over.

Barr pushed back his chair and laughed. He tried to control his laughter, but he couldn't. He saw his laughter was hurting her; still he couldn't stop. Finally he said, "Honey, that's the oldest gag in the world." He began to laugh again.

She was hurt and angry. "I'd like to know about it so I could laugh, too," she said tartly.

Barr stopped laughing. "Honey," he said soberly, "if a woman doesn't have a physical deformity, there's no such thing as being too big. And there's no such thing as a man being too little, if he's got anything at all."

"Well, he said . . ."

"I don't give a damn what he said," Barr said. "If you were worried about it, why didn't you go to a doctor?"

"I did," she said triumphantly, "and he said that for a woman who had borne a child I was fine!" She looked at him defiantly across the table. "That's why I was willing to marry you."

Barr nodded. "But still you got to worrying about what he said, is that right?"

"That's part of it," she said.

"What's the rest?"

She said sadly, "Thirteen years is a long time, Grady."

Barr placed his knife and fork on his plate. "Arlene, in a movie this would be the time for me to come around the table and hug and reassure you. Well, I'm not going to do it. You don't need it. I told you early this morning that we'll make love when we are damned well ready to do it. So don't sit there worrying about me. I'll survive, I promise you."

But she was not to be shaken out of her sad mood. "I wouldn't blame you if you got up from this table and went right back to Caracas."

Barr said, "I'm going to get up from this table and go brush my teeth, like any good dentist will tell you to do after every meal. Then I'm going to lie down for thirty minutes or so and rest the kinks out of my back I got from sleeping in that damned chair. And you—you're going to get yourself pretty and we're going to take a drive around town. They lay out a new street or put up a new building every day, and I want to catch up."

She woke him by snuggling up against him. There had been a dramatic change in her attitude while he slept for she was now naked and her hands were removing his pajama bottoms. She brushed her breasts roughly against the hair on his chest again and again, and when he kissed her mouth it opened, and she sucked his tongue greedily. "Harder!" she said; the friction between her breasts and his chest hair had her frantic. But Barr kissed her breasts before he pulled them back against his chest. She scraped herself against him, and almost immediately was in the throes of orgasm.

While she was still gasping, she grasped Barr's penis and pulled it toward her vagina. Barr mounted her. Barr prided himself that even on first encounters he could control his ejaculations, but before he fully entered her she started coming, and his hunger and her passion combined to drive him to an explosion. Even so, she came several more times, and even when his passion was spent and his penis was growing flaccid, she ground herself against him and had another orgasm. They lay together without speaking.

A half hour passed. Barr was still resting on her, and his penis was still inside her. Then she began moving her hands on his body, very slowly, and Barr found her lips with his. She had not cried out during the first coupling, but now she moaned as she felt his penis harden inside her. He began to make love to her slowly, using all the skill he possessed, talking to her, telling her how wonderful her pussy felt, telling her how sweet and tender were her breasts, rubbing his chest hair against her rosy nipples, kissing her mouth and eyes each time she came but giving her little time to relax between orgasms. He made love to her this

290

way until he sensed she was nearing exhaustion, then they came together in a climax that had Barr tearing at the bed sheets.

Later, when they had regained their breath, Arlene chuckled and said, "I've got to write Harley and tell him how much I appreciate those books he sent me."

"Books?"

"Uh huh. When I told him I was going to marry you, he sent me about a dozen 'how to' sex books." She giggled, and Barr slapped her on the ass.

They were drinking cold beer in the breakfast nook. "Grady," Arlene said, "I didn't know . . ."

She got no further. Barr had placed a hand over her mouth. "I know what you were going to say, Arlene, and I don't want to hear it. Not from you. That's a whore's line."

Her eyes showed her hurt. "Listen," Barr said, "a man of experience can judge pussy. He can look back and remember what was good and what was better. But a woman can't do that, Arlene. Not a woman who isn't promiscuous. With a normal woman, the last she gets, if it's any good at all, is the best she ever had. If it's any good at all, I said." He shook his head. "Maybe a woman just can't help saying that she didn't know it could be so good, or 'I didn't know it could be like this.' I guess it's been said a million times and written about the same amount. It's flattering, I guess, to a man the first time he hears it, but he learns eventually that every whore says it to any john who gives her twice what she thinks her pussy is really worth."

"Thank you for the lecture," she said tartly.

Barr grinned. "I'm just filling in the gaps in those 'how to' books Harley sent you. Why don't you get us another beer?"

She took his hand and placed it on her breast.

Barr had little time for reflection. For three days they never left the house, and the hours were filled with lovemaking and learning about each other. Even when she slept while he was awake his thoughts were on her. He was honest enough to admit to himself that one of the reasons he had married her was that he simply wanted to get married. He hadn't been sure that he loved her because he hadn't been sure that he really knew what the word meant. Now he did.

He had been disturbed that he did not lust for her as he had for other women. Now he knew he had been practicing a restraint he had not known he possessed. Now he wanted her all the time, it seemed, and sex with her was the best he had ever had.

He thought of Millicent. Her father had neglected her, according to Arlene. "She never wanted to leave my side," Arlene said. "That's why I insisted that she go to school in Dallas. I knew she had to get away from me. She's smart. She's smart enough to know she's plain, and she's terribly shy. If this doesn't work, Grady, her being away at school, you're going to have to help me think of something else." Barr had said that he would.

On the second night after the wedding, they had called Millicent at her dormitory. "Remember," Barr had told her, "you promised to come to Caracas at Christmas." Later, Arlene had told him, "I think she already loves you, Grady," and he had been pleased . . .

On the third day, at five in the afternoon, Charles Cannon called. As calmly as if he were issuing instructions to a secretary, he said, "Grady, somebody shot Roberto Fontenot about an hour ago. We want you to get back there. We'll have a company plane ready in an hour."

"Is he dead?" Barr asked.

"He wasn't when Gurwell called a few minutes ago. Either way it will be bad enough, don't you think?"

"Uh huh."

"Get packing then. A car's on the way to pick you up."

"All right, Charley," Barr said.

He told Arlene what had happened. "I'll call you as soon as I can, honey."

"Call? I'm going with you!"

"No, honey," he said gently. "This is not the time for you to be there."

"You mean it may be dangerous, don't you? Now I *know* I'm going!"

Barr took her by the shoulders. "You're not going, and I haven't got time to argue with you about it. You know damned well that I'm going to see you just as soon as I can, here or there. Now help me pack." He kissed her. "And don't cry."

She clung to him, but she didn't cry. Barr finally had to tear loose from her. They were naked, and she reached down and squeezed his penis. "Don't you dare let anyone else have any of that candy leg," she warned.

292

Barr laughed. "You didn't read *that* in one of Harley's books."

"No, but a woman friend told me she says that to her husband every time he goes off on a business trip." She smiled. "I thought it was kind of cute the way I did it."

Barr said dryly, "It *was* cute, but you'd better let go of it or I'll never get to Caracas."

"That's the point," she said, but she released him and set about helping him pack.

Fontenot was not dead, but soldiers were patrolling almost every Caracas street, and Barr's limousine was stopped for inspection five times between the airport and his office. "He's not in any real danger of dying," Gurwell told Barr, "but his left shoulder was shattered, and there's talk that he may lose the arm."

Fontenot had been shot twice with a high-powered rifle, the second bullet striking him in almost the same place as the first. He was struck as he got out of his car at the site of a planned housing development. No one had seen the rifleman, and two hours had passed before police found two empty cartridge cases in a second-floor room of a deserted building. "The son of a bitch must be dead-eye dick," Gurwell said. "That building is a good two hundred yards away from where Fontenot was standing."

"They don't have a lead on him at all?" Barr asked.

Gurwell snorted. "These goddamned Caracas cops couldn't find a ten-ton truck in a one-car garage."

"Well, who's getting the blame for it, the oil companies or the commies?" Barr asked.

Gurwell's laugh held no mirth. "Right now I'd say we have a slight edge. The newspapers haven't hinted at anything, but I've had our people out on the streets since the shooting. The so-called man on the street knows the commies hate Fontenot, but they figure we're all pissed off because he took that big tax bite out of our asses."

"I'd figure the guy to be one of Medina's buddies, or somebody they hired. Wouldn't you? I'll bet that's the angle the other junta members are working on."

"Sure, but that's too simple for the man on the street."

"Has Fontenot issued any kind of statement?"

"Not a word."

"Well," Barr said, "I'm going to see him."

"You'll never get through the hospital door," Gurwell said.

"What are our blood brothers doing?"

"Same as us. The workers are milling around the fields like a herd of longhorns, and we're trying to get them back to work."

"That's why I'm going to see Fontenot, Ed. He can do the job for us."

"Well, you ought to at least shave before you go."

Chapter Twenty-One

Freedom of the press had been restored, and to Barr it seemed as if every newspaper and radio station in the republic had a representative at Saint Joseph's Hospital. He worked his way through them, but was stopped several times by soldiers or policemen before he reached the hospital entrance. He was being denied admittance to the hospital when Eduardo Vigas came out the door on his way to the street. He stopped when he saw Barr.

"How is he, Eddie?" Barr asked. "I just got back from Houston."

"He'll make it. And he's not going to lose his arm."

"I have to talk to him, Eddie. It's important, or you know I wouldn't be here."

"You're crazy!"

"Listen, Eddie. I know he's in bad shape. But he's not a sissy, he's the head of a state, and sometimes heads of state have to suck it up and do more than we ordinary mortals can do. I'm asking you, get me in to see him. If you don't, I'll try some other way, and I'll keep on trying."

Vigas studied him for a moment, then nodded to the soldier to let Barr inside. Vigas led Barr down a long corridor where soldiers paced while nurses and nuns scurried among them at their duties. Two soldiers were stationed at the door of Fontenot's room.

"Wait here," Vigas said, and the soldiers allowed him to enter, holding Barr back with the force of their presence. Barr longed for a cigarette. Vigas came back outside quicker than Barr had anticipated. He held the door open for Barr and they went into the room.

Fontenot was propped up in bed, and his face was as gray as ashes. Only his eyes seemed alive. A bearded doctor stood at the foot of the bed, and next to him stood a slender captain with a hawk-like face. Before Barr could speak, the captain snapped, "Speak Spanish—if you can!"

Barr repaid his insolence by ignoring him and by saying to Fontenot, "I am happy to see that you are hardier than the bullets."

Fontenot nodded.

"I will not tire you," Barr said. "A common cause has brought me here. The workers in the fields and stations are idle because they lack direction." He smiled. "I need not remind you that fifty percent of the time they're wasting belongs to the administration. The administration needs greater production now more than ever before so it can launch its many social programs. I . . ."

The captain interrupted. "In a democracy, we do not *order* the workers to produce!"

"In a democracy," Barr said, speaking to Fontenot and ignoring the captain, "we *appeal* to the workers to produce, for the good of the country and a bright future."

Fontenot nodded. "Are there reporters outside?" His voice was weak.

Barr grinned. "About a million."

The captain broke in. "And what do you think he should say?" His voice was venemous.

Barr looked at him. "No one has needed to tell Roberto Fontenot what to say and how to say it since the day he first opened his mouth." He turned back to Fontenot. "I ask this selfishly; if there is anything you can say to absolve the industry in this affair, it would ease my mind." Looking back at the captain, he added, "Of course, if a clue to the rifleman has not been found even at this late date I would imagine that every citizen in the republic is suspect." He turned back to Fontenot and smiled. "Fifty-fifty. We've both got to do our part."

Barr headed for the door. Behind him Fontenot cleared his throat. Barr stopped and faced him. Fontenot said, "Thank you for coming." He closed his eyes.

Barr and Vigas went into the corridor. Vigas said, "You know what they say in East Texas, Grady—You're as tough as a bodark stump."

Barr looked at Vigas quizzically. "Are you trying to make up with me, you son of a gun?"

"No. Just making a comment," Vigas said, and walked away.

From the Caracas *Daily Star* of November 25, 1945:

> Pale and obviously still in great pain, Roberto Fontenot assured the nation that he is on the road to recovery and appealed to all workers to return to their jobs to build a greater Venezuela.
>
> He said he was appealing particularly to the oil workers. "It is they who primarily will produce the wealth that will allow us all to accomplish the great social programs for which we have so long yearned. I entreat them to go about their jobs as if this incident had not occurred."
>
> Meanwhile, both police and the military said they had found no clue to the identity of the rifleman who shot the junta leader. . . .

Fontenot mended rapidly, though his left arm remained practically useless. The rifleman was never found. Neither the attack nor the bad arm appeared to diminish Fontenot's energy. He and the other members of the junta set about constructing their conception of an ideal democratic state. Dozens of social programs were initiated. Voting rights were extended to all Venezuelans eighteen years and older, without distinction as to sex, and excepting only those serving prison sentences. Any citizen twenty-one or older was eligible for for public office.

In this new air of freedom, thirteen political parties were legalized, and to Barr it seemed as if the country had turned into a nation of orators. Fontenot had said that he and other junta members would not run for office, and they didn't. In the first national election, ninety-two out of every one hundred registered voters cast a ballot. Candidates of Accion Democratica won handily in almost every section of the country.

And when the promised presidential election was held, the Accion Democratica candidate, Romulo Gallegos, a respected writer and teacher, received 870,000 votes; his nearest rival received only 273,000; the Communist Party candidate received 37,000 votes.

Fontenot was President Gallego's chief advisor, and the administration's strength. As promised, the administration supported the oil workers in demands for sick pay, vacation periods, increased supplies in company commissaries, better working conditions. The companies met these demands, and Barr and the Shell man instituted a pension plan for their employees. But the pay structure Barr had worked out with Leonel Castillo remained intact.

When the Communists tried to foment a strike in the lake region fields, the administration made no move to interfere. Barr called on Castillo in his Cabimas office. "I have gone even farther than I intended to go at first, which makes you look like an even smarter union leader," Barr said. "Is this true?"

"It's true," Castillo said.

"Then I want you to kick those Communist bastards out of the union," Barr said, "and don't tell me Leonel Castillo can't do it."

"All of them?"

"No, just the leaders. The ones pushing for a strike."

Castillo nodded. "Consider it done."

"No strike?"

"No strike."

The Communist leaders were expelled from the union.

The stability in the fields was coupled with a new energy. Each month production records toppled as Cajun and the other companies drilled new concessions and increased their production in the old ones. Cajun was the brightest jewel in the SCI crown, and Barr received much of the credit for it.

Barr was almost serene. Arlene had joined him within a week of his return to Caracas, and he had bought her a beautiful home in a small canyon. With her at his side he became more involved in the city's social life. He became devoted to Millicent, and encouraged her to visit them at every opportunity.

And it was at this time, when President Gallegos had served but a portion of his five-year term, that Senator Filemon Vela's "tub of shit," Colonel Marcos Perez Jimenez, joined with other army officers in overthrowing the duly elected government. President Gallegos, his cabinet, most of the Congress, and thousands of other Venezuelans were jailed. Perez Jimenez' chief rival in the new junta was murdered, and the country had a new dictator.

Roberto Fontenot escaped the dragnet as he had escaped one

before. He lived underground briefly, then made his way out of the country. Eduardo Vigas escaped with him.

Ed Gurwell lit two cigarettes and handed one to Barr. "Grady, this new son of a bitch makes Lopez Contreras and Medina look like a couple of pansies. He's as mean as Gomez ever hoped to be. Do you think we're going to be able to deal with him?"

Barr blew a gloomy smoke ring at the ceiling. From his desk he took a page from the Houston *Post* and slid it across the desk to Gurwell. "I got this in the mail yesterday." The headline on the page said: OIL OUTPUT PASSES WORLD DEMAND.

"It means production cutbacks and layoffs," Barr said. "I can see where it's going to be great fun to tell that to Perez Jimenez the first pop out of the box. He may have a little trouble believing that the coup and oil problems are purely coincidental."

Gurwell sighed. "Have you discussed this with the blood brothers?"

"Uh huh. They want me to explain to him that his income is going to be dramatically curtailed." Barr smiled weakly. "That's the Shell man's description of the situation, of course."

"Jesus!"

"And I've got to talk to Leonel Castillo, and I'd just as soon take a beating with a wet rope."

"It would be a good lick if you could talk to both of them at the same time," Gurwell said.

Barr sat upright in his chair. He grinned at Gurwell. "Now I know why I keep getting SCI to give you those fat raises instead of transferring your ass to India or Lapland. You come up with an idea every once in a while."

"I thought it was because I keep you in cigarettes," Gurwell said.

Once again Barr sat in the office in Miraflores Palace where years before he had sat with Lopez Contreras and Charles Cannon. With him this time was Castillo, stolid but impressive in a white suit.

For this occasion Perez Jimenez wore a civilian suit of soft gray. He was a soft-bodied man, round-faced, short-legged, and his plump hands were in constant motion as Barr explained to him the financial facts of life. Behind the heavy tortoise-shell glasses his dark eyes seemed to be fixed on Barr's mouth.

"In the contract with the workers, the companies have agreed to retain all features of the contract during and after any changes in the government," Barr said. "We hope we will be able to honor that obligation. And, as I said earlier, we will try to cut production and drilling as little as possible and lay off as few workers as we can manage to do."

The dictator shifted his gaze to Castillo. "You will excuse us, please." He spoke slowly, and Barr realized he did so to keep from stuttering. Castillo got to his feet and left the room. Perez Jimenez looked back at Barr.

"You were a friend of Senator Filemon Vela. You were involved in the action against Isaias Medina. To what degree is not important. What is important is that from this date you confine your activities to the oil business. I am not being unfriendly. I am saying this: You run the oil business and I will run the government. I am depending on you to see that the government receives its proper share of oil income and the workers are treated with concern. Come to me only when you feel you need my help." He smiled. "Let us hope that I never have to come to you."

"That's plain enough," Barr said. "I appreciate your candor." He prepared to leave, but the dictator motioned for him to remain seated. "You have noticed that there are many beautiful women in this country?"

Barr smiled. "One of the true blessings of the land."

The dictator was shifting his short legs and his nervous hands seemed to be seeking a place to hide. "Some day soon I will invite you to a place you will not forget." His smile, Barr thought, was disgustingly lascivious. "Would the thought of many beautiful women in one place intrigue you? It is said you have an eye for beauty."

Barr said with mock gravity, "I can't see how that could interfere with the oil business *or* administering a government."

The dictator rose and offered his hand to Barr. "Life must not be all work." Barr shook the proffered hand, rising as he did so. The dictator waved the hand when the handshake was completed. He smiled. "Go make us some money."

Production and drilling *were* curtailed. Workers *were* laid off. And 1949 marked the first time since 1943 that production did not increase over the previous year.

It appeared that 1950 would be even worse, but in June North Korea launched an attack against South Korea, and demand for oil skyrocketed. Cajun began drilling in almost every section of

300

Venezuela, including the vast mud flats of the Orinoco delta, and the refinery on the Dutch island of Aruba was enlarged. And, under the fifty-fifty law which mandated future refinery construction on the Venezuelan mainland, both Cajun and Shell erected new installations on the mainland.

Barr was kept so busy that he was neglecting Arlene, and she made it clear with increasing intensity that she resented it. Barr considered her outbursts as harassment, and their quarrels became as frequent as their lovemaking. She demanded that he take a long vacation; he refused, declaring it an impossibility. Later she suggested that they return to the States. "We've got enough money to live where we want to and how we want to. You're killing yourself and destroying our marriage." Barr told her to go home if she wanted to. She cried, and he held her to him. But both knew they were losing something vital to their relationship.

Roberto Fontenot's name was never mentioned in the Venezuelan newspapers except when the dictatorship decided to castigate him for one reason or the other. However, SCI in Houston kept Barr informed of his activities as he moved between the few capitals in the western hemisphere where he was welcome. He spoke often, and the oil companies noted with relief that now his target was always the new dictatorship.

Eduardo Vigas surfaced in the Middle East. "He's covering more ground and preaching harder than Billy Graham," Ed Gurwell reported to Barr from Houston where he was vacationing and spending most of his time, it appeared, at the SCI office. "He's preaching the fifty-fifty law to the heathen, and the heathen are listening."

"Who's financing him?"

"Nobody knows. Maybe he's getting the dough from down there."

"And you think they're listening to him, eh?"

"I know it. Cannon was telling me that the old king in Saudi Arabia has already asked about it. I don't see how the old bastard can spend any more money than he gets now."

"He might want to spread it out among the people," Barr said dryly.

Gurwell snorted. "There must be a hundred people in his family, and every damned one of them has got everything from a solid gold Cadillac to a solid gold shithouse."

"Allah be praised! When are you coming home?"

"I'll see you next week," Gurwell said.

Three weeks after Gurwell's return, Barr received a letter from John Henry Craig. The old man was retiring as SCI board chairman, and Barr thought at first the letter was just a friendly note. But Craig had written: "To bring you fully up to date on developments outside your sphere, Eduardo Vigas has sold the fifty-fifty law to every oil producing nation in the Middle East. Indeed, the consortium has just concluded such an arrangement with the King of Saudi Arabia.

"It has not been a disaster, however, or even a blow of any consequence because of an idea you held in 1943 when you were dealing with Medina. If you recall, you suggested that the American companies approach the U.S. government with a proposal that the increase in royalty payments to Venezuela be regarded as a tax increase, and thus deductible from our U.S. tax bills.

"We have done just that as regards Saudi Arabia. We found support for our proposal in Washington, and the job is done. We estimate that the consortium will save about $50 million in the first year alone by this device; all of the companies will be doing this very soon in the other countries, I am sure, as will SCI.

"Perhaps someone else would have thought of this idea if you had not, Grady, but I want to praise you for what I consider a monumental contribution to the international oil industry.

"Please come to see me when you come to Houston."

And there was a footnote: "There will be no publicity about this, of course, since the U.S. Treasury is being deprived of this money and the U.S. taxpayers, in effect, are footing our bill for it."

The letter caused the final break between Barr and Arlene. In the recent past she had accused him of philandering, and he had not replied to the accusation. She had acted as if his silence were an admission of guilt, and he had left the house rather than argue about it. When he had returned after several hours' absence, she had refused to acknowledge his presence in the house. That had lasted for several days, but finally they had edged toward an uneasy truce. So they at least were on speaking terms on the day she found Craig's letter among some papers Barr had brought home from the office. Going through the papers to put them in their proper places in his den office, she noticed Craig's name on the envelope.

"I see you got a letter from Mr. Craig," she said. "Is it a farewell note to an old comrade-in-arms?"

"Matter of fact, he wrote to compliment me about something," Barr said. He was fixing drinks for them.

Arlene said, "How nice of him," and she took the letter from the envelope and began reading it. She had read it through when Barr brought her a scotch and soda. He was surprised at the fury he saw on her face. She shook the letter at him. "Compliment? One thief complimenting another thief!"

Barr said nothing.

"You'll admit it's a tax dodge, won't you?" she demanded. "You're honest enough for that, aren't you?"

Still Barr said nothing.

"It's stealing, pure and simple," she said in a calmer voice, "and you're the bright boy who dreamed it all up." She tossed the letter on the floor. "I'll never have any respect for you again, Grady."

Barr was tense and on edge himself, but he tried to hold himself in check. "I think I can explain it," he said.

"Explain it? A child can explain it! Why don't you admit it's a tax dodge?"

"It's a tax dodge," Barr said stiffly. "A goddamned *big* tax dodge. And it's going to get bigger." He extended his hand holding the scotch and soda. "Now that I've confessed, can we have a drink?"

She slapped the drink from his hand, and ran out of the room.

Three days later she left him; Barr did nothing to stop her. Six weeks later he received a letter from one Alton Rippy of White, Bassett & Rippy, Houston attorneys, saying that Arlene wanted a divorce, inquiring if Barr had any intentions of contesting it, and asking what if any ideas Barr had in regard to a settlement of property.

Barr wrote back that he would not contest a divorce action, that he wanted nothing from Arlene and that she needed nothing from him. He said he would sell the house in Caracas, which he no longer needed, and send her half of the proceeds.

A week later he received a letter from Millicent in Dallas. The paper was stained where her tears had fallen on it as she wrote. It was incoherent, but Barr gathered from it that she loved him.

And then his mother called from San Antonio to wish him a happy birthday. He was still living in the house. After they had chatted for a while, his mother asked to speak to Arlene. Barr had to tell her the truth. "She's been gone a good while, Mama."

"Grady, your daddy was a fine man, and he was a fine-looking man, and he ran around on me, and I knew it, but I loved him, and I knew he loved me, and I knew he would never leave me for anybody else."

"Yes, Mama."

"Now Arlene is a lot like me, Grady, way down inside her. She wouldn't leave you for that. Were you running around on her?"

"No, Mama."

"Did you hit her or anything like that, Grady? Don't lie to me."

"No, Mama."

"Grady, I want to know why she left."

"She thinks I did something dishonest."

"Was it?"

"I guess so, Mama, but not in a business sense. She should have understood that."

His mother's voice softened. "Grady, I knew it way back there when you were a fancy man for bad women. You never said so, and I never asked you about it because I knew you were doing it for me and your sisters, and for your daddy while he was still alive. I never asked where the money came from, but I knew, or I guessed, but I was afraid to ask because we needed it so bad with your daddy the way he was and all."

"I know, Mama. I know."

"It was against all my teachings, Grady." She was crying now. "I grew up knowing better, and I tried to teach you better."

"I'm not a bad man, Mama, not anymore. Not since I came down here, and that was a long time ago."

"I was always mixed up about you, Grady."

"I always hoped you were proud of me, Mama. I mean since I came down here."

"I can't talk anymore right now," Margaret Barr said. "Just tell me one thing, Grady. Is there a chance of yawl getting back together?"

"I don't think so."

"You're not going to try to get her back?"

"No," Barr said, "I'm not. And she wouldn't do it if I tried. Can we quit talking about it, Mama?"

"Good night, Grady," Margaret Barr said. "Happy birthday." And that hurt him worst of all.

* * *

The dull pain of Arlene's leaving was constant, but it was not obvious in Barr's conduct. He remained hard-working and cheerful. He began exercising regularly and cut down on his eating and drinking. He was in his early fifties and looked like a healthy man of forty. Women many years his junior found him attractive, and frequently let him know it. The physical examinations he took twice a year always earned him a clean bill of health. And he began playing tennis twice a week.

"I'd rather play pool by a hell of a lot," he told Ed Gurwell, "but it's too undignified for a man of my stature in the community, don't you agree?"

"I wish you knew how undignified it is to be a cigarette bum," Gurwell said. But Gurwell was grumbling from habit. He had been praised highly in Cajun's annual report, and had received a substantial salary increase as a result.

Barr had sold Perez Jimenez on his old dream of cleaning out the sand bars in Lake Maracaibo. "Right now," Barr had told him in one of their rare meetings, "all you have in the lake area is oil. Open up that lake entrance and it will be a shot in the arm for agriculture and all kinds of industrial development."

"And it will help the oil companies also," the dictator had said with his soft smile.

"Of course it will," Barr had replied.

Barr talked the other oil companies into joining Cajun in buying the bonds, government guaranteed, to finance the project. The fleets of saucy little lake tankers were mothballed, replaced by deep-draft, ocean-going tankers capable of lifting full cargoes from the lake.

The dictator seldom showed his rough side to the oil companies, granting concessions frequently and generally leaving them alone, as he had told Barr he would do. To the people, however, he was an iron-fisted tyrant. There were no political parties and the unions were impotent. The prisons were full. Tales of his greed and cruelty were accepted instantly and completely.

"All that son of a bitch wants to do is make Caracas into a show place and ride that fucking motorcycle," Ed Gurwell said.

Indeed, it did appear that Perez Jimenez was determined to make Caracas into the most beautiful city in the western hemisphere. He slashed a speedway through the mountains from Caracas to the port of La Guaira. Tall public buildings of futuristic design towered over magnificent cathedrals of an earlier day. Wide boulevards were built to handle the increasing automobile traffic. Vast apartment projects of multi-colored stone and glass were erected to shelter the thousands who lived in hovels on the valley's sides. And, to keep the military happy, he constructed a military club in the city at a cost of twelve million dollars.

"You can go outside town in any direction and tell he's not spending a dime anywhere but here," Gurwell said. "I don't want to sound like Roberto Fontenot, but that twelve million bucks he spent on that military whorehouse would have built lots of schoolhouses out in the boondocks."

Gurwell's remark about Perez Jimenez riding a motorcycle was inspired by a story that had circulated about what was said to be his favorite sport. On one of the Caribbean islands off the coast, so the story went, PJ, as the people and the press called him, maintained an establishment filled with lovely girls. Naked, they would be set free on the beach, and Perez Jimenez would pursue them while mounted on his Italian-made motorscooter.

"I hear he rounds them up like cattle, then screws the one who's panting the worst," Gurwell said.

Barr suspected that the island establishment was what Perez Jimenez was talking about when he had told Barr at their first meeting that someday he would invite Barr to a place he wouldn't forget. The invitation had never come, and Barr had never regretted it.

Although there was no pressure from the government, Barr insisted that the companies continue to deal with the union. He met stout resistance from some of the newer companies. "PJ won't listen to them if they do complain," said the head of one of the more successful newcomers.

"He might," Barr said mildly.

A group of company leaders was meeting in a private dining room at Casa del Sol, and the newcomer, a stocky, powerful redhead from Oklahoma, stood up to make his point. He glared at Barr. "I'm telling you, he won't! We've got the world by the tail with a downhill pull, and I want to keep it that way!"

"There's a lot more to it than that," Barr said patiently.

"All I know . . ."

Barr interrupted him. "I think you've told us all you know, Clyde. *I'm* going to sit down with Castillo, and I think I can safely say the older companies will go along with any agreements I make with him—if I make any. I'd advise you to cool off."

"Sit down, Clyde," said the Gulf man quietly. "We've got other problems to discuss. This one is already settled."

Muttering, Clyde sat down.

Later, when Barr invited Castillo to his office, even Castillo seemed a bit surprised that Barr wanted to talk contract. Seeing this, Barr plunged immediately into a discussion of present business conditions and what he thought the future might hold. But Castillo's eyes were questioning him all the while.

"Damn it, Leonel," Barr said finally, "we understand each other. We've helped each other. The first time we met you told me the military was a weather vane, and PJ made you a prophet. Now, let's deal for one year, and you don't be greedy and I won't be tight-fisted. If times get bad, I expect your support. Fair enough?"

"You speak for everyone, as usual?"

"As usual," Barr said.

While the Venezuelan oil companies flourished under the dictatorship, all was not serene in other oil provinces. In Iran there was an argument over implementation of the fifty-fifty law, revolution, and finally nationalization. The international oil cartel boycotted Iranian oil, bringing the country economically to its knees. The British and American governments got involved, another revolt restored the deposed shah to his throne, and Iranian oil began to flow once more.

In 1956 Egypt nationalized the Suez Canal. Israel, France and Great Britain attacked Egypt, and sunken ships blocked the canal, effectively shutting off the flow of oil from Middle East fields.

Independent oilmen in the United States, who were allowed to operate their wells only a few days a month under proration laws supported by the international oil cartel, now were permitted to open up their valves, and Europe was supplied with oil from the U.S. and Venezuela while the crisis lasted.

When the crisis ceased and the canal eventually was reopened for tanker traffic, U.S. producers were ordered by the various regulatory agencies to cut back on their production. They did so because they had to; the major oil companies refused to order U.S. oil when their cheaper oil from abroad again was available for import to the U.S., Europe and elsewhere. In Texas, for example, wells were allowed to produce only eight days a month, and each well could produce no more than thirteen barrels per day.

The U.S. independents rallied together, demanding that the

government act in their behalf. They insisted that imported oil was not supplementing U.S. production, as the cartel argued, but supplanting it. Millions upon millions of acres of land were being untouched by the drill, they said, because there was little reason to find oil that could be sold on such a limited basis. The American independent oilman was being forced out of business.

President Eisenhower eventually succumbed to the pressure. He announced that he would shortly institute a system of limiting imports by what he called "voluntary controls."

"Here we go again," the Gulf man said in a phone call to Barr. "Looks like those Texans got a taste of the watermelon during Suez and they can't forget how good it was."

"That's not all," Barr said. "I smell another glut coming on. There's as much oil being produced around the globe as this old world can consume."

"Are you going to discuss the bad news with PJ?"

"Not right away. We've got some grace time."

"All right, Grady. And don't forget my cocktail party Saturday. It ought to be pretty nice. You haven't been getting out enough lately."

"I'll be there," Barr promised.

Chapter Twenty-Two

Barr decided he had never seen a more beautiful woman. He had arrived at the cocktail party, been handed a martini by a roving waiter, and had for the past five minutes been watching the woman as she talked with two others about twenty feet away from him on the patio. She was an American, with long blonde hair that fell in waves below her shoulders. Her complexion was flawless and her features perfect, Barr decided, and her body in the yellow cocktail gown made him forget that he was nearing sixty, that his golden ringlets were graying at the temples, and that only two weeks earlier a dentist had placed a bridge in a space once occupied by four lower teeth.

"Stunning is the word," the Shell man said as he sauntered past Barr on his way to the bar.

"Gorgeous," Barr whispered to himself.

The three women were talking and laughing. The blonde turned toward Barr, apparently looking for a roving waiter, for her glass was empty. She saw Barr staring at her. Immediately and quite unabashedly her gaze shifted to his groin—and Barr became aware that an erection was bulging his trousers. The blonde turned back to the other women and resumed her conversation. Barr sidled off the patio into the garden to give himself time and opportunity to relax. He was so embarrassed he decided to excuse himself to the Gulf man and leave the party.

But the Gulf man wouldn't hear of Barr leaving. "You haven't got a goddamned thing else to do, and you know it. Get out there and mingle and meet some people. Do you want everybody to think you're a hermit?"

Barr asked him about the blonde.

"Jesus!" said the Gulf man. "Did you ever see anything like it?"

"Not lately," Barr said.

Her name was Regina Ruiz, the Gulf man said. She had come down from the States two or three years ago for Pan American airlines, and promptly was wooed and won by Julio Ruiz, one of the country's leading industrialists. Julio was out of the country on business. "You know Julio, don't you?"

"I've met him a couple times," Barr said. "I never had any kind of conversation with him."

"Bright and tough," the Gulf man said. "One of the few who will stand up to PJ."

Barr mingled, as the Gulf man had suggested, moving from group to group, joining in a conversation occasionally but generally just listening. He moved out on the patio again and was leaning against the railing when he sensed someone behind him. He turned around. Regina Ruiz had come out on the patio a few steps. As Barr faced her she moved back inside the house.

Was she trying to entice him inside? he wondered? Barr didn't think so. It was more likely, he thought, that she had come outside for a breath of air and his presence had driven her back. In any event, Barr was certain he was not going to pursue her. He had been far from celibate since Arlene's departure, but he had selected his paramours with care. Regina Ruiz was half his age and, more, he had no desire to become entangled with the wife of one of the country's leading industrialists. Particularly when he had the task of soon facing PJ with bad news.

He stayed at the party another hour, then left despite the Gulf man's protests.

Barr slept late the next day, a Sunday, and awoke thinking of her, seeing her clearly in his mind in all of her beauty. But he shrugged and rolled out of bed. "To hell with it," he muttered. He cleaned up, combed his hair, and was having his first cup of coffee when his phone rang. The caller was his liaison man with the Congress. "Did you hear about what the archbishop said at the cathedral last night, Mr. Barr?"

"I haven't read the papers yet," Barr said.

"It won't be in the papers."

"Oh."

"He spoke reproachfully about the construction of so many garish buildings in the city while so few schoolhouses are being built. I believe he specifically mentioned the military club."

310

"And PJ won't let the papers print that kind of criticism . . . is that what you mean?"

"But it will be all over the country in a day or two."

"And?"

"It will be like the words came from the lips of God, Mr. Barr. It will spread courage across the land. There probably is more unrest among the people than we know about. There always is."

"Yes," Barr said. And, he thought, there'll be a hell of a lot more when we have to cut back production and lay off people. He thanked his man and praised him for his alertness. He was happy he had negotiated the ten percent pay hike for the workers with Leonel Castillo. That should take some of the sting out of the layoffs. Arlene, he thought . . . In honoring a commitment PJ wouldn't have forced him to acknowledge he had been taking a little of the sting out of the tongue-lashing she had dealt him. No, he told himself, that's bullshit. I did it because it was smart; neither Arlene nor the long-dead Endicott had a damned thing to do with it.

He called Ed Gurwell at home and told him what he had heard. "Have you noticed anything, Ed? I haven't."

"No, but I've got a suggestion for you. Don't go see PJ. He reads the newspapers. He knows what Eisenhower is going to do. So write him a letter and let him know what to expect. Don't put yourself in a position where he can explode at you if he's really worried about the archbishop."

"A very good idea, Edward," Barr said approvingly.

"Well, I've heard you say you've had some good teachers. I've had a good one, too."

"That's so touching."

"All right, fuck you. What are you going to do when I retire? I'm up for it pretty soon."

"You don't want to leave Caracas, so I'm going to keep you on the payroll as a consultant, whatever that is."

Barr wrote the letter to PJ. He discussed the situation with Leonel Castillo, and was tempted to ask the union leader whether the archbishop's remarks had generated any unrest. He decided against it. The following week the "voluntary" controls were implemented from Washington. Barr received a note of thanks from PJ for Barr's explanatory letter, but that was all. There was no reaction from the workers.

"It looks like both of them have their minds on other things,"

Barr said to the Gulf man on the phone. "Do you sniff anything on the wind?"

"You're getting jumpy, Grady," the Gulf man said. "You know you ought to relax more."

"Maybe so," Barr said.

Now it seemed that he saw Regina Ruiz everywhere he went. He saw her dining at Emiliano's with a slender man he took for Julio Ruiz. She was at the restaurant a few days later with two women, having cocktails, and shortly thereafter she was at a party given by Bethlehem Steel. She was alone, and someone said that Ruiz was out of the country. Barr did not approach her at the party and, if she saw him and recognized him, she gave no sign of it. He saw her again a week later, lunching with the two women.

That night he dreamed about her. He was pursuing her in the great bullring, Nuevo Circo, losing sight of her entirely at times as she sped from tier to tier, catching glimpses of her as she darted up one aisle and down another, plodding after her step after agonizing step, hearing her mocking laughter, seeing her wrap her flowing silken robe close to her body to tease him into haste. She flew up aisles he climbed with pain. He was still plodding after her when he awoke . . .

Three nights later he saw her at a party at the Shell man's house. She looked exquisite in a cocktail gown of palest blue. Her husband was not in sight. Barr knew that the young woman had invaded his mind, had captured his imagination, and that he had invested her with mystery. He told himself that his age probably had something to do with it. And he told himself to stay away from her.

Nursing a tall drink, he began wandering about. The Shell man took his arm. "I saw you gazing at the lovely Mrs. Ruiz," he said. "Have you met her formally?"

Barr said he hadn't, and the Shell man steered him toward the small group where she was chatting and sipping her drink. The Shell man pulled her aside to make the introduction. "I didn't realize you two people weren't acquainted," he said. "I'll leave you alone to rectify that." He left them, and the woman looked up at Barr, her face expressionless.

It was one of the few times in his life that Barr was ill at ease. "I'm Grady Barr, of Cajun," he said after a pause.

"You're the man that insulted me," she said with a Kansas

312

accent. Her voice was low-pitched and pleasant on the ear. "You're lucky I didn't tell my husband."

"I was as embarrassed as you were," Barr said. "I'm sorry about it, and it will never happen again."

"It better not happen again, you old goat," she said, turning away. She went back to her group, leaving Barr standing there as if he had asked for alms and had been denied. He knew his face was flushed. He finally got his feet to move and walked right into the smiling Shell man.

"Deflated, old boy?" the Shell man asked, greatly amused.

"Completely," Barr said ruefully.

The Shell man nodded. "You're one of a million, I'd say. She's castrated that many, I'm sure. She's a breezy girl. Tart of tongue, and she can tell a dirty story with the best of them. But she won't tolerate anyone making a pass at her."

"I didn't make a pass at her," Barr said.

"You didn't?"

Barr shook his head. And he told the Shell man what had occurred at the Gulf man's party, and what Regina had said minutes ago.

"What a delightful story," said the Shell man. "I shall do my very best not to yield to temptation and spread it around." Laughter shook his portly frame. "Called you an old goat, did she?"

"She did," Barr said, and he couldn't help grinning.

The Shell man had to hurry off to welcome a newcomer to the party, and Barr took the opportunity to leave the house by a side door. Driving home, he writhed in his car seat, reliving the scene with Regina over and over, but laughing a little more heartily each time when he thought of the Shell man's delight. To hell with it, he thought. I ought to be grateful to the damned woman.

Her flat statements had erased his obsession with her beauty, but he knew that he would think of her from time to time, and with regret.

The next day Leonel Castillo called and invited him to lunch at Emiliano's. As they sipped their pre-lunch drinks, Barr said, "This is a pretty fancy place for a labor leader to be picking up the tab. What would your boys say?"

Castillo was somber. "My boys trust me."

"So do I," Barr said.

313

"And I trust you," Castillo said, looking at his hand holding the martini.

Barr began adding up the archbishop's remarks, the lack of interest shown by PJ and Castillo in President Eisenhower's voluntary import controls, the out-of-the-country trips by Julio Ruiz. Ruiz, the Gulf man had said at his cocktail party, was one of the few Venezuelans who would stand up to PJ.

"Look, Leonel, I think something is going to happen, and I think it's going to happen pretty damned soon."

Castillo raised his gaze from his glass.

"I *know* nothing, you understand," Barr hastened to assure him, "and I haven't said a word about my thoughts."

Castillo sighed.

"Don't think I don't appreciate what it has cost you to invite me here for a talk, old friend," Barr went on.

Castillo grunted.

"You should know this," Barr said. "I think PJ at least suspects something is up."

Castillo's dark eyes glinted. "Why do you think that?"

Barr smiled. "Because he has been as unconcerned about the cutbacks in production as you have been about the layoffs. Both of you have been thinking of other things."

Castillo shook his head. "It must be something else with him. If he suspected you could hear the screams of the tortured across Caracas valley."

"All right. But how can it be done? He has the army and the police. I ask not as his friend but yours."

"There is also the navy, the marines and the air force, and he has neglected them. Particularly the pilots of the new jets your country forced on him."

"And the people?"

"Priests will fight shoulder to shoulder with Communists," Castillo said. "Believe me, this will be a true revolution—not an exchange of power as in the past." He smacked his lips. "*Not* an exchange of power." He swallowed the last of his drink. "Now it would be better if we say no more about it."

"Why did you want me to know about it?" Barr asked.

Castillo shrugged. "How else could I explain to you why you should stay in your apartment on New Year's Day and listen to the radio?"

"Thank you," Barr said.

* * *

314

A jet fighter streaking across the valley was the signal for the revolt to begin. Barr heard its screaming passage not in his apartment but in his office. The office was *his* command post, and four days and nights he stayed there, trying to keep abreast of work in progress in the various oilfield districts and of the blood being spilled across the land.

The navy, marines and air force launched the assaults on the army's installations, but it was the people who spelled out the difference. Priests *did* fight shoulder to shoulder with Communists, as Castillo had said they would. They fought with bricks and bottles, knives and clubs, and they were mowed down by the hundreds by the soldiers' submachine guns. While Barr listened, the government radio station changed hands three times in a single day. The end came when a platoon of soldiers defected, and turned their weapons on those who remained loyal to PJ.

Smoke was still rising from burning wreckage in the streets when PJ fled the country by airplane; he wound up his travels in Florida where he tallied up the millions of dollars he had deposited over the years in Swiss banks.

A junta headed by a handsome admiral, Wolfgang Larrazabal, sat in Miraflores Palace. Larrazabal spent much of his time assuring everyone that the junta was provisional, that an election would be held shortly and that his prime interest was in maintaining the status quo until election time.

But in a shabby office in a downtown building sat another junta, and Barr knew that the decisions which would effect his company were being made there. Its members were representatives of the four major political parties—Accion Democratica, Republican–Democratic Union, Copei and the Communists. Exiles streaming back into the country reported in at the dingy office. Conflicting statements were issued from it and found their way into newspapers eager to reassert their independence.

An Associated Press story of February 11, 1958, which was printed in many newspapers in the U.S. and throughout Latin America summed up the situation best, it seemed to Barr.

> It is generally accepted that the international oil companies operating in Venezuela will face four major problems after the promised election: 1) A move to revoke the 50-50 law to give the government a larger share of oil income; 2) A round of pay raises and benefits that will cut deeply into company profits; 3) A determined bid by powerful political

factions to put the government in the oil business in competition with private enterprise, a plan that could eventually end in complete government ownership and operation; 4) An investigation of the 1956–57 concessions granted by the dictatorship to both established and new oil companies. . . .

But where was Roberto Fontenot?

He was in Washington, perhaps. Or perhaps Mexico City. Or San Juan, Puerto Rico.

A month had passed and other political aspirants had grabbed platform space almost daily. The people had shouted *bravos* to them all. But no one in his right mind doubted that the people were waiting for Fontenot's return. Word had been widespread that he had helped in the planning of the revolution, and with every day that passed his absence was more keenly felt.

"He's letting tension build," Barr told Ed Gurwell. "The first time I ever heard him speak he took so long to get started he had everybody sitting on the edge of their seats. He'll know when to show up. The rest of these politicians just as well ask for a law making him president by acclamation."

Then the word came: Fontenot was in New York. He would be flying in to Venezuela on Sunday afternoon, and would greet the people in El Silencio, a business and housing area in the heart of Caracas.

"It's going to be like Lindbergh landing in Paris," Gurwell said.

The people filled El Silencio and strung out along the route all the way to the airport. Thousands more gathered at the airport itself, wanting to get the first glimpse, the first touch. When Fontenot's plane landed, police were pushed through hedges and around building corners by the shouting throng. The *bravos* and *vivas* followed his limousine to El Silencio where a platform had been erected for him.

In his black suit, his left arm hanging loosely at his side, he mounted the platform and took his time adjusting the microphone to his liking. At the last moment, he stepped down from the platform and picked up a handful of wind-blown dust from the paving. He went back up on the platform.

He faced the microphone, and as the dust trickled from his fingers to be caught by the breeze he said, "It's good to be home."

Eduardo Vigas was waiting for him when Barr arrived at his

316

office the next morning. Vigas was graying at the temples and looked a little plumper to Barr, but otherwise he had changed little in nine years of exile. He was reading a newspaper in Barr's outer office, and stood up when Barr entered.

Barr grinned and stuck out his hand. "Been expecting you, Eddie." Vigas shook hands, but didn't return the grin. Barr said to his secretary, "Get someone to bring us some coffee, will you please."

"I don't have the time, Grady," Vigas said.

Barr waved a hand at his office door. "Can't you come in for even a little while?"

Vigas was expressionless. "No, I just dropped by to tell you to start thinking in terms of seventy-five and twenty-five."

Barr was now also expressionless. "I know that if we have an election Fontenot will win by a landslide. And if that happens, I know the petroleum law is going to be revised. You know the business as well as I do, Eddie. You know there's a hell of a glut with new fields being found in new countries every day. And Mr. Eisenhower's recession has spread to Europe. What you're talking about is simply unrealistic."

"To you," Vigas said. "To us it makes sense, for the present."

"And just across the horizon is nationalization . . . is that what you're telling me?"

Vigas smiled faintly. "As you say."

Barr couldn't help grinning. "You bastard, you *would* remember that."

But it was obvious that Vigas wished he hadn't remembered, wished he hadn't said the old familiar words. He turned on his heels and left the outer office. Barr stared at the empty door a moment, then told his secretary, "I'd still like that cup of coffee."

That night at his apartment Barr made himself a drink and sat down to count his blessings. Not a single oilwell in the country had been damaged during the fighting. With the revolution secure, Leonel Castillo had sent the workers back to their jobs; the loss in production had been small . . . Those were the blessings.

On the other hand, he knew the voluntary controls on imports to the U.S. were a farce. Only Venezuela was being penalized; the international oil companies were increasing their imports from the Middle East to take up the slack. So there would be no relief for the American independent oilmen; they would shout for mandatory controls and Eisenhower would have to institute them. And again only Venezuela would be hurt, Barr reasoned. With the U.S. government—the State Department—supervising the control system, imports likely would increase, not decrease, as the politicians hastened to kiss the asses of the various Middle East countries they were courting for reasons other than oil.

He fixed himself another drink. And suddenly the calm reasoning with which he had analyzed his position deserted him, and he was gripped by a terrible feeling of aloneness he had never before experienced. He wanted desperately to reach out and touch someone. He went to the phone to call Louise Bremond in Maracaibo, but when he placed his call it was to Arlene in Houston. He thought it miraculous when she answered the phone.

"Arlene?" he said.

"Grady? I'm surprised I recognized your voice, it's been so long since I heard it."

"I know," Barr said.

She waited for him, and finally Barr said, "There's hardly a night that passes that I don't think about you." At the moment he believed his words were true. "Sometimes I wake up at night and reach for you, Arlene," he said, and these words *were* true.

"I'm not being mean, Grady, but I imagine you can always find someone to share your bed."

"It's not the same," Barr said. "That's not what I'm talking about."

"Grady, I think about you more than I like to, more than is good for me, I have to tell you that. But I'm glad I left you when I did. It would have gotten worse if I had stayed."

"Maybe," Barr said.

"I've thought about it, Grady. "You shouldn't have married me. You were already married to that oil company. You didn't *need* a wife. All you needed was someone to make love to you when you felt like it."

"Arlene . . ."

"It's the truth, Grady. No woman could compete with that damned company."

Barr asked, "How do you look honey? Much different?"

She laughed. "Some people say I'm the best-looking fifty-five year old woman in Houston, but that may be because I've got so much money."

"Millicent, how is she?"

"Slim and attractive enough now to be married to a fine lawyer

318

here in town. They live here with me." She paused. "Are you showing your years, Grady?"

"I'm sure as hell feeling them," he said with some fervor. But he laughed—and realized his depression was lifting.

"I'm glad you called," she said abruptly, and Barr thought he heard the echo of a sob.

"I'm glad, too," he said.

"Well then, hang up, you damned fool!"

The click was loud in his ear, and he knew she had slammed the receiver to the cradle. He put down the receiver and went to the bar to revive his drink.

"Married to the company, am I?" he said to his reflection in the bar mirror.

The reflection grinned crookedly. "If you are, you sure as hell are being cuckolded."

Later that night he was awakened by a telephone call from his sister Kathleen in San Antonio. Their mother was dead. A case of the flu the past December had weakened her more than she knew, and now her old heart had failed.

"I'm on my way, Kat," Barr said.

Chapter Twenty-Three

From the Caracas *Daily Star* of May 10, 1958:

President Roberto Fontenot told the Congress today that he had no present plans to alter the tax increase placed on the oil companies by the provisional junta shortly after his election and just weeks before his inauguration.

The provisional junta decreed that the government receive a 60–40 split of oil revenues instead of 50–50, while it was believed that the Fontenot administration had plans for a 75–25 split once it assumed power. The provisional junta, under law, was in power until the day of Fontenot's inauguration.

It is widely believed that the junta's action was a result of the oil companies' insistent declarations that a 75–25 split under present economic conditions would create chaos. Fontenot rebutted the companies' contention time after time during the presidential campaign.

While accepting the 60–40 split, the President made it clear that creation of a state oil company was in the planning stage. "The remaining national oil reserves will be turned over to this company," the President said, "and not a single centimeter more of national territory will be awarded as concessions to foreign oil companies."

He also said that a state oil refinery will be built, and the state oil company will market its products.

Once again the President lashed out at U.S. President Dwight D. Eisenhower for instituting mandatory controls on oil imports to the States, calling the action "discriminatory and unjust."

He concluded his remarks by announcing that Petroleum Minister Eduardo Vigas was in Cairo as an observer at the newly-formed Arab Petroleum Congress.

Barr shook his head. "Observer, my ass! He probably *called* the meeting."

The Shell man laughed. "Ah, Grady, must there be a specter at every feast? You couldn't get three Arabs to agree on how your throat should be cut. I thought we were here to drink to what I consider a major victory over the powers of darkness." He smiled fondly at Barr. "How hard you strove, and what a magnificent job you did, Grady. Your arithmetic was so splendidly confusing I couldn't understand it half the time, much less the junta."

They were having a drink in a booth in Emiliano's, and the newspaper was on the table in front of them.

"As for the Arabs," the Shell man went on airily, "two or three of them took a little price cut a while back, the way I understand it. They simply want to meet and shout at each other and swear by the prophet that the companies best not make any more cuts without consulting them."

"I know that," Barr said irritably. "It's Vigas I'm worried about."

"Well, you know him better than I do."

Barr said grimly, "You're goddamned right I do."

As he lifted his glass to finish his drink, Barr saw Regina Ruiz being welcomed into the restaurant by Emiliano. With her was the slender man he assumed was Julio Ruiz. It had not been publicly acknowledged, but Barr had heard that Ruiz had been a courier and fund-raiser for the revolutionists. The Shell man's back was to the entrance. Barr hoped he wouldn't turn around and see them; he would surely invite them to the booth if he did.

Seeing Regina moving to her table in all her youthful beauty, Barr realized how hard he had fought for his company's rights, how utterly tired he was, how worn he must look—and how old.

"A centimo for your thoughts, old man," the cheerful Shell man said.

Barr chuckled at the "old man," and at his moment of self pity. "I was just thinking about what an old friend of mine named Bandera used to say," Barr lied. "He said a gentleman never fucks a hungry woman on a cold floor." He laughed more heartily now, remembering Bandera and his own youth with wry affection.

"Sounds like an interesting fellow," the Shell man said in a puzzled tone.

"Very," Barr said. He was now impatient to be gone, and he stood up. "I'm going to push off. A friend called me this morning and said he had a pot of chili on the stove."

The Shell man made a face. "I've eaten it only once, on a tour of our Texas properties, and it made me violently ill."

"It does that to some people," Barr said. "Now don't sit here and drink too much and get a bad reputation."

"Our reputations are bad enough as it is," the Shell man said.

Barr left the restaurant hurriedly and without a glance in the direction of Regina Ruiz . . .

But he dreamed of her several times during the night, and awoke long before his alarm sounded at seven in the morning. He was pleased that his penis was standing at attention. He laughed, recalling something Bandera had said when Barr had wondered about a senile old man who regularly visited one of Bandera's girls. Bandera had winked and said, "The older the buck, the stiffer the horn."

Weeks passed without Barr seeing Regina Ruiz, and eventually he stopped anticipating it. By then he had taken to bedding a handsome widow who owned and operated a high fashion shop. She was entertaining, thoughtful, and competent in bed.

But she was his only pleasure. It seemed to Barr that Cajun was under constant attack from the Ministry of Petroleum. Several times a week he would he hailed to the ministry to explain some company act or intention. Cajun had a board of directors and high-ranking officers, but it was always Barr only that the ministry insisted on seeing. A paper had been filled out incorrectly; a new regulation was not being obeyed to the letter; a well was being drilled improperly. It was harassment, in Barr's opinion, and that his blood brothers were receiving such treatment did nothing to alleviate his dull anger.

Meanwhile, the Fontenot administration was busily creating a new life for the country, and Barr privately acknowledged a grudging admiration for the President. Marcos Perez Jimenez had looted the treasury. The provisional junta had spent oil income wastefully if not wickedly. But Fontenot was putting to good use the oil income as the government received it. He was

322

doing what others who had sat in Miraflores Palace had said they would do but had never done. He was "sowing the petroleum."

But Barr would grant him nothing else. His plans for the oil companies made him the enemy.

The slow dissolution of Barr's marriage with Cajun began with a phone call from Charles Cannon on the afternoon of what had already been a very trying day. Cannon was now SCI's executive vice-president as well as a board member. John Henry Craig had been replaced as board chairman and chief executive officer by Woodrow Ralston.

In his calm voice, Cannon said, "Grady, Ralston is going to cut the price we pay for Venezuelan and Middle East crude by ten cents a barrel."

Barr was stunned.

"Did you hear me, Grady?"

"I heard you, but I can't believe it," Barr said. He wanted to shout at Cannon, beat his fist on the desk. His head began aching.

"Next week," Cannon said.

"When did he and the other company bigshots make this decision?"

"The other companies don't know about it. Ralston doesn't want to waste time arguing with them about it now. They'll fall in line later."

"No, Charley. Not a unilateral move." Barr was fighting for calm. "I've had two or three years of solid hell down here, and you know it. If Cajun cuts the price, and the others don't, Fontenot will string me up on an old derrick."

"Grady—"

"It would be bad enough if everybody cut the price, Charley, but a unilateral action by Cajun will wreck our position here."

"There's a glut, Grady, the greatest glut," Cannon said, "and the Russians are selling crude at much cheaper prices than we are. They're underselling us in Italy, in India, and in Japan. We've got to cut our selling price and that means cutting our buying price."

"Why doesn't he talk to the countries involved? Tell Fontenot and the Arabs about the glut. Tell them about the Russians. Tell them *all* his goddamned problems. A cut is going to knock hell out of their revenue. Hell, maybe he could even offer to share that loss with them."

"That was suggested, Grady."

"And he didn't like it. Well, tell the son of a bitch to increase the company's marketing profits to make up for the production losses."

"That also was suggested, and he said no. The majority of the board supports him."

Barr sighed. "I ought to pack up and leave this fucking place."

"I understand the Venezuelan situation better than he does," Cannon said. "Perhaps I can talk him into excluding Venezuela from the cut. I believe I can get some support from other board members."

Barr grunted. "That would tickle hell out of Eduardo Vigas."

"Vigas?"

"Vigas. The guy I write all those reports on. The one who keeps everybody stirred up in the Middle East."

"I know who Vigas is."

"I can see it now," Barr said. "I can see him telling the others all the benefits of being tough with the companies. 'Look at Venezuela!' he'll say. 'SCI was *afraid* to cut us!'"

"I'll talk to Ralston and some others," Cannon said. "You'll hear from me soon."

Barr said solemnly, "Charley, we're damned if we do and damned if we don't in this case. If we cut Venezuela along with the Middle East, I can't guarantee our position here, and I don't know if I want to try. If we *don't* cut Venezuela and cut the others, I assure you that Vigas and some of the friends he's made over there will make the Middle East as much of a hellhole as this place has been."

"I'll be back in touch," Cannon said. He laughed. "As I have heard you say, simmer down."

Barr missed Ed Gurwell. Barr had managed to keep him on the payroll as a "consultant" after Gurwell had reached the mandatory retirement age, but during the past year's election campaign Gurwell's ailing wife had convinced him that they should return to the States. While Barr had learned to appreciate the virtues of Gurwell's successor, and he had many, Barr knew he lacked Gurwell's alley-cat shrewdness and mental toughness.

So Barr kept his own counsel, and waited alone for Cannon's call. He avoided his blood brothers. He sent others to the Ministry of Petroleum in his stead. When the widow intuited that he had a troubled mind, she became more tender with him but otherwise left him to his own devices.

324

He worked harder than ever, pushing for improvement in every department of the company. He inspected the refineries, and found little to his liking, or so it must have seemed to those who accompanied him. He visited various new fields, observing everything with his driller's eye, climbing up a rig floor occasionally as he had done in the past to demonstrate the proper function of some tool or design. He dropped in at pipeline pumping stations, and stormed about the condition of a dock at Lagunillas.

All the while he knew he was fighting off the feeling that he had been betrayed.

"We're going to announce the cut tomorrow," Cannon said, "and you've been excluded."

"Charley . . ."

"I didn't say so in so many words, Grady, but I strongly implied that you would resign if we cut Venezuela. Would you have resigned, Grady?"

"I don't know," Barr said honestly. "I really don't know."

"Well, the board has a lot of respect for you and the job you've done down there."

"Thank you, Charley . . . for everything."

With uncharacteristic enthusiasm Cannon said, "There's going to be an opening on the board next year, Grady, and I wouldn't be surprised if you were the top candidate."

"Again, I say thank you, Charley."

"Well, don't worry about your Mr. Vigas and the Arabs. We'll handle them, I assure you."

Barr sat staring at the window for almost half an hour after the call. The news should have elated him, but it hadn't. Not even the strong possibility of a promotion to the SCI board had stirred his blood. He still was resentful that Ralston and the board had decided to cut Venezuela without discussing it with him first. He was grateful that Cannon had interceded for him, but he gained no pleasure from knowing it had been necessary. Finally he turned back to his desk to deal with the paperwork he detested.

When the price cut in the Middle East was announced the next day, August 8, 1960, Barr had only a "no comment" for the reporters who called him. With Venezuela excluded from the cut, his "no comment" suggested that Venezuela had no basic relationship with the Middle East. He assumed, correctly, that harsh and bitter words were being transmitted to SCI headquarters from the offices of the six other members of the international oil cartel: Shell, Gulf, Texaco, Mobil, Standard Oil of California and British Petroleum, once the Anglo-Iranian Oil Company. But he also assumed that they would fall in line with SCI on the cut and within a week they did.

He told his blood brothers that he had been informed of the cut only an hour before it was announced publicly, and he refused to speculate on why Venezuela had not been included. "I don't give a damn why were were spared, as long as we were," he said, "and I'm not going to ask any questions about it."

"I thank God for it," said the Gulf man, "I'm due for retirement in six months, and I haven't got the heart for another battle with Fontenot and company. Or anybody, for that matter."

"Still and all," said the Shell man, "I must say it was despicable for SCI to act unilaterally, and after the cut was accepted, the Hague and London almost talked themselves into cutting Venezuela as well. Wouldn't that have been a fine kettle of fish?"

"It would have been enough to upset Jack Bolton," Barr said.

"Who's Jack Bolton?" the Gulf man asked.

"Some fucking Irishman, I think," Barr said, and the Shell man chuckled.

Then Barr received a phone call from Miraflores Palace. Fontenot wanted to see him, and Barr went. The Presidential office was alive with color, the walls decorated with pastel paintings by Venezuelan artists. Behind the presidential desk was a portrait of Simon Bolivar. Fontenot was working with his coat off. He was younger than Barr, but like Vigas he was graying. Heavy horn-rimmed glasses rode on his strong nose. He took off the glasses when Barr entered.

"I need glasses," Barr said when he took his seat, "but I'm too vain to buy any."

Fontenot laughed and said, "Be as honest about something else. Tell me why our country was passed over in the price cut."

"You won't like the truth about the price cut," Barr said evenly, "so let me say first that I think your administration is doing some fine things for the country. I hope your successor will do half as well."

Fontenot nodded his acknowledgement of the compliment. "I am pleased to hear you say that."

"I have told no one this," Barr said, "but I implied I would resign if Venezuela was cut. I ask you not to repeat that."

Fontenot nodded. He was waiting.

"Frankly, I was afraid of what you and Eduardo Vigas would

do to my company. Vigas is obsessed with nationalization, and an obsession blurs a man's judgment. I don't think he could have pushed you that far, to nationalize my company, but you would have been angry as hell and ready to punish me in some way."

"You think that Vigas has great influence with me, and the wrong kind?" Fontenot's eyes were angry.

"He stands between you and the companies, Mr. President. You hear him and not us."

"You see him as Iago to my Othello?"

"No. He's not a liar and you're not stupid. You're one of the most effective men I know. But he does have your ear, and he's ready to risk economic death to achieve nationalization. And, as I said, you would have been mad as hell and ready to listen to suggestions for reprisal."

Fontenot shook his head and said, more in resignation than anger, "You have a strange view of us, Mr. Barr."

"I've known you both for a long time," Barr said. "Can you honestly say that you wouldn't have taken some kind of action against my company if SCI had cut Venezuela? With or without Vigas?"

"Some action would have been justified, called for. But not something foolish, in the heat of anger."

"I couldn't take the chance. You've stung me in the past for less reason. And there's Vigas."

"Your relationship with him has been disturbed, hasn't it?"

"I spoke some foolish words about personal matters," Barr said. "It has nothing to do with this business."

"I'll say nothing of it to him, but it's a shame," Fontenot said. "He had a special regard for you as a person."

"And I for him, and I still do. His obsession is my enemy."

Fontenot smiled. "And I'm the enemy when I act against the company, that corporate citizen your public relations department is always writing about."

Barr returned the smile. "Exactly."

Fontenot was through with the subject. "Do you ever hear from Teresa?"

Barr grinned. "We corresponded for a while, for several years, but Teresa is Teresa, and I was busy. You?"

"About the same," Fontenot said. He stood up, signifying the meeting was over. As Barr rose to his feet, Fontenot said, "Whatever your motive, I am happy your protest saved us from the price cut, and I thank you."

"I'd like to hear that from Vigas, too," Barr said.

"He's out of the country."

"I supposed as much."

"There's no reason the producing countries shouldn't discuss mutual problems created by the international cartel," Fontenot said.

Barr nodded. "Thank you for inviting me over, Mr. President."

"I'm glad you could come," Fontenot said formally.

From the Caracas *Daily Star*, Baghdad, September 9, 1960:

Delegates from five countries that are responsible for eighty percent of the world's exports of oil met today in this historic city to form the Organization of Petroleum Exporting Countries, or simply OPEC.

The five countries are Venezuela, Saudi Arabia, Iran, Iraq and Kuwait. Venezuela was excluded from last month's price cut imposed by the seven members of the international oil cartel, but the country's petroleum minister, Eduardo Vigas, said his government strongly supports an OPEC resolution to fight for restoration of prices to the level prevailing before the reduction.

Most observers here see little chance that the previous price will be restored, despite the display of unanimity among the five countries. On the other hand, they believe this show of strength may prevent the companies from making further cuts without first consulting with the countries involved.

Asked by reporters if he thought the companies would take OPEC seriously, Vigas said, "They had better take it seriously. For us it is an instrument by which we can confront the companies as one country."

Asked if he believed that countries with different backgrounds, different nationalities, religions and forms of government could act together effectively, Vigas said, "We are determined to do so. We will quarrel occasionally, I'm sure, but we will never forget that our common interest binds us together."

But one observer told reporters, "They'll be in disarray before the year is out."

The posted price for crude. . . .

* * *

328

Barr pushed the paper aside and lit a cigarette. All of the city's newspapers had published the story, some in greater detail, but he doubted if half a dozen newspapers in the States had taken note of the meeting. He called the Shell man. "It looks like our friend is ramrodding things in the fabled city of Baghdad," he said.

"I just got off the horn with London on another matter," the Shell man said. "I mentioned this OPEC and our friend Vigas. I gather that their position is to ignore it and it will go away. They're still too angry with SCI for forcing the cut to be concerned with anything else. But really, Grady, how can this OPEC be naughty to us?"

"I don't know," Barr said, "but I'm afraid to find out."

"That's a glum attitude. Why don't we have a drink at Emiliano's?"

"Not today, thank you. I've got a mountain of paperwork in front of me."

"Perhaps tomorrow, then."

"Perhaps," Barr said.

With a sudden burst of energy, the Shell man said, "Grady, what is really troubling you?"

"For one thing, I see more price cuts coming, and this time we won't be missed."

"But Grady, that would be a foolish thing to do!"

"They're already being foolish," Barr said.

Barr shed his gloom, but he continued to keep track of Vigas' peregrinations in the Middle East, and noted them in his reports to SCI headquarters as the months passed. He pointed out that representatives of the OPEC countries would meet in Caracas during the first week of January 1961; he would attempt to have the sessions monitored. In return he received a chiding note from Charles Cannon: "Grady, sometimes I think you are as obsessed with Vigas and OPEC as you say Vigas is obsessed with nationalization."

Barr politely turned aside several invitations to parties, and he and the widow greeted the new year with champagne in her apartment. Standing at a window with his arm around her waist, listening to the ringing of the cathedral bells, Barr thought wryly that he should be celebrating *his* survival of the old year while he welcomed the new.

* * *

The OPEC meeting was closed to observers and to the news media. Eduardo Vigas explained the reason to reporters outside the meeting room in Casa del Sol. "Several representatives have asked that the meeting be closed, and as a proper host our country has no alternative. However, I have been permitted to say this much, that the sessions will be devoted primarily to arriving at an equitable pricing formula." This seemed to satisfy the reporters; Barr wondered if it was because they lacked interest or lacked enterprise.

When the sessions ended and the representatives had gone their ways, there was no official statement as to what, if anything, had been accomplished. Cornered by reporters, Vigas said only, "There is much to be studied in this matter, and it would be imprudent to discuss it at this time."

Near the end of the week Barr received a mimeographed letter from the Ministry of Petroleum signed by Vigas. It said: "It has come to my attention that for several months last year and in the recent past the chief executives of the oil companies were subjected to petty treatment by this office. It was not ordered or endorsed by the Petroleum Minister, and it will not occur again."

Barr smoked his way through three cigarettes before phoning the Ministry and getting Vigas on the line. Barr thanked him for the note. "It's close to quitting time for all hands, Eddie, and I'll buy a drink at Emiliano's."

"See you there in fifteen minutes," Vigas said.

Emiliano escorted them to Barr's favorite booth at the rear of the restaurant. While the waiter went for their drinks, Barr grinned and said, "Well, Eddie, why did you accept my invitation . . . to ask me about the price cut or tell me about OPEC?"

Vigas smiled faintly and humor glinted in his eyes.

"You've got a right to gloat a little," Barr said. "You came out a winner on both ends of the stick."

The waiter brought the drinks. Barr lifted his glass for a toast, and Vigas clicked it with his own. "Now that we're halfway friends again," Barr said, "tell me who financed those Middle East trips of yours while you were in exile. When you went over there and preached fifty-fifty to them?"

"Arabs," Vigas said, as if surprised Barr didn't know.

"Arabs?"

"Young Arabs going to school in the States. They read about PJ's coup and knew I was familiar with fifty-fifty, so they ran me down in San Juan."

330

"Wanted you to teach their elders the error of their ways, eh?" Vigas nodded.

"And now the young ones are back home and helping you with OPEC," Barr said.

"They're older and smarter now," Vigas said. "They can read and write and add up a row of figures. Some of them don't even ride camels."

"I'll bet they don't," Barr said. Then, "Do they want nationalization as badly as you do, Eddie?"

"They're going to have it. *We're* going to have it." Vigas took his first sip of his drink. "Then we'll be the oil kings, not the cartel."

Barr drank.

"We'll decide who gets the oil and how much it will cost them," Vigas went on, speaking as if by rote. "Venezuela is showing the way with its state oil company and state refinery."

"Going to have your own tanker fleets, Eddie? Going to send them where you want to?"

Vigas flushed, but Barr said quickly, "I'm not being facetious, old friend of mine. After all, I saw you make fifty-fifty happen over there."

Vigas was mollified—too easily, Barr thought. "There's no reason why we can't control it all," Vigas said. "It won't come quickly, but it will come. If they regard us lightly, it will be their asses, not ours." Barr knew he had made the statement many times. He signaled the waiter for another round of drinks.

Vigas was still talking. "We're going to be in the position where we can turn the valves on and off when we want to, not the cartel. We'll be the oil kings."

The waiter brought fresh drinks, and Barr sipped his. "Haven't you got one good thought about the companies, Eddie?"

Vigas laughed. "Sure. We'll let you run the filling stations."

Barr laughed with him, lifting his glass and saying, "Fill 'er up!"

But Vigas did not touch his fresh drink. "You know how I am when I drink too much," he said with no hint of friendliness. "I talk too much."

Barr nodded. "Seems to me you've said about all you've been aching to say to me." Then he asked casually, "Did you ever run across Naomi Boxer while you were rambling around those nine years?"

Vigas picked up his drink. "I never saw her. I never looked for her. I never think about her anymore." He drank, licked his lips, then smiled at Barr. "Are you still getting all the good pussy in town?"

Barr chuckled and ran a hand over his graying locks. "I still like it as much, I think, but I don't pursue it as vigorously as I used to." He chuckled again. "I think that about sums it up."

"I thought you'd cornered the market, because I haven't been getting my share," Vigas said, and they both laughed.

They both drank, then Vigas said seriously, "You told me when Naomi left here she was still in love with her dead husband. I think you were probably right. She used to talk about him a lot when we'd be drinking. You know?"

"She'd talk about him when *we'd* have a drink," Barr lied. "When she left you, she did it so she could be loyal to him . . . to his memory."

"I think you're right," Vigas said.

"I *know* I am," Barr said. "She loved you, but she couldn't betray him."

Vigas nodded, and finished his drink. He said apologetically, "I've got to be going, Grady. I've still got work at the office."

Barr did not try to dissuade him. "It's been good to see you, Eddie. I've enjoyed it."

Vigas stood up and tossed money on the table. "I did all the talking so I'm buying."

Barr winked at him. "As you say."

Smiling, Vigas walked away.

Barr ordered another drink . . . He was thinking of the time, so many years ago, when he was twenty-five or six and Vigas was nineteen or twenty, and they were standing in front of the Bull Wheel in Maracaibo with Christina in the Studebaker at the curb, and Vigas, bright-eyed and eager, was telling Barr he wanted to help him try to drill the well in the lake . . .

"Little did I know . . ." Barr said softly to himself.

Chapter
Twenty-Four

Barr waited three months before he wrote the letter to Charles Cannon. During that time he did not once mention Eduardo Vigas or OPEC in his reports. He wrote the letter at night in his apartment, and with a restraint Cannon would have envied. He knew he was risking a tongue-lashing, if nothing more. To be effective, Barr thought, the letter had to be read by the other board members and by Woodrow Ralston himself. Ralston, Barr thought, might resent its implication.

The Suez Crisis of 1956 clearly demonstrated that SCI's supplies of Middle East crude can be cut off by actions beyond SCI's control.

The formation of OPEC, in my opinion, increases the likelihood of such actions occurring. It is the practice of SCI and the other international companies to deal with each country separately. It is OPEC's aim to halt this practice and force SCI and the other companies to deal with its members as a unit—one cartel confronting another cartel.

Smaller companies are testing several African countries. From the reports that cross my desk, their chances of finding crude are excellent. If they hit, SCI will have to move into these countries to protect its position. This will add more crude to the glut and, in my opinion, force these countries into OPEC.

OPEC's ultimate goal is nationalization. I think it will be achieved eventually. A further price cut, particularly a unilateral one, will hasten the day.

At that time SCI's crude supplies will be subject to the politics, whims and angers of OPEC's leaders. To quote Eduardo Vigas after the Caracas meeting: "We're going to be in the position where we can turn the valves on and off, not the cartel."

I suggest that SCI immediately begin exploring for reserves elsewhere, particularly in the United States where there are vast areas untouched by the drill. Knowledgeable independent oilmen have been insisting that there is more oil yet to be discovered in the States than has been found to date. From our reports, I gather that some of our geoscientists agree with them.

I am aware that SCI has pared its U.S. exploratory staff considerably, but it could be beefed up quickly. I also am aware that the program I suggest would be costly, but it could be financed by setting aside a portion of the profits now being derived from Middle East and Venezuelan crude.

I think I know the arguments against pursuing the course I have suggested, but they do not outweigh the reality of a maturing OPEC.

Barr saw the letter mailed without much hope of hearing back from Cannon quickly; it had even occurred to him that he might not hear at all. Five days later he received a letter from Woodrow Ralston. "Dear Grady," the letter said, "Charles Cannon took the liberty of handing me your letter before beginning an inspection tour of our Canadian subsidiaries. I would appreciate it if you would find the time to be in my office at 2 PM next Thursday. It will be good to see you."

He's not a wordy bastard, Barr thought as he lit the third cigarette of the day. He was apprehensive, and admitted it. The note left too much unsaid. There was no hint of what was in store. Well, Barr thought, he's got a wide range of alternatives, everything from firing me to putting me in charge of a stateside drilling program. He could say: You suggested it, now run it. Or he may eat me alive . . .

On the flight to Houston Barr couldn't decide if he should try to see Arlene, and he took his indecision as a bad sign. Ralston, who had disrupted the economies of several countries with a unilateral price cut, would make short shrift of an indecisive man. He wished suddenly that he was flying to see John Henry Craig, and just as quickly frowned the thought away as a sign of weakness.

The plane landed in Houston at midnight, and it was after two o'clock before Barr had registered and bedded down at the Shamrock-Hilton. He didn't sleep well, so he slept late. He ate in his room. He dressed carefully in his best suit, and rode a taxi to the SCI tower on Fannin Street where Woodrow Ralston sat in power on the 55th floor.

He hadn't called Arlene.

Barr had seen Ralston several times over the years when he had been called to Houston to appear before the board on various matters. Once he had spoken briefly with the man, but he couldn't recall the nature of the conversation. He knew that Ralston was a petroleum engineer, and that he had been president of an SCI domestic subsidiary before being selected for the SCI board. Now, as board chairman and chief executive officer he had reached the pinnacle.

Coming from behind his desk to greet Barr, he looked to Barr like the movie actor Vincent Price playing the role of a business tycoon. He was tall, wide-shouldered and immaculate in a dark suit, white shirt and dark tie. His wavy gray hair looked as if it had been marcelled. He was brown from the sun. Green eyes shone under heavy graying brows, and a trim graying mustache added the final touch.

He shook hands with Barr, saying in a pleasant, nasal voice, "Glad you could make it, Grady." He pointed Barr to a chair and returned to his own behind his wide mahogany desk. The office was a perfect setting for him, the carpet, furniture, the appointments glowing with a subdued opulence. On the polished desk was a manila folder, and Barr suspected it contained his letter to Cannon.

"Nice flight up?" Ralston asked.

"Nice enough. No bumps." Barr smiled.

Ralston clasped his hands on the desk. "Let's see, Grady, how old are you now?"

"Sixty-two. I'll be sixty-three in September."

"And the first well in the lake was drilled in twenty-three or twenty-four, wasn't it?"

"It overlapped. It started in—"

"So you've been in Venezuela a long time, haven't you? A long time in one place."

"After I became president of Cajun, I thought about asking for a transfer every now and then," Barr said, "but always there was some kind of crisis, or one brewing, and Mr. Craig would encourage me to stand pat."

"Yes."

"I consider it an honor," Barr said evenly.

"Of course," Ralston said brusquely, "but I think you've been there long enough." He unclasped his hands and leaned back in his chair. "I'm sure we can find a position of responsibility for you in some other subsidiary. Here in the States, if you would prefer. Or perhaps you would prefer Colombia or Argentina." He smiled thinly. "Take your time about letting Cannon know what you want."

Barr was surprised at his self-mastery. He said calmly, "What did you think about my letter to Cannon?"

"Oh," Ralston said, as if just remembering. With a long forefinger he pushed the manila folder across the desk, and Barr took it. If there was malice in his green eyes Barr could not detect it. "Your fears are groundless, and your suggestions unrealistic," Ralston said.

Barr stood up, clutching the folder.

With no emphasis, Ralston added, "Ridiculous, in fact."

Barr nodded slowly. He turned and went to the door. He opened it and said to Ralston's secretary, "Honey, will you please bring your pad and pencil in?" She was a voluptuous brunette in her middle forties. She studied Barr with curious eyes for a moment, then got her pad and pen. Barr opened the door wider so she could enter Ralston's office. She was several feet inside the office when Barr said, "That's all right, honey. That's far enough." She turned to face him.

"I want to dictate, honey. Today's date, Mr. Woodrow Ralston, blah, blah, blah. All right?"

She nodded.

"Please accept my resignation as of this date." Barr smiled at her. "Type that up and I'll sign it on my way out."

Barr watched her go out the door. Behind him, Ralston said, "That was childish."

Barr turned his head and grinned at him. "Ridiculous!" he said, and left the office. He stood by the secretary's desk until she handed him the paper. Barr leaned over and signed it on her desk. As he was writing his name, the woman said, "He'll never forgive you for that."

Barr smiled at her. "You're wrong, honey. He's already forgotten it."

He was able to restrain himself on the taxi ride back to the hotel, but once in his room a wild rage shook him. He sat on the side of the bed and in a monotonous sing-song cursed Woodrow Ralston, pouring out his bitterness and grief.

"*My* company, you goddamn rotten son of a bitch, *my* company, *I* built it, you stupid bastard, fought them *all,* you silly motherfucker, took the chances, by God, got the wells dug, goddamn you, lied and cheated and stole and everything else a son of a bitch can do, you miserable motherfucker, *built* it, goddamn you, made it number one in Venezuela, number one in your goddamn corporate checkbook, you fucking idiot son of a bitch, drilled where you *couldn't* drill, you bastard you, where you were *afraid* to drill, and schemed and conspired and fucked everybody that got in the fucking way, goddamn you, oh god-*damn* you, you loathsome son of a bitch . . ."

He was spent, his anger exhausted; the tears were running down his cheeks and spotting the carpet. The incredible sadness. The sense of loss. The emptiness without purpose. "Oh, fuck it!" he said softly, and he got to his feet and began to pace the room. He wanted a cigarette and didn't have any. He wanted to get drunk, but knew he shouldn't, not now. So he paced.

Finally he undressed, showered, and flopped across the bed. "That was childish," Ralston had said when Barr had dictated his resignation to the voluptuous secretary. But it hadn't been childish. It had been the only route to take. Ralston had probably thought that at sixty-two, growing on sixty-three, Barr would take any kind of shit Ralston was ready to dish out. Well, fuck him, Barr told himself. He had eaten his rations of shit but he had eaten them for Cajun—

And he could see Ralston behind his desk in the opulent office, and he knew that Ralston, for all of his cold-blooded suavity, would have been afraid to take the route Barr had taken had he been in the same position. He would have thought about his retirement pay, the stock options, and he would have said, "Whatever you say, send me where you want to send me, I'll do a good job, I'll accept the challenge."

Cannon, too, for that matter.

But not Ralph Lytel. Lytel had quit in disgust when Cannon's geologists had insisted on drilling on the llanos in the east instead of the jungle where Lytel had said the oil was. Against orders Barr had drilled where Lytel had pointed, and had brought in the Quiriquire field. But Lytel had been gone by then. He would have told someone like Ralston to kiss his ass.

Likewise Steve Boosie, the maverick geologist Cannon had sent to Barr in the east. He had discovered the Peanut Field from the airplane flying out from Caracas to Caripito, and had gone on to discover many more for Barr. He had left Cajun when Barr went to Caracas as president; the excitement for him had died, and he wanted a change of scenery. He, too, would have told someone like Ralston to kiss his ass.

And Ed Gurwell. That snotty bastard may have pissed on Ralston's carpet, but he would have told Ralston to kiss his ass.

And there were others.

The phone rang. Barr crawled across the bed to answer it. The operator said Mr. Charles Cannon was calling from Ottawa, and Barr told her to put him on.

"Grady . . . ?"

"Hi, Charley."

"I just got off the horn with Ralston and he told me you'd resigned. I figured I'd catch you at the Shamrock if you were still in town. What happened, Grady?"

"Didn't he tell you?"

"Only that you had resigned. Said he would give me the details when I get back. I don't understand it, Grady."

Barr told him what had occurred in Ralston's office. There was a long silence, then Cannon said vehemently, "That ice-cold bastard!"

Barr couldn't help but chuckle. "Was that the undemonstrative Charley Cannon who said that? The imperturbable Mr. Cannon?"

Cannon laughed with him. "All right, what are you going to do?"

"I don't know yet. I'll *have* to go back to Caracas if for nothing else than to settle my accounts and get my stuff. And I may stay there."

"Doing what?"

"For Christ's sake, Charley, I just got unemployed. I don't know what in the *hell* I'm going to do."

"I'm sorry. I just don't want to lose sight of you."

338

"You won't, old friend of mine. Wherever I land, I'll let you know."

"You know, Grady, that . . ."

"I know, Charley," Barr said. "I'll be in touch. The word of a Barr."

"All right, Grady."

In one of the hotel dining rooms he gorged on oysters, shrimp and stuffed flounder. Back in his room, he ordered a bottle of brandy. He stayed up until midnight, sipping brandy and watching television. He went to bed sober, and slept better than he had expected to. Much of his depression was gone when he rolled out of bed.

He ordered coffee from room service, and exercised on the carpet with a solemn determination until the waiter knocked on his door. He drank the coffee in quick gulps. He cleaned up in the bathroom, and while he was splashing after-shave lotion on his face, he grinned at the mirror. "All right, you crooked-nosed son of a bitch," he said to his reflection, "let's see if we've got sense enough to make it in this cold, cruel world."

There was no Ralph Lytel listed in the phone book, but under consulting geologists in the yellow pages was the name of Stephen J. Boosie. Barr dialed the number. A pleasant female voice answered. "Mr. Boosie's office."

Barr identified himself. "Years ago I worked with a geologist named Steve Boosie in Venezuela. I wonder if he and your Mr. Boosie are one and the same."

"Could be, Mr. Barr. I've heard him talk about working there when he was much younger."

"My Steve Boosie was about as big as a barber pole," Barr said. "He was cotton-headed then, and his ears looked like a couple of dinner plates."

The woman laughed. "Don't you dare let him know that I said so, but that fits him exactly." She paused. "But he's not here, Mr. Barr. He's in Europe. He'll be there another week, until next Friday."

"Europe," Barr said stupidly.

"London, really, He's attending a seminar."

Barr sighed. "Tell me, ma'am, is he still a maverick?"

She laughed. "I'll say he is!"

"Does he think there's plenty of oil left to be found in this country?"

"You *do* know him." She laughed. "He'll stop people on the street to say that."

"Well, please tell him I called, and that I'll call again. I want to see him."

"I'll sure do it, Mr. Barr."

Barr thanked her and hung up the receiver. He stared glumly at the wall a moment, then went downstairs for a late breakfast. After that he sat in the lobby and glanced without much interest through a newspaper. He tossed it aside. He had finally made up his mind about Arlene. If she was at home or in town and wanted to see him he would see her. If not, he would catch an evening flight for Caracas.

She answered the phone when he called, and he could hear people talking in the background. "Are you holding a convention out there?" Barr asked.

"Grady! Are you here . . . in town?"

"At the Shamrock. May I call on you, ma'am, at your pleasure?"

She said in a rush, "Listen! The kids are in New York for three weeks, but Harley is here, and he has some people with him. They'll be leaving about four or four-thirty, and Harley has to leave here by six to catch the plane for Washington."

"Slow down," Barr said, laughing.

"No. Why don't you come out about five so you can spend some time with Harley before he leaves. Is that all right?"

"Will you fix me dinner afterward?" Barr teased.

"You be here at five o'clock, young man! I am expecting you."

"Yes, ma'am," Barr said.

Arlene opened the door for him. Her face was flushed with nervousness and Barr felt the old tenderness for her grip him. "Come in, come in," she said in the hurried way she spoke when she was excited. She waved a hand. "They're still cleaning up in there. Do you mind the breakfast room?"

Barr grabbed her hand, but she already was moving away, and Barr laughed because it looked as if she were pulling him across the huge foyer. He could hear the hum of a vacuum cleaner from the direction of the den. He let her lead him down the long corridor to the breakfast nook, and all the while she was talking, explaining that Harley had been a member of a task force helping President Kennedy select his cabinet, that he had come to Houston to tidy up some loose ends, and that she had let him use the

340

house for the tidying. It was as if she were trying to get trivia out of the way so she could better concentrate on Barr.

Harley was lounging in the doorway to the nook, looking like a college dean with his curved pipe and tan jacket. He was smiling, and he shook Barr's hand with enthusiasm. "You know why I'm here. Now have a seat and tell us why *you're* here." He helped Barr with a chair. Arlene went to the refrigerator and came back with a can of beer for Barr.

Barr made a great show of opening the beer while saying, "I am no longer the president of Cajun Petroleum Corporation or employed in any other manner by SeaCoast International."

Harley was impassive; Arlene was looking at Barr with amazement.

"I'm not sure whether I quit or got fired," Barr said, and he could see the joy spreading across Arlene's face.

"I don't understand, Grady," Harley said. "What in the world happened?"

Barr told them, beginning with Cannon's phone call about the impending price cut and Barr's implied threat to resign. He told them about Vigas and the birth of OPEC, about Barr's more than occasional mentions to SCI of OPEC's apparent growing strength. He told them about the letter, the summons to Houston, and what had occurred in Ralston's office. It was cathartic for Barr; his hand trembled when he took the letter from his pocket and placed it on the table.

Arlene covered his hand with hers. Harley picked up the letter and read it. He handed it to Arlene. Neither he nor Grady spoke while Arlene read. She punched her finger at the letter. "Here it is," she said. "Where you're talking about nationalization and you say that a further price cut, particularly a unilateral one, will hasten the day." She looked at Barr. "That's what he resented, Grady."

"Maybe," Barr said. "That and Cannon implying I'd quit if he cut Venezuela."

Harley had picked up the letter and was toying with it. Looking steadily at Barr, he said, "You've spent most of your years away from the land of your birth, Grady. Do you consider yourself an American?"

"Of course he's an American!" Arlene said.

Barr said, "Why do you ask?"

"Because all of your fears are for SCI's crude supplies. Your suggestions are on how to improve its position outside OPEC."

Harley paused. "Don't you have any fears for the American economy? The American people? Can't you imagine what would happen to this country if your fears materialize?"

Barr said honestly, "I haven't given it much thought, Harley."

Harley nodded. "Do you mind if I show this letter to President Kennedy? In confidence?"

"Hell, Harley, he knows about OPEC. I imagine he feels just like Ralston and Shell and everybody else."

"I'd like to show it to him," Harley insisted. He stood up, the letter in his hand. "I'm going to have to run to make it to the airport on time."

Barr stood up. "You can tell him what's in the letter, Harley. You don't need it."

"The letter is the best evidence. And it will be in confidence. I need it, Grady."

Barr shrugged. "If it's important to you."

Harley put the letter in a jacket pocket. "It may be important to us all," he said.

She was in his arms before Harley's rental car had cleared the long driveway to the street. She was kissing his cheeks, his mouth, his eyes, crooning his name, touching his hair, his neck with tender hands, celebrating the death of her rival for Barr's love.

Still holding on to him, touching him, squeezing him, she led him back to the breakfast nook. As they sat down, she said with her impish smile, "You're not going to leave here. Ever!"

"Not even for my clothes and things?"

"To hell with them. We'll get you new ones."

"I have to go back for a few days, honey. There are things I have to do." Among them, Barr thought, was to say goodbye to the widow properly; he owed her that much.

"I'll go with you," Arlene said.

"No, I'll be rushed for time. I want to be back here by next Friday." As he said the words, Barr realized how badly he wanted to talk to Steve Boosie.

"Friday? Why Friday?"

He told her about Steve Boosie. "If there's oil anywhere, he can find it, honey, and I'm the guy who can get it out of the ground."

"It'll take a lot of money, won't it?"

"I'll find investors," Barr said confidently. He grinned. "I think I'll be very good at charming ladies out of their money."

342

She didn't rise to his words. "You don't have to do anything. You don't have to work. We can just live, Grady."

Barr shook his head. "I couldn't stand that, Arlene, and after a while you wouldn't be able to stand me."

She said sadly, "It will be just like it was before."

Barr took her hand. "No, it won't, honey," he said softly. "I'll be doing it for us, not Cajun or some other company. We'll be partners. Everywhere I go, you'll go, if you want to."

"You just want to show that man Ralston and the others what a good oilman you are."

"That's part of it," Barr admitted, "but mainly I want to show myself." He paused. "I've got to show myself I can still cut the mustard without the trappings of a big company. Please understand that, honey."

She wouldn't give up. "What if this man Boosie doesn't want to join you?"

"What a stubborn hussy," Barr said with mock sadness. "If this man Boosie doesn't want to join me, I'll find somebody else." He looked to the ceiling as he said, "Man experienced in all phases of oil drilling and production seeks geologist as partner in exciting venture. Fringe benefits include plenty of booze and women." He looked at her and grinned. "That kind of ad in the newspapers will have them flocking to my door."

She sniffed. "You could go on television."

"Why don't you shut up and lean over here and kiss me?" Barr said.

She started to but stopped. "Grady, how did you feel when that man said he was taking Cajun away from you?"

Barr said candidly, "It liked to have killed me, honey."

"I knew it," she said with satisfaction.

"I'm recovering nicely," Barr said dryly.

She kissed him then, and put her hand on his inner thigh, nudging his penis. With her mouth against his cheek, she said, "You don't have to go back to Caracas tonight, do you?"

"Not hardly," Barr said.

Their physical reunion that night was a passionate milestone in Barr's journey through women, combining the wantonness, the tenderness, the touching, the feeling, the love talk, the small talk, that made him feel like a king among men. He would fix them drinks at the bar, and as they drank their free hands would be caressing each other. In orgasm she would cry out as if her soul

343

was on fire, and it would thrill Barr to the core of his being. But simply holding her brought him such great satisfaction that he could have wept at the sweetness of it.

At one point, Arlene said, "Grady, wouldn't it be wonderful if we could do this until the end of our days."

"Bandera used to say that people who keep on fucking can fuck until they die," Barr said. "I intend to live until the twenty-first century. Is that long enough?"

"You and your Bandera!"

"Well," Barr said, "he was as smart as Woodrow Ralston, and better at his job."

The next morning over coffee they decided that Barr didn't have to be in such a hurry to get back to Caracas after all; he could leave the next day, Sunday. So Barr made a hurried trip to the Shamrock in her car, checked out, and returned with his luggage. At brunch he said firmly, "We're going out to dinner tonight. The last time I was in this town you kept me locked up here and this time I've been in such a daze I wouldn't have noticed if the streets were painted red. I want to see how this place has grown."

Arlene made a face. "It's just another town."

"Dinner," Barr said, "with plenty of time for a sight-seeing tour."

While they were dressing that evening the phone rang, and Arlene answered it. Barr was hooking her brassiere. She held the receiver to her ear for a long moment, then turned and handed it to Barr. Her eyes were wide with wonder, and Barr thought she had been listening to an obscene caller, but she whispered, "It's Harley!"

"Harley . . ."

"Glad I caught you, Grady. I'm at Camp David with the President and some others, and he wants to talk to you. He wants to see you Monday, at the White House."

Barr was annoyed. "Well, *I* want to be in Caracas Monday. I've got to get back there and close up shop and such."

"Grady, this is the President of the United States we're talking about. He doesn't invite just anybody to his office. You ought to feel honored."

"I'll be back next Friday, and we can talk about it then. All right?"

"Grady, the man read your letter. He wants to ask you some questions. And he wants to do it Monday. You've *got* to do it."

344

"I'm not a politician," Barr said shortly. "I can't help him. What the hell do I know about his problems? And I don't like the idea of fooling with a government. I've fooled with governments too much already."

Arlene jerked the receiver from his hand. "Harley! He'll be there! *We'll* be there! What time does the President want him there?" She nodded. "Ten-thirty in the Oval Office. That's fine. Will you make us a reservation for tomorrow night at the Mayflower? We'll fly up tomorrow." She thrust the receiver at Barr, defiance written all over her face. "He wants to talk to you again."

Barr put the receiver to his ear. "Thanks for the invitation, Harley," he said dryly.

Harley laughed. "She's right, Grady. This is an opportunity you can't miss."

"Will you be there?"

"No, that's why I wanted your ear again. I'm flying to California tomorrow. But the White House guards will be alerted, and someone will take you to the Oval Office."

"But *when* will I see you?"

"Soon, Grady. This is my last government stint. I'm coming back to Texas to fish and golf." He laughed. "Remember, don't let Arlene talk you into going by my house. My wife doesn't like her."

"It seems impossible, doesn't it?"

"Doesn't it? Well, I'll make your reservation and pave the way. And, Grady, thank you . . . and good luck."

"Uh huh," Barr mumbled, and hung up. He turned slowly to Arlene. She was standing with an impish grin on her face, wearing only her brassiere. "All right, blabbermouth," Barr said sternly, "but we're going out to dinner and to see the sights if it's the last thing I ever do."

She went into his arms. "Oh Grady, I'm so proud of you!"

345

Chapter
Twenty-Five

The Oval Office was not as spacious as Fontenot's Miraflores office, not as ornate, but to Barr on this bright morning it seemed as massive as a cathedral and as indestructible as a fortress. There was a solidity about everything in the room; the walls, the furniture, the artifacts suggested a continuity, emitting a power that flowed toward, and through, the young President behind the desk flanked with flags. Through the tall bow windows Barr could see a garden, exuberant with greenery and color.

Seated at one end of the desk was a bulky man with a wide face and big hands, which held Barr's letter to Charles Cannon. Barr recognized him from newspaper photographs—Lyndon Johnson, the vice-president. He stared at Barr impassively.

The President rose and reached across the small desk to greet Barr with a firm handshake. Barr read geniality and wit in the blue eyes, and there was something about the tough, masculine face that hinted at the sardonic. "I thank you for coming, Mr. Barr," he said. "I have asked the vice-president to sit in with us." He smiled. "He's a Texan, too, you know. The whole world knows it."

Johnson rose and Barr moved to shake his hand. Johnson smiled while his eyes measured Barr, head to foot. "Glad to know you, Mr. Barr," he said finally.

"I'm glad to know you," Barr said.

Kennedy waved Barr to a chair at the opposite end of the desk, and Johnson immediately sat down and began reading the letter.

Kennedy lounged back in his chair. "Tell me about President

Fontenot," he said. "I've talked with him on the phone a couple of times. What kind of man is he?"

Barr was surprised at the question. He thought of Fontenot in hiding, in exile, his shoulder shattered by a rifle bullet, and he saw him in the great bull ring calmly explaining his position, saw him in Miraflores directing a government wrested from a brutal dictatorship, and he wondered about the telephone conversations. He said carefully, "He wouldn't pick me to be his press agent, I assure you. In all of the years I've known him, we've been at sword's points. But I think he's intelligent. I think he's capable, and I think he's dedicated to his country's welfare."

Kennedy laughed. "I gathered that on the phone. He lectured me on the economy and a few other things."

Barr nodded. "He's apt to do that."

"Do you think his administration is stable? The country?"

Barr thought of Leonel Castillo's remark about the military being a weather-vane. "It's a different country now," he said. "I don't believe the people would tolerate a military coup, and I believe the military knows it. The people have confidence in Fontenot, as far as I can tell, and his administration appears to be acting on the people's needs."

"What about the Communists?"

"He accepts them. I think it would be against his principles to have any political party outlawed."

"Are they a significant force?"

"They're noisy, and they harass Fontenot's administration, but they don't have much voting strength."

"President Eisenhower and Mr. Nixon thought they were a significant force," Kennedy said.

Barr nodded. "That was because the Perez Jimenez government labeled all dissidents as Communists. He blew it out of proportion for his own purposes."

"They couldn't affect the outcome of an election?"

"Not in my opinion, Mr. President."

Kennedy glanced at his wristwatch, and Barr said quickly, "It's an honor to be here, Mr. President, but you could have gotten this kind of appraisal from your own people."

Kennedy grinned. "Not this succinctly, Mr. Barr."

Johnson spoke, his voice heavy as he were just arousing from a deep sleep. "*If* these people stick together, and *if* they nationalize, and *if* they shut off their valves, what are they going to do with the oil?"

347

Barr said calmly, "A better question would be, what are *you* going to do *without* it?" He turned back to Kennedy. "Your dependence on them is so great now, and your reserves so small, they could outwait you." He pointed to the letter which Johnson had placed on the desk. "When I wrote that letter, I was trying to help SCI, but I've done some thinking since Harley Bowie said you wanted to see me. OPEC can hurt you more than it can hurt SCI, Mr. President. It can make a shambles of your economy."

Kennedy was thoughtful. "Mr. Barr, the Iraqis hate the other Arabs, the other Arabs hate the Iraqis, and all of them hate the Iranians who hate them in return. I don't believe hate is too strong a word. And in this mixture you've got Venezuela. What a strong glue it would take to hold such an alliance together!"

"Hate," Barr said promptly. "Exactly the word you used. Hatred for wrongs done, real or imaginary, to them all. And the profit motive, of course. Greed, if you prefer."

Johnson spoke. "The way I understand it, your company didn't think much of this letter, is that right? Woodrow Ralston didn't like it."

Barr smiled. "He said my fears were groundless and my suggestions unrealistic. Ridiculous, in fact."

"Woodrow Ralston is supposed to be the smartest man in the oil business," Johnson said.

"I suppose he is," Barr said.

"The other companies feel like he does, don't they?" Johnson asked.

"I suppose so. They feel that if they ignore OPEC it will go away." Barr was weary now, and it showed.

Kennedy said, "Do *you* think there's as much oil left to be found in this country as has been found to date?"

"I don't know, Mr. President. A man I respect says so. Some others agree with him. They all could be wrong. But if you wait until OPEC turns off the valves to find out, it will be too late to play catch-up."

"But if the oil companies don't want to launch a massive exploration and drilling program here, what can the government do?" Kennedy asked.

"I don't know, Mr. President. I've had unhappy experiences with government involving itself in business."

Barr stood up. In Venezuela he always had waited until he had been dismissed before he left the seat of power. He didn't have to wait here. He was tired of the questions, tired of OPEC, tired of the ignorance and the obvious disbelief in anything he said about OPEC. He wanted to get about his own business.

Kennedy stood up and said quickly, "This Eduardo Vigas. The Minister of Petroleum. You think he's the real glue, don't you?"

Barr nodded.

"Tell me about him," Kennedy said.

Barr shook his head. "I don't know how to tell you about him. Have somebody look him up in the files. Or have somebody go down and interview him." He picked up his letter, put it in his pocket and nodded to both men. "It was an honor to be here," he said. He started for the door.

"Mr. Barr."

Barr turned around and Kennedy had his hand outstretched. Barr shook it. "Thank you for coming," Kennedy said.

Barr turned again to leave and Kennedy again stopped him. "If the Arabs and Iranians decided to close their valves, what would President Fontenot do? As a fellow member of OPEC?"

Barr faced him and smiled his nicest smile. "Why, Mr. President, I'm sure he'd do what he thought was best for Venezuela." Barr turned away then for the last time and left the Oval Office.

Kennedy said, "Well, Mr. Vice-President, what do you think?"

"Bullshit," Johnson said. He stood up and shook his trousers. "It's all bullshit."

Barr got into a cab outside the White House. The driver peered at him through the rear-view mirror. "You from Texas?" he asked Barr.

Barr fingered the brim of his Stetson and smiled. "Yes, I am."

"Lot of oil down there, ain't it?"

Barr looked out the window. "Oil," he said, "is where you find it."